ATTACK ON FORT HALL

A fire arrow lit the night as it soared up and came down, missing a wagon by only a few feet. Several men jumped up and started to move to the flames.

"Get down!" Preacher called. "Let it burn out! And save your powder and shot. This ain't St. Louis. You can't go to a store and buy more." He dropped back down beside Greybull. "Damn pilgrims anyway."

"Them Blackfeet are workin' in close and then they'll jump us," Greybull said, never taking his eyes from the area in front of their position.

Preacher stared into the darkness. "See that stump over yonder? It wasn't there two minutes ago."

"You're right. You want the honors?"

"I believe I will." Preacher pulled his Hawken to his shoulder, took careful aim, and let her bang.

The "stump" grunted when the ball struck him. A war axe went flying into the air and the brave fell forward and lay still. Suddenly the night was filled with darting shapes as the Indians worked their way closer to the fort and the wagons.

"Here they come!" Greybull shouted. The fight was on.

BOOK YOUR PLACE ON OUR WEBSITE AND MAKE THE READING CONNECTION!

We've created a customized website just for our very special readers, where you can get the inside scoop on everything that's going on with Zebra, Pinnacle and Kensington books.

When you come online, you'll have the exciting opportunity to:

- View covers of upcoming books
- Read sample chapters
- Learn about our future publishing schedule (listed by publication month *and author*)
- Find out when your favorite authors will be visiting a city near you
- Search for and order backlist books from our online catalog
- Check out author bios and background information
- Send e-mail to your favorite authors
- Meet the Kensington staff online
- Join us in weekly chats with authors, readers and other guests
- Get writing guidelines
- AND MUCH MORE!

Visit our website at
http://www.zebrabooks.com

THE FIRST MOUNTAIN MAN
WILLIAM W. JOHNSTONE

Zebra Books
Kensington Publishing Corp.

http://www.zebrabooks.com

This novel is a work of fiction. Names, characters, places, and incidents are either the product of the author's imagination or are used fictitiously, and any resemblance to actual persons, living or dead, events, or locales, is entirely coincidental.

ZEBRA BOOKS are published by

Kensington Publishing Corp.
850 Third Avenue
New York, NY 10022

First Printing: December, 1991
10 9 8 7 .6 5

Printed in the United States of America

One

"When you call me that, smile!"

Owen Wister

He was on the east side of the Absaroka Range, in the timber, heading down toward the Popo Agie. He was in no hurry, and there was no real reason for him to go there. He just had him a hankering, call it. He felt he might run into some old friends around there who, like the lone rider, had felt the calling for companionship.

He hadn't been down there in some time, not since the last rendezvous back in '30, he thought it was. He was pretty sure it was the year of our Lord 1837. Had to be close to that, anyway. If the year was as he figured, he was about thirty-five years old, near as he could figure. And he'd never felt better in his life.

The rider was of average height for his time, lean-hipped and rawhide tough, with tremendous power in his upper body. What women he'd run into over the last seventeen or eighteen or so years in the mountains considered him handsome. He tried to recall the last time he'd seen a white woman. Two, three years at least.

5

Just thinking about the rendezvous got him all lost in memories — but not so lost that he forgot where he was and to keep a sharp eye out for Injuns. He rode with his Hawken rifle across the saddle horn and had another one shoved into a saddle boot. He carried two .50 caliber pistols behind his waistsash and two more hung in leather on the saddle horn, one on each side. He'd always boasted that he was a peaceful man, but Injuns is notional folks. You never really know how to take them. A man can nearabout always ride into an Injun camp and they'll feed you and bed you down for the night. They'll usually treat a body right well. 'Course, depending on the tribe and the general mood of the day, the rub comes when you try to leave the next morning. They might decide to have some fun and skin you alive. He had seen what was left of a man after that. It was a disheartening sight, to say the least. He didn't expect the other feller cared much for it either.

The lone rider rode easy, ruminating on this and that. He'd seen a white man up the trail about five months back, when the snow was thick, and he'd told him it was Christmas. That had got him to feeling all maudlin and the like, thinking about folks and family he hadn't seen in years and would probably never see again on this side of the grave.

Time gets confusing up in the High Lonesome. The months and years just blend together and don't take on a whole hell of a lot of importance.

He reined up at a creek and swung down from the saddle, getting the kinks out of his muscles and bones and giving his horses a chance to drink and blow. He rode a mountain horse he'd caught and gentle-broke. Called him Hammer for no particular reason. Hammer was a gray, tough as a mountain goat and stood eighteen hands high. His good pack horse was also a gray, just as tough as Hammer and just as smart: he wouldn't tote no more than he felt he could comfortable carry. Overload him and he just wouldn't move. Stand there and look at you with them eyes telling you to get that crap off his back. Smart.

The rider looked all around him careful, then stood still and sniffed the air. He could detect nothing in the cool mountain air except the scent of nature's own growth in springtime.

There was no Injun smell. After so many years in the mountains, he had learned that all men have a distinctive scent that can be picked up by others if you just teach your blower to do it.

He stretched out on his belly by the creek and took him a long drink of cold clean water. He thought about taking off his moccasins and sticking his bare feet in the crick and splashing around some, like a kid, but some poor critter downstream that wasn't hurtin' nobody and who just come out of the woods for a cool drink would be sick for a week.

He did take off his moccasins and rub his feet, though. Felt good.

He rubbed his feet dry on the grass and slipped back into his moccasins. He chewed on a piece of jerky and wished long for some coffee, but he'd been out of coffee for weeks. That was another reason for this trip. He had to resupply with salt and beans and coffee and the like. He also had to get him a new pair of longhandle underwear. His was plumb wore out. And his buckskins were thin.

He was known from the Northwest to the deserts of the Southwest as Preacher.

He was far from being a man of the cloth — about as far as a man could get, even though he'd been raised in the church as a boy. When he was new and green to the High Lonesome, Injuns had grabbed him and was planning on slow-roasting him to see how well he stood pain. If he stood it well, they would praise him and sing songs about him. 'Course, those songs would be sort of hard to appreciate from the grave. So he started preaching. He preached all day and all night. The Injuns finally figured he was crazy as a lizard and turned him loose. The nickname stuck.

Preacher had been in the mountains since he was just a boy; he had run away from a good home and reached the mountains a year later. And while he had left the mountains many times to see what was over the next ridge or river, he always returned to the High Lonesome. He had lived with a number of tribes, and gotten along with many of them. He'd had him a squaw from time to time, and a few offspring.

But unlike many of his counterparts, Preacher could see the

7

writing on the wall, so to speak, even though he might have some difficulty reading actual words. The beaver market was glutted. Man was hard-pressed to make a living anymore, and it was only going to get worse. He knew that while most of the other mountain men did not, or would not accept it.

Preacher could do a lot of things besides trapping. He could pan for gold, he could scout for the Army or for wagon trains, he even knew a little about farming — although he kept that to himself.

He cut his eyes to Hammer as the horse raised his head and pricked his ears up. He was over to him in a heartbeat, stroking his neck and talking to him low, so he wouldn't whinny and give away their position. He spoke to the pack horse and rubbed his neck. They stood quiet, but they weren't liking what they smelled one damn bit.

Then Preacher smelled what the horses had smelled, and he heard them coming. Injuns, and their scent was strong. With it came the scent of blood. Fresh blood.

He picketed both horses on graze and pulled the pistols from the saddle horn. He slipped to the top of a rise and peeked through the brush. What he saw below didn't set well at all. Five young bucks and they had prisoners. The Injuns looked to be Arapaho, and Preacher never had got on too well with that tribe. They just didn't much like the white man. Preacher lay still, moving only his eyes, carefully checking everything out. But it appeared five was all there was. But five bucks on the warpath was plenty. He could see fresh scalps on the manes of their horses and on their war lances. And they weren't Injun scalps.

The bucks had two white women and two white men, and from the looks on their faces, they were all plenty scared. And they had a right to be.

A lot of wagon trains were pushing west, to Oregon or California. Wagons had been rolling to Oregon for several years. Nat Wyeth, Preacher thought it was, took the first emigrants over the Oregon trail back in '31 or '32. Been a lot of them since then, and a lot of them hadn't made it.

Preacher had him a thought that these poor, scared pilgrims

was part, or had been part, of a small wagon train that just ran out of luck.

"The Lord will see us through, brother and sisters," a man said. "Put your faith in the Lord."

Missionaries, Preacher thought. Come to the wilderness to bring Jesus to the savages. Damn fools bringing womenfolk out here to preach with them. Injuns don't think like white people. It's not that the whites is right and the Injuns is wrong, it's just that they're two very different ways of life. Whites and Injuns don't think alike. Injuns don't steal 'cause they're bad people. It's more of a game to them, and right and wrong doesn't enter into it. Courage and dying well and bravery mean a great deal to Injuns. They can't none of them abide a coward.

Preacher had tried to tell a few missionaries that the Injuns didn't need or want their religion; they had a religion all their own and they practiced it and lived by it. But you'd have better luck trying to tell a lawyer to shut up than you would with a Bible-thumper.

Preacher watched as one young buck pulled at himself and grinned at the others. He knew then that one of the young women — and they were both lookers — was fixin' to get hopped on right then and there in front of God and everybody else.

Then the buck said as much. Preacher spoke some Arapaho, and heard him tell the woman what he was gonna do. She looked up at him from the log where they'd plopped her, confusion and fear on her face. Then that buck just reached down and run his hand up under her dress. That woman squalled something fierce.

"Here now!" a man blustered up. "You stop that barbaric behavior, you hear me?"

The woman's hands was tied behind her back, but her feet were free. She kicked that buck right between his legs and he went down howling and puking, both hands holding onto his privates.

Preacher winced and he was thirty feet away.

Preacher knew if he was to do anything, it had to be now. He eased the hammers back on his old .50 caliber pistols and

9

laid them on the ground. He took the second brace — hoping the powder was dry on them all — and eased the hammers back on them. Another buck jerked out a knife and whacked an ear off one of the men prisoners. The man screamed and the blood poured. The buck then proceeded to make it clear to the lady — using sign language that an idiot could understand — that if she didn't hike up her skirts and do it real quick, he was gonna cut something else off the man, and it was located a mite lower than his remaining ear.

"Melody!" the man with one ear hollered.

Preacher figured he got the message, too.

The buck she'd kicked in the privates was still on the ground, rolling and moaning and being sick all over the place. She had really put her little foot in him.

There wasn't any other option left Preacher. He lifted his pistols with the double set triggers and let 'em bang. He had double-shotted these and the first ball hit the buck with the knife in the chest; the second ball hit him in the belly. Both balls from the second pistol hit a brave smack in the face. He was a real mess when he hit the ground.

Preacher grabbed the second brace of pistols and let the lead fly. He couldn't hardly see a thing for the gunsmoke but knew he had put four Injuns on the ground and the other one was just getting to his moccasins, still bent over in pain. Preacher jerked his long-bladed knife from its sheath and ran down the short slope toward the scared pilgrims.

He ran right over that skinny Injun with the bruised privates and knocked him sprawling back to the ground. He jumped up, a war axe in his hand, and he was some mad. Preacher told him in his own language what he thought of him, his family, and his horse. The buck screamed and charged. Preacher ducked and cut him from brisket to backbone. That blade was honed to a fine edge and went in easy. The skinny Injun was out of it. Preacher ran back to his guns and loaded up again as fast as he could.

The women were in a shocked silence. The man with one ear looked at Preacher like he was some sort of devil. And, Preacher thought, maybe he did look like one. He hadn't shaved in a month or so and his clothes were made from what

10

he could kill and skin and cure. His hat was so old and floppy it had no shape. Preacher reckoned he did look like a wild man to these city folks.

"Praise be!" Melody found her voice. "The Lord has sent us a warrior!"

"He ain't done no such of a thing," Preacher told her, while cutting her bonds loose. "I just happened to be close by. Now get them others untied and let's get the hell gone from here 'fore more Injuns show up."

The second man put his mouth in motion and stuck his two pennies worth in. "We're all Christians, brother. And we don't hold with strong language in front of ladies."

Preacher spat on the ground. "That's your damn problem. I don't hold with fools comin' into the mountains and stirrin' up the Injuns. So I reckon that makes us even." Preacher cut the others loose.

He helped Melody to her feet and she swayed against him for a moment. She was all woman, that one. And when their eyes met, Preacher could see that she knew he was all man. A high flush came to her cheeks and her smile was tight and her eyes bright, like with a fever. They had a fever all right, but it wasn't brought on by sickness. Preacher released her hand and she stepped away, each knowing what the other was thinking, and Jehovah didn't have a damn thing to do with it.

"You don't have to worry about the other savages," the man with one ear and bloody face said.

Preacher knew then he was dealing with a real pilgrim. In the mountains, a man *always* worries about Injuns.

Preacher grunted in reply.

"You see," one-ear said, pulling a fancy handkerchief out of a jacket pocket and pressing it to the side of his head. "The other savages fled in a different direction after the attack."

"They didn't flee nowheres," Preacher told him. "They own these mountains; they got no reason to be afraid. All they did was split up to divvy up the booty. But how do you know they didn't plan on meetin' up agin, right here?"

That shut one-ear right up.

"We must get Richard to a doctor," the haughty-acting fellow said.

11

Preacher laughed at him. "Shore. They's one about two hundred and fifty miles from here. Won't take us more'n a month to get there. What we'll do is get gone from here and then I'll take a look at your partner's head. Clean it out good. I'd pour whiskey on it but I ain't got none."

"You probably drank it all, lurching about in some drunken debauchery," the second female spoke up. She had her color up and was climbing up on her soapbox. "Cavorting about with a loose woman, more than likely a pure, simple, ignorant savage you took advantage of."

"Amen," the mouthy man said. "It's not only the savages to whom we must introduce God."

Preacher chuckled and shook his head. "For shore I drank the whiskey. As to the second part, no. Let's go. When we make camp I'll fix up a poultice for one-ear there. You ain't hurt bad, mister. But you're gonna be tiltin' your hat to the other side of your head for the rest of your life. Now, all of you, move, goddammit!"

Two

They were in trouble and Preacher knew that for a hard fact. The Arapaho bucks back yonder had been wearing red streaks on their faces. To an Arapaho, the color red could mean three things: earth, man, or blood. In this case, Preacher pretty well knew it meant blood, and they weren't in the best of positions, either. They were caught with the Shoshoni just to the west of them, the Blackfoot to the north, the Crow to the east, and the Arapaho and the Cheyenne to the south and everywhere in the immediate surroundings.

All in all, it was not a good place to be. Preacher, traveling alone, never gave it much worrying time. He knew how to stay alive in hostile country. But with four pilgrims — that was quite another matter.

And two of them females, no less. That only added to the problem.

"Git up on them horses," Preacher told them.

"We don't have the proper saddles for the ladies," the mouthy man said. "And by the way, my name is Edmond. You know Melody and Richard. This is Penelope."

"Well, I am just thrilled beyond words. Now, get up on them damn horses!"

Nobody moved.

With a snort of disgust, Preacher climbed up the gently sloping bank, slid down the other side, and fetched his own animals, leading them around to the others. They still hadn't made a move toward the ponies.

He swung into the saddle and led an Indian pony over to the group. He looked at Melody. "Mount up, sister. I'll get you outta here. Move, woman!"

Melody didn't hesitate. She stepped up on a log, hiked up her skirts, and swung onto the horse's back. Preacher handed her the reins. "Let's go."

"What about us?" Penelope shrieked.

"Keep your voice down, woman!" Preacher said. "You'd put a hog-caller to shame. If you wanna come with us, put your butt on that pony's back and come on."

"Barbarous cretin!" Edmond said. "You'd leave us, wouldn't you?"

"You see my back, don't you?" Preacher called over his shoulder. "That tell you anything?"

"Are you really going to leave them?" Melody whispered.

"Naw," Preacher returned the whisper. "But they don't know that."

She grinned at him. Preacher winked at her.

"I'm a worker in the house of the Lord, sir," she reminded him.

"You're a woman first," he told her. "And a hell of a woman, at that."

She blushed and tried to adjust her bonnet, pushing some blonde hair back under the brim and almost fell off the pony.

"Hang on, sister," Preacher told her. "You're all lucky them Injuns took saddles from the dead pilgrims for their ponies. You'd be plumb uncomfortable if you was ridin' bareback."

"I can just imagine," Melody muttered.

"I bet you cain't, neither. Here come the others. I figured I'd get them movin'." He looked with approving eyes at the way the men sat their saddles. They could ride. Penelope, on the other hand, was bouncing up and down like a little boat on a great big lake in the middle of a storm. "Grab ahold of that

14

saddle horn, sister," Preacher said. "And hang on. The damn thing ain't for tootin', you know."

She gave him a dark look and muttered something under her breath.

"Must you use profanity?" Edmond said.

"Will if I want to, and I want to, so hush up and stay in line. And don't get lost. Which way's what's left of the wagon train?"

"On the Oregon Trail," Richard said.

Preacher whoaed up and twisted in the saddle. "Somebody's been playin' games with you folks. The Oregon Trail is 'way, 'way south of here. People, you was *lost!*"

"As a goose," Melody said. "I knew that, but nobody would listen to me."

Richard and Edmond both looked embarrassed. Richard said, "I suspected our guide didn't know what he was doing. He drank a lot."

"I know lots of guides who drink a lot," Preacher said. "That ain't got nothin' to do with it. Where'd you folks outfit and jump off from?"

"Missouri," Melody told him. "Our guide told us we would bypass Fort Hall because he knew a better route."

"Damn fool," Preacher muttered. "All right. How far north is the train?"

"I would say about fifteen miles," Edmond said. "No more than that, I'm sure."

"Probably not that far," Preacher said. "Injuns wouldn't travel that distance in these mountains 'fore torturin' and rapin'. If that's what they had in mind."

"Perhaps you could take us on to Oregon?" Edmond suggested.

"I'll take you somewheres," Preacher said, and pointed his horse's nose north.

Night draped the mountains before they could reach the site of the wagon train. Preacher killed a couple of rabbits with a sling and stopped before dark to build a small fire. While the meat was cooking, he said, "We'll eat, then move on a couple of miles and make camp for the night. It's gonna be cold, so you folks use your saddle blankets for warmth."

"But they *smell!*" Penelope complained.

"You will too 'fore you get where you're goin'," Preacher told her. "Like a bunch of polecats—but you'll be alive. So shut up."

Preacher let the others eat the rabbits while he chewed on jerky and ate a handful of some berries he'd picked. He was used to lean times. These pilgrims looked like they'd never missed a meal in their lives.

He carefully put out the fire and moved them north a couple of miles for a cold camp. Melody was the only one who didn't complain, even though she was just as uncomfortable as the others.

She'll do, Preacher thought. *She's tough.*

Their eyes met in the darkness through the dim light of the quarter moon. She blinked first, then laid her head on the saddle. Preacher grinned and rolled up in his blankets.

Across the small clearing, Edmond had watched the silent exchange through hot eyes, and bristled in anger.

They all saw the buzzards long before they reached the site of the ambush and massacre. Those carrion birds who had not yet feasted on dead flesh soared and circled and wheeled and waited their turn in the sky, while the others staggered around on the ground, too full and heavy to lift off.

"It ain't gonna be pretty," Preacher warned. "I've seen it before. When you puke, don't get none on me. Where are you folks from anyways?"

"Philadelphia," Richard said.

"Shoulda stayed there. This country's too crowded as it is. Can't ride five days without seeing some damn body."

"It's called progress," Edmond said.

"It's a damn nuisance, is what it is," Preacher retorted.

"Must you swear constantly?" Melody asked.

"Yeah, I must. I'm gettin' in practice for our rendezvous down south. Although it don't look like I'm gonna make it."

"I've read about those affairs," Richard said. "Then you're a real mountain man."

"I am."

"What drove you to this horrible existence?" Edmond asked.

16

Preacher turned to look at the city man. *"Horrible?* What's so horrible about it? I'm as free as an eagle, wild as a grizzly, mean as a wolverine, tough as a cornered wolf, and quick as a puma. I can out drink, out cuss, out fight, out dance, out sing, ride farther and faster than any man, and tell more lies than any ten men. And I'm good-lookin', too."

Melody laughed at his words.

"You should be ashamed of yourself," Edmond admonished him.

"Why?" Preacher asked. "For bein' what the good Lord intended me to be? You are what you are, I am what I am. It's just as simple as that." He reined up and let the horses drink. "This here's what we call Shine Crick. I know what your guide was up too, now, but he was flat out wrong. He'd been listenin' to lies about a trail through the wilderness just to the west of us. There ain't no wagon trail through there. You'd have to go north over a hundred miles and then cut west. But even then, that would be a tough pull. Windin' way. Get caught there in the winter, and you'd die. You people were listenin' to a fool. What happened to him anyways?"

"When the savages attacked, he ran away," Melody said. "I watched him leave."

"You know his name?"

"Jack Harris," Edmond said. "I did not like him. He was a lot like you."

"Jack Harris ain't nothing like me," Preacher told him. "Jack's a back-shooter and a coward. Brags a lot about how brave he is, but when it comes down to the nut-cuttin', he ain't nowheres to be found."

"He claimed to be a mountain man," Melody said.

Preacher snorted. "He's a hanger-arounder, is what he is. He tell you about the time I whupped him down at Bent's Fort? No, he wouldn't mention that. I whupped him to a fare-thee-well, I did. He ain't liked me to this day."

"What was the fight about?" Richard asked. Although the man was in considerable pain, he'd come up in Preacher's eyes by not complaining about his missing ear and by pulling his weight.

"He insulted my mother. Now, you can insult me all day

17

long — if you do it in a friendly manner — and I'll just insult you back. But leave my dear sainted mother out of it. Or get ready to get bloody."

The wind shifted and brought a horrible stench with it, wrinkling the noses of the missionaries.

"That's . . . the wagon train?" Melody asked, getting a little green around the mouth.

"Yep," Preacher said. "What's left of the bodies, that is. Buzzards'll try for the soft parts first. Belly and kidneys. It ain't a real pretty sight. I've seen yards and yards of guts all strung out like rope. Why, I recollect one time, I come up on this Pawnee village that'd been hit by a band of Injuns that didn't like 'em very much — nobody likes the Pawnee. And I seen . . ." Preacher went into great long gory detail until the sounds of retching stopped him. Penelope and Edmond were off their ponies, kneeling down in the trail.

"What's the matter with you two?" he asked, with a very definite twinkle in his eyes. "Something you ate don't agree with you, maybe?"

Richard and Melody dropped off their ponies and headed for the bushes when they approached the wagon train. It was evident that the Indians had spent several hours torturing some of the survivors, and many Indian tribes could be very inventive when it came to torture.

"Savages!" Edmond blurted. "They need the word of God even more than I thought."

"Is that right?" Preacher asked with an odd smile. "Savages, huh? 'Ppears to me I read where they was still cuttin' off folks' heads in France and drawin' and quarterin' folks over in England. Big public spectacle. Ain't them religious countries? Would you call that civilized?"

Melody and Richard returned from their hurried trip to the bushes, both of them pale. The stench from the bodies was horrible. Articles of clothing and broken pieces of furniture were scattered all over the area, along with what remained of tortured men and women and older kids.

"Where are the young children?" Penelope asked, her voice no more than a whisper and her face very pale under her bonnet. "There were a dozen or more boys and girls."

"Injuns took them to raise," Preacher said. "They do that sometimes. If the child behaves, they'll live. Some tribes won't harm a child at all. Others will kill them outright. Injuns are notional. Just like white folks, you might say."

"I don't know any white person who would harm a child!" Edmond said.

"Then you don't know many of your own kind," Preacher told him shortly. "You folks start gatherin' up clothing you think might fit you and what food and powder and shot that might be found. Get yourselves some warm clothing."

"Stealing from the dead!" Penelope said.

Preacher turned slowly and looked at her. "Lady, you are beginnin' to wear on me. Do you—any of you—know the trouble you're in? I don't think so. We're smack in the middle of hostile Injun country, and from the paint on them dead bucks, they're on the warpath. Somethin's stirred them up. And it's reasonable to think that they ain't the only tribe that's took up their war axes." Preacher knelt down and began drawing in the dirt. The others leaned over to watch him.

"Now pay attention," Preacher said. "We're here. Dry Crick is behind us here. The South Fork of the Shoshone is to our west. The Oregon Trail is 'way to hell down here. 'Way I see it is like this: we got hostiles on the warpath all around us. We'd be damn fools to try to make it south to the wagon trail." He looked at all of them for a moment, then sighed. "I reckon I'm stuck with you. I can't in no good conscience leave you. Hell, you'd all *die*. Don't none of you seem to know north from south or what's up or down."

"Now, see here!" Edmond protested.

"Shut your fly-trap," Preacher told him. "And don't argue with me. I been makin' it in these mountains for years. You're just a helpless baby in the wilderness. And folks, if you think *this* is wild, you ain't seen nothin' yet. We couldn't make it with wagons where I'm thinkin' of carryin' you, but on horseback . . ." He shrugged his shoulders. ". . . We got a chance. We're goin' into the Big Titties . . ."

"The *what?*" Penelope blurted, high color springing onto her cheeks.

"Mountain range that was named Les Grande Tetones by a French trapper 'cause they reminded him of big tits," Preacher said, ducking his head to hide his grin. The grin did not escape Melody. "It's wild, people. It's the most beautiful and wildest thing you'll ever see. And it's slow goin'. But it's the safest way. We might run into some Bannocks in yonder; but I get on well with them. Likewise the Nez Perce further on west and north. Good people. It's our only shot, folks, and we got to take it. Now look around for a bottle of whiskey."

"My word, man!" Edmond said. "Are you thinking of getting drunk at a time like this?"

Preacher gave him a look of disgust. "No, you ninny. Take a look at your friend's head. Where his ear used to be. It's fillin' up with pus—infection, to you. I got to open it up, clean it out, and cauterize it with a hot blade. The whiskey's for him, to ease the pain. Even with that, y'all gonna have to hold him down. If we don't do that, he'll die. So shut your mouth and get to lookin'."

Preacher slowly circled the ambush site on foot and concluded that the Injuns who had done this had not been back. No need to, for at first glance there was precious little left to plunder. He began searching the rubble, grateful that the Injuns had not burned the wagons. They had raped and killed and tortured, run off the horses and mules. They'd eaten the oxen, then lay up in a stuffed stupor for a day or so. But this was a sight that Preacher had seen more than once since pilgrims began pushing west. He knew all the secret places where folks liked to stash valuables.

He found a cache of food in one wagon, including several pounds of coffee. Preacher immediately set about building a small smokeless fire out of dead wood and made a pot of coffee.

"Man, we have to bury the dead!" Edmond said.

"You bury 'em, if you're in that big a hurry," Preacher told him. "There ain't enough left of most of 'em to bother with. You'd best worry about stayin' alive. The dead'll take care of themselves. I'm fixin' to have me some coffee."

Preacher drank the hot strong brew while the others rummaged around, picking up this and that, stepping gingerly around the torn and bloated bodies.

"You women find you some men's britches and get in 'em," Preacher called from the fire. "Be easier ridin' that way."

"I most certainly will not!" Penelope squalled in outrage at just the thought.

"Either you do it, or I'll snatch them petticoats offen you and dress you myself," Preacher warned her. "I ain't gonna put up with them dresstails gettin' snagged on bushes and such. My life and your lives are at stake here. Damn your modesty."

Preacher looked westward and shook his head. He'd been in the Tetons, but never with a bunch of persnickety pilgrims, and certainly with no females draggin' along.

"Disgraceful!" Penelope said, holding up a pair of men's britches and shaking them.

"Just get in them," Preacher said. "Be right interestin' to see what you ladies look like without all them underthings hidin' your natural charms."

"You are a vile, disgusting man," Edmond told him.

"Maybe," Preacher said, sipping another cup of coffee. "But I'm the only hope you got of stayin' alive. I'd bear that in mind was I you." He looked at Richard, standing with the bottle of whiskey Preacher had found. "Drink it down, missionary. Get stumblin' drunk." He took out his knife and laid it on the stones around the fire. "This ain't gonna be no fun for neither of us."

Three

Preacher had to practically sit on the man to get him to take the first couple of slugs. After that, it got easier and Richard got sillier and looser than a goose. He passed out right in the middle of his story concerning the time he peeped in on his sister taking a bath. "Lord, what wonders I did behold that evening," said he, then fell backward, out cold.

Preacher grabbed his knife and went to work. He opened the wound, let it drain, cut away the infected skin, then applied a poultice he'd made. Long before Richard woke up, Preacher had cauterized the wound with the hot blade. Edmond got sick.

"It ain't as bad as it looked," Preacher said. "He's gonna have him a nub of an ear. Leastways his hat won't fall down that side. But he's gonna be hard to get along with for a couple of days. High as we are, wounds heal quick — air's so clean and pure. Won't be for long, the way folks keep showin' up out here," he added.

Preacher prowled around some and found more articles he could use, including some soap and some store-bought britches and shirts that looked like they might fit him. There was a nice lined Mackinaw coat that had only been burned a little bit, and he took that. Best looking coat he'd ever had. And bless Pat, he found him some brand new long-handles in the bottom of a trunk. In the same trunk, he found him a fancy razor and new strop and a mug with soap. He was tempted to take some boots off the dead, but he knew he'd worn moccasins for so long his feet would not be comfortable in anything else.

He wandered off down to the crick.

"Glory be!" Melody said, upon sighting him an hour later. "You are a *fine* looking man!"

"Melody!" Penelope admonished her brazenness.

Preacher had shaved, leaving only a moustache. He had bathed from top to bottom—he hoped nobody downstream tried to drink out of that crick for a day or two—and had dressed in the new clothes. He really felt a little self-conscious. He took the whiskey bottle and dabbed some on his freshly-shaved face.

"First time in ten years I been without a beard," Preacher said. "Feels funny." He looked at Richard. "He made a sound yet?"

"Moaned a couple of times," Edmond said. "I'm beginning to get concerned about him."

Preacher shook his head. "He's just passed out drunk, that's all. I been that way myself a time or two."

"I'm sure," Penelope said, giving him an acid look.

Preacher just grinned at her. Penelope needed a good man to roll around in the blankets with her for a night or two. He figured that might change her whole outlook.

Of course, he admitted, he could be wrong. It happened from time to time. He was wrong back in '26 or '27, he recollected.

Rather than break their backs burying the dead, they dragged the bodies to a shallow ravine and then caved earth in over them. Preacher, Edmond, Melody, and even Penelope pitched in to drag small logs and then spent the better part of an hour placing rocks over the mass gravesite. It wouldn't prevent digging and burrowing animals from get-

23

ting to the bodies, but it was the best they could do under the circumstances.

Preacher stood holding a new hat he'd found to replace his old one and listened to Edmond deliver a long-winded eulogy. Five minutes passed. Ten. The sun beat down mercilessly. Fifteen minutes, and still Edmond droned on.

Preacher couldn't take it anymore. "Amen, brother!" he shouted and walked off.

They pulled out the next morning, heading into a wilderness that only a handful of white men—and no white woman—had ever seen. Richard was in some pain, but he never complained. The man might be a Bible-thumper, but he was steadily rising in Preacher's estimation.

The man asked sensible questions, trying to learn about the land and its people, and Preacher answered each question as best he could.

"Is this the Shoshone River we're crossing now?" he asked, as they forded the stream.

"Nope. It's a fork off of it, though. This branch splits off east of what some folks call Heart Mountain. Injuns call it Spirit Mountain. It's sacred to some of them. Bear in mind to keep out of Injun buryin' grounds. That'll bring bad medicine on you. We won't cross the Shoshone this day. Tomorrow, 'bout noon, if all goes well."

"What do you mean by bad medicine?" Melody asked. "You don't believe in Indian superstition, do you?"

"What's the difference in what Injuns believe and what you're tryin' to bring to them? Only difference is the Injuns don't have no book like the Bible. Their religious ways is passed down by mouth. And each tribe has their shamans; they're like you folks, sort of. They believe in the Great Spirit, and life after death. That Happy Hunting Grounds claptrap is white man's bullshi . . . dooky."

Even Edmond and Penelope had pulled closer and were paying attention and not bitching about this, that, and everything else. For a change.

"Injuns is real good to their kids. Very kind to them. Once you get to know them, and they like you, they're good people. I've lived with them, I've fought them, and I've killed them. And likely I'll do all three things again. And don't you think that most Injun women is loose, 'cause they ain't. An Injun father is just like any father anywhere. You start messin' with his daughter, and he'll kill you.

"You take the Cheyenne tribe, for instance. Tough, mean fighters. Everybody's scared of the Cheyenne. But for all their fierceness, they hold women in high regard. A girl's comin' of age is a big deal in a lot of Injun tribes. And any number of tribes worship dogs and wolves. If one has to be killed for whatever reason, they'll apologize to it. And to a Cheyenne, a dog is damn near a god. They even have a warrior society called the Dog Soldiers."

"It sounds to me that you actually *like* the Indians," Edmond observed.

"Oh, I do. You can't blame them for fighting the whites. Hell, this is their land. It's been theirs for only God knows how long. Thousands of years, probably. If they'd let me, I'd never strike a hostile blow against any of them."

He thought about that for a moment. "Well, exceptin' maybe them goddamn Pawnees."

When they made camp that afternoon, Preacher figured they were within a half day's ride of the Shoshone. As soon as they crossed it, he'd cut south, down toward Togwotee Pass. He sure wasn't going to attempt to take them across the Snake and over the middle part of the Tetons. At least he hoped he wouldn't have to.

While they had been resting back at the ambush site, two horses had wandered back into camp, anxious for human closeness. Preacher had rigged up frames and they were used for pack horses. He'd found enough canvas that hadn't been burned to use as shelters for the pilgrims. While it wasn't any fancy Eastern hotel, it did offer a small creature comfort.

"It's a great, vast, lonesome place, isn't it?" Melody asked, sitting close to the fire as the sun sank past the towering mountains.

"It's big, all right," Preacher told her. "But lonesome?

25

Well, I never dwelled on that too much, though some folks do call it the High Lonesome. I've knowed men who've gone crazy out here, sure enough. And a lot more men who gave up and headed back to towns and people and such. Takes a special breed to make it out here. I knowed one old boy who lost his horse and was afoot during the winter. He fought him a puma to the death. We found 'em both come the spring. Both of them froze stiff to a tree. He had his hand on that big cat's head, like he was sayin' 'It's all right. No hard feelin's. We both was just doin' what come natural.' "

"Did you bury him."

"Not right then. Ground was too hard. We come back about a month later and put them both together in a cave and sealed it shut."

"That was a nice gesture," Penelope said.

Preacher looked at her. "I reckon. Howsomever, we didn't have much choice in the matter. They was both still froze together. It've took an axe to get them apart."

By noon of the next day, Preacher knew they were being followed. Problem was, he didn't think they were Injuns. If they were renegade white men, they could turn out to be worse than Injuns. The mountains weren't exactly overflowing with renegade white men, but there were enough of them to cause trouble every now and then. They'd knock trappers in the head, or even shoot them for their pelts or for food or their boots or coats, for that matter. And, he thought, trying to cheer himself up, it could be a party of government surveyors or explorers.

But he couldn't quite make himself believe that.

He figured they were renegades after the women. Two beautiful white women could make even a good man go bad. Especially men who hadn't even seen an *ugly* white woman in years.

When he called a break and the women stepped behind some bushes to do their business, Preacher got Richard and Edmond close.

"We're bein' followed," he told them. "I don't think it's In-juns, and it ain't the Army—I'm sure of that. They'd have seen 'way back that we're not a hostile party and they'd have closed with us. Any good scout would have seen the sign that women leave and they'd be mighty curious. I think we got us some renegades on our trail and I think they're after the women. So keep your powder dry and be ready to fight and fight quick. 'Cause when they come, they'll do it one of two ways, they'll either come real sudden like, or they'll hail the camp and get in amongst us. That's what we don't want. We can't let 'em get in amongst us. I know you two think of yourselves as highly principled men, but you just remember this: there ain't no law out here except the gun, the knife, and the war axe. And if they're renegades, missionaries or not, they'll kill you both and do it without blinkin' an eye. You got the women to think about. They got to come first."

"Neither one of us has ever used violence against another human being," Edmond pointed out.

"Well, you're about to do so," Preacher said, "unless you want to die. Make up your minds. I don't think we got a lot of time to ponder it."

"We should warn the women," Richard said. "I feel they have a right to know about this."

"It's only a suspicion," Edmond said. "Why alarm them unduly?"

Preacher walked away, leaving the two men arguing. When Melody and Penelope stepped out of the bushes, he walked up to them. "You ladies stay put with the men. Rest awhile. No fires. You understand me?" They nodded. "Good. I'll be back in an hour or so."

He took his Hawken and set out at a ground-covering lope. Preacher could run all day, and had done so several times during his time in the mountains. He'd had more than one horse shot out from under him, by both white men and Injuns, by bullet and arrow, and been forced to run for his life.

He ran for a couple of miles, then scrambled up on a ledge. He squatted down, studying their back trail. Far below and behind them, he could pick out tiny doll-figures moving toward them on horseback. He counted eight riders, and they were not Indians. They had only two pack horses, so they were not trappers. They were not dressed in uniform, so they were not military. That left government explorers or renegades. Preacher had him a strong suspicion they were the latter.

"Damn!" he said. As if he didn't have enough problems without this being added. If that was Bum Kelley's bunch, they were in real serious trouble.

Bum had come out back around '28 or '29 and immediately started making trouble wherever he happened to be. He always had anywhere from ten to fourteen thieves and killers and toughs hanging around him, and the gang ranged from the Utah Territory up into the British-held lands. There wasn't nothing Bum and his bunch wouldn't do, and precious little they hadn't done—and all of it bad.

He wished he had him a spy-glass, but then figured as long as he was wishing he might as well wish for a detachment of soldier boys and about half a dozen of his good friends, like Thumbs Carroll, Nighthawk, Tenneysee, and some others. They'd probably all be 'way south of his position, though.

"Might as well wish for the moon," Preacher muttered, and then picked up his rifle. He paused as four more riders caught his eye, one of them leading a pack horse.

"That's about right," he muttered. "Twelve bad ones and me with a one-eared gospel shouter, a smart-aleck missionary, and two faithful female followers. Lord have mercy on a poor mountain boy."

He picked up his Hawken and loped back to where he had left them. "Mount up," he told them, bending over to catch his breath. "We got big troubles about five miles behind us."

"You ran five miles?" Penelope asked.

"I've run all day, lady, and half into the night 'fore. I'll tell you about it sometime. But not now. Let's go!"

Preacher pushed the group. He knew where he wanted to

go. It wasn't no more than a day's ride, and he set a hard pace. They had crossed the Shoshone and now, instead of cutting south as he had planned, Preacher rode straight west, toward a place he'd once wintered. He figured the hidden cave was still there. He had no idea what it would take to make it disappear. Other than God.

He rode into a tiny creek and told the others, "Stay right behind me. Don't get out of this crick. It won't fool them for long, but it will slow them up tryin' to figure out where we left it." He chuckled. "And that, boys and girls, is something that's gonna take them a-while to do."

They rode for several miles, always staying in the creek, until coming to a sandy, rocky flat. "We'll leave it here," Preacher told them, as he swung down from the saddle. "Stand down for a couple of minutes and rest; let the horses blow. I got to do something."

He had saved his old buckskins and now he cut them up to make socks for the horses' hooves.

"Why are you doing that?" Richard asked.

"So's the steel hooves won't scar the rocks and leave a trail," Preacher told him. "Get that old ragged blanket off my pack horse and do the same with it. Quickly, people. Every minute counts."

When the hooves were covered, Preacher led the group to the timber and told them not to move from that spot. Then he led the horses over, one at a time and had each one mount up.

"Stay with me," he told them. "Don't snag a thread on a branch. If you do, holler and stop and pick it off. They'll find this trail, eventually, but let's don't make it any easier for them."

Preacher led them deep into virgin forests, forging his own trail, the needles and leaves making only faint whispering sounds under the hooves. He pointed to a tree, which had strange markings some twenty feet off the ground. "Grizzly. And a big one. He'll stand twelve feet high and weigh damn near half a ton. If a grizzly gets after you, climb a tree. They're so big and heavy they don't climb.

Usually," he added with a smile.

Edmond looked up at the scratchings and shook his head, wondering what it would be like to come face to face with a beast that large.

It was a trail-weary and saddle-sore bunch that finally slipped out of the saddle just at dusk. Preacher had set a grueling pace. And he didn't make matters any better when he said, "Cold camp. No fires. Roll up in your blankets now and stay there. Cool clear night like this, the odor of food cookin' or coffee boilin' would travel five miles. This spruce and pine's got an odor to it, too."

"Not even a little fire?" Penelope asked.

"No. See to your horses, rub them down good, and picket them careful on graze."

"Tyrant!" she muttered.

Preacher slept well but cautiously that night, as he usually did in the mountains. He did not awaken at natural sounds. The sounds of a hunting owl seizing a mouse or rat or rabbit would not pull him awake. The lonesome call of a coyote or the talking of wolves would not alarm him. A breaking twig would pull him instantly alert, for deer or elk or most forest creatures would not step on a branch unless they were frightened and running. Man steps on twigs and branches.

The rain woke him several hours before dawn would touch the high country.

He quietly climbed out of his blankets and rolled them in his ground sheet. The others slept on, unaware of anything that was happening around them; they would have to learn the woods, or they'd die.

With it raining, he would chance a small fire for coffee, built under an overhang to break up the smoke. He checked the snares he'd set out the evening before and found two fat rabbits. He skinned them out and carefully scraped the meat from the skin and rolled them up from habit. They made good glove linings. He had the meat cooking before the others began stirring.

Melody was the first up. She completed her morning toilet and joined Preacher by the small fire, both of them waiting for the coffee to boil and the meat to sear.

"We're in trouble, aren't we?" she asked.

"It ain't the best situation I ever been in," he acknowledged. "But it ain't the worst, neither. I get to my secret hidey-hole — and it is a hole — we can all get some rest and figure out our next move. It'll take Bum and them others some time to find us there. They might never," Preacher told her, knowing it to be a lie.

He poured them coffee, both of them cupping their fingers around the tin, warming their extremities, for the morning was very cold this high up. The others slept on.

Preacher met her blues across the fire. "Edmond's sweet on you."

"I know. But I don't share his feelings. At all. He's not a bad person, really, Preacher. He's just far out of his element. And he's scared. Like all the rest of us. Except you."

"I'd be scared in a big city like Phillydelphia. Too damn many people for my tastes." He shook his head. His hair was long, hanging well past his ears, for he hadn't cropped it all winter. It helped to keep his head and face warm during the brutal mountain winters. "You don't act like no gospel-shouter I ever seen, Melody. Richard and Edmond, yeah, and Penelope, too. But not you. How'd you get tied up in an outfit like this one?"

"Through a society I belong to. We all thought it would be a grand adventure and we could help bring the Lord to the savages. I'm afraid we didn't think it out very thoroughly."

"You sure didn't. No place for a woman out here. Not yet. Someday, yeah. Someday this country will be ruined with people." The last was spoken with some bitterness.

Melody smiled at him across the flames. "It has to be, Preacher. The nation is growing. People want to build new lives, to explore, to expand. Do you know about the steam locomotives?"

"The what?"

"Locomotives that run by steam. It's true. We've had

31

them for almost six years now. Soon the railroads will be running everywhere."

"Not out here!"

"Oh, yes, Preacher. Even out here. A true visionary by the name of Doctor Hartwell Carver is proposing a transcontinental route."

"A trans-what?"

"Coast to coast railroad tracks. You wait and see. It will happen."

"Stars and garters! I never heard of such a thing. Why, I had a man tell me that no more'un five or six years ago, they wasn't but a hundred miles of track in the whole United States."

"That's true. But I assure you, there are many many more miles of track than that now."

Preacher shook his head. "Makes a poor man like me feel plumb ignorant."

She smiled. "No, Preacher. Never ignorant. You've just been isolated, that's all. When was the last time you read a newspaper?"

"I . . . don't remember. I can read," he quickly added. "I went to the fifth grade. But it's been so many years since I read a word I'd have trouble, I 'magine."

"I understand that there is talk already of an expedition to chart a route from St. Louis to San Francisco, although I'm sure it will be several years before that happens. Can you just imagine that? A railroad from St. Louis westward all the way across the nation? It's mind-boggling. Preacher, the government will be looking for men like you to lead those scouting parties. Men like you who know the wilderness that so many of us have only read about. Ignorant, Preacher? No, you're far from being that. You've been to California?"

"Oh, yeah. I seen the blue waters a couple of times. I been to California and Oregon. Hard, mean trip from here. A railroad? That's *impossible!* You can't build no damn railroad through these mountains." He again shook his head. "That's a pipedream, Melody. It ain't possible. You can't hardly get a wagon through. You can't even do that in most spots."

"But you are going to take us to Oregon, aren't you, Preacher?"

"I shore ain't gonna leave you out here alone," he hedged the question slightly.

She smiled and kissed him right on the mouth. Startled Preacher so bad he spilled the hot coffee right on his crotch and he jumped up, hollering and bellering and slapping at himself. The others thought they were under attack and went into a panic. Penelope got all tangled up in her blankets, shrieking like a banshee, and Richard jumped out of his blanket, the back flap to his underwear hanging down. Edmond flew out his blankets and ran slap into a tree, knocking himself goofy—which wasn't that long a trip.

Melody and Preacher hung on to each other, laughing so hard they had tears in their eyes.

Four

"Lost their tracks," the renegade reported back to Bum. "He took 'em into that crick yonder. I don't know whether he went up or down. Down, if he was smart."

"Preacher is anything but smart," Bum replied, knowing he was telling a lie. Preacher was as wiley a mountain man as ever tracked a deer, and as dangerous as any puma. He remembered that time down on the Poison Spider Crick when an ol' boy name of Jason Dunbar got to needlin' Preacher about his name. Preacher took all he could stomach and told him to lay off or stand up and get ready to duke it out. Dunbar was a good foot taller than Preacher and out-weighed him by a hundred pounds. But when Preacher got through with Dunbar and finally let him fall, Jason Dunbar didn't have no front teeth left him a-tall, couldn't straighten up for a week, and only had half of his left ear. Preacher had bit off the top half. Preacher had put a thrashing on Jason that was talked about for years afterward.

Bum shook his head. "No, Luke, I done told you a tale. Preacher's smart, he's mean, he's tough, and he's quick. And when we catch him—and we will catch up to him and them folks—he won't go down easy. We'll lose some people. Bridger and Broken Hand Fitzpatrick and Carson and

Beckwourth all speak highly of the man. Them boys don't give praise lightly. Bear that in mind."

"Two women out there," another thug said, pulling at himself. "White women. Been a long time since I had me a taste of white women."

"Hell, Slug," another man said. "I ain't even seen a white woman in more'un two year."

"Jack Harris was leadin' them pilgrims straight to us," Bum mused aloud. "How the hell was I supposed to know a bunch of Arapaho was waitin' in ambush?" He cussed and kicked at a rotten branch and it flew into a hundred pieces. "Damn the luck, anyways."

"And where the hell did Jack get off to?" another questioned.

"Runnin' for his life, probably," Bum said. "He's probably settled down and huntin' our trail now. He'll be along. Come on, let's fan out and try to pick up Preacher's trail."

"South?" one of his gang questioned, looking down the little creek.

Bum shook his head. "No. By now, Preacher knows we're trackin' him. He ain't gonna do this the easy way. George, you take a few boys and head south aways just to make sure. Beckman, you take the west side of the crick, Moses, you take the east side. You both work north. Rest of us will wait here so's not to crap up any sign. Take off. Adam, you build us a fire and we'll boil some coffee." He bit off a chew from a twist and looked up the crick. "White women," he muttered. "And them men with 'em is totin' gold, too. I got a good feelin' about this. A real good feelin'."

Several miles from his destination, Preacher halted the short column and once more sacked the horses' hooves. He then led the group up a gently sloping hill to a jumble of rocks on a ledge. A towering mountain loomed high above them, snow-capped all year round.

"It gets right close in here, folks," Preacher told them. "So mind your feet and knees."

He led them into a narrow twisting passageway that was just wide enough for them to pass with not three inches to spare on either side. There was just enough light filtering in from the crack high above them to illuminate their way.

"Eerie," Melody muttered.

With the sacking still on their horses' hooves, the party made very little noise as they moved along. The narrow fissure suddenly opened up into a high, huge, cathedral-like cavern with a bubbling stream running right through it. About a hundred feet long and several times that in width, the other end opened up into a beautiful little valley, about twenty-five or thirty acres of lush grass and a winding little creek.

"I don't think anybody else knows about this place," Preacher said. "Them drawin's on the walls was done hundreds of years ago, I reckon. Lord knows, I ain't never seen no beasties that look like some of them animals yonder. If you was to talk to an Injun about this place, he'd tell you it was the People Who Came Before who done this. Sounds reasonable to me."

"Is the way we came in the only way in?" Richard asked.

"Nope. They's another way. See that waterfall over 'crost the valley? They's another cave under that, leads into a blow-down on the other side."

"A what?" Edmond asked.

"Long time ago, years, must have been a terrible storm struck here. Tore up several hundred acres. Huge trees tore up by the roots and tossed ever whichaway. Piled on top of one another and flang willy-nilly about. The cave comes out direct into all that mess. Them chasin' us might look a little ways into that blow-down; but they ain't gonna give it no good looksee. Too wild a place. Now in here where we is, the smoke filters up through them cracks in the ceilin' and disappears somewheres else. I built me a roarin', smokin' fire in here one winter's morning and spent the rest of the day outside. I never seen no smoke nor smelled none. We're as safe as I can make us. Now what I want you folks to do is this: strip the horses and put them out to pasture. I'm gonna take my bow, go out into that blow-down, and kill us a deer or two so's we'll have some meat to go along with the beans and bread that you ladies is gonna make from the flour we salvaged back at the ambush site. They's fish in that stream in the valley that's mighty good eatin'. I'm gonna be gone the rest of the day and maybe the night. Don't worry. I'll be back if a rattler don't bite me, a bear don't tree me, a puma don't jump on me and claw me to death, an Injun don't kill me, or I don't die from phewmona after gettin' soakin' wet duckin' under that waterfall yonder."

"I hate to be macabre," Edmond said.

"Whatever that means," Preacher said.

"But, what happens if you *don't* return?"

"You sit tight until your supplies is just about gone. By that time, if you don't eat all the damn day long, Bum and his boys will have given up and gone. Then you head west. That's the direction the sun sets. If you come to a great big body of water, that's the Pacific Ocean. You'll either be in California or Oregon country."

"You don't have to be insulting," Penelope said.

Preacher stared at her for a moment, then shook his head. He was muttering as he got his bow and quiver of arrows and left the cave and headed out into the meadow, walking toward the waterfall.

Melody stood in the mouth of the cave and watched him until he ducked behind the cascading water and was gone from sight. Penelope was lying down, exhausted from the travels, and Edmond was seeing to the horses.

"He's quite a man, Melody," Richard said softly. "But not the man for you."

She turned slowly and faced him. "Whatever in the world do you mean, Richard?"

"It's easy to see that you're quite smitten with him, Melody. We've all commented on it. But I urge you to think about what you're doing and to try and curb your emotions. The man is a wanderer, a will of the wisp. He'll only break your heart."

"It's purely platonic, Richard," she lied. "Nothing more. I enjoy his company, that's all. He's a fascinating man who has packed ten average lifetimes into one."

"Melody, I don't want to appear ungrateful for all he's done for us. He saved our lives and continues to do so hourly. But the man is only a cut above a savage. I doubt he's had a fork in his hand in ten years. He eats with his fingers. The two of you come from different worlds."

She smiled and patted his arm. "You worry needlessly, Richard. Come, let me change the dressing on your ear. In years to come, no matter where we might be, we'll look back on this episode and enjoy a good laugh."

Preacher got his first deer within moments of entering the blow-down. He quickly but carefully skinned and butchered it, leaving the waste parts for critters of the forest to eat. There would be no trace of the animal come the morning. He put the eatable parts in the hide and using a length of rope he'd brought, he hung the meat high from a limb to protect it. It took him an hour to find, stalk, and bring down the second deer. He heard a rustling in the dense brush and knew that wolves had caught the blood scent and were closing. Three big gray wolves, a male and two females. Preacher tossed them liver, intestines, and other scrap parts, shouldered his load and headed back toward the valley. Lots of folks feared wolves, but most of that fear was groundless. Preacher had never known of a healthy, full-grown wolf ever, unprovoked, attacking a human being. But a starving or hurt wolf was quite another matter. And when any animal is eating a kill or hiding the carcass for a later snack, you best leave that animal alone. And they also get mighty protective when it comes to their young.

He left the wolves snarling in mock anger and tearing at the meat parts. "Enjoy, brothers," he said.

Preacher rather liked wolves. He'd had several as companions from time to time. They had not been pets, for a wolf cannot be domesticated like a dog. And if you're going to be around them, you got to know their ways. They don't conform to human ways; a man's got to conform to *their* ways. Once that's settled, a man can be fairly comfortable around wolves. You just can't never let them get the upper hand. For once they do, it takes a fight for dominance to regain it. And you ain't likely to come out in too good a shape fightin' no two hundred pound buffalo wolf.

Preacher figured he was packing close to a hundred and fifty pounds of raw meat, for the deer had both been sleek and fat. It had been an early spring, with lots to eat. But he'd carried more than that for longer periods of time.

He was back in the cave by nightfall and had some steaks sizzling moments later. "We'll smoke and jerk the rest of it," he told them. "Tomorrow, I'll pick some berries and we'll make pemmican."

"What in the world is that?" Richard asked.

"After the meat's dried, that's what we call jerky, I'll pound it into a powder and mix it with pulped and whole berries and the fat I saved from the venison after I cook it down. You mix all that up and it keeps for a long time. I got some over there in my parfleche. Try some. It's good."

"What is a parfleche?" Melody asked.

"Rawhide case yonder. Hand it here." Preacher stuffed some pemmican into his mouth and smiled. "I ain't kiddin' y'all. It's really good."

He passed the parfleche around and the others reluctantly tried some of the concoction. They all smiled as they chewed. "It really is good!" Edmond said.

"Y'all gonna bring Jesus to the savages," Preacher said, "I reckon now is a good time to start your learnin'. You got to know something about these folks."

"We were to be instructed in Oregon," Richard said.

"Wagh!" Preacher said in disgust. "Them's coast Injuns. Klamath and Tillamook and Chinook and Spokan and Pomo and Chumash and the like. Hell, they all 'bout either civilized or whupped down by now. I'm talkin' *Injuns,* folks. Scalp-hunters and warriors and the finest horsemen on the face of the earth. Comanche, Pawnee, Ute, Shoshoni, Apache, Blackfoot, Arapaho, Crow, Kiowa, Flathead, Assiniboin, Dakota—that's Sioux to you—and Nez Perce. They's more, but them's the important ones you'll be seein', I 'magine. Most of the ones I just named is hunters and warriors. Only ones I know of that'll grow anything to eat to amount to anything is your Hidatsa, Navajo, Pima, Pueblo, and Papago. Most of them is down in the Southwest. Except for the Hidatsa, and what's left of them is scattered along the northern borders. Mandan and Pawnee will raise a few crops, mostly corn, beans, squash and pumpkin. They trade a lot with other tribes. You watch a Pawnee when you're tradin'. They're slick. Blackfoot, Crow and Comanche won't eat fish. It's taboo to them. Your desert tribes roast snake and insects.

"Richard, you asked me couple of days back about how Injuns cook and what they eat. You'd be surprised. I've lived with Injuns that could whup up a buffalo stew that'd leave you smackin' your lips for days. Injuns ain't like white folks in that they don't waste nothin'. And I mean nothin'. They break the bones and boil the marrow or just suck it out. They clean and scrape out the guts and make sausage cases out of 'em, stuffin' 'em with seasoned meat. They're good with nature's own wild things. They season with sage and wild onions and milkweed buds and rosehips. They peel the prickly-pear cactus and add that to stews and soups. It was Injuns that taught me to peel fresh sweet thistle stalks and eat it. Tastes kinda like nuts.

"Injuns ain't got pots like we use, so when they make a stew, they use the linin' from a buffalo stomach. You get you four poles, secure the ends of the linin', dump in some meat and stuff like prairie turnips and wild peas. To make the water boil, the women drop in hot rocks. The pouch will last three/four days until it gets soggy, then you eat the linin'. They don't waste nothin'.

"Injuns use ever' part of the animal they can. The thick pelt from a buffalo's neck can be made into a shield. Animals killed in winter has a special use cause the hair is long and thick. They use 'em for blankets and robes. Rawhide is made into strings and ropes. Buffalo hair is woven into ropes. Buffalo horns is used for everything from spoons to gourds. Injuns used to make knifes out of buffalo bones. Injuns use buffalo hides to make their tipis. And a tipi is not only a home, it's a sacred place to the Injun. The floor means the earth that they live on. The walls, which is peaked, is the sky. They round 'cause that is the sacred life circle, which ain't got no beginnin' or no end. Get it? A circle. And Injuns will always burn something that smells good in their tipis. Sage or sweet grass. It's an altar to them. That's where they pray to *their* gods."

An inference that none of the missionaries missed.

Preacher took one of the deer steaks out of the pan and fell to eating. With his knife and fingers. Around a mouthful of meat, Preacher said, "The tipi belongs to the Injun women of the plains, and don't ever let nobody tell you no different. The women make em, they put 'em up, they take 'em down, they haul 'em around. A man lives there only if the woman wants him to. She can chuck his possessions outside and the marriage is over. And he damn well better scat."

"How many hides does it take to make a tipi?" Melody asked.

"Anywhere from seven to thirty. Depends on the size of the lodge. It's a social thing for the women. Kind of like a barnraisin' to you folks. Say a Cheyenne needs a new lodge, the word goes out and the women gather, among them, one woman who is the official lodge-maker. After the woman who's needin' a new lodge feeds them all good, they start sewin' the skins together, usually startin' early in the mornin'. Then they'll eat again, and it's back to sewin' and gossipin' and gigglin' and singin' and carryin' on. Takes a day and a new lodge is up."

"Then they have order in their societies?" Edmond asked.

"In a way. The Plains Injuns don't much cotton to someone tellin' 'em what to do." Preacher stuffed the last of his meat into his mouth, chewed for a moment, swallowed, then belched loudly. "You got to belch after a meal. Means the grub was good. If you don't belch, your host might be offended 'cause he'll think you didn't like his woman's cookin'. Always belch after a meal with the Injuns. 'Least the ones I been around.

"Injuns is pretty much free to come and go as they please in the tribe. Contrary to what you probably been taught, the Plains Injuns ain't got no elected nor passed-down leadership. Even a chief ain't got the power to punish nobody. To get to be a chief means that the rest of the tribe respects that man's wisdom, his courage, or even how well he can talk. Every male is a member of the council, and every man has the right to state his opinions. And they all do. It can go on for days!

"I reckon tradition might be the glue that keeps tribes together. I don't know what else could do it. All the tribes is different, but yet they're strangely alike in a lot of ways. When the white man finally gets up a head of steam and starts comin' thisaway, and they will, they's gonna be a lot of blood spilt. On both sides. At first it's gonna be mostly white people who die. But that won't last long. From what I've been able to pick up durin' the past few years, east of the Big Muddy is fairly overflowin' with people. They got to come west. The Injuns ain't gonna adopt the white ways, and the whites ain't gonna adopt the Injun ways. So what we re gonna have—to my way of thinkin'—is a great big bloody mess that's gonna go on for years."

"Then the savages have to be convinced that they cannot stand in the way of progress," Edmond said. "That's where people like us can help."

Preacher looked at him in the dancing light of the fire. He smiled rather sadly. "White man's way is the only way, huh?" He shook his head and poured a cup of coffee. "We shore take a lot upon ourselves, don't we?"

"Civilization and progress must continue if we, as a nation, are to survive," Richard said. "That's the way it's always been, and must continue to be."

"Says who?" Preacher challenged.

"This discussion is silly," Edmond said. "You obviously are not prepared to meet the challenge of a changing world. You miss the point of it all."

"Oh, I get the point," the mountain man said. "And lots of other folks will, too. The point of an arrow."

Five

Preacher spent the next morning backtracking the way they entered the cave, carefully erasing all signs of anyone ever having come that way. He spent a couple of hours inspecting the sides of the narrow passageway, picking off hair the horses left as they rubbed the sides here and there. When he was satisfied he could do no more to insure their safety, Preacher rejoined the group in the cave.

"Any sign of them?" Edmond inquired, lifting his eyes from the Bible he'd been reading.

"No. But they'll be along. White women's too grand a prize for them to give up on. And they probably figure you're carryin' gold."

"That's ridiculous!" Richard said.

"Really? Them money-belts y'all totin' don't fit too well. They pooch out from time to time."

Richard and Edmond automatically put hands to their bellies.

"Yep," Preacher said, pouring coffee. "Gold and women. Many a man has died for that combination. How much you boys carryin'?"

"That is none of your affair," Edmond bluntly stated.

"You're right," Preacher replied easily. "It ain't. But if I'm to put my life on the line for you folks, I figure I at least ought to know what I'm dyin' for."

"This money," Richard said, patting his belly, "must get to our new mission in Oregon. It isn't ours. This is money raised by our organization back East. Contributors' money. This is money that will be used to further God's work."

"You ain't got no poor folks back in Philadelphia could use a helpin' hand? Must be quite a prosperous place," Preacher said sarcastically. "Rich folks aboundin' ever'-where. I shore wouldn't fit in."

Richard sighed heavily and Melody laughed at the expression on her friend's face.

"And didn't nobody ever tell y'all that it ain't fittin' for unmarried young men and women to go traispin' off unchaperoned? What does you girls' mommas and daddies think about this trip?"

"We left with their blessings," Penelope said. "They know that we are both very trustworthy and level-headed women." She looked at Melody. "One of us is, anyway."

Melody reached over and patted the young woman on the leg. "Don't worry, dear. I'll look after you. I did promise your mother."

Bum Kelley and his boys patiently searched and, as Preacher had predicted, found the trail after Preacher had left the rocks of the creek.

"He's headin' into the wilderness," Beckman said, just a touch of awe in his voice. "You know that country, Bum?"

Bum shook his head. "Can't say as I do. I've skirted it a time or two taking the south route. But that damn Preacher seems to know every rock between the borders and between the Big Muddy and the ocean. And he turned north, right into the Tetons. Damn his eyes."

The outlaws stood on the fringe of the mountain range and gazed at the towering peaks that stood silently before

45

them.

"How old a man is this feller, anyways?" a man called Keyes asked.

"Thirty-five or so, I reckon. He come out here, so the stories go, back when he was about twelve or thirteen years old, and he ain't never stopped explorin'. So he's got twenty or so years of experience behind his belt. And he's as tricky as they come."

"He know you, Bum?" Bobby asked.

"He knows me. And he don't like me."

"Hey!" Slug shouted. "Here comes Jack Harris. I knowed he'd catch up with us."

Jack swung down from the saddle wearily. His clothing was in rags and he looked gaunt. "Put some grub on, boys," Jack said. "I ain't et in days."

A fire was hurriedly built and a thick deer steak jammed on a pointed stick. A blackened coffee pot filled with creek water was soon boiling and the coffee dumped in.

Jack was so worn out he could hardly keep his eyes open. A cup of thick strong coffee perked him up enough to talk, while the cooking steak caused drool to appear on the man's lips.

"What happened back yonder at the wagon train, Jack?" Bum asked.

"Them Injuns came out of nowhere, I tell you. I didn't have a clue they was there. I jumped off the flat and hit the timber at the first yell 'cause I could see we didn't have a chance. The outriders went down first. I don't know what happened after that. I was too busy floggin' my good horse gettin' away from there. I waited two days, I think it was, and went back lookin' for food. But I couldn't find nothin' 'ceptin' some bloody bandages and shod tracks headin' west. You boys' and somebody else's. I just started followin' along."

"Preacher," Bum said. "I recognized that big gray of his through my spy glass. He's got them gospel shouters and the women with him. He knows we're on his trail and he's wary."

Jack was instantly alert. *"Preacher!* What the hell's he doin' up here? He's supposed to be down on the Popo Agie at the rendezvous."

"Well, he ain't. And he's tooken them folks into the wilderness." He pointed. "Yonder."

"In *there?"* Jack said with horror in his voice. "Northwest to the talkin' smoke?"

"I don't think so. I think he's got him a hidey hole in the lonesome yonder and he's all tucked away, thinkin' he's safe."

"He's pretty damn safe in there, Bum. I don't know that country. Hell, don't *nobody* really know that country. Well, a few does. And Preacher's one of them."

Bum looked hard at the man. "You want to give up?"

Jack jerked the half-raw steak from the stick and went to gnawing. He finally shook his head and wiped the grease from his mouth with the back of his hand. "No. Them two men was carryin' heavy with gold." He belched and farted and tore off another hunk of bloody meat. "And them women, boys, I swear I ain't never seen nothin' so fine in all my days."

"How fine?" a thug named Leo asked, leaning closer to Jack, his thick lips slick with spittle.

"Fine enough to fight a grizzly for."

"Bet they smell good, too," Bull said. "I just cain't hardly wait!"

The ladies had gone down to the waterfall to bathe and wash clothes, using soap they had salvaged from the ruins of the wagon train. Preacher sat on the outside of the cave exit, overlooking the valley. He had carefully cleaned his weapons and placed them at the ready. He knew it was only a matter of time before they would be found. No one is good enough to obliterate all signs of their passing,

47

not if there is a good tracker behind them. And while Bum's people were no-goods, they had survived in the mountains for years, so that made them professional in anybody's book.

Preacher doubted that Bum's boys would have the patience to explore the blow-down, so the rear entrance was reasonably secure. But one or two of them would be brave enough or curious enough to follow the twisting passageway once it was located—and it would be located, he felt sure of that. So let them come on. They would die in that twisting maze and the silent rock walls would be their coffins.

Preacher had spent that morning rigging dead-falls and other traps in the darkness of the twisting entranceway. He had warned the others not to enter there. To make his point, he had showed them one of his traps, and how lethal it was.

"Hideous," Edmond had said.

"Awful," Penelope whispered.

"Such a terrible thing to do to a person," Richard said.

"I just hope it works," Melody said.

It'll work, Preacher thought, as he honed his already sharp knife to a razor's edge. The first one to hit the traps will make the others awful cautious. But they'll press on. The second trap will stop them cold; maybe for a day. *By that time, we'll be far away and pushing hard.*

"You didn't just stop here for safety's sake, did you, Preacher?" Richard asked, breaking into the mountain man's thoughts.

"What else you think I had on my mind?" Preacher looked at him.

"You knew we needed several days of rest," the missionary said, and pegged it right. "My wound needed to heal and we all needed to lay about and eat and regain strength. But you, alone, would have been a hundred miles away by now. You're risking your life for people you hardly know. You're a very brave and complex man, Mister . . . what *is* your Christian name?"

"Preacher'll do. Yeah, they's some truth in me wantin' to get you folks rested some. When we leave here, we're gonna be pushin' hard, with not much time to rest. They's a small fort down near Massacre Rocks on the Snake. Fort Hall, I believe it's called. Few soldier boys down yonder. But it's gonna be hell gettin' there. If I can get y'all to the fort, that'll put you back on the Oregon Trail and it bein' springtime and all, chances are good a wagon train is there or one will be along shortly."

"And you'll leave us there?" Edmond asked.

"Why should I stay any longer?"

"Melody, if I may speak frankly," Edmond said.

"Fine-lookin' woman. Good woman, too, I believe. Got stayin' power to her. I like her. I'll say that in front of God and ever'body. And it's both an uncomfortable and yet nice feelin'. Been a long time since I experienced anything like it. But our worlds is different. Too far apart. I don't fit in hers and she shore as hell don't fit into mine. So relax, pilgrim. You won't see me again. This is my world, the mountains, the wilderness, the open sky. I plan on dyin' out here. My good horse will stumble, or an Injun's arrow or war axe will find me. I might get cornered by a bear, and we'll have us a high ol' time, a-roarin' and a-yellin' and a-clawed and a-bitin' and a-stobbin' 'til one of us is down." He smiled, showing amazingly good teeth and softened his facial features. "She don't fit in them plans."

Richard smiled. "I believe she might have something to say about that."

"She might think she do. But she don't. Oh, I know the signs, all right. I can see 'em on her face and in her eyes. But once I leave the lot of you at Fort Hall, I'm gone like the wind. I got mountains to climb and rivers to ford. I got valleys to cross where the grass is so lush and high it brushes the belly of my horse. I got to see country I ain't never seen before. I can't do that with no woman taggin' along. Not unless it's a squaw who's used to the hard ways of the trail." Preacher stood up. "You boys stay put. And when the women gets back, y'all start gettin' your possiblies together. I'm fixin' to move some things close to that blow-down hole."

"You think those hooligans are close?" Edmond asked.

"I think they're right outside."

Preacher scrambled up the sloping sides of the valley and stepped into a maze of virgin brush and timber. The bench that encircled the little valley was about three hundred yards deep. He made his way carefully to the outer edge and was not surprised to see Bum and several of his gang moving slowly toward the rock face, a tracker on foot, carefully studying the ground. Preacher backed off and silently made his way back to the cave.

"No talkin'," he whispered. "They're outside now. Get your gear together and get gone to the waterfall. You'll see a natural lean-to on the north side of the falls. It's big enough for all of you and the horses. Take my packhorse with you. There's my gear. No fires. Get gone. Like right now."

The men were gone in ten minutes, gathering up their gear and heading out toward the horses. Preacher quickly packed up what he would carry out and set the pack by the mouth of the cave. Then he drank what coffee was left in the pot, packed the pot away, and carefully put out the fire. He went outside and saddled his horse, then sat back and waited, his .54 caliber Hawken at the ready.

He knew it was only a matter of time now, and probably not that much time. He had lied to the others about how safe they would be in the cave in order to give them some comfort and let them relax. It had worked and all of them, even Richard, were back up to snuff and ready for the trail.

Preacher knew that a good tracker would find the cave opening. Whether or not they would search the entire twisting, turning passageway was up for grabs. Preacher

50

had, years back, but he'd also been wary of running into a bear or a mountain lion. He hoped the men out there now would be twice as wary as he was, but they had women and gold on their minds.

He heard a very faint scraping sound and slowly rose, moving silently toward the entrance to the passageway. They had found the opening.

He had rigged the first dead-fall in such a manner that as dark as it was in that narrow passage, they would probably think it was just an accident.

The second trap would be a hell of a lot more obvious to anyone that it was man-made.

"Dark in there," Bull said, his words not reaching Preacher, who was crouched near the opening, waiting.

"What the hell did you think it would be?" Beckman asked. "A lamp-lit roadhouse? Can you see anything at all?"

"Nothing. Narrow trail, is all. Don't look wide enough for no horse to get through."

Jack Harris shouldered his way into the passage. "It's wide enough. Dirt's too smooth for my likin'. It looks like it's been smoothed out by a branch to me."

"Maybe," Bull said. "There damn sure ain't no puma or bear tracks in the dirt."

"There ain't nothin' on that dirt. See that openin' high up?" He pointed upward to the tiny crack. "It's rained lately here. Drops would have cut a groove in the dirt. He had to hide his tracks, but Preacher was hopin' we wouldn't notice that. I noticed. They's in yonder somewheres, boys."

"Knowin' Preacher is a-layin' in wait in that dark don't make me feel real good, Jack," Beckman said. "You know damn well he ain't no pilgrim."

"He ain't but one man," Jack replied. "Move. Let's search this place. See where it leads."

Preacher had heard only the murmur of voices. He had not been able to make out any of the words. He really

51

didn't need to; he figured they were coming on in.

Bull was the first to inch forward into the dimness of the passageway, moving in a crouch, and advancing very carefully. He was a thug and a murderer, but not an idiot. He knew perfectly well that if Preacher was at the end of this winding, twisting passageway, it would mean a fight to the death.

His fingers touched a rock about the size of a human head. He pushed it aside. That released a tight rawhide thong that whipped out and up, disappearing out of sight and releasing about a dozen other large rocks.

"Slide!" Jack hollered, jumping back as he heard the sound.

Bull jerked back, but not fast enough to avoid getting conked on the head by a rock. The impact laid him out cold on the ground, a swelling knot on his noggin.

"Pull him out of there," Jack said, and he and Beckman tugged at the limp Bull and dragged him out of the passageway, back out into the light.

"Is he daid?" Leo asked.

"I don't think so," Beckman said. "But he's shore gonna have him a headache."

"I think he moved a rock and that triggered the slide," Jack said. "It was a trap."

"You think Preacher done it?" Bum asked.

"Yeah. I do. And they's probably more traps in yonder."

"And Preacher and them others could be long gone," Keyes pointed out.

"Could be," Bum said. "But I don't think so. I think they holed up in yonder for rest. One of 'em's hurt; we've all seen the bloody bandages. The size of 'em tells me it's either a thigh or head wound. Moses, fetch us some long poles to push along ahead of us and wave in the air. That'll set off any traps Preacher might have laid."

All but the last one.

Preacher had taken a small keg of powder salvaged from the wagon train and rigged up a fuse. He had placed the keg between a large rock and the face of the stone wall. When it blew, he felt there would be enough force behind the blast to bring the boulder down and block the passageway.

Preacher could now hear the sounds of sticks whapping the sides of the passageway.

Smart, he thought. *I ain't dealin' with idiots. I'll have to remember that.*

Preacher grinned as the sounds of the sticks striking the earth and the rock walls drew closer. He cocked one of his pistols and let it bang. The sound was enormous in the cave. And he got what he was hoping for.

"Oh, my God!" Beckman hollered in pain, as the wildly ricochetting lead struck him in the leg. "I caught me a ball. Oh, God, it tore up my leg. Git out of there. Git me outta here."

Preacher let bang another ball. He could hear the ugly sound of the ball as it howled from wall to wall, bouncing and careening, looking for a place to strike.

"Get back!" Jack hollered. "Drag Beckman outta there. We got to come up with another plan. It's a death trap in yonder."

"I cain't walk!" Beckman bellered. "Oh, my leg's tore up bad, y'all."

Preacher was reloading as fast as he could, with ball, patch, powder, and ram. He capped his pistols and waited.

"Preacher!" Bum yelled. "You give us the women and the gold and you can walk free. That's a promise, man."

"Go to hell!" Preacher shouted.

"Don't be a fool, Preacher. You're trapped in yonder. Think about it. All we got to do is wait and starve you out. We got the time and you ain't. Them pilgrims ain't worth your dyin' for, man. Give it some thought."

"Ask him if he's got some whiskey to pour on this leg," Beckman said.

Bum gave the man a disgusted look.

53

Preacher waited.

"One way or the other, we're gonna get you, Preacher," Bum yelled, his words echoing around the twisting passageway. "All you got to do is walk out of there and you're a free man."

"In a pig's eye," Preacher muttered. He knew they'd kill him on sight.

Preacher settled down for a long wait.

Six

"So who's got a plan?" Jack asked.

The gang was sitting well away and to the side of the opening in the mountain. They had dug the flattened ball out of Beckman's leg and he lay moaning in pain while Moses rambled around in the woods, gathering up various leaves with which to make a poultice.

"Why not smoke 'em out?" Leo suggested. "It's a cave, ain't it?"

"That ain't a bad idea," Bum said. "As a matter of fact, it's a damn good idea. Let's start gatherin' up all the wood we can tote." He thought for a moment. "No. I got a better idea. We'll build us a shield outta small branches. Lash half a dozen good-sized branches together and stay behind it while we advance. That'll protect us from ricochets and we can get right up on Preacher. When we get close enough we can toss burning pitch over into the cave proper and really smoke 'em out."

The thugs all agreed that Bum had come up with a fine plan. The first log shield they lashed together was too wide and got hung up in the first turn in the passageway. Preacher sat back in the cave and listened to them cuss and holler. He chewed on jerky and waited.

When they finally got the right size shield lashed together, it didn't take them long to get close. Preacher had bellied down on the dirt, his .50 caliber pistols in hand. When the men rounded the long curve that would lead them to the cave, Preacher smiled at the sight. The men were holding the shield about six inches off the passageway floor. Preacher fired both pistols, keeping the muzzles about three inches off the ground. Two of the thugs started squalling in pain as the balls tore into one's foot and the other's ankle, shattering bone.

The shield was dropped to the earth and forward movement halted while the two wounded men were stretched out on the earth, to be dragged out into the clearing.

"I'll kill you for this, Preacher!" Slug bellered. "I'll skin you alive, damn your eyes!"

"I'll do worser than that, Preacher!" Bobby screamed over the pain in his shattered foot. "You'll rue the day you shot me, you dirty bastard! You tore offen some toes, damn you. When I git my hands on you, it'll take you days to die, you sorry son."

"Yeah, yeah," Preacher muttered, reloading. "Flap your mouth, boy." He chuckled. He had put three of them out of action so far. He was cutting down the odds right good, he figured.

Preacher popped another piece of jerky in his mouth and waited.

Then the gang got real quiet. He knew they were up to something, and he didn't think it was going to be pleasant.

It wasn't. They started chucking lit torches into the cave. Preacher grinned and began chucking them right back, figuring he might get lucky and set someone on fire.

He did.

"Halp!" Keyes yelled. "My britches is on far. Halp me beat it out, boys. Jesus Christ. Oh, Lord, hit's a-burnin' my leg. Halp!"

Preacher chucked several more burning brands behind the shield.

"Goddammit, Bum!" a man yelled. "This ain't workin' out like you said it would."

"Well, hell's fire, Adam. I never said it would be perfect, now, did I? Oowww! Somebody kick some dirt on my britches leg. Jesus, it's on fire. Hurry up, dammit!"

"Now you know how I feel!" Keyes hollered.

Preacher felt it was time to add even more confusion to the yelling knot of thugs. He had prepared a small bag of powder—a bag-bomb as Richard had called it while watching the mountain man make it—and now he took it out of his possibles pouch and lit the fuse. He tossed it over the top of the log shield.

"Holy Christ!" he heard a man yell. "Run. It's a damn bomb."

The small grenade really didn't do a lot of damage when it exploded. But in the confined space of the passageway, it sounded a lot more dangerous than it really was. It also peppered the thugs with small rocks and pebbles when it blew, stinging and bloodying the men.

Preacher leaned back and laughed at the sounds of panic echoing all around him.

"Damn you, Preacher!" George hollered, then immediately fell into a coughing fit due to all the dust. "Why don't you fight fair, man?"

"Idiot," Preacher muttered. "There ain't no such of a thing as a fair fight."

"Oh, I cain't walk!" Rod moaned. "The bomb done crippled me. Don't abandon me, boys."

"Fool!" Bum yelled. "That's Leo sittin' on your legs. You ain't hurt."

"The whole side of my face is bloody," Adam squalled. "Look at me. Did it blow my face off, boys?"

Preacher scooped up a double handful of dirt and wrapped it up in a piece of cloth. He fashioned a fuse and lit it. He yelled, "Here comes another one, boys!" Then he chunked it over the logs.

Wild panic broke out in the narrow space as the outlaws began screaming and cussing and literally running over each other in their haste to depart the scene. Preacher crawled forward, pushing the burning brands the thugs had tossed into the cave in front of him. He stacked them up all around the front of the lashed-together logs and then hustled back around the bend in the passageway to safety.

"It was a dud!" Jack shouted.

"Long-burnin' fuse!" Preacher yelled.

"You're a liar, Preacher," Bum shouted.

"Look!" Moses shouted. "The barricade's on far."

"Grab some dirt and put it out, boys!" Bum yelled.

Preacher decided he'd had enough fun and lit the long fuse leading to the charge behind the rocks above the barricade. He grabbed his gear and headed out the mouth of the cave. He figured he had maybe thirty seconds to vacate the area before all that powder blew.

He misjudged it slightly. The fuse burned quickly and then touched the powder. The concussion rocked the ground beneath his moccasins when it exploded.

The huge rock and dozens of smaller ones came tumbling down, completely blocking the passageway and sealing that entrance to the little valley.

One rock bounced off Moses's head and knocked the thug sprawling to the earth, addling him. Jack Harris took a stone right between the eyes and it knocked him cold.

Bum Kelley assessed the damage and threw his hat to the ground and cussed.

In the valley, sitting his saddle, Preacher threw back his head and howled like a great gray wolf. Then he laughed and headed for the waterfall.

Preacher led his party through the blow-down and headed westward into the Grand Tetons. He figured he had bought them at least two days and maybe as many as four.

Behind him, Bum Kelley and his outlaws had staggered out of the passageway to fall exhausted on the ground. All of them were cut, bruised, and bleeding from wounds ranging from minor to serious.

"Let's start checkin' each other out," Bum finally spoke, heaving himself up off the ground. He swayed slightly on his boots. "Unless you boys want to give up on gettin' the gold and them women."

The outlaws gave him grim looks.

"Not damn likely," Bull muttered darkly. "But I want Preacher worser than I want anything else. I want to stick his feet into a far and burn him slow."

"Yeah," Bobby moaned the word. He looked at the bloody bandage that covered where some toes had been. He was alternately working on a piece of deerskin, making a crude moccasin, and moaning through his pain. "I wanna gouge his eyes out."

"I'm gonna cut him," Beckman said. "And that's just for starters." He looked at his wounded leg and cussed.

Slug was splinting his broken ankle over the damage done by the .50 caliber ball. "I'm gonna rape both them women and make Preacher watch. Then I'm gonna skin him. Slow."

Bum smiled grimly. He knew there would be no stopping these men now. Now it was a matter of honor with them. Preacher had shamed them all and if need be, they would track him right up to and through the gates of hell for revenge.

But, Bum thought, to make matters even worser, as soon as Preacher reached some post or settlement, he would tell the story, and really juice it up. Unless he was stopped, Bum and his boys would be the laughing stock of the territories. He knew the others had the same thought.

They couldn't none of them allow that to happen. They had to close Preacher's mouth. Forever.

Preacher would chuckle occasionally as he built a fire to cook their supper.

"I fail to see what is so amusing about inflicting pain and suffering upon your fellow man," Edmond said.

Preacher looked at the missionary. "Do you have any idea what them ol' boys back yonder will do to you if they catch you?"

"Rob us."

Preacher chuckled. "You really are a babe in the woods, ain't you? Well, let me tell you something. If they catch you people, after they get tired of usin' the women, then they'll use you men. You get my drift?"

"I don't believe that!" Edmond said. "That would be— well, barbaric!"

"It sure would. But they'd still do it. Then they'd torture you just to listen to you scream. They've done it all before. Ain't nothin' new to none of them. They been doin' it for years and years."

"Why don't the authorities stop them?" Richard asked.

"Good God, people!" Preacher blurted in exasperation. "Look around you. What authorities? There ain't no law out here. This is wilderness. Can't you people understand that?"

"The *Army* is the authority in wilderness areas, I believe," Edmond said. "When we reach this fort you spoke of, we shall certainly report the reprehensible behavior of those ruffians who attacked the cave."

"Sure," Preacher replied. "People, this land is in dispute 'tween England and the U-nited States. There might not be soldiers there. 'Sides, ain't but about five hundred million billion acres out there. Hell, they oughtta be able to search that in no time a-tall." He shook his head. "Foolish, foolish people."

Preacher fell silent as the little something that had been nagging at him all day finally settled down in the light of his mind. He had known about half of the men behind the voices back yonder in the cave. But yet another voice had been awful familiar to him.

"Jack Harris!" he blurted.

"What?" Richard said, looking at the mountain man. "What about our guide?"

"I *knowed* that voice was familiar. He was one of them back at the cave. I'm sure of it!"

Melody scooted closer to him. "If that's correct, Preacher, then that means that . . ." Her voice trailed off, her face frozen in shock.

"Yeah," Preacher spoke the word softly. "The whole thing wasn't nothin' but a set up from the git-go."

"Whatever in the world do you mean?" Penelope asked.

"Them Injuns spoiled Bum and Jack's plans. They wasn't figurin' on them Injuns attackin'. *They* was gonna ambush the wagon train. That's why Jack took y'all so far north of the Oregon Trail."

Edmond was speechless—which, to Preacher's ears, was a great relief.

Penelope sat on the ground, her mouth open.

"Yes," Richard finally said. "Yes. It has to be. What a thoroughly untrustworthy, black-hearted, and totally reprehensible individual."

"Does that mean he's a dirty, low-down, sorry skunk?" Preacher asked.

"Yes. That sums it up quite well."

"Thought so. Well, it means something else, too: it means they got to kill us all. You see, no tellin' how long Jack's been doin' this. You say Jack hooked up with y'all in Missouri?"

"Well . . . not exactly," Richard said. "Ten days out of Missouri, our guide suddenly disappeared. He'd been out scouting, I think. Well, you can imagine our predicament. We were beside ourselves with worry. We were *lost*. The next morning, Jack Harris rode in. He was so strong-appearing and full of confidence. We practically had to beg him to take on the job of guide."

"Where was your wagon master?"

"Why . . . I don't suppose we had one."

"Just how much beggin' did y'all have to do 'fore Jack agreed to sign on?"

"Well, actually, not very much."

"I thought not. Well, let's fix some vittles and eat up. We got to push hard come the mornin'. There's some damn rough country ahead.

They crossed the Yellowstone and Preacher took them straight west. He took them over the Divide and headed for the Snake. By now, he knew that Bum and his boys would have circled the small range in which the cave was located. They would pick up their trail and be hard on it.

"By the Lord!" Edmond exclaimed one frosty morning in the high-country. "This land is exhilarating!"

"Does that mean you like it?" Preacher asked.

"My word, yes!"

"You ain't thinkin' of settlin' here, is you?"

"We've discussed it," Melody said sweetly. "After all, savages are savages, whether on the west coast or here. Of course, we shall have to push on to deliver the monies. But we think we shall return to this wonderful and primitive land."

"Is that a fact?" Preacher's words were glumly spoken.

"Yes!" she said brightly. "Aren't you excited with the news?"

"I can tell you truthful I am purt near overcome."

"I knew you would be . . . darling," she added softly.

Preacher felt like he was standing in quicksand, and slowly sinking. Movement caught his eyes. He looked up. First time in his life he was happy to see a band of Indians.

Seven

"Relax," Preacher said. "They're Bannocks. I know that brave in the lead. His name is Bad Foot."

"Bad Foot?" Edmond said. "Why would anybody name a child that?"

"Probably 'cause he was borned with a club foot. Sometimes that's the way Injuns name their young. If I knowed y'all better I'd tell you a story about a brave I knowed once called Two Dogs Humpin'."

"Please don't," Penelope said quickly.

"Sounds like a delightfully naughty story," Melody said, her eyes bright.

"I'm sorry I brung it up," Preacher said, getting to his feet and making the sign of 'Brother' to the Indian on the lead pony.

Preacher began speaking to the brave in his own tongue, Snake. Bad Foot grinned and nodded his head and began rubbing his belly.

"They been buffler huntin'," Preacher explained. "And they gonna give us some steaks. We got some mighty fine eatin' comin' up, folks."

"Ask him if he's ever heard of God," Edmond said, digging in his pack for one of the many small Bibles he'd salvaged from the wagon train ambush.

"Ask him yourself. He speaks pretty good English. I's just bein' polite speakin' his tongue."

Edmond approached the Indian cautiously, holding a Bible in his hands. Bad Foot stood smiling at him. Edmond held out the Bible and Bad Foot took it.

"Thank you," the Indian said. "My woman thanks you. She will take it as soon as I return to the lodge. She will use it much more than me."

Edmond's face brightened as he watched Bad Foot finger the pages. "Your, ah, woman is a Christian?"

The others wondered why Preacher was laughing so hard he had to sit down on the ground, holding his sides.

"No Christian. I take all Bibles offered me."

"She studies them? My word. We've got to return and live with this tribe."

"Studies? No study. Can't read. Pages thin. Make good ass wipe."

They stopped early that afternoon. Preacher wanted to get the buffalo steaks on while they were still fresh. Besides, if he was tired, Lord knows what the others were feeling. They camped on the west side of Pacific Creek. Preacher wasn't too worried about Bum and his bunch; he figured they were at least three days ahead of them. They'd eat good this afternoon and just lay around and rest. Give the horses a much needed break, too.

He glanced over at Edmond, who still had his lower lip all poked out over Bad Foot's refusal to return the Bible. Preacher had been forced to step between the two men before Bad Foot forgot he was a peaceful Bannock and went on the warpath.

Before leaving, Bad Foot had grinned at Preacher and pointed at Edmond. He extended the index finger of his left hand and held it straight up in the air, cupping it with his right hand, making and up and down motion.

"What did that savage call me?" Edmond demanded, after the Bannocks had left.

"An asshole," Preacher told him. "Among other things."

"Well! I *never!*" Edmond said.

"I shore hope not," Preacher replied, hiding his grin, and certainly not telling the man everything the hand signals had implied. "Although Injuns tolerate that type of thing better than whites do."

"Whatever in the world are you babbling about?" Edmond asked, irritated.

Preacher shook his head. "Skip it." He looked up at the sky. The weather had been perfect ever since leaving the cave and the little valley, but now it was about to turn foul. Preacher figured they'd be in a hard, cold rain long before dusk.

He set about building the ladies a crude lean-to. If the men wanted one, they could damn well build it themselves. As for himself, he'd just get up under a tree and sleep with his robe wrapped around him, his back to the tree. Richard and Edmond watched him for a few moments, then set about building their own shelter. Preacher eyeballed them for several minutes and concluded their rickety shelter would collapse before the night was over.

Preacher did build a small shelter over the cook-fire and then set about broiling the thick buffalo steaks. He got the shelter up just as the rains came.

The others watched him and marveled at how much a man Preacher's size could eat. He was gnawing on a half-raw steak while cooking the others.

"Learn this," Preacher said. "Eat when you can, drink when you can, and sleep when you can. 'Cause you don't know when you're gonna be able to do any of the three again."

"We've been eating rather well and often on this sojourn," Richard pointed out.

"You ain't never wintered out here," Preacher told him, not quite sure what sojourn meant, but not wanting to appear plumb ignorant. He kind of figured it had something to do with traveling. "Snows can come a-howlin' this time of

66

year. Catch you flat-footed. Makes a fat rabbit look as good as airy steak you ever et."

"Will you please stop speaking like some ignorant savage?" Edmond yelled at him, startling them all. "You have some education. I know you do. Why do you persist in speaking like some addle-brained buffoon?"

"Bothers you, do it?" Preacher adjusted the steaks over the flames. "Why is that, Brother Edmond?"

But Edmond sulled up and sat under his leaky lean-to, refusing to speak.

"You got something stuck up in your craw, spit it out, Brother," Preacher told him. "Anger's a vile thing to keep all bottled up. Might even make a feller sick. You liable to come down with the collie-wobbles or the nobby-noddles or something worser than that."

"There you go again," Edmond broke his silence. "I won't even ask you what those ridiculous illnesses might be."

"They ain't nothin', Brother."

"And stop calling me Brother. I am not your brother. You don't even worship God. How could you be my brother?"

Preacher smiled. "You still got your lips all pooched out 'cause of what Bad Foot done. And who says I don't worship God? I do in my own way. Who says your way is right and mine is wrong? Why, I've even worshipped the Almighty at the Great Medicine Wheel over in the Bighorns. I bet that's something you never studied in your fancy Eastern colleges."

"I've never even heard of it," Edmond muttered.

"High up in the mountains, it is. 'Bout ten thousand feet or more. White stones in a circle, measurin', oh, 'bout seventy-five or eighty feet. Got twenty-eight spokes. And on a river 'bout fifty, sixty miles to the west of there, they's a great stone arrow, pointin' direct at the wheel. Lots of stories 'bout them things, but the Crow say the Sun laid out the wheel to teach the tribe how to make a tipi. I told y'all how the Plains Injuns feel about the sun and the earth. I'm gonna tell you something else: when I stood there in that circle, I got me a strange feelin', I did. Spiritual feelin'."

"Are the Crow dangerous?" Richard asked.

"Depends on how you look at it. They love to steal horses. They're fine horsemen. I know an ol' boy name of William Gordon. Mountain man. He had him a Crow chief tell him that if they killed the white man, they wouldn't come back, and they couldn't steal no more of the white man's horses. So they'll steal from the white man, but they won't kill him. Howsomever, that don't hold true all the time. You get some young buck lookin' to make a name for hisself so's he can impress the girls, he might just take your hair. It don't happen often, but it do happen. All in all, though, I trust the Crow not to kill me. But I sleep with one eye on my horses when I'm in their territory."

Preacher looked at the steaks and said, "They's ready. Come get this food and eat good."

Over supper, Melody said, "The Indians who attacked the wagon train, Preacher—what did you say they were?"

"Arapaho. Strange bunch of people. They stay to themselves mostly, but sometimes they will hook up with the Cheyenne. They ain't got no use for most white people. They's been talk of the Cheyenne and Arapaho comin' together to fight. Both tribes hate the Kiowa. I been hearin' talk that they's goin' to band together and head on the warpath against the Kiowa. Odd, 'cause the Kiowa and the Cheyenne used to be friends. I don't know what happened. The Arapaho will tell you he s your friend, but he ain't—not really. How's your meat?"

"It's delicious," Edmond said. "And please let me apologize for my earlier outburst. It's been, well, a trying time for all of us."

And it ain't nearabouts over, Preacher thought.

"I can't figure where he's takin' them," George said. "He's headin' straight west."

"Has to be Fort Henry on the Yellowstone," Bull said.

The huge knot on his head had gone away, but the memory of who gave it to him had not. He dreamed nightly of killing Preacher.

"But there ain't no soldier boys there," Bum said. "That's a civilian fort. And that shore ain't gettin' them folks no closer to the Oregon Trail."

"Maybe it is," Jack Harris said. "Preacher knows everybody in the wilderness. They's bound to be some trappers and the like hangin' around Henry. He could get some of them to ride with him down to Fort Hall for protection and then get them pilgrims hooked up with another wagon train headed west. Once that was done, we'd be out of luck."

"How many days you figure they're ahead of us?" Bum asked.

"Maybe two—three at the most. We're travelin' a lot harder than they is. But if we're gonna catch up, we got to push harder still."

"This ain't gettin' us no closer," Bobby said, lurching to his feet with the help of a branch he was using for a crutch. "Let's ride."

Slug, also using a tree limb for a crutch, rose painfully to his one good foot. "I'll follow Preacher clear to the blue waters if I have to," he said, his face tight with the pain from his broken ankle. "I owe him, and this is one debt I damn sure intend to pay."

Beckman hobbled to his feet, grimacing at the pain in his wounded leg. "Let's ride, boys. Hell, even if we get to Fort Henry and they're still around, there ain't no law there. Cain't nobody do nothin' to us. If them pilgrims say we attacked them, it's our word agin theirs. And they's more of us than there is them. If anything's said about our wounds, we'll just say we was attacked by Injuns."

Moses dumped water on the fire and stirred the ashes. Outlaws they were, but none of them wanted to be anywhere near a raging, out-of-control forest fire.

"Get the horses," Bum said. "We got to put some miles behind us."

None of them—Preacher included—knew whether Fort Henry was still operating. Andy Henry had built several forts, beginning back in 1807 when he built a fort on the Yellowstone at the mouth of the Big Horn. Then another fort was built in 1810 near the confluence of the Jefferson and Madison rivers. Blackfeet destroyed that one. Then in 1811-1812 another fort was thrown up on Henry's Fork of the Snake. Blackfeet and hard winters put that one out of business. Back in '23 another, sturdier fort was built and so far as any of the men knew, it was still operating.

They could only hope.

Preacher plunged them across the Snake and into the wildness of the Teton Range and into Washington Territory. He picked up the pace, knowing by now that those behind him would have figured out where he was going. Problem was, Preacher didn't know if the fort was still standing, much less in business. He hadn't been over this way in several years. There had been several Injun uprisings in that time. He'd asked Bad Foot about it, but the sub-chief had only shrugged his shoulders in reply. Which might have meant anything or nothing.

With an Injun, you just never knew.

The side of Richard's head was still tender to the touch, but the wound had healed nicely. Edmond had gotten over his mad with Preacher, Penelope was still a bitch, for the most part, and Melody, seeing her advances thwarted, had taken to not speaking to Preacher. Which suited Preacher just fine. He didn't have time to fool with some love-struck female.

If he had any kind of luck, in a couple of weeks he'd be done and through with the whole damn bunch of them and the entire misadventure would be behind him.

With any kind of luck.

They rode right into a storm and had to seek shelter from the cold driving rain that had bits of ice in it. The ice,

70

driven by high winds, cut like tiny knives on bare skin.

"These late spring storms can be pure hell," Preacher said, almost shouting to be heard over the howl of the wind as it came shrieking down off the mountains. "We might wake up in the mornin' and they'll be a foot of snow on the ground. You just never know this high up."

"It sounds like the wailing of a million lost souls," Edmond said. "I've never heard or felt anything like this."

"That's a right good way of puttin' it," Preacher agreed. "Never had thought of it like that."

"But if we can't travel," Richard said, shouting the words. "Neither can those behind us."

"Don't bet on it," Preacher told him. "This storm might be local. It might not be doin' nothin' fifteen miles to the east of us. Sorry."

Preacher managed to throw up a windbreak and get a fire going. But all in all it was going to be the most miserable night the pilgrims had yet spent on the trail. Preacher took it in his usual manner: calmly and philosophically. He knew there was no point in bitching about it; wasn't nothing he nor anyone else could do about it.

The rain soon changed to snow and in a very short time, the land was covered in white. The snow, whipped by the high winds, soon reduced visibility to near zero.

"Don't no one stray from camp!" Preacher yelled. "You got to relieve yourself, you just step behind the nearest tree. You stray from camp in this, and you'll get lost sure as shootin'. You'll be froze to death 'fore we could find you."

For once, no one argued with him. The pilgrims were scared, and looked it.

About midnight, the lean-to that Richard and Edmond built gave up and collapsed. Preacher, wrapped up in a ground sheet and buffalo robe, his back to a tree and his hat brim tied over his ears with a scarf he fastened under his chin, opened one eye and chuckled at the antics of the men as they thrashed around in the cold and snow.

One thing about it, the mountain man thought, all four

of these people will be a sight smarter about the wilderness when this is over. If they survive, he added. Then he closed his eye and went back to sleep, snug in his robe.

Neither Richard nor Edmond was in a real good mood come the morning.

"I have a head cold," Edmond complained. "I am in dire need of a plaster for my chest and some hot lemonade."

"Jesus Christ!" Preacher muttered.

"I simply must have a cup of hot tea," Richard said. "Do you have any left, Penelope?"

"I'll make us some. I have a few leaves left."

Preacher had been ruminating on their situation. "Y'all don't need to hurry none," he told them. "We shore ain't goin' nowheres. We'd leave a trail a drunk blind man could follow."

"That means the hooligans behind us will gain on us," Richard said.

"They'll gain," Preacher admitted. "But I left the trail and turned gradual north early yesterday mornin'. I didn't figure none of you would notice, and you didn't. Then I cut back south for a few miles, then headed west again about noon. That's when I led y'all into that little crick. If y'all had paid attention, you'd have noticed that crick cut back south. A lot of cricks and rivers do flow that way," he added drily. "Howsomever, Goose Crick does run north. It's a weird crick. But that ain't got nothin' to do with us." He pointed. "That mountain right there, it's got about fifteen different names, but the Injuns call it Mountain That Takes Life. They say it's evil. I 'magine what happened was some sort of sickness killed a bunch of them years back and they just figure the mountain is evil and won't go near it. That's where we're goin' soon as the sun melts this snow. Reason I'm tellin' you all this, is that I took us 'way, 'way off the trail. Now with the snow, if we just sit tight and don't build no big fires, Bum and them others won't have no idea where we is. They'll just think we kept on the trail westward and that's the way they'll go. They might even make the fort—if it's still there—two or three days ahead of us."

"Well, what would be the advantage of them doing that?" Richard asked.

Preacher smiled. " 'Cause we ain't gonna go to the fort. Soon as the snow melts, I'm takin' y'all southwest to Fort Hall."

Eight

Bum and his party of no-goods pressed on, never leaving the westward trail. They had lost the trail, but were all convinced that Preacher was heading for Fort Henry on the Yellowstone. It was the only logical thing for him to do. South was very rugged country.

A dozen miles to the south, Preacher and his pilgrims sat it out until the snow was completely gone. By that time, everyone was well rested, including the horses. Preacher had listened to Edmond bitch about his head cold until he knew if they didn't get on the trail, he was really gonna give Edmond something to complain about. Like maybe a poke on the snoot.

"Pack it up," Preacher told them. "We got about a hundred miles to go."

Preacher led them straight south, toward Teton Pass. His plan was to take them through the pass, then cut more to the west, leading them through the Caribou Range, staying north of the great dry lake some called Gray's Lake, cross the Blackfoot Mountains, then on into Fort Hall. That was his plan, but in Indian country, plans were subject to change.

Once clear of Teton Pass, Preacher cut southwest and pushed his party hard. They were becoming used to the trail, and Richard had become a fair hand. Preacher began ranging far out in front of them whenever he felt it safe to do so — safe was his being fairly sure Richard would stay on the trail Preacher forged and not get the others lost. He tried to stay apart from the group as much as possible, for Melody had once more begun speaking to him and batting her blues and shaking her bottom at him. Damn woman was about to drive him nuts.

Bum and his bunch had found themselves smack in the middle of a Blackfoot uprising. A friendly Bannock had told them the Army was warning all people to leave the area north of the upper curve of the Snake. And the Bannock also had told them, that everybody was gone from Fort Henry until the Blackfoot had been settled down. They'd been gone for several weeks. He knew that for a fact, 'cause he'd been there.

"Tricked us," Bum said. "He cut south during the snow, and holed up until it melted 'fore pullin' out. That has to be it."

"Then we're out of luck on this run," Jack said. "No way we can make Fort Hall 'fore they do."

Bum thought about that while he was warming his hands over a small fire. "You know where Red Hand is?"

"Yeah. But you ain't thinkin' of trustin' that crazy renegade, is you?"

"I don't see that we got a whole lot of choice in the matter. With his bunch, and with us maybe pickin' up eight or ten other ol' boys, we could take on any wagon train. We could hit them anywheres between Fort Hall and Oregon Territory."

"I don't like it. Why would Red Hand even want to join up with us?" Bull asked.

"For prisoners and booty. We could make a deal with him. He will keep his word on certain things. I've worked with him before and always been careful not to try to rook him. We can pick our spot once they leave Fort Hall, 'cause there ain't no Army forts along the way until you get to Oregon Territory, and I think them's all British, far as I know. And them silly people don't worry me none. Hell, they'll stop and drink tea right in the middle of a damn battle."

"Them women we been chasin' might get killed," Keyes pointed out.

"And they might not. 'Sides, all the gold them Bible-toters is carryin' will make up for the women."

"True," Moses said.

"So what do we do?" Slug asked.

"Git our butts outta Blackfoot country first thing. When that's done, we head south to find Red Hand and his bunch and to find us some more ol' boys that we can trust. When we talk to him, we don't mention nothin' 'bout the gold or the women we're after. Luke, do Preacher know you?"

"No. I ain't never laid eyes on the man."

"Then you'll be the one to ride into Fort Hall and find out what wagon train them pilgrims is leavin' with. We'll be camped 'bout fifteen miles southeast of the fort, down close to the Portneufs. That's where Red Hand hangs out. Let's get the hell gone from here. I don't wanna tangle with no damn Blackfeet."

"Two days from the fort," Preacher told the group. *And then I'll be shut of you,* he silently added. Praise be! "We'll stop at a crick just 'fore we make the fort and you ladies can bathe and whatever and change back into them dresses you toted along. Howsomever, it's gonna be right difficult for y'all to ride properlike in them saddles."

"We want to pay you for all your troubles," Edmond said.

Preacher fixed him with a bleak look. "I did what I done cause it was the right thing to do. So don't you be tryin' to hand me no money. I don't want your damn money." *I just want to get shut of you and I hope I don't never see none of you again.* "I feel bounden to see you hooked up with a wagon train, and I'll do that. Then I'm gone."

"Where will you go, Preacher?" Penelope asked. Now that

salvation — in the form of less cretinous people — was near, she felt it wouldn't hurt to be at least cordial to the man. To a degree.

"Don't know. Furrin's about played out. I can see that while most of the others can't. But I'll tell you what I ain't a-gonna do. I ain't a-gonna guide no gawddamn wagon trains full of pilgrims."

He would live to eat those words. Without benefit of salt, pepper, or anything else. And a lot sooner than he could possibly know.

Preacher had tucked them all in a natural depression off the trail. The fire was built against a huge rock so the rock would reflect the heat back to the group. They were running out of supplies, and Preacher had not wanted to risk a shot bringing down a deer, and had not been able to get close enough to one to use an arrow. He had managed to snare a few rabbits, and that was what they were having this evening.

"A paté would be wonderful," Penelope said, holding a rabbit's leg.

"Yes," Edmond agreed. "Or one of your mother's wonderful meat pies."

Preacher rocked back on his heels and gnawed at his meat.

"I dream of being warm again," Melody said. "The luxury of sitting in a chair, snug and warm by the stove, and reading poetry, while the elements rage outside the window."

"Stimulating conversation over tea and cookies," Richard said.

"Luxuriating long in a hot, soapy bath," Penelope said. She gingerly took a dainty little bite of rabbit.

Preacher broke the bone and sucked out the marrow. He muttered under his breath.

"I beg your pardon?" Edmond inquired.

"Nothin'," Preacher said, reaching over and slicing off a hunk of rabbit. He tensed only slightly as an alien sound came to him. He shifted position and continued to eat. But

77

he had moved closer to his saddle and the extra brace of pistols. The move also put his back to a large rock. The others did not seem to notice.

Preacher glanced over at the horses. They had stopped grazing and were standing very still, their ears all perked up.

Preacher ate the last of his meat and then picked up a handful of snow that remained on the shady side of the small boulder. He rubbed the snow on his hands to clear away the grease and used more snow to wipe the grease from his mouth. He dried his hands on his britches and wiped his mouth with his jacket sleeve. Free of the odor of grease, he took a deep breath. He picked out the tangy odor of old woodsmoke. There was no way he could tell by smell what tribe the Indians were from, but he'd bet ten dollars they were Blackfeet. And there wasn't no fiercer fighters anywhere—unless it was Red Hand and that bunch of half-crazy renegades that run with him. But this was just a tad north for Red Hand, although Preacher had once run into Red Hand a hell of a lot further north than this.

This bunch was slipping up from behind Preacher. To the front was clear, as was to his left. He stretched and scooted back another foot or so, putting himself in the shadows. Using as little movement as possible, he slowly eased both his pistols from his sash and cocked them. The pilgrims were busy discussing poetry and the latest fashions back East.

Preacher figured this was a mighty small bunch of Injuns. If they'd had any size to them a-tall, they'd have already attacked and done the deed. These were probably young bucks, out to take some hair so's they could impress the girls back at the village.

"Richard," Preacher said in a soft whisper.

The man cut his eyes to Preacher while the others kept talking, unaware of any trouble.

"Real easy like, now, without you sayin' a word, you put your hand on the butt of your pistol and be ready to jerk and cock and fire."

78

"What? What?" Edmond said. "What's this about discharging a weapon?"

Penelope jumped up. "Are we under attack?" she screamed.

Melody looked up just as braves came leaping into the camp. She jumped to her feet and let out a shriek that would put a mountain lion to shame.

Preacher put two bucks on the ground and crippled a third when he fired his pistols, both of them double-shotted. He grabbed up his second brace and let them roar. His left hand gun was a clean miss and his right hand gun misfired.

Richard fired, the ball catching a brave in the stomach and stopping him cold. The missionary stood rock still for a second, looking at the gore he'd caused, then vomited down the front of his coat.

Preacher was on his feet, his long blade knife at the ready when a buck came screaming at him, a war axe in his hand.

Preacher side-stepped the blow from the axe and cut the buck across the back, from his shoulder down to his buttocks, the big blade slicing deep. The Indian screamed and rolled on the ground, coming to rest near Penelope. He reached out and clamped one hand around her ankle. Edmond picked up a rock about the size of a grapefruit and smashed the buck on the head, cracking his skull.

Preacher jumped for his Hawken and cocked it, leveling the .54 caliber rifle just as a brave leaped at him. At point-blank range, he fired. The ball struck the Indian in the center of his chest and turned him in mid-air. He was dead when he hit the ground.

"Reload, goddammit!" Preacher yelled, dropping the rifle and hurriedly trying to charge his pistols. "Edmond, see to the horses."

A brave leveled his bow and Melody screamed at Preacher. Preacher threw himself to one side and the arrow whizzed past him, embedding into a tree. Preacher charged the lone brave and clubbed him with his pistol, smashing his head on the way down.

Edmond never made it to the horses. He was on the ground, unconscious, and a Blackfoot was grappling with Richard. Richard was holding onto the buck's wrists.

"Kick him in the parts, Richard!" Preacher yelled.

The Blackfoot kneed Richard in his groin and the man went down, moaning.

Melody grabbed up a burning brand from the fire and jammed it against the Indian's arm. He screamed in pain and slapped her in the face, knocking her down. Preacher leveled his pistol and fired, the ball striking the brave in the head and doing terrible damage to the man's face, tearing away part of his jaw and slamming the man to the ground.

A young buck, armed with only a war axe, took a vicious swing at Preacher. Preacher clubbed him with the butt of his Hawken just as another brave jumped onto Preacher's back, screaming his defiance. He tried to ride Preacher down. Preacher flipped the brave off his back. The buck hit the ground, rolled, and came to his feet just in time to receive the full length of Preacher's knife in his belly, the cutting edge up. Preacher jerked the knife upward, the heavy blade ripping through stomach and into lung and heart. The Blackfoot was dead before he stretched out on the cold ground.

The fight was over. If there were any more Blackfeet, they decided their medicine was bad this night and vanished back into the timber.

Edmond was getting to his feet with the help of Penelope, and Melody was trying to get Richard to his feet. Richard wasn't having any part of that. He lay on the ground in a fetal position, moaning, both hands holding his privates.

Preacher reloaded his pistols, then his rifle. He walked over to Edmond and looked at the man. The missionary had a lump on his noggin but other than that was unhurt. Melody's face was red and swelling where the brave had smacked her. She'd have a pretty good bruise there come the morning.

Penelope pointed to the dead Indians. "What are we going to do with them?"

"We're not doin' nothin' with them," Preacher told her. "We're packin' up and gettin' the hell gone from here. Injuns will come back for them." He shook his head. "Injuns must really have their dander up to attack at night. They don't usually do that."

"Why?" Edmond asked, fingering the knot on his head.

"Most tribes believe that if they're killed at night, the spirit wanders forever. Some believe that if the body is not recovered and properly buried the spirit wanders." Preacher inspected each of the dead braves. All young men. "Mosquitoes," he said.

"I beg your pardon?" Richard said, finally able to get to his feet. He was still all hunched over.

"Pack up. I'll tell you while we pack. We got to get gone from here, people. Them Blackfeet'll be back. Bet on that. Get busy. Move." Preacher began rolling his blankets. He said, "Each tribe has several warrior societies. These here Blackfeet are in the middle society. That's reserved for young men between the age of nineteen and twenty-three. They're called Mosquitoes. The one they're in before that is called the Doves. Them's all boys between fifteen and eighteen. That's how they learn to be warriors. These bucks got so excited about attackin' us, they forgot their teachin's."

Preacher started saddling up, leaving the others to finish packing.

"How far do we ride tonight?" Melody asked. "I'm really very tired."

"I don't know that I *can* ride," Richard said.

"You'll ride. And you'll all ride just as far as we dare push it," Preacher told the group. "Unless you'd rather be dead. People, I don't think this was just a chance attack. Something's got the Blackfeet all riled up and they're on the warpath. We all best close up the distance 'tween us and the fort. Now stop flappin' your gums and get to work. I got things to do myself that might buy us some time."

Preacher went to work dragging all the bodies to the center of the camp and lined them up neatly. He put their war axes on their chests and tidied up as best he could.

"Whatever in the world are you doing?" Richard asked, eyeballing the work.

"Showin' them Blackfeet that'll shore come back here this night that these here bucks fought bravely and we all respect them for it. We'll leave the rabbits cookin' on the spit and some of the supplies we got left we'll set out for them. I'll arrange it so's they'll know it's an offerin'. Injuns set a mighty lot of store by that. It might not help us, but then again, it might. You just never can tell about Injuns. It's best to cover all your bets out here."

He looked at the fat rabbit cooking on the spit. Preacher smiled and reached out and tore off a hunk and popped it into his mouth. He chewed thoughtfully for a moment. "We don't want them to think we're too respectful, though."

Nine

When they finally stopped and made a cold camp, Preacher figured it was about near midnight. And he had him a group of tired, butt-weary pilgrims. They were all asleep moments after crawling into their blankets.

Preacher checked his pistols and his Hawken and wrapped up in his buffalo robe, his back to a tree. He would sleep there, and sleep very lightly. Just before he closed his eyes, Preacher reminded himself that he'd better stock up on copper caps for his rifle at Fort Hall.

He slept well, but lightly, and was up long before the others. He made a small fire and used up the last of their coffee. With the distance they'd traveled during the night, Preacher figured to see the walled stockade called Fort Hall by late that afternoon.

Providing the Blackfeet didn't make another appearance.

Richard rolled out of his blankets and joined Preacher by the small fire. "Not far now, right, Preacher?"

"As the crow flies, just about two hours. It'll take us eight or ten. Did I teach y'all anything out here, Richard?"

Richard smiled and poured a tin cup full of coffee. "More than any of the others will probably ever admit. At least to you. This is the last of the coffee?"

"That's it. Enough for everyone to have a cup and then

some. We're sitting right on the western slope of the Black-foot Mountains. The Snake makes a big curve not too far ahead. We'll cross it and then about ten miles further, they's a crick where the ladies can bathe and get all gussied up. I know a spot where they's plenty of privacy. After that, it's the Fort."

Richard studied the man for a moment, peering at him over the rim of his cup. "You'll be glad to be rid of us, won't you, Preacher?"

The mountain man sighed. "Tell the truth, yeah, I will. We been lucky, missionary. I can't tell you just how lucky we've been. Y'all must have God ridin' on your shoulders. This ain't no place for pilgrims."

"Maybe God sent you to us?" Richard suggested.

"Doubtful," Preacher said with a shake of his shaggy head. "I ain't set foot in a church in nigh on twenty-five years."

"Of course you have, Preacher. All this," he waved a hand at the lonesome splendor, "is God's work. His cathedral. My word, but I can feel His presence out here more strongly than I ever experienced it in my life."

"Are you a minister?"

"Yes, but not a practicing one. I graduated seminary. But administration is my field. Edmond is the one who was called."

"How much money are you carryin', Richard?"

"We're each carrying several thousand dollars."

Preacher whistled softly. "That's a fortune. Don't let no one on the train know you're totin' that much. But now you're gonna have to use some of it to get outfitted. You know that, don't you?"

"We have a fund for that purpose. Don't worry."

"I'll help you choose the mules, if they got any at the fort. Some folks prefer oxen, but I'll take a big red over an ox any day. It'll be easier goin' for y'all over the others. You ain't tryin' to haul no heavy family heirlooms. As I'm sure you seen comin' out here, the trail is littered with posses-

84

sions folks tried to bring along and was forced to leave along the way. Once you leave the fort, Richard, y'all is on your own. They's damn little 'tween here and the blue water. Miles and miles of nothin' but wilderness and Injuns and bears and puma and danger. But you folks has toughened up considerable. You'll make it, I'm thinkin'."

"After we leave the fort, how far to the next settlement?"

"Fort Vancouver, 'less they's others built that I don't know about. Long, long way. I keep hearin' 'bout a mission of some sort that was built up near where the Snake and Columbia meet. In the Blue Mountains. But I ain't talked to nobody yet that's been there and seen it. So don't count on it."

The others began rising stiffly from their blankets, and Preacher noted with some amusement that they were a bedraggled-looking bunch. A lot of the haughtiness had been drained right out of them. The wilderness can do that to folks who try to fight it. You can't fight the wilderness. You got to work with it. You got to know the rules and stick by them. But men and women and whole families was pushin' west, and they was bringin' their civilized Eastern ideas out into the wilderness. That's why so many people was already buried alongside what was being called the Oregon Trail.

And they'd be hundreds, maybe thousands more buried along the way 'fore it was all said and done, Preacher figured.

Preacher noticed that the hands of the ladies was all cut and dirty and the nails broken. But that was all right, it showed the females had toughened and that's what it took to make it out here. And they'd get tougher 'fore they reached Oregon Territory. They'd either get tougher mentally and physically, or they'd die—and that was all there was to it.

Preacher watched as the ladies poured coffee and sat down quite unladylike by the fire. They just plopped down on their rear ends. He hid his smile as Penelope reached out and tore off a leg from one of the rabbits he'd snared during the night and was now cooking over the fire. It wasn't quite done, but she didn't seem to pay that no mind.

Melody, too, ripped off a hunk of meat and fell to gnawing, eating with her fingers. Even prissy-pants Edmond was eating with his fingers just like he'd been doin' it all his life and it was the natural thing to do. And maybe it was, Preacher thought. None of us was that far removed from the dog-eat-dog ways of our ancestors, and it sure didn't take a body long to fall back on those ways.

He'd miss these folks; he admitted that to his mind. It had been right pleasant to have folks to palaver with—at least part of the time. And Preacher was some sorry he hadn't taken Melody into his blankets for a night or two. But that would have only complicated things and he'd probably have never gotten shut of her if he'd done that.

She'd make someone a good wife; but that someone would not be Preacher.

She lifted her blues and looked at him across the fire. She reached out and cut off a hunk of meat and offered it to him. He nodded his thanks and took the offering.

Preacher ate the rabbit and then abruptly left the fire and walked to his horses, holding the bit of his good riding horse under his coat to warm it 'fore he tried to put it in Hammer's mouth. How'd you like to have an ice-cold hunk of steel jammed into your mouth?

He spoke to his horses for a moment, then saddled up Hammer and fixed the frame on his pack horse. He glanced back at the forlorn-looking group. "Fifteen minutes, people. Then we ride."

The day turned warm and pleasant, the miles passed quickly and uneventfully, and by the time Preacher led the group up to the creek several miles from the Fort, he figured the water would be plenty warm enough for a bath. For the others, not for him.

"Y'all go on," he told them. "I'll stand watch."

Before the women did anything, they shook out their

dresses and hung them up on bushes to get some of the wrinkles out. Then they peeled right down to the skin and hit the water, rag and soap in hand.

Preacher hadn't heard such gigglin' and carryin' on in his life. Richard and Edmond wasn't no better. They was duckin' and dunkin' each other and altogether the whole bunch was actin' like a gaggle of schoolkids.

Be a hell of a time for a bunch of Blackfeet or Arapaho to show up.

The pilgrims showed up about forty-five minutes later lookin' a whole hell of a lot better than the last time Preacher had seen them. The men was all duded out in suits and white shirts and ties and the women was gussied up to the nines. Then damned if the men didn't grunt and strain and work to arrange the women proper on the saddle, with one leg hooked around the horn.

"Ain't that uncomfortable?" Preacher asked.

"I will not ride into the fort astride this mount like some common whore," Penelope said.

"Nor will I," Melody echoed.

"If we have to make a run for it, y'all are gonna fall off smack on your behinies," Preacher told them.

"We shall cross that river when, or if, the need arises," Penelope informed him.

"Oh, my God!" Preacher pointed, jumped about a foot off the ground, let out a wild whoop and ran for his horse. "Injuns!" he squalled.

Penelope and Melody jerked up their skirts and under-coats—exposing some right shapely ankles and knees and a lot of milky white skin that was further up and wasn't never seen by no man—and was astride their horses before Preacher could reach Hammer. Preacher lay down on the ground and kicked his feet up in the air and hoo-hawed with laughter.

"Fooled you!" Preacher said, wiping the tears from his eyes. "That was a right good sight to see, ladies."

"You, sir, are no gentleman!" Penelope said.

"Eh, eh, eh," Preacher chuckled, getting to his feet. "No, I reckon I ain't. I been called a lot of things, but never no gentleman. I . . ." He looked up the little valley. "Oh, *shit!*" he hollered, leaping onto Hammer's back. "Come on, people, rake them cayuses! Here comes a whole passel of Injuns. Move, dammit, this ain't no joke."

"Now, see here, sir!" Edmond protested. "I must insist that this sophomoric behavior you are displaying cease immediately. It's crude and disgusting. You are frightening the ladies and I—" He looked behind him as a wild savage yell reached his ears. His eyes widened. "Son of a bitch!" the missionary bellowed, and kicked his pony in the slats.

About a hundred braves were thundering toward the creek, their war cries and the pounding of hooves filling the warm spring air.

"Stay on the trail!" Preacher hollered. "It'll lead you straight to the fort." He made sure the others were ahead of him and wheeled Hammer, cocking his Hawken and bringing it to his shoulder. He compensated for the distance and squeezed off a round. The ball struck a lead rider and knocked him off his pony and under the hooves of the other hard-running horses. If he wasn't dead when he hit the ground, the hooves finished him.

Preacher gave Hammer his head and the horse took off like shot from a cannon. Hammer didn't like the sound of those wild screamin' Injuns no better than Preacher. And the pack horse, light-loaded now, after weeks on the trail, was keeping up all his own. He didn't like what was coming up behind him either.

Preacher tied the reins on the horn, turned in the saddle, and pulled his other Hawken from the boot, booting the empty rifle. "Give me a nice steady run, old hoss," Preacher said. "So's I'll know when to pull this trigger."

The horse seemed to understand and steadied down. Preacher let the muzzle wag up and down a few times, to get the rhythm of it, then fired.

He hit a horse right in the head and the animal dropped,

creating the biggest pile-up Preacher had seen in many a year. "Sorry, hoss," Preacher muttered. "I musta lost the rhythm."

He turned around in the saddle, but not before he saw a dozen or more Injuns all crippled up and sprawled around both sides of the trail after their mounts piled up.

"The fort!" he heard Edmond shout, after a couple of miles of hard riding.

Preacher put the reins in his teeth and pulled out both .50 caliber pistols and let them bang to warn those in the fort that trouble was coming hard on the hoof.

The gates swung open and they were inside.

"Yee-haw!" Preacher heard the call just as he was jumping from his horse. He grinned and turned around to face a grizzled mountain man, looking to be much older than he was.

A huge bear-like man, dressed all in skins and fur, lumbered toward Preacher. "Preacher, you old hoss, you! You bring all this trouble down on us?"

The defenders of the fort — more civilians than soldiers — were on the ramparts, blasting away at the attacking Indians. Most of the Indians were armed only with bows and arrows and the guns of the defenders were swiftly driving them back. But all knew that come the night, it would be a much different story, for the Indian was a master at stealth.

"Wagh!" Preacher shouted. "Greybull, you old bear, you. How come you ain't down on the Popo Agie?"

The two men bear-hugged each other while the pilgrims looked on. The battle raged around them and these two were behaving as if nothing were happening.

Greybull held Preacher at arm's length. "Did you find these poor lost children in the woods?" he asked, glancing at the four missionaries.

"Wagon train attack over crost the Tetons," Preacher said. "The Good Lord delivered them into my hands."

Greybull glanced at the nattily dressed men. "You shoulda throwed 'em back. What are they?"

89

"We are under attack, gentlemen!" an Army officer shouted at the men. "We must defend this post."

"Aw, keep your britches on," Greybull told the young man. "This ain't nothin'. Wait 'til the night comes. Then you'll see trouble lookin' you in the face."

"Wild Indians do not attack at night," the young officer said.

Greybull and Preacher grinned at each other. "He's new out here," Greybull explained. "He knows ever'thing there is to know 'bout Injuns. Just ask him. He gradeeated from Sandhurst."

"Do tell. What's a Sandhurst?"

"Some fancy soldier school. Teach 'em how to walk nice and give orders in a military manner."

"I say, sir," Richard butted in. "My companions and I survived an attack on our wagon train. We—"

"What happened to your ear, sir?" the officer asked.

"Injuns cut it off," Preacher told him. "He was defendin' the honor of these ladies here."

"Oh, I say now," the officer beamed. "That was gallant of you, sir. I'll have the post surgeon take a look at it."

"No need," Preacher told him. "It's all healed up now. I fixed it good."

"Indians are breaking off, sir!" a soldier yelled from a lookout tower. "They're fleeing."

"Fleein'?" Greybull asked.

"They'll be back come the night," Preacher told the young officer. "Mighty young soldier boys," he remarked, looking all around him. "Why, there ain't a one of them dry behind the ears."

"The Injuns are fleein'?" Greybull muttered.

Penelope batted her eyes at the young officer and he about melted down into his boots.

"Where's the regular Army?" Preacher asked. "Hell, these ain't nothin' but kids!"

"We are British troops, sir," the officer said. "And I am in command. Lieutenant Jefferson Maxwell-Smith at your service. The troops who were garrisoned here were transferred west to Oregon Territory."

"Any of you ever been in a war?" Preacher asked.

"Only a few minor skirmishes like the one we just repelled, sir."

"You didn't re-pell nothin', boy. Them Injuns'll be back come the night. You best double the guards and keep a sharp eye out, or they'll be comin' over these walls."

"Indians do not attack at night, sir." Jefferson Maxwell-Smith stood his ground.

"You in for a big damn surprise, boy," Preacher told him. "Whether they attack at night depends en-tarly on how they feel their medicine is workin'. If they medicine is good, they'll attack."

"You are wrong, sir."

"They flee-ed," Greybull said. "The Injuns flee-ed. I got to 'member that. Tell Dupre about how the Injuns flee-ed."

"Incredible!" Maxwell-Smith said, looking at the huge mountain man.

"They gonna be fleein' back here in about three, four hours," Preacher said. "Come on, Greybull, let's us flee over yonder to the sutler's store for a drink of whiskey."

"Shore won't be time for drinkin' tonight," Greybull said. "Not once them Injuns flee back at us."

"Come, ladies," the lieutenant said to Penelope and Melody. "Let's see about making you comfortable in quarters. I assure you, you are quite safe here. The savages have gone and will not return."

"They flee-ed," Greybull said.

"Yeah," Preacher said. "Right over that damn hill yonder to make more medicine."

Ten

At the sutler's store, a dark and crowded low-beamed building, the men each ordered a cup of whiskey and settled down at a table.

"So how you been, Preacher?" Greybull asked. "I ain't put eyes on you . . . how long? Two years?"

"Sounds about right. I think it was over on the Powder, wasn't it?"

"I believe so. 'Bout the time Lazy Bob got scalped by them renegades of Red Hand."

Preacher drank his whiskey down and chuckled. "They jerked Lazy Bob's hair off his head so fast they didn't even check to see if he was dead. He run into Red Hand 'bout a year later and scared that Injun so bad Red Hand turned around and run screamin' off into the woods."

Preacher got Greybull another cup of snake-head whiskey and sipped on his first one. "Bring me up to date on the Injuns' uprisin'."

"Don't nobody seem to know what kicked it off, but the Blackfeet is damn shore on the warpath. We got three wagon trains backed up here and the wagon masters done quit on two of them. The one bossin' the third one is about to quit. One train already tried to get through this spring. Didn't none of them make it. I led the party out to what was left of it. Turrible sight to see."

"You scoutin' for the Army now?"

Greybull shrugged his massive shoulders. "Got to do somethin'. Beaver's about gone. I noticed your packhorse ain't carryin' no heavy load of pelts."

"Shore ain't," Preacher said morosely, looking down into his cup. "You like scout work?"

"It beats starvin' to death."

"I reckon."

"What you plannin' on doin', Preacher?"

"I ain't made up my mind. But I ain't gonna work for that damn kid lieutenant bossin' this garrison. Greybull, that youngster ain't got no sense."

"He's got some growin' up to do, fer a fact. And out here, he'll either do it quick, or get dead."

"Yeah. But how many others is gonna get kilt with him?"

There were a lot of Flathead Indians and some Mandans living close to the fort, but they had long since been tamed and posed no threat to anyone. The Methodist church had sent missionaries several years back, in April of '34, with Nat Wyeth's second expedition. The mission of the church was to find the Flathead Indians and to live with them and wrest the heathen nation from the clutches of Satan. It had proved to be a major undertaking.

Preacher knew several of the Flatheads and squatted down to palaver with them about the Blackfoot uprising. Both the Flatheads and the Nez Perce were, for the most part, friendly to the white man, and neither tribe cared for the warlike Blackfeet.

"It will be very bad before it is better," a Flathead told Preacher. "The young man directing the soldiers is brave, but foolish."

"We agree on that," Preacher told him.

"The Blackfoot say they are going to drive the Bostons out of this area."

Both the Nez Perce and the Flatheads called the trappers

and mountain men Bostons, since many of the pelts were sold to Boston based companies.

"They ain't done it yet."

Preacher walked the sturdy walls of the fort, and they were stoutly constructed. That was due to the efforts of one Nathaniel J. Wyeth, who back in '34, after being treated very rudely by Fitzpatrick and Sublette (of the Rocky Mountain Fur Company), moved on to the Snake River Bottom and walled in what is called Fort Hall. The timbers were cottonwood, very close-set, and stood fifteen feet high. He built bastions, a log storehouse, and many cabins. That troops were here was a surprise, for the garrisoning of troops at company forts, while not rare, was not customary.

Well, even green troops were better than nothing. Although not by much, in Preacher's mind.

He walked outside in the waning light and shook his head at the slap-doodle manner in which the wagons were placed. "Idiots," he said. "You can't tell a pilgrim nothin'." He stalked around the wagons until he found the one remaining wagonmaster and confronted the man. "Tell them pilgrims of yourn if they wanna live through the night, they'll circle their wagons, stock inside the circle, and keep weapons at the ready and a sharp lookout this night. You ought to have had sense enough to know that. How many wagon trains you ramrodded?"

"This is my first," the man said stiffly.

Preacher spat on the ground. "Then whoever hired you was a goddamned fool!" He walked back inside the fort.

He found the young lieutenant and the young man's manner had changed noticeably toward Preacher, probably due to talking with Richard and Edmond.

Preacher put a hand on the young officer's shoulder. "Son," he said, even though he was probably no more than ten or twelve years older, "I got to say this to you. You might feel hard towards me afterward, but I still got to do it. What you know about Injuns is mighty thin; 'bout as thin as frog hair. You'll learn. But that ain't helpin' you none now. Them Blackfeet's gonna be back. If their medicine is good to them, it'll be tonight. Forget all that 'bout Injuns not fightin' at night. Sometimes they do, sometimes they don't. You're thinkin' war as a white man. Injuns don't think like us. Injuns think like Injuns."

"I'm . . . beginning to understand, sir. I feel rather like a fool, not listening to Greybull from the start. I'm afraid my behavior has been boorish to say the least."

"I don't know what that means. But I do know this: we got to get ready for an attack. And we ain't got a whole lot of time to get set."

"Tell me what you want done, and it shall be done."

"Fine. This is what we'll do . . ."

Preacher left the lieutenant readying his troops, while he and Greybull concentrated on the outside, where both of them intended to be when the attack came. And both of them felt an attack was not far off.

They helped hitch the teams and pull the wagons into a box, with the rear of the box against the walls of the fort. "Fill all your buckets and barrels," Preacher told the pilgrims. The Injuns will be sure to use fire arrows to set the canvas ablaze."

"Our children?" a woman asked.

"Inside the fort, if they'll go. If not, under the wagons we got in the center of this box. I can't believe y'all come all the way from the Big Muddy to here without no Injun fights."

"The wagonmasters all said we were very lucky," a pioneer stated.

Greybull shook his shaggy head. "Damn sure was that," he muttered.

Like Preacher, the mountain man was loaded down with weapons, and after the wagons were in place, he and Preacher went off into the gathering gloom of evening to find a good spot from which to fight and to check their weapons.

"The lieutenant's took a likin' to you, Preacher," Greybull said, once the two had settled down near a wall. "I bet he'd hire you on if you'd ask."

"I ain't made up my mind," Preacher said. "I ain't never worked for nobody but me in all my life. I don't know how I'd be takin' orders from fresh-faced kids."

"It ain't so bad. The lieutenant the kid replaced was a real horse's butt, though. You'd a-killed *him,* for a fact. I damn near did."

"What was his problem?"

"I just told you. He was a horse's butt."

"Oh."

"I say, gentlemen," Lieutenant Maxwell-Smith said from above them.

The mountain men looked up. The young officer was standing on the rampart looking down at them.

"Git down, Smith," Preacher told him. "Your noggin makes a dandy target all stuck up there. In case you ain't noticed, they's timber all around us. Speak through the gun slits."

"Oh. Yes. Quite right." He ducked down out of sight. "The missionaries you rescued speak highly of you, sir. But I must fill out a report concerning the wagon train attack and those ruffians following you. What is your Christian name?"

"I ain't got one. Preacher'll do just fine."

"But are you a man of the cloth?"

Greybull started giggling. "Not likely, Lou-tenant. I been knowin' him over twenty years and never knowed him to go to church yet." He scratched his head and frowned. "Course, they ain't been no churches out here 'til recent. That might have something to do with it."

Jefferson Maxwell-Smith walked away, muttering under his breath.

"You didn't say nothin' 'bout no one followin' you, Preacher," Greybull said.

"Bum Kelly and his gang. Jack Harris has hooked up with 'em, too."

"Wagh! That no-count."

96

"That ain't all." Preacher told Greybull about his suspicions of Jack deliberately leading the train north so Bum and his gang could ambush it.

Greybull was thoughtful for a time. "That'd be a low thing for any man to do, Preacher. But Harris is that low, I reckon. Reckon, hell, I know he is. Yeah. It has to be like you say. Ain't no way even a fool like Jack Harris could get that far north of the trail."

Then, as night touched the wilderness around the fort and the wagons, Preacher set Greybull to chuckling when he told him about the antics in the cave.

"He's got to kill you, Preacher. Bum and all the rest of them bad apples. It's a matter of honor now. They'll never give up. And I hope you ain't forgot that Bum has been in cahoots with Red Hand and his renegades more'n one time in the past."

Preacher bit off a chew of twist he'd bought at the store. "I ain't forgot."

Both men tensed, then glanced at one another as the unnatural sound of silence settled around the fort. Nothing moved in the forest. No birds called.

"Here we go," Greybull muttered.

"I'll warn the pilgrims to get ready," Preacher said. "See if you can get some soldier boy's attention and tell them to pass the word and get set."

"Will do."

Preacher found the wagon master. "Get your people in place. The Injuns will be along shortly."

"I've never been in an Indian attack before," he admitted.

Preacher studied him closely in the faint light. The man was scared and showed it. "Where in the hell did you ever get the experience to be called a wagon master?"

The man sulled up and stuck his chin out. "I drove a freight wagon out of Pittsburgh," he said defensively. "I traveled all over Pennsylvania and Ohio. It's plenty wild back there, mister."

"Oh, I know it is," Preacher said. "I can just imagine. Injuns on the warpath at every turn of the road. Get your people ready to fight."

He got back to Greybull and made himself comfortable on the ground. "How many men's the kid got under his command?"

"Forty. All green 'ceptin' the senior sergeant. Just got to the coast by ship not six months ago. I think they come the long way around. Some of 'em still looked sick."

They watched as several dark shapes flitted from stump to tree several hundred yards out.

"Workin' in close and then they'll jump us. You reckon they'll try to breech the walls?"

"That's the word I get. They gonna try to burn it down. They want the fort and the soldiers and the Bostons gone from this country. And all these wagon trains comin' in sudden really got em mad."

"Well, they better get over it. Them holy-shouters I brought in told me folks was fixin' to pour into this country like ants to honey."

"You don't say?"

"I do. Thousands of people." He shuddered at the thought. "Gonna be a lot of folks killed, too. I just can't understand how these folks come all the way from the Muddy and didn't get set upon by Injuns."

A fire arrow lit the night as it soared up and then came down, missing a wagon by only a few feet. Several men jumped up and started to move to the flames.

"Let it burn out! Get down!" Preacher called. "Don't show yourselves. And save your powder and lead."

"Was we that stupid when we come out here, Preacher?" Greybull asked, never taking his eyes from the area in front of their position.

"No. 'Cause times was still wild where we come from. We growed up more cautious than these pilgrims. And do you know what else I learned from them soul-savers?"

"What?"

"They's people in the big cities back east puttin' crappers

in their *houses!*"

"You mean like a chamber pot?"

"No. I mean like a regular room where they go to take care of business."

Greybull blinked. "You mean to tell me they shit in their house?"

"Right next to where they sleep."

"I can't believe it!"

"That's what them folks told me. I think it's disgustin'. Who'd wanna do something like that?"

"Shorely not me. Why, I never heard of nothin' like that in my life. And I bet they's some of them same people that says folks like you and me ain't civilized 'cause we live in the mountains. Tsk, tsk, tsk."

"Look sharp now, Greybull. They's workin' closer. See that stump over yonder? It wasn't there two minutes ago."

"You're right. You want the honors?"

"I believe I will." Preacher pulled his Hawken to his shoulder, took careful aim, and let her bang.

The 'stump' grunted when the ball struck him. A war axe went flying up into the air and the brave fell forward and lay still.

"Here they come!" Greybull roared, and the fight was on.

Eleven

The Indians became darting shapes in the night, utilizing every bit of cover as they worked their way closer to the fort and the wagons. So far, although two dozen shots had been fired from the defenders, Preacher was the only one to have scored a hit.

"Don't fire until you're sure of a target!" Preacher yelled. "Goddammit, save your powder and shot. This ain't St. Louis. You can't go to the store and buy more." He dropped back down beside Greybull. "Damn pilgrims anyways. I'd hate to be saddled with guidin' them fools."

Another fire arrow lanced the night and this one landed on the canvas of a wagon, igniting it almost instantly. Greybull drilled the Indian who fired the arrow and the brave doubled over, mortally wounded from the .54 caliber Hawken.

Men and women ran to put out the fire and the Indians showered them with arrows. One woman was struck in the throat and died horribly, the life gurgling out of her, and a man went down screaming with an arrow in his stomach. Children were laying under their parents' wagons, many of them screaming in fright.

"Welcome to life on the frontier, folks," Preacher muttered without malice. "I 'spect it ain't at all like the big adventure it was painted to be."

"They're using ladders to breech the north wall!" a young soldier shouted.

"Did you tell the kitchen people to have lots of boilin' water ready?" Preacher asked his buddy.

Greybull chewed and spat. "Yep."

"Well?"

"The lieutenant said he wouldn't do nothin' like pourin' no boilin' water on folks. Said that was agin the rules of war."

"Until that boy grows up, we're gonna be in trouble, Greybull."

"Yep. Must be two, three hundred Blackfeet out yonder." Both men were lifting their rifles to their shoulders.

"At least," Preacher said.

"Wait a minute," Greybull said, lowering his rifle. "What the hell's that chantin'?"

Preacher listened for a moment. "Them back over that ridge is singin' their death songs. But . . . why? And why the rush to attack us? Ain't none of this makin' no sense, Greybull."

From out in the darkness, far away from the light of the burning wagon, came the angry shouting voice of a Blackfoot. Greybull and Preacher listened intently to the hard words.

"My Sweet Jesus," Greybull whispered. "Is he sayin' what I think I'm hearin'?"

"Yeah," Preacher told him, his words hard and grimly offered. "He damn shore is." Preacher tapped on the logs of the wall. "Can anybody hear me in yonder?" he called.

"Right here, Preacher," a trapper he knew slightly said. "I heard them words, too."

"Get to usin' an axe, Jim. Get some men choppin' and make us a space big enough to get folks through and do it quick. And get the lieutenant over here."

"Right, Preacher."

101

Only a few heartbeats passed before the voice of Maxwell-Smith came through the logs. "Yes, Preacher?"

"Now listen to me, Lieutenant," Preacher said, steel in his words. "I ain't gonna say this but once. Don't let no Injun come over the walls. Don't touch none of them. We got to get all these pilgrims inside the walls and keep the Injuns out. Now you get them goddamn pots filled with water and keep it hot. When they try to come over, you dump it on them. You got all that, Lieutenant?"

"I hear you, Preacher. Boiling water poured on the flesh of those poor wretches out there. But can you give me a reason for the barbaric behavior?"

"Them's their death-songs they's singin' out yonder, boy. The white man's done brought smallpox down on them. Whole villages has been wiped out. And them out yonder got it too. They want to die in battle—but not before they infect us. Now, is that good enough for you?"

"I'll get right on it," Maxwell-Smith said, his voice filled with horror.

"You do that." He turned to Greybull. "Them on the other side'll be through in two jigs. Soon as the hole's cut, I'll start workin' them pilgrims over here. We got to do this fast." He handed him his Hawken. "Little extry fire-power, Greybull. I'm gone."

The wagon was almost burned down to smoldering char as Preacher made his way into the knot of men and women.

"They're through!" Greybull called.

"Get to the wall," Preacher told the first bunch. "Grab what you can and run like hell. Move, people. *Move!*"

"What's the meaning of this?" the wagon master confronted him. "I give the orders out here."

"Not no more, partner," Preacher told him. "If you want to live, you do what I tell you to do."

"I don't take orders from you . . . you smelly, shaggy reprobate!"

"Then you can go right straight to hell," Preacher replied. "I ain't got the time to fart around with someone as dumb as

102

you." He shoved the man out of the way.

The wagonmaster grabbed him by the shoulder and spun Preacher around, his fist drawed back for a blow. He never got the chance to throw it. Preacher put him on the ground, butt first, with a hard left and right to the jaw. Then he went about his business of gathering up those pioneers who would go into the fort.

And not all of them would.

"I don't believe you!" one man said. "And I'm not leaving my wagon out here for the savages to plunder and burn."

"Then stay here," Preacher said, and pushed past him. It was cold on the mountain man's part, but he was doing what he felt was necessary, and he didn't have much time. And he also knew what smallpox could do. He'd had it and survived it, as had Greybull. They'd been with some Mandans when it struck their village, and it was a horrible sight to witness.

About half of those in the wagon train chose to leave their wagons and run for the fort. Preacher held several sets of parents at pistol-point while Greybull and two young soldiers forcibly took their young children from them and ran for the fort.

"I'll see you in hell for this!" a man shouted.

"You'll be there 'fore me," Preacher told him.

Then the enraged Blackfeet struck the fort and there was no time for anything except survival as the infected and sick and dying Indians threw themselves against the thick walls of the fort. They came out of the night in silent waves of fury and hate.

The first wave was repelled by shot. On the heels of that one came another with makeshift ladders. Boiling water was poured on them and they ran shrieking into the night, burned horribly.

Those pilgrims who had refused to leave their wagons fared not well at all. It did not take the Blackfeet long to overwhelm them, and the Indians were in no mood to take prisoners for slavery or barter.

The screaming of those being tortured played hell on the nerves of the defenders inside the fort.

"What are they doing to them?" Edmond asked nervously, standing beside Preacher on a rampart.

"Injuns can get right lively with their torture," the mountain man replied. "And if they're a mind to, they can make it last for days. Each tribe has its own favorite way of torture, and there ain't none of it very pleasant."

"What happened to the tame Indians who were living around the fort?"

"They run off 'fore the Blackfeet got here in force."

Flames from the burning wagons illuminated the night, highlighting the bodies that littered the ground around the walled fort. Moaning from the wounded mingled with the screaming of those being tortured. A man from the wagon train came stumbling out of the night, his head on fire and his hands tied behind his back. His shrieking was hideous.

Preacher lifted his Hawken and shot him dead.

"My God, man!" Edmond said.

"I put him out of his misery," Preacher said. "They'd gouged out his eyes and set his hair on fire. You ever seen a man who's brains was cooked?"

"Ah . . . no."

"It ain't a nice sight."

An arrow whizzed between them and fell to the earth on the grounds inside the walls.

"When we whup them," Preacher said, "and we will do that, eventually, we got a real problem. Those of us that's had the 'pox has got to go out there and burn them bodies to kill the germs. You been scratched, Edmond?"

"Yes. All of my party received the cowpox."

"Good. Y'all can help then. Hudson's Bay sent supplies of smallpox vaccine to all its forts. The lieutenant said his people had been vaccined."

Greybull came hunched over to them. "From what I been able to pick out of the night, the Blackfeet's lost a lot of people. Whole villages wiped out. A Mandan just slipped through and he sayin' that all along the Missouri there ain't nothin' but death. His whole tribe was wiped out. He says that folks is runnin' away from it, headin' west, and that's how it got here so fast. He says that people of his tribe is killin' themselves right and left. Said the talk is it started over at Fort Union. Brought in by someone on a keelboat."

Preacher nodded his head. "Listen to that," he said, as the chanting and singing grew louder, coming to them from out of the night. "Them Blackfeet's gone crazy. They're workin' themselves up into a killin' rage."

"Can't say as I blame them," Greybull replied. "I'd rather die quick than linger in pain for days with the pox, havin' the skin rot off me."

Edmond shuddered. "You are rather graphic in your description, sir." He paused. "A thought just occurred to me. Those savages we encountered the night before we reached the fort. Do you suppose . . . ?"

"Yeah, they probably had it, or suspected they did. But you all been vaccinated, so you ain't got nothin' to worry about. What you got to worry about is right out yonder."

The singing and chanting stopped. The sudden silence gathered all around them.

"What does that mean?" Edmond asked.

"It means they comin' straight at us," Preacher said. "Like right about now!" He lifted his Hawken and blew a hole in the chest of a running brave.

The ground on all sides of the fort was suddenly transformed into a mass of charging Blackfeet, some of them carrying makeshift ladders. They threw ladders against the log walls and began climbing up. Buckets and pots containing hot water were dumped on the Indians, scalding them. They flung themselves off the ladders, screaming in pain, running away into the night. Men were firing straight down from the ramparts, the heavy caliber rifles and pistols inflicting horrible damage on the Indians at close range. The cool night air became thick and choking with gunsmoke and the stench of death.

Although outnumbered by at least twenty to one—and probably more than that—the defenders of the fort held the high ground, so to speak, and fought savagely, once again breaking the Indian attack.

Lieutenant Maxwell-Smith made his way along the ramparts to Preacher. "While it is quiet, I am going to stand half of my men down for a rest and some tea."

"Good idea. They damn sure earned a rest," he complimented the young officer. "We just might have broken their spirit this last charge. Them Blackfeet might think their medicine has turned bad and fall back to ponder on it some."

"I'll have the men in the towers keep a sharp eye out."

Preacher watched the young man leave and said, "I think he learned something about the frontier this night."

Edmond mopped his grimy, sweaty face with a handkerchief. "I know I certainly did."

Most of those inside the fort managed to catch an hour or so of sleep that night. The Indians made no more charges against them. They settled back to harass them with arrows and an occasional gunshot, for many of them did not have rifles, and those that did were not very good shots, not having sufficient powder and shot to practice.

The sun rose to a sight of mangled bodies on all sides of the fort. More than a dozen of those men and women who had refused to leave their wagons had been stripped naked, tortured, then tied to a wagon wheel and burned alive. Even the children had been killed, a sure sign of the Indian's rage over the white man bringing his deadly diseases to them.

"I 'spect we can salvage 'bout half them wagons," Preacher opined. He glanced at Richard, looking out grim-faced at the carnage that lay before them. "Any clothing found out yonder will have to be handled careful-like, with a stick,

106

and boiled 'fore anyone uses it."

"Yes. Have the Indians gone?"

"I don't know. I doubt it. Mad as they is, 1 don't 'spect they'll give up too easy." He was studying the body of a Blackfoot that lay on the ground at the base of the walled fort. "Cut his claws off," Preacher muttered, just as Greybull walked over to them. "You noticed that, Greybull?"

"What?"

"Them Blackfeet done cut their claws off 'fore this battle. Strange."

"Claws?" Richard asked. "Claws? Like in animal claws?"

"Thumbnails," Preacher explained. "Blackfeet men let their thumbnails grow until they crook like a claw. Something else, too. See them dead ponies out yonder? Look at the symbols painted on the necks. Them's the ponies of war party leaders. We just may have broke this bunch. They've pulled 'way back now, busy electin' new chiefs and leaders."

Preacher glanced to his left. Lieutenant Maxwell-Smith was standing silently, watching him and listening intently. The young officer had learned many things during the past twenty-four hours. One important thing was that these disreputable-looking mountain men knew what they were talking about when it came to Indians and how to fight them, and if he was going to survive out here among the savage heathens, he'd better shut his mouth and listen and learn.

"You done just fine, Lieutenant," Preacher told him.

The young officer smiled through the grime that covered his face, most of it residue from the black powder of pistols and rifles. "Thank you, Preacher. For a lot of things." He smiled again, and it made him look very, very young. "I'm afraid that Sandhurst did not adequately prepare me for life on the American frontier."

"This is a land and a people that nobody else can learn you, Lieutenant," Preacher said. "It's just so damn . . . *big* out here."

"Yes," the officer said, stepping closer and speaking quietly. "I was quite awed by the vastness of it; I still am. England pales by comparison. Although I wouldn't want the men to hear me say that."

"Let's get a report from the men in the towers," Greybull said. "Then we got to make plans about draggin' off and burnin' them bodies out yonder and roundin' up all the pioneers' stock that run off."

"We got to see who all ain't been vaccined against the pox and get the company doctor to fix 'em up."

"I'm ahead of you there, Preacher," Maxwell-Smith said. "I've already canvassed the group and the doctor is preparing to scratch people now."

"Good, good!" Preacher clasped the man on the arm, and was not surprised to find it heavily muscled. "Let's go see what the lookouts can tell us."

"They're still out there," the only senior sergeant in the garrison reported. "Over those ridges. See the faint smoke?" He pointed. "But none of us can detect any movement in the woods near the fort."

"You wouldn't be able to," Preacher said. "And I ain't castin' no doubts on your soldierin' abilities by sayin' that. Injuns is the greatest fighters and hiders and ambushers in the world. Settlers down in the southwest tell a story about an Apache who found himself out in the desert with no place to run and the army comin' hard up the trail. That Injun wasn't twenty feet from what passed for a road. Well, he just laid down on the sand and didn't move and he blended right in. Problem was he didn't figure on two patrols, back to back. When he got up the second patrol was toppin' the rise and they shot him dead.

"Out here, be scared when you see Injuns. Be twice as scared when you *can't* see them."

Maxwell-Smith said, "It's going to be a very warm day, gentlemen."

"Yeah," Preacher said. "And them bodies is gonna bloat and stink before long. And we can't allow no buzzards in to tote that infected flesh off and spread the pox. We got to kill ever' one of 'em that lands. See 'em circling high up? They'll be comin' in for breakfast right shortly. Ever seen a buzzard a-tearin' at human flesh, Lieutenant?"

"Thankfully, no. I have yet to witness that disgusting sight."

"I have," the grizzled sergeant said. "In India. I hate the filthy buggers."

"No need for that," Preacher said. "They're just doin' what God put 'em on earth to do. They don't know no better. I don't much care for rattlers, but I don't hate 'em. Human bein's now, that's another matter. We got a brain, and God give us the power to think and reason things out. But there ain't no earthly reason for a human person to do bad things. I ain't got no use for human trash. None a-tall. I'd just as soon shoot 'em as have to look at 'em. And have, more'n once."

"Law out here in the wilderness is, ah, primitive, to say the least," Maxwell-Smith said.

Preacher cut his eyes to him. "What it is, is final."

109

Twelve

By noon, the health hazard was becoming a real concern. The day had turned off unusually warm and the bodies were beginning to bloat and stink.

Not one Indian had made a sound that the defenders could hear, shown himself or fired a ball or arrow.

The defenders had stayed busy killing the buzzards that had swooped in to dine on the dead.

Finally, Preacher made up his mind. "I got to go out there," he said to Greybull.

"Either you or me," the mountain man replied. "And I think it ought to be me. I'm takin' money from the soldier boys to scout."

"It better be me. You're as big as a damn grizzly bear and as clumsy as a armadiller. You'd stumble around out yonder and them Blackfeet would be sure to catch you and I don't want to have to spend the rest of the day and night listenin' to you holler. You beller like a damn constipated hog."

"Mayhap you be partly right," the huge mountain man said. "Even if they catch you, you so damn ugly and misera-ble-lookin' they'd prob'ly feel sorry for you and run you off 'fore you frightened their horses and caused their wimmin to go barren."

"You can make yourself useful whilest I'm gone by

gatherin' up some ropes and gettin' ready to drag them bodies off aways so's we can burn them. I know if I don't tell you what to do, after I'm gone you'd just sit around lookin' like a fat dumb child and do nothing."

"Them Injuns is over that ridge, Preacher," Greybull pointed and continued the insults. "That's south. As foolish as you are 'bout directions, I want you keep that double-humped ridge to your skinny rear end at all times. That way you might find your way back here by this time next week."

"Thankee kindly for the consideration. It's nice to know somebody cares."

"Oh, I don't care a twit for you," Greybull told him. "I'm just tryin' to keep you alive long enough so's you'll pay me that fifteen dollars you borrowed from me ten year ago over on the Platte."

"It was more like two dollars and it was on the Missouri, you ox. And I paid you back at the rendezvous the next year. You was so drunk you don't 'member."

"Git outta here 'fore I throw you over the damn walls!"

The mountain men grinned at each other, for the moment satisfied with their insults. Preacher checked his pistols and his Hawken and dropped down from the ramparts, walking over to Lieutenant Maxwell-Smith.

"I'm goin' out yonder to eyeball the situation," he told the officer. "I got me a hunch the Blackfeet's done pulled out, figurin' their medicine is bad for this fight."

"I thought the savages always returned for their dead?"

"They usual do. But in this case, they probably got so many dead and dyin' all around them they just don't care no more. There ain't enough livin' to take care of the dead. We'll see. I'll be back." Preacher wheeled about and walked to the rear of the post. The other trapper, wounded in the shoulder by an arrow, lay on a pallet near the rear gate.

"How's your wing?" Preacher asked him, squatting down beside the man.

"Pains some. But I been hurt worser. If the Injun who handled that arrow had the 'pox, I reckon the infection was on the point."

111

"Probably. You been scratched with vaccine?"

"Last year. Made me sicker than shit, too."

"I do know the feelin'. I wintered with the pox some years back. You heard anything movin' out back?"

"No. And I been listenin' careful and peeking out through the logs, time to time. Ain't seen nothin', neither. I think they's gone, Preacher."

"Me, too. I'm goin' out for an eyeballin'."

"You watch your top-knot out there, boy. These Blackfeet don't care no more."

"I gleamed that right off. See you."

"Don't step on that damn stinkin' swole-up body layin' next to the logs. It might blow up."

Preacher cracked the gate and squatted for a time, moving only his eyes, searching the hills and timber very carefully. The dead Blackfoot by the gate was all puffed up and smelled really bad. From the looks of him, he'd taken a full vat of boiling water and it cooked him proper. He had died hard, but not as hard as lingerin' at death's door with the pox.

Preacher dashed out and made the timber. There, he squatted down and listened just as hard as he looked. In the distance, the birds had returned and were singing. That was a good sign. He worked his way up a ridge, moving carefully. He almost stepped on the body of a pilgrim the Injuns had dragged off and tortured. Looked like they had kept him alive for several hours while they had their fun. From the looks of him, the pilgrim didn't appear like he'd thought it a damn bit funny.

Preacher stepped over him and moved on to the crest of the ridge. He found another body there. It was an eastern woman and she'd been used hard 'fore they cut her throat and scalped her bare. She'd been a blonde, and that was a much sought-after trophy for a war lance.

She lay on her back, bare legs spread wide, her eyes open and bugged out in shocked death. Preacher tried to close her eyes but the lids were stiff and would not close. He gave up and moved on.

He came upon a Blackfoot, badly wounded and dying.

112

The brave was so weak he could not lift his war axe at Preacher's approach. The Blackfoot cursed Preacher, heaping great insults on Preacher and his entire family, including his horses, his dogs, and his bastard children, if any.

"Left you here to die, did they?" Preacher asked, when the brave ran out of steam.

The Blackfoot curled his lip and snarled at Preacher.

"No need to feel hard at me," Preacher told him. "I didn't shoot you. If I'd a shot you you'd be dead."

"Finish it," the brave gasped, speaking English.

"All right," Preacher said, and bashed him on the head with the butt of his Hawken.

It was done with no malice. If Preacher had been found bellyshot as bad as the brave, with his guts hangin' out the hole in his back, knowin' there was no hope, he'd want someone to do the same to him. Preacher was a lot of things; mainly he was a realist.

He stayed in the timber and brush, moving carefully and silently, and skirting a little meadow, he worked his way up another ridge.

The sight before him brought him up short.

Row after row of dead or dying Indians lay in the shallow meadow. Preacher squatted down by a tree and eyeballed the gruesome sight. He had never seen anything like it in all his years. There must have been five hundred or more Blackfeet all laid out in rows, most of them dead. But Preacher knew the defenders of the fort hadn't killed near that many. Most of the dead and dying had just been too weak to go on; they'd used up everything they had during the night fighting and staggered back to this place to die. Probably the place had been all picked out beforehand.

Damnest thing he'd ever seen.

He made his way back to the fort and hailed the front gate. "Preacher!" he called. "I'm comin' in. Lieutenant, you got to see this sight. It's something you can tell your grandbabies about, for sure."

Lieutenant Maxwell-Smith took ten men with him, leaving the senior sergeant commanding those troops back at the fort. Greybull walked with Preacher back to the little valley of death.

Maxwell-Smith removed his tunic and laid it over the body of the raped and dead woman.

"Dumb move," Preacher told him.

"What do you mean, sir?" the young officer said, his eyes flashing. One simply did not say something like that to an officer in front of his men.

"She'd been hopped on half the night by Injuns dyin' with the pox. Pox germ stays alive a long time, so I'm told. Now you got to fetch your jacket back with a stick and boil it out good 'fore you even think about puttin' it back on." Preacher turned his back to him and walked on.

Maxwell-Smith arched one eyebrow and slowly smiled very ruefully, indeed. "Yes. Quite right. Come on, men," he said to his troops.

They stood on the crest and looked down into the small valley. "Incredible," one of the enlisted men said.

"We best start gathering up brush and pile it on the bodies Preacher said. "Greybull, you want to take a couple of the men and start some backfires so's we don't set the whole damn forest ablazin'?"

"I'll do 'er."

"Some of those savages are still alive out there," Maxwell-Smith pointed out.

"They won't be for long," Preacher told him.

"Preacher," the officer said softly. "I won't permit you to burn people alive."

Preacher stared at the man for a moment. "I was plannin' on shootin' the ones near death, Smith. Believe me when I tell you they'd want it that way."

"I won't permit that either."

"You ever seen pox close up, Smith? The flesh rots. Go down there and take a good look."

There was anguish in the young officer's eyes. This was a decision that no man should be forced to make; Lieutenant Jefferson Maxwell-Smith was going to have to make it. And do it quickly, for the stench from the little valley was already getting strong.

"Do what you think is right," Preacher finally told him, after several moments of silence, while the two men stared at one another. Neither of them had blinked. "I'll leave Greybull here with you and I'll go back to the fort and start burnin' the bodies back yonder. Just 'member this: you been scratched, but that don't mean you can't catch you a small dose of the pox. You work careful, now, you hear?"

"I hear you, Preacher," Maxwell-Smith said, his tone low.

Preacher went back to the fort and organized volunteers to help drag off and burn the bodies of the dead. They tied rags around their mouths and pulled on gloves. Those that did not have gloves wrapped rags around their hands in an attempt to avoid flesh contact with the dead.

Those at the fort would not know it until months later, but this epidemic of smallpox killed nearly two thousand Mandan and nearly six thousand members of the Blackfoot tribe. The Blackfoot's power on the plains was greatly reduced and they were never again the power they once were. From the Missouri River westward, thousands of Indians died from the white man's disease. In the year 1837, doctors were aware that injections of the cowpox virus would immunize people against smallpox. The Hudson's Bay Company had sent great amounts of smallpox vaccine to its traders, and many Indians were saved because of that vaccine. Most of the Indians who refused to be inoculated died.

At the fort, Preacher and the others worked swiftly to drag off the bodies of the dead and burn them, while others stood guard, attempting to frighten away, or as was usually the case, killing the many buzzards that angrily fought to tear and rip at the dead and bloated and infected flesh.

Women kept huge vats of water boiling constantly, for every bit of clothing had to be boiled and sterilized. The smallpox virus could survive for months in the most unlikely of places. Knowing that, nothing could be left to chance.

Before the epidemic would run its course, entire tribes would be wiped out, or very nearly so. Some of the Indians attempted to combat the disease by rolling in fire, giving

115

everything they had to medicine men, taking sweat baths. Many killed their own families in desperation, killed their horses, and killed themselves by the most gruesome of methods, often shoving arrows, knives, or other sharp objects down their throats. Of the Mandans, only a handful survived. All in all, more than fifteen thousand Indians would die. That is more than would die fighting the Army and the settlers during the rest of the century, before the western frontier was finally tamed.

It was a grim-faced, haggard and haunted-eyed young British officer who, along with his men, dragged back into the fort just before dusk. Preacher did not ask him what he had done back in the valley of death. He did not have to. He had heard the shots and seen the smoke.

"Bad," Greybull told Preacher. "That boy growed up a whole lot this day."

"So did the pilgrims," Preacher replied. "It's been tough on them buryin' them folks they come westward with. It's been hard on me buryin' the young children them foolish parents kept out of the fort. But I can't get the thought outta my head that they's a lot of grievin' Injun mommas and daddies that it's just as tough on."

"It's gonna be a turrible thing when the whites really get to crowdin' in this country," Greybull opined. "It's got to the point now where a man can't hardly ride four or five days without seein' a white family. I tell you, Preacher, the ruination of the high country is fast comin' on us."

"Makes a man just wanna sit down with a jug of good rye whiskey and get drunk, don't it?"

"That might not be a bad idea."

"They's a small problem there, Greybull. 'Cause they ain't no more whiskey to be had here at the fort."

"What?"

"It's true. The company doctor used it all easin' the pain of them that got wounded."

"That's disgustin'!"

"But true."

Several rather matronly-looking ladies marched up to the two mountain men and stood glaring at them, hands on hips. "Into the fort," one told them.

"Go waggle your bustle and flap your mouth somewheres else," Preacher told her.

One of the ladies, just about the same size as Greybull, grabbed him by one ear and marched him off toward the front gate, with Greybull hollering and bellering loud enough to wake the dead.

"Don't crowd me," Preacher warned the group, which was growing in number.

"Get in there and strip down to the buff," another of the ladies told Preacher. "We got fresh hot water and lots of soap waiting for you."

"I'll take my bath in private, thankee," Preacher told her. "Now be off with you."

"Move," she told him.

Preacher noticed there was a wicked look in her eyes. He really got nervous when Melody appeared in the group, holding a towel and a bar of strong lye soap. She smiled at him.

"Git away from me," Preacher warned them all.

About nine hundred pounds of determined female, and in most cases, dubious pulchritude moved closer.

"You're a rake and a reprobate," one lady told him. "And most likely those terms are mild, but you are going to take a bath, and take it now."

"You'll play hell givin' me one."

Four of the larger ladies moved in and grabbed him by legs and arms and bodily lifted him off the ground and toted him inside the walls of the fort.

"Unhand me, goddammit!" Preacher roared.

"Right down to the buff," Melody said, then started laughing.

Thirteen

"Them women took my damn clothes!" Greybull roared as he sat in a wooden tub filled with hot water. The water had already turned black. "I ain't got nary a stitch on."

"Well, what the hell do you think they done to me!" Preacher bellered. "I ain't sittin' in this tub with no suit of clothes on myself."

"That big fat one wanted to know if I needed some help in awashin' myself! Damn women is shore gettin' pushy nowadays. Next thing you know they'll have the vote, too!"

"That'll never happen," Preacher said, finding the bar of soap and working up a lather.

Melody walked up behind him and dumped a bucket of hot water on his head. Preacher jumped up with a roar.

Melody eyeballed him from knees to neck. "My, my!" she said approvingly.

"You brazen hussy!" Preacher hollered. "You 'bout as much a missionary as I is President of the U-nited States."

Laughing, she strolled away, humming and swinging the bucket. Among other things.

"That woman's got her bonnet cocked your way, Preacher," Greybull warned. "You bes' make tracks quicker'n a 'coon can wash his supper. At least as soon as you get your clothes back. And sit down. You ain't no sight to behold in your altogether."

When a nearby gaggle of women started pointing at him and giggling, Preacher sat back down in the tub. He was red with embarrassment from his nose to his toes.

"I reckon I was some dirty," Greybull said, looking down at the dark water which had dead fleas floating in it. Lye soap was hell on bugs.

"I ain't never knowed you when you wasn't."

"Preacher?"

"What?"

"When I come out here, feller by the name of Jim Madison was President. Who is now, you reckon?"

"Last I heard, when I was in St. Louis four or five winters ago, it was a man name of Jackson. I reckon he still is. But I can't rightly say."

"That woman that's got her eye on you—she really a missionary?"

"I don't much think so. I never seen no Bible-thumper that sassy. Where in the hell is our clothes?"

"They burned 'em," Greybull said mournfully.

"Burned 'em! Why didn't they just boil 'em good? I ain't had them clothes on more'n a month."

"I'd had them skins of mine on considerable more than that," Greybull admitted. "I reckon they was kinda greasy. You feel all right, Preacher?"

"Oh, hell, yes, Bull. I'm fine. I'm sittin' here nekked as a jaybird, a gaggle of females done burned my clothes, and a half-crazy woman is makin' improper advances toward me. I never felt better."

"That ain't what I meant."

"Oh. Yeah, I'm all right. I wasn't even scratched the last time I was around the pox and I didn't catch it. I reckon oncest you got it two or three times you can't take it no more. I just want to get gone from this place. If you got any sense, you'll come with me."

"I made my mark on a Company paper. I signed on to scout for the Army. I think the lieutenant is gonna ask you to help out with the wagon train, Preacher. That foolish wagonmaster was kilt last night."

"The lieutenant can go kiss a buffalo. Lord God in heaven and all his angels, man! You think I wanna lead them pilgrim-people through the wilderness? Do I look like an Israelite? I'd be a stark ravin' lunatic 'fore we got there." Preacher threw back his head and roared, "Where's my gawddamn clothes?"

The trapper with the busted shoulder had a brand new set of buckskins a Mandan woman had made for him. He gladly gave them to Preacher to shut him up. Said all that bellerin' was causin' his shoulder to ache.

Preacher, clean from the top of his head to his toes, thought he'd best save the skins for the trail. He put on some homespuns the ladies gave him to wear for what time he would remain in the fort. And that wasn't going to be very long if Preacher had anything to say about it.

Everybody was breathing as shallowly as possible, for the stench of death was still very strong around the fort. Workers kept the funeral fires blazing throughout the night. Lieutenant Maxwell-Smith and the sergeant stayed busy recording the names of the pioneers who died in the fight, and any addresses of relatives back east.

The next day, Preacher and Greybull went out to gather up the loose stock and drive them back to the fort, while the survivors set about trying to piece together wagons from the wreckage. Of the more than fifty odd wagons that had been gathered around the fort, the men managed to put together twenty wagons that looked like they might be able to stand the trek westward to Oregon Territory.

Maxwell-Smith called Preacher into his office and asked him to have a chair.

"Don't want one," Preacher said with a straight face. "Ain't got no reason to tote one around."

"Sit, sir!"

Preacher sat.

"Tea?" Maxwell-Smith offered.

"Whiskey'd be better. But I reckon coffee will do. I ain't

never developed no real taste for tea."

"As you wish." The officer asked his orderly to bring them refreshments. He and Preacher sat and stared at one another until the coffee was poured and the tea was steeping.

"What you got on your mind, Lieutenant?"

"You are aware, sir, that you are in British-held territory."

"The land's in dispute. I reckon it'll soon be in American hands."

"Don't count on that, sir. You colonists might have a fight on your hands."

"Y'all tried that a couple of times, as I recall. Seems like you'd learn after awhile."

The lieutenant's smile was very thin, indeed. "Be that as it may, sir, I am in command here. Solely in command. I give the orders, to both civilian and military personnel who are at this fort."

Preacher stood up. "I'll be gone 'fore you can blink."

"Preacher, sit down, please."

Preacher sat.

"I need your help, Preacher."

"I ain't guidin' no damn wagon train."

Maxwell-Smith leaned back in his chair and smiled. "I can promise you more pay than any guide ever received before you."

Preacher slowly shook his head. "I ain't got no use for riches. What am I gonna spend 'em on? Hell, man, I know where they's gold nuggets big as your toe. I got a sackful out there in my possibles bag. They's enough gold in that bag to last me the rest of my years. I ain't got the patience to guide no bunch of hollerin', squallin' runny-nosed kids and whinin' complainin' women, and foolish men. You got Greybull on the payroll. Give the job to him."

"We have to keep him here. What is that man's Christian name?"

"I ain't got no idea. He got his name cause he nearly drowned in the Greybull just west of the Bighorns."

"I beg your pardon?"

"Twenty year or more ago. 'Round '15 or '16, I think it

121

was. He got drunk and fell off his horse. He's been called Greybull ever since. Names ain't very important out here, Lieutenant. It's what's inside a man that counts."

"By that you mean personal courage, the keeping of one's word when given, never shirking one's duty, and of course, helping those in need." The last was spoken with a slight smile.

"Ah . . . yeah, something like that." Preacher had the feeling he was being pushed into a box canyon. This young officer might not know doodly-squat about the wilderness, but he sure was good with words.

"*I* am in need, Preacher. Those poor pioneers out there are in need."

Preacher held up a hand. "Whoa, now. Just back up. I didn't tell them folks out yonder to head west. They done that all by theyself. Didn't nobody force them to do nothin'. Them folks ain't my responsibility. And the truth be known, they ain't yours, neither."

"So you would just have me send them off westward, into a largely unexplored land that is fraught with danger. A land that no man knows—"

"I know the damn country!" Preacher exploded. "Unexplored? Why hell, they's been trappers and traders and the like all over that country for years now. Why I—" He closed his mouth. *Just diggin' your hole deeper ever' time you flap your gums,* he thought.

"Precisely, Preacher!" Maxwell-Smith said. "*You* know the country they have to travel through. You're the best. You're a legend, Preacher. I marveled about your exploits in England. You—"

"All right!" Preacher said. "That's enough grease. You slop anymore lard on me and I'll be so slippery I won't be able to sit a saddle. I'll guide your damn wagon train." He shook his head. "Lord have mercy on a poor mountain boy like me."

"It's the pox!" Luke reported back to Bum. He had not entered the fort, only watched from far off and talked to

122

some Mandans he met on the trail. "The Blackfeet took the disease and then attacked the fort. They died by the hundreds. But not 'fore they kilt more'n half of them movers and tore up a whole bunch of wagons. Them folks is busy piecin' together wagons, so they gonna keep on their journey."

"Did you see Preacher?"

"Yeah. And the missionaries. They made it through and is all right, 'pears to me. What's Red Hand say about this plan of yourn?"

"He's thinkin' about it. Gone back to his camp to talk it over with his bunch." He eyeballed Luke suspiciously. "You didn't bring nothin' back with you, did you?"

"Huh? Oh! No. I never got close enough to catch nothin'. And them Mandans I talked to had already been scratched for the pox." He looked over at the new men that had joined the group since he'd left. "I know Burke and Dipper. I figured they'd hook up with us. Who's them others?"

"Jennings and Penn rode with the Hawkins' gang up in the northern territories. They're good boys. Halsey and Wilson busted out of jail back in St. Louie in the winter. Olson's a farm boy from back east. He's wanted for murder."

"Who'd he kill?"

"His parents. I think he's a good man."

"Sounds like it. I got more news. They's another wagon train comin' in later this month. The commandin' officer at the fort sent some of his men to make sure it got in all right. They's some talk about the guide a-fixin' to quit the train. What's left of the pilgrims at the fort is gonna wait and hook up with this new train."

"Who'll be guidin' it?"

"Don't know. But Greybull's there. I seen him. Hard to miss a man his size."

"Greybull's scoutin' for the Army. I know that to be true. Trappin's about played out." Bum smiled. "Preacher. Has to be Preacher."

"Doin' what?"

"Guidin' the damn train, idiot! Ever'thing is workin' out

just right. We'll get the gold, the women, and have Preacher to torture."

"So we'll just stay right here and keep low and by the time the trains link up and get ready to pull out, the boys will be healed up for the most part."

Bum looked at him. "Sometimes you can make sense, Luke. Not often. But sometimes."

Luke grinned like a fool.

Preacher carefully inspected each wagon. If he found something wrong, he ordered it fixed. From Fort Hall to Fort Vancouver was a long, hard, dangerous pull, with Indians being only a part of the problem. There were rivers and streams to cross, and many of them would be running over their banks this time of the year. There would be broken bones and sprained limbs and squabbles among the movers.

And Bum Kelley and his gang.

There would be wagon breakdowns, wheels would come loose and have to be repaired. Tongues would break and harnesses would rip. Kids would get sick and probably one or two would get lost in the woods. A couple of these silly females were pregnant and that meant they would probably birth along the trail.

And Bum Kelley and his boys would surely be cookin' up something unpleasant to spring somewheres along the way.

He would have to see that additional canvas was brought along 'cause sure as shootin' some pilgrim wouldn't have his lashed down proper and come a high wind it'd go sailin' off to China. Better lay in a stock of nails and shoes for the animals and make damn sure there was plenty of powder and shot and lead and copper caps and spare bullet molds. There would be weapons aplenty, what with the ones taken from the dead pioneers.

And he wished he knowed where Bum Kelley was plannin' on stagin' his little surprises; and whether he had throwed in with that damn no good Red Hand.

Preacher paced the lines of wagons and went over them again. The men and women and children watched him in silence, the kids big-eyed. He knew what he looked like to them, all dressed out in skins, from his feet to his jacket. He looked like some grim-faced wild man, with pistols and knives ahangin' all over him as he prowled up one side of the line and down the other, never speaking to anyone.

He stopped when he came to Richard and Edmonds wagon. The wagon was loaded with new supplies but none of the quartet was anywhere around. One of the teenage boys in the train was sitting on the seat. "What you doin' up there, tadpole?"

The boy, maybe fourteen at the most, red hair and freckle-faced, grinned at Preacher. "Mister Richard employed me to drive the wagon through the wilderness, sir."

"Did he now?"

"Yes, sir, he did. And the money will come in handy when we get through the wilderness and start to homesteading."

"I reckon so. Your parents don't object to you doin' this, do they?"

"Oh, no sir. Not a bit."

"You figure on handlin' that team of mules all day, by yourself, do you?"

"I'm going to try. We had mules back in Missouri. Big reds. Just like the ones I'll be driving here." He frowned. "The ladies don't know how to drive a team. I never heard of anything as silly as that. But Misters Richard and Edmond said they would spell me from time to time."

"That's right considerate of them. What are they goin' to be doin'?"

"Riding their mounts, sir. I believe they said something about assisting you."

Preacher choked on his 'baccy and coughed for a spell. He spat and said, "They's plannin' on doin' *what?*"

"Assisting you, sir."

"Ass-istin' me doin' what?"

"Scouting, sir, I suppose."

Preacher looked at the lad, blinked a couple of times, and walked off, muttering "Sweet Baby Jesus. Them two couldn't find their ass-ends if they britches was on fire."

He spied Melody heading his way and ducked between wagons. Preacher sighed. It was hard to believe that about six weeks back, he was headin' down to rendezvous without a care in the world. Now he was saddled with a wagon train load of pilgrims, with more coming in, a gang of outlaws on his trail, and dodging a love-struck female who could raise the temperature of a room by ten degrees just by walking into it.

He had even offered Greybull two of his gold nuggets to take the train westward.

"Not for that whole en-tar poke of yourn," the big mountain man told him. "And I'm sorry 'cause I'll prob'ly never see you no more after you pull out."

"What are you talkin' about, you big ox?"

"Why, hell's far, that blue-eyed, honey-haired missionary lady's got marriage on her mind. And you're the man she plans on hitchin' up with. She's gonna have you out hoein' gardens and pluckin' petunias, and totin' her little bag whilest she shops and the like."

"Have you lost your mind? I ain't gonna marry nobody, you mule-brained, goat-headed giant!"

"Yep. I can see it now," Greybull said somberly and sorrowfully, but with a definite twinkle in his eyes. "You clerkin' in some store, strainin' your eyes sortin' ribbons and socks and drawers and the like. You be goin' home to the little lady after work—only by this time she'll prob'ly weigh about as much as a buffalo, and have seven or eight kids a crawlin' around on the floor, a-squallin' and a-dirtyin' their diapers and a-hollerin' for their daddy and—"

The pioneers stood in shocked silence, wondering what was going on as Preacher chased a laughing Greybull around the fort, the smaller man waving a tomahawk and cussing at the top of his lungs.

Fourteen

Preacher had done everything he knew to do to make the wagon train ready for the trail. Oddly enough, he felt good about what he had done. Even Greybull and another trapper, Jim, had noticed the subtle change in the mountain man.

"You've changed, Preacher," Jim pointed out. "I can't put no finger on it. But they's something different about ye."

Greybull smiled. "I think it's 'cause he knows they's love at the end of the trail."

Preacher sighed and held his tongue.

Even though several weeks had passed since the pox had struck the Blackfeet and their bodies had been burned, the smell of death still hung faintly over the area, for not all bodies had been found and burned.

"The patrol that just come in says the second train is 'bout five days out." Greybull wisely changed the subject, not wanting to be again chased around the fort by a toma-hawk-wielding Preacher. "Twenty-five or thirty wagons. With them three wagons that rattled in last week, you'll have near 'bouts sixty wagons to guide through the wilderness."

"The soldier boys say anything about the guide and the wagonmaster?" Preacher inquired.

"Only that they picked the guide up in St. Louie and the wagonmaster is original from back East somewheres."

"Wonderful," Preacher muttered. "More pilgrims a-comin' to the promised land."

Maxwell-Smith walked up in time to hear the last couple of comments. "This train started out with more than forty wagons," the officer said. "They survived half a dozen major engagements with hostiles along the way. That tells me that they are at least trail-wise."

Preacher nodded. "Mules or oxen?"

"More ox than mules," Greybull said. "That means they won't be totin' no heavy supply of grain."

"But they'll be slower," Preacher countered. "On the other hand, Injuns don't steal oxen as a rule. I reckon it'll all balance out. Mainest thing is gettin' these pilgrims through with their hair."

Preacher turned to Maxwell-Smith. "You had any word on Red Hand?"

"Nothing," the British officer replied. "And I was specifically warned about that renegade."

"That worries me," Preacher admitted.

"You think Bum may have hooked up with him?" Greybull asked.

"He's done it before," Trapper Jim answered for Preacher. "I'd like to see the end of both of them. And soon."

But Preacher's thoughts had again shifted to the monumental task that lay before him. He said, "Best you can expect from ox is twelve to fifteen miles a day. Mules can give you eighteen to twenty. We're lookin' at near 'bouts the end of summer 'fore we reach Fort Vancouver. Is losin' ten percent of these people along the way off the mark, 'Bull?"

"I wouldn't think so. Prob'ly more'n that 'fore it's all said and done."

"Twenty percent of 'em," Trapper Jim said.

"I want the post surgeon to check these new people over good," Preacher told Maxwell-Smith. "My bunch is clean of

128

cholera and I want it to stay that way. Has he got enough laudanum to give us a goodly stock?"

"Yes. Since the trains started coming this way, he's tripled his orders from the Company." He held out several pages. "And this is not going to help matters any."

"What's all them words say?" Greybull asked.

"A financial panic has struck the people back East," Maxwell-Smith said. "Newspapers are calling it the panic of '37. And according to this newsletter, thousands of people are making plans to come westward."

"Shit!" Preacher summed up his feelings with that one bitter word.

"There is more," the British officer said, "and none of it is good. Andrew Jackson has retired from office and nearly all the major New York City banks have closed their doors. A massive financial depression has enveloped the land. Farmers can't sell their agricultural products, farm surpluses are clogging the markets and farmers are being forced off the land because they have no money. A massive movement is on for the free lands of the Pacific."

"That's the end for us," Greybull said. "Folks that ain't got no money shore can't buy pelts. You was right in what you said two year ago, Preacher. You said the end was in sight and we'd all better brace for it. Them that laughed at you is eatin' mighty bitter words now."

"Bein' right don't make me feel good, though," Preacher said. He looked at Maxwell-Smith. "What else is writ on them pages? I know that ain't all. Your jaw is hangin' low enough to touch your boots. So let's have it all."

"Sickness. Back East there are epidemics of typhoid, dysentery, tuberculosis, scarlet fever, and malaria. New Orleans is very nearly quarantined. Cholera is being brought over from Europe and is trekking westward with the human movement."

"Ain't they nothin' good a-tall in them pages?" Preacher asked.

"I'm afraid not, Preacher."

129

Someone among the wagons started singing, the voice liltingly Irish.

"Will you go lassie,
go to the braes of Balquihidder,
where the blackberries grow,
mang the bonny highland heather . . ."

"I've tried to tell these folks about this northwest trail," Preacher said. "Tried to talk some sense into they heads. But they don't wanna listen. Ol' Joe Walker blazed one trail back in '32 or '33. I went over it with him. That one was hell, boys, pure hell. This one is only slightly better."

"Fools and dreamers," Greybull said quietly. "But, hell, wasn't we the same when we pushed out here, Preacher? I was at Pierre's Hole back in '32 when one of the first bunch of colonizers came a-staggerin' in. John Wyeth was one of them. But he tried again and I was told he made it. You'll get them through, Preacher. I kinda wish I was goin' along."

"Please feel free to take my place," Preacher said dryly.

Preacher laid around the fort for the next several days, waiting for the second train to roll in. Then he would carefully inspect the wagons and give the people a good eye-ballin'. 'Sides, them folks would be trail-worn and sufferin' bad from the wearies. They'd need some rest.

He didn't have to work at avoiding Melody now. She'd changed her tactics and had latched onto Lieutenant Maxwell-Smith, hoping to make Preacher jealous. The lieutenant squired her about, with her hangin' on his arm, shakin' her bustle and battin' her eyes at him.

Preacher only made matters worse by tipping his hat at them every time they met and saying, "Mighty handsome couple you are. Yes, siree. You shore do compliment each other. Mighty handsome couple." Then he would go away chuckling.

"You tryin' to get the lou-tentant kilt?" Trapper Jim asked one afternoon, after Preacher had tipped his hat and Melody had bared her teeth at him like a mad puma.

"The boy needs some excitement in his life." Preacher

jerked his head toward a man over by the company store. "You know that hombre over there?"

"Cain't say that I do. He drifted in last evenin'. Names Luke."

"Trapper?"

"No traps or pelts on his pack horse. I don't much cotton to him, Preacher. He's a tad shifty-eyed to suit me."

"What's he ridin'?"

"Big gray with a reworked brand. 'Course, that don't mean nothin'. As many folks that's been kilt tryin' to come west, that horse could have belonged to anybody."

"Yeah," Preacher said, but he was unconvinced. After Jim had wandered off, Preacher walked over to the store to eyeball the man called Luke. He stood on the rough-hewn log porch and stared at the young man.

Luke smiled at Preacher. He did not receive a returning smile. "You want something?" Luke asked in a nervous voice. Preacher was known from the Big Muddy to the blue waters as a man a body had best not mess with.

Preacher didn't immediately reply. He was busy studying the clothes the young man had on. He had a feeling he'd seen that jacket somewheres before. Yeah, he knew he had. But where? Then it came to him. At the ruins of the ambushed wagon train. He'd tried that jacket on himself and found it too tight across the shoulders.

'Course that didn't mean the feller had done anything wrong. Preacher had taken clothes there himself. Only a damn fool leaves useable clothing to rot in the weather if he is able to put them to use — but not to sell or barter. A man had to draw a line somewhere.

Luke's right hand drifted to the pistol tucked down behind his belt, a movement that did not escape the eyes of Preacher.

Then something else returned to Preacher. Edmond had knowed the man who owned that coat. He had found his body and put the coat on over his tortured flesh before they dragged off the bodies and caved the earth over them.

That meant . . .

"Goddamn grave-robber," Preacher told the young man.

"What'd you mean, Preacher?"

"How'd you know who I was?" Preacher demanded.

"Uh . . . I asked and somebody tole me."

"Who?"

"I . . . ah, disremember 'xactly."

"You're a damn liar!"

Lieutenant Maxwell-Smith and Melody came strolling by about that time. They both was gonna have to buy new shoes if that second wagon train didn't soon get here and they all could get gone.

"Here, now!" Maxwell-Smith said. "What's going on here?"

"Look close, Melody," Preacher said. "You recognize the jacket this grave-robbin' scum is wearin'?"

"Why . . ." She peered at the frightened Luke. "That's the suit coat we buried poor Mister MacNally in! Edmond put it on the poor man himself."

"That's right," Preacher said grimly.

Luke grabbed for his pistol and Preacher kicked the young man on the knee, knocking him off balance. Preacher stepped forward and busted Luke on the side of the jaw with a big hard fist. Luke went down, addled to his toes.

Preacher jerked the pistol out of the man's britches and looked at it. The name Blaylock was carved in the butt, along with Boston, Mass., 1832.

Greybull had come at a running lumber and jerked the now very badly frightened Luke to his feet, holding him by his neck with a huge hand.

"Where'd you steal this, boy?" Preacher said, holding up the pistol.

"I ain't stole nothin'. It's mine. My pa give it to me."

"What's your pa's name?"

"Wilbur Mason."

"From where?"

"Mary-land."

Preacher smiled. "Do you know what's carved here, boy?" He traced the words with a blunt finger.

"Yeah! My pa's name."

"Where was your pa back in '32?"

"In the ground dead. Fever got him and my sister."

"Then how come this pistol's got the name Blaylock carved on it? Along with Boston, Mass., 1832."

"I . . ." Luke shut his mouth and shook his head.

"I thought you told me you couldn't read words?" Melody asked the mountain man.

"I lie on occasion," Preacher told her. "And I didn't say I couldn't read. I said it'd been a long time since I had, that's all."

"What else have you lied about?" she pressed him.

"This ain't the time to go into that." Preacher looked at Luke. "You ride with Bum and his trash, don't you? You come in here to spy for him, didn't you?"

"I don't know no one named Bum Kel . . ." Luke's eyes darted from person to person like a child caught with his hand in the cookie jar as he realized he had, more than likely, just stuck his head into a hangman's noose. He knew the British had issued death warrants against Bum and anyone who rode with him.

"Then how did you know his last name?" Maxwell-Smith asked.

"I heared it one time," Luke told them. "But I don't ride with no gang. I ain't done nothin' wrong 'ceptin' take this here coat offen a dead man. Critters had pulled him out from under the cave-in and the brush and had been eatin' on him. I took his coat 'cause I needed it and then I buried him proper. Took me the better part of an hour to dig the hole. I even spoke words over the grave."

"You're a lyin' son!" Trapper Jim said, walking up and eyeballing the young man. "I know you. You're Luke Chatfield. You're wanted for murder back in the Ohio Territory."

"It's a state now," Melody said. "Admitted and recognized

in 1803, I believe. My heavens! How long have you been out here?"

"I was borned here," Jim said. "My daddy was half grizzly and half wild tornader and my momma was a Pawnee."

Preacher looked at him. "Wagh! Pawnee!" Preacher grinned. "I knowed there was something I didn't like about you."

Luke was tossed into the post stockade and would be taken—sooner or later—to the northern territories for trial. Bum was a gutsy outlaw, but all suspected he was smart enough not to attack a fort under the protection of the Crown. Not for someone as unimportant and blantly worthless as Luke Chatfield.

Luke had given up protesting his innocence the same day he was tossed in the stockade. Now he was offering to make a deal in return for his neck.

"What do you think?" Maxwell-Smith asked Preacher.

Preacher shrugged. "He's gonna tell you that Bum has hooked up with Red Hand and they's gonna ambush the wagon train somewheres between here and Fort Vancouver. Big deal. As far as him takin' us to where they's camped, forget it. When he don't return on time, they'll know he's either dead or captured and shift camp. But it would be nice to know the size of Bum's gang and how many renegades Red Hand has with him."

"And what do we offer him in return for that information?"

"We don't hang him."

Fifteen

Luke took the offer without hesitation. "Bum's got about twenty men, and he's lookin' for more. Bum wants the gold them missionaries is carryin' and he wants the white women. Red Hand's got near'bouts forty bucks with him."

" 'Way more'n enough to give us hell out yonder on the trail," Preacher said after they left the stockade building. "Red Hand's people would hay-rass us at night, stealin' and killin' stock and cripplin' the wagons. They'll try to drag us down slow and then move in for the kill."

"And your plan is . . . ?" Maxwell-Smith asked.

By now this had become a challenge to the mountain man. "I'm takin' the wagon train through to Oregon Territory. To hell with Bum Kelley and Red Hand."

"I really wish I could let you have some men, Preacher. But I don't have the authority to do so."

"I'll get them through. They'll be some that don't make it. I'll lose some to accidents, some will probably fall to diseases, and Bum and Red Hand will get some more. But most of them will get through. Or I'll be buried along the trail with them."

Preacher fixed up one wagon and with Lieutenant Maxwell-Smith's permission, commissioned Trapper Jim to drive it through. The wagon would be filled with gee-gaws to trade with the Injuns they would encounter along the way. Preacher stocked the wagon with bolts of calico and Hudson's Bay blankets. He laid in a stock of metal knives and a trunk filled with three pound carrots of tobacco. He put in several dozen one pound metal kettles and lots of cheap but flashy trinkets.

The second wagon train finally rumbled up to the walls of the fort and Preacher stood and watched as more kids than he'd seen in many a year poured out of the wagons. Seemed like they never would stop coming, all of them yelling and shouting and giggling and runnin' around like a bunch of idiots.

"I sure hope some of them is midgets," he said to Greybull.

The huge mountain man slapped Preacher on the back. "I got to go a-scoutin, ol' son. We'll say our hail and farewells now, I reckon."

"You be careful out there, you moose," Preacher said, shaking hands with the man. "Stay with your hair now, you hear?"

"You ride easy in the saddle, Preacher. And try not to get hitched up with that honey-haired filly."

The men grinned at each other and Greybull was gone, walking to his horse to begin his lonely and dangerous job. Preacher stood in the open gates of the fort and watched him until he was swallowed up by the wilderness.

He wondered if he would ever see the man again.

He'd wondered those thoughts many times. He wondered them when Jed Smith went off on his last adventure back in '30. Commanches got him.

Preacher shook such thoughts from his head and set about locating and acquainting himself with the guide and wagon master of the train.

"There appears to be a small problem," Maxwell-Smith said, stopping Preacher along the way.

"Well, hell, when ain't there been?" Preacher said. "What's wrong now?"

"The guide just quit. Said he was going back to St. Louis."

Preacher dismissed that with a wave of his hand. "I don't need no second opinion in gettin' this train acrost the wilderness. How about the wagon master?"

"He seems to be a good, solid man. He's staying on."

"Let's go meet him."

He introduced himself as Swift and Preacher immediately sized him up as a man who would brook no nonsense from anyone. Swift was a well-built man of middle age with quick intelligent eyes. Preacher knew that he was also being sized up by the wagon master.

"You've been over the trail?" Swift asked.

"More'n once."

"How bad is it from this point on?"

"You ever been to hell?"

"Can't say that I have."

"You're about to get a goodly taste of it. You got any sickness with you?"

"No. At least nothing more serious than blisters and sore muscles. My bunch are all in good shape. I insisted that all people be scratched before we left."

Preacher's first impression of the man had been correct. Swift knew his business.

"We've got sheep, goats, milk cows, and extra mules and oxen," Swift said. "We hooked up with a small train three days ago. We are thirty-one wagons and more than a hundred and twenty people."

"Most of them kids," Preacher remarked.

Swift smiled. "Correct, sir. But I've found them to be well-behaved and they've become trail-wise. You'll find none of them dashing off to become lost in the woods. One did, back in Wyoming. We never found him. That settled the rest of them down."

"It usual takes something like that to do it, so I been told. Sorry you had to lose the kid. I got things to say, and I be honest with you, Swift. I been a mountain man for all my life—since I was twelve year old. I come out to this land— *this land*—fifteen year after Mackenzie. I wasn't the first. But them that was first, they left. I stayed. Blackfeet probably wouldn't hate the white man so much if Lewis hadn't shot one he caught stealin' rifles . . ."

A crowd of people from the fort and both wagon trains had gathered around, listening to this buckskin-clad, shaggy-haired, wild-looking man of the mountains.

". . . But they ain't nobody blamin' Lewis. He done what he had to do. But the Blackfeet still tell the story about how, not too long after that, one of Lewis' own party accidental shot him in the ass. Lewis had to be toted around on a litter for some time. Blackfeet still get a big laugh when they tell that story.

"Now I'm gettin' to what it was I was original gonna tell you, Swift. I know the trail. I been over it and back. But I ain't never guided no wagon train filled with females and squallin' kids. I ain't got no patience with young'uns. So I'll stay shut of the train as much as possible.

"One more thing and then I'm done. Don't cross me when I tell you something to do. If I tell you to gather the wagons, you give that order right then and there. If I tell you we're stoppin' early in the day—I got a reason for it. And I warn you now that we got a bad bunch of outlaws on our trail and they've hooked up with some renegade Injuns who's headed by a Blackfoot called Red Hand. And so's I won't have to answer a bunch of gawddamn foolish questions, Red Hand was named cause they's a big birthmark on his hand that's red." Preacher caught Penelope's eyes and said, "Kinda like them two dogs I was tellin' y'all about."

"Well!" Penelope tossed her curls and marched off.

"I beg your pardon?" Swift leaned forward. "Did I miss something?"

"Naw. Where was I? Oh. That's about it, I reckon. You folks have put some hard miles behind you, and you've got some hard ones ahead of you. You folks get busy checkin' out your wagons and the like. We'll start whenever you

138

people have rested and resupplied. Until then, don't bother me. I don't have the patience for a bunch of damn fool questions from a pack of pilgrims that shoulda stayed to home in the first place."

Preacher nodded his head at Swift, then wheeled about and stalked off without another word.

"What an ill-tempered, sharp-tongued, savage man!" one woman observed of the mountain man.

Maxwell-Smith smiled and said, "Be thankful you have him to guide you, madam. There is no more qualified man in all the western lands. However, he does take some getting accustomed to."

Melody looked at the young lieutenant and rolled her eyes at what had to be the understatement of the year.

Preacher squatted on his heels and with a stick, drew a crude map in the dirt for Swift and a handful of men from the newly arrived wagon train.

"We're here, on the Snake. Once we leave here, we'll dip south just a mite, then start anglin' some north and west. What's left of the Blackfoot is north of us. Also north of us, but that don't mean a whole lot, 'cause Injuns is roamers— they apt to pop up anywhere so don't never take nothin' for granted—also is the Nez Perce, the Flatheads, and some Crow and Shoshone. Over here," he jabbed the stick, "is the Bannocks and here is where you'll find the Paiutes. The Yakimas is all over this area here.

"Don't worry about the Paiutes. They's pretty peaceful Injuns. War ain't very high up their list of things to do. In their society there ain't no glory or honor in fightin' and killin'. When a Paiute hears a bunch of whites is comin', they been known to hide their kids in brushpiles or run off in a panic.

"Shoshone ain't quite that kind to the white man. I get along with them alright, though. I ain't never had no problem with the Washos neither. Tell the truth, I ain't expectin'

139

much in the way of Injun troubles. This is probably gonna be the largest wagon train most Injuns west of here has ever seen. Injuns ain't foolish; they ain't gonna attack nothin' that they think is gonna beat them back or cause a lot of deaths and injuries. Them that attacked us here at the fort did so out of rage and desperation. It's Bum Kelley and Red Hand that's gonna be causin' us the problems."

"My people will be ready to go in two days," Swift said.

Preacher stood up. "That's when we'll stretch 'em out, then."

On the morning of the pull-out, Preacher rolled out of his blankets while the stars were still bright overhead. He saddled Hammer and rigged up his light-loaded pack horse—most of his things were in the wagon—and tied the reins to the back of the wagon driven by Jim.

Richard and Edmond had made their appearance in their new trail gear the day before. Preacher had been wondering about those two, so he was not surprised when they showed up all in buckskin. They'd arranged for one of the Flathead women who'd returned to the fort to make the skins.

Damnest lookin' sight Preacher believed he'd ever seen in all his days.

Melody and Penelope had come up with sidesaddles—only God knew where—and they had announced that they would be mounted at least part of the way.

"Don't make no difference to me if you ride a camel," Preacher told them.

"You don't have to be rude," Melody told him.

"I ain't," Preacher replied. "Just truthful."

"Don't you think the new attire of Richard and Edmond makes them look quite dashing?" Penelope asked.

"I can say truthful say that I ain't never seen nothin' to compare it with."

"Oh, good!" Melody clasped her pretty little hands together. "They were afraid you might laugh at them."

"Cry might be a better word," Preacher muttered.

"Beg pardon?" Melody asked.

"Nothin'."

Melody found Preacher as he was squatting down drinking coffee and chewing on a biscuit filled with salted fatback. It was still dark and the morning was pleasant.

He looked up at her. Both women had been doing a lot of sewing and each had put together several fashionable riding outfits. She sat down beside him.

"I'm so excited I could just fairly burst!"

"Yeah, me too."

A very large, muscular, and smart-aleck teenage boy about fifteen or sixteen that Preacher had taken an immediate dislike to let out a wild yell of excitement.

"Idiot," Preacher muttered. "If he does that on the trail somebody's gonna shoot him. And it might be me."

"Avery is just full of himself, that's all. He's been flirting with all the girls. Why, he even made eyes at Penelope."

"Better watch him around the sheep, then," Preacher muttered.

"Beg pardon?"

"I said did you get enough sleep?"

"Oh, yes. How far is it, Preacher?"

"In miles, I ain't got no idea. We'll be weeks on the trail. We'll do good to average, ten or twelve miles a day over much of this country. They'll be days we'll push fifteen, days we'll do four or five. They'll be days we'll never leave camp 'cause of the weather."

"You always look on the gloomy side of things, Preacher."

He cut his eyes to look at her. "I look at the way things is, Melody. Not the way I want them to be." He tossed the dregs of his coffee to the ground and stood up in one smooth, effortless movement. "Get your kit together. We'll be pullin' out at first light." He turned to leave.

"Preacher?"

He stopped and looked back at her.

"Why do you dislike me?"

Preacher stared at her in the semi-gloom. Many campfires were now being lighted, the pioneers stirring from their blankets, ready to begin the second phase of their long journey to the promised land. The smell of coffee brewing filled the early morning air. "I don't dislike you, Melody," Preacher spoke the words softly. "Matter of fact, I like you more'n I have any woman 'fore in my life. And mayhaps that's the problem. This is my world, Melody. The mountains and the valleys and the plains and the wild things. Yours is all different. I don't fit in your world, and you don't fit into mine. So there ain't no point in startin' nothin' that neither of us can finish. It's not that I won't change. I *can't* change. I'm as much a part of this land as the mountains I live in and the winds that blow through the passes. This is where I'll die. You folks back East, you read all about the carryin's-on of Kit Carson. Melody, I was out here *years* 'fore that squirt showed up.

"I was the *first* white man to see much of this country. It was me that opened up many of the trails that folks are now usin'. I wasn't alone in doin' it, but I was there. I can't leave this country for no length of time. It just keeps pullin' me back. It calls to me, Melody. Sings to me. It's a part of me and I'm a part of it. I can go for weeks without hearin' the sound of a human voice. And I love it, Melody. I love it. I don't need people the way you do. Hell, I don't even *like* most people. They want ever'thing that I don't see no need for and ain't got no use for. I got my good horses, a fine saddle, my guns, and a good knife. What else do I need? Nothin'. Not a thing. You desire a roof over your head. Woman, I can't hardly sleep under no damn roof. Not for no length of time. It hems me in. Makes me nervous when I can't look up at the stars.

"You're a fine woman, Melody. I believe that. A looker, too. You 'bout as easy on the eyes as any female I ever seen. But I ain't the man for you. I got to say that I'm prideful you like me. Any man who wouldn't be is a pure damn fool. So lets us be friends. No more than that. 'Cause it can't be, Melody. You and me . . . just can't be."

He turned and walked away.

Richard stepped out of the shadows, moving quietly in his fringed buckskins. Melody turned to face him.

"You heard, Richard?"

"Not intentionally, Melody. I was bringing you a cup of coffee and a biscuit when I heard you talking. I didn't want to interrupt Preacher. He was telling you the truth, Melody. Heed his words."

She took the tin cup and the biscuit with thanks. "I've never had a man affect me the way he does, Richard. And I've never said that to anybody."

"Melody, I had a pet wolf once. I raised it from a cub. Found it when I was summering on my grandfather's farm in the country. I loved that wolf. But I had to let it go. I cried like a baby, but I still turned it loose. It belonged to nature. It was a wild thing—just like Preacher. This is where he belongs, and he knows it. Just like that wolf longed to be free. I truly believe that wild animal loved me, in its own way. But it loved the land more. I finally saw that and let it return to its rightful heritage."

Richard saw that Melody was crying, silent tears streaming down her cheeks. He stood for a moment, then turned away and walked back to their wagon.

Preacher was in the saddle, restlessly walking Hammer up one side and down the other of the wagon train. Faint streaks of gray were slowly highlighting the eastern horizon.

He stopped by the gee-gaw wagon. Trapper Jim sat on the seat, the reins in his big, work-hardened hands. "Are ye filled with excitement and wonderment at the journey ahead?" Jim said with a twinkle in his eyes.

"Where'd you hear that?"

"One of the movers said it about fifteen minutes ago. I like to have fell offen this seat."

"What I'm filled with is coffee and biscuits and fatback. You et?"

"A right good meal. One of the movers hailed me and fed me. Right nice folks. Preacher, I had me a run-in with that boy called Avery. Last evenin'. He's gonna cause us some woe, I'm feared."

"I got the same thoughts. What'd he do?"

"Sassed me right smart. I was of a mind to box his ears. But ifn I'd a-done that, I'd prob'ly had to kill his pa. He was a-watchin' close. Shootin' the man wouldn't a been no way to start off a trip."

"It would have spoiled his evenin', for sure," Preacher agreed. "Yeah . . ." He sighed. "The boy's gonna be trouble. I gleamed that right off. Swift thinks so too. He told me he come close to banishin' the wagon from the train but he just couldn't do it in the middle of hostile country."

"You might have to do it, Preacher. Some of the other movers wanted to call a meetin' here at the fort and discharge the family. Some others talked 'em out of it."

"I guess we'll cross that river when it comes time." Preacher lifted the reins. "Be shovin' off in a few. Talk to you later."

"I'll shore be creepin' along," Jim said with an easy grin. "All filled with wonderment and excitement."

Preacher laughed and moved up the line. "Get the kids that's ridin' into the wagons!" he yelled.

Preacher moved up to the rear of another wagon. "Replace that rope on your grease bucket, Sanders," he told the man standing beside the oxen. "You'll lose it 'fore the day is gone."

At another wagon, he said, "Secure your canvas back here, Smithers. A good gust of wind and she'll rip and sail clear to the blue waters."

Wagonmaster Swift was mounted on a fine-looking black. He blew his bugle and called, "All know that those not yet ready to take their place in the line of march must fall to the dusty rear for this day. Get in place!"

"All fires out!" Preacher yelled.

Preacher eyeballed Lieutenant Maxwell-Smith, all decked

out in his dress uniform, as he rode out of the fort on his pony, a-bouncin' up and down on his silly little saddle like the British is trained to do.

"Count your young uns," Preacher yelled.

"Drovers to the livestock in the rear," Swift yelled, and tooted on his bugle again.

"That damn bugle is gonna get old 'fore this journey is done," Preacher muttered.

Edmond and Richard rode up, all splendid in their new buckskins and wide-brimmed hats. Preacher noticed that Bible-thumpers they may be, but they were both armed with a brace of pistols and rifles in the boot.

As dawn split the skies, Edmond took off his hat, waved it over his head, and yelled, "Onward to our western destiny!" He jerked on the reins, his horse reared up, and Edmond fell out of the saddle, landing on his butt on the ground.

"Lord, give me strength," Preacher said.

Book Two

One

"If God will only forgive me this time and let me off I will leave the country day after tomorrow — and be damned if I ever come into it again!"

*John Colter at Lisa's Fort
on the Yellowstone River, 1810*

"Did he ever return, Preacher?" Swift asked, after Preacher had told him about John Colter and his promise to God.

The men were riding together, ranging ahead of the slowly plodding oxen.

"Nope. He died in St. Louie a few years later. He was a hell of a man, though. I never knowed him, but nearly everyone speaks highly of him. He was captured twice and tortured by the Blackfeet, and both times he broke loose and escaped. One time he ran nekkid for miles after they'd tortured him. Finally hid out in a river. I'd like to have known him. I think he was probably a hell of a man."

"What are you going to do after the train is safely placed in Oregon Territory, Preacher?"

"Head back just as fast as I can. You?"

"I'm going back to take another train through. There is good money to be had doing this sort of work and I like the open skies of the trail."

"Lots of folks want to come out here, eh?"

"Thousands."

"Plumb depressin'."

They were on the south side of the Snake River. Across the river to the north lay the Snake River Plain, lava beds, and totally inhospitable terrain. They would not cross the Snake for several weeks, and that was if nothing went wrong.

For the first several days, it would amount to a shake-down. The movers would adjust to life on the trail and each would find their place in the long train. Those in command could pinpoint the trouble-makers and the whiners and complainers. All would soon know if the repairs made back at the fort would hold.

The first several days passed uneventfully, the weather was near perfect, and the wagon train soon settled into a routine. In four days, Preacher figured they had covered about thirty-five miles. He could ask for no better than that.

Preacher was not worried about Bum and Red Hand attacking this close to the fort. They would wait until the train was a good hundred miles out, then they would make their move. And they were about; Preacher had ranged out far and picked up their sign. Bum and Red Hand had gone on ahead, to pick out their ambush site, leaving scouts behind to watch the train for weak points. Soon they would start harassing the train.

Preacher was up early the morning of the sixth day out, earlier than usual. He had quickly put a stop to the sentries' habit of discharging their rifles at four o'clock in the morning to awaken the encampment. The first time they did it he damn near shot a man.

"Toot on that goddamn bugle to wake folks up," he told Swift. "I don't want no guns goin' off in my ear at four o'clock in the morning."

Preacher wasn't sure why he awakened so early, but many of his hunches had kept him alive in the wilderness, and he never questioned them.

Preacher moved silently past the sleepers, most of whom slept under their wagons, for the bed of any wagon was filled with precious possessions the movers had carefully packed, from woodburning stoves to coffee grinders to violins. They took whatever they could, for supplies were very scarce and very expensive on the coast.

Preacher stopped and gazed out at the blackness of night. Storm clouds had moved in during the night, and the stars and moon were unseen this early morning.

But something was out there in the darkness. Something that had triggered the mountain man's survival instincts and brought him out of sleep. He wasn't sure, but Preacher had him an idea that Bum or Red Hand was about to make a move. Probably to slip in, cut a throat or grab a child, and leave without disturbing anyone's sleep.

There! Preacher's eyes focused on a very slight movement in the gloom. Was that object — whatever it might be — there the night before? No. He stood motionless just outside the circled wagons, standing beside one of the nearly six foot high rear wheels, nearly two feet higher than the front wheels. The front wheels were smaller to allow for sharp turns.

The object that Preacher had spotted moved ever so slightly. Preacher smiled and quietly pulled out his long-bladed knife from its sheath. Preacher opined to himself that he'd been playing at this game longer than that fellow out there in the night . . . and doing a better job of it.

He was still alive, wasn't he?

Preacher motionlessly stayed his position, holding the big bladed knife close to his leg, to prevent any glimmer of light from reflecting off the polished metal, the heavy blade held edge-up for a gut-cut.

The man Preacher watched moved closer to the encircled wagons, moving expertly and soundlessly on moccasined feet. Preacher caught the glint of faint light off a blade.

Come to do some dirty work, eh? Preacher thought. *Well, just come a little bit closer and you'll find your work's is gonna be a tad more difficult than you figured.*

The man made the circle of wagons with one final and swift dash. Preacher could smell the grease and smoke on the half-naked flesh of the renegade Indian. The buck took one more step and grunted in surprise as his eyes picked out the shape of Preacher, standing not two feet from him.

It was the last sound the Indian ever made. Preacher whipped his knife and laid the razor sharp blade under the Indian's jaw, cutting off any further sound from the savaged throat. He grabbed the Indian by the hair and soundlessly lowered him to the dewy ground.

Not one mover had heard a thing, even though an entire family of husband and wife and two kids was sleeping under the wagon not five feet from the death scene.

Preacher stood for a moment, waiting to see if the renegade had come alone or had some help waiting for him in the night. After several moments, Preacher concluded the buck had been working alone. He relaxed some.

Preacher squatted down and contemplated on whether to scalp the renegade. He decided against it. These movers might think him to be a terrible savage if he done that. Most of them thought that anyways. Preacher wiped his blade clean on the Indian's leggings. He left the body where it was and walked off toward the center of the encirclement for some coffee. He smiled, figuring it was gonna be right interestin' in a few minutes. Just as soon as Swift tooted on his bugle.

Preacher almost scared the crap—literally—out of the man whose job it was to keep a small fire burning and the coffee hot for the sentries when he approached him as silent as a ghost and said, "Howdy."

"Lord God!" the mover said, whirling around, his rifle at the ready. "You took ten years off my life."

"You wouldn't have had ten seconds left you if I'd been a hostile," Preacher told him. "Dwell on that for a time."

Preacher squatted down and took a tin cup and poured it

full of strong coffee. "I figure it's near'bouts four o'clock. You got airy watch?"

The mover reached into a vest pocket, clicked open the lid, and consulted his timepiece. "Five minutes 'til four," he said. "My woman made panbread last evening. It's there." He pointed. "And there's some jam to spread on it."

"Kind of you," Preacher said, helping himself. "Where y'all from?"

"Ohio. Lost my farm when the depression struck. Couldn't sell my pigs. I went bust. Had to do something and this seemed like the thing to do."

"Goin' to the promised land, eh?"

"Beats watchin' my woman and kids starve."

"I reckon. What's your name, pilgrim?"

"Prather."

"Well, Prather, let me give you some advice about guard work. Don't stand in one spot for very long. Move around. And when you're stationary, stay in the shadders. Move your eyes, not your whole body. We got people after us that can come into a camp like this, cut a throat, and be gone and won't nobody know they's done it 'til the body's found."

"I do not believe that, sir."

"Is that right?" Preacher did not take umbrage at the words. One of the many things he'd learned about these eastern people was that they thought they could flap off at the mouth and not be held to account for their remarks. "Well, I reckon in about two minutes you gonna have to be eatin' them words. We'll see." Preacher chuckled.

"I see nothing amusing," Prather said.

"Neither will them folks sleepin' warm in their blankets under that wagon yonder, I 'spect. But it might just teach them a hard lesson."

"You're a strange man, Preacher."

"I been called worse." Preacher ate his panbread and drank his coffee. "Just about now," he said, as Swift tooted on his bugle.

"Holy Christ!" a man yelled and his wife began screaming and the kids rolled out from under the wagon.

151

Preacher guffawed and slapped his knee. "Hee! I called it right, didn't I, Prather?"

"There's the body of a savage over here!" the mover yelled. "And his throat's been cut."

Preacher looked at Prather. "Don't never call me no liar again, pilgrim. I don't like it. It's bad business out here in the wilderness. I cut that Injun's throat. Cut it 'fore he could cut yours or grab some child or jerk the hair off a woman. You got a lot to learn about this country, mover. You folks think you're goin' to a city that's got boardwalks and streetlamps and the like?" He laughed. "You're all in for a surprise, you are."

Preacher rose and walked over to the wagon, stepping over the tongue and pointing to the dead Indian. "Red Hand's got a dozen different tribes in his bunch. All of 'em bad poison. But this one's a rogue Kiowa. See that raggedy sash hangin' over his shoulder? That means at one time he was a Principal Dog. One of the ten bravest men in the tribe. Or wanted Red Hand to think he was. If he was a Dog, he musta done something turrible to get kicked out of the whole damn tribe."

"How could he get this close without one of the sentries seeing him?" a woman asked.

Preacher smiled at her. "You traveled twelve hundred or so miles and still don't understand, do you, ma'am? The Good Lord alone only knows how you folks made it this far." Preacher shook his head and walked away.

"Here now, sir. What about this dead savage?" a man called after him.

"You wanna bury him, hop to it. Was it up to me, I'd just roll him 'bout fifty feet away from the wagon and leave him lay. Some of his own will come fetch him. If they don't, the buzzards or varmits will take care of him."

"That's disgusting, sir!" a woman called.

"Practical, is what it is," Preacher called over his shoulder, and kept walking.

In the years ahead, when thousands of movers would attempt either the Oregon or California Trail, they would not be so kind to their own dead. Between 1837 and the late 1860's, more than half a million people would try those trails. It is not known exactly how many died, but twenty thousand would not be an unlikely number. Many times wagonmasters simply would not halt the train for a lengthy funeral, and the bodies were buried in very shallow graves — if they were lucky — or simply stretched out alongside the trail for the elements and the varmits. Old diaries have writings in them telling of the callousness toward the dead. People rolling or riding, or in most cases walking across the trail have written of witnessing human hands and feet and even heads sticking up out of the ground. And still they came, but the Great Adventure illusion had long been shattered. It was either broiling hot or bone-chilling cold. Across the plains the dust would pile three or four inches thick inside the wagons. Animals and humans alike dropped dead from exhaustion, or lack of water, or disease. Wheels splintered and wagons collapsed on people, crushing them to death, or shattering bones so badly that the movers had to be knocked on the head, held down, and the limb crudely sawed off before gangrene set in.

And still they came, by the thousands. In what is now Wyoming, the ruts of their passing wagons are still there, visible after a century and a half, hundreds of miles of them. Silent ghosts of the past. Of humankind's insatiable urge to move, to settle, to strive for a better life.

They rode and drove and walked through dust storms so violent they could not see the wagon in front of them. Cholera struck them hard, due in no small part to crowded campgrounds where bacteria thrived on mounds of garbage and excrement. Cholera killed by horrible degrees: violent dehydration, uncontrollable diarrhea, vomiting, sweating, death. When cholera struck on the trail, many times those afflicted were abandoned by their fellow movers and left to die alone in the vast stillness of what many called the Big Lonesome.

And still they came.

Those who took the route to California faced hardships not known on the northern route to Oregon Territory. They faced deserts seemingly so cruel many thought they had been guided straight to Hell. Tongues became so swollen from thirst people actually tore their lips off in panicked frenzy. Christianity received a lot of converts on the way west.

Starvation took its toll. Canvas rotted or was ripped away and when the oxen or cattle dropped dead, they were skinned and the hides used as a roof over the ribs of the wagon—until hunger drove the people to tear down their roofs and eat the hides.

On occasion, some of the graves were dug up by scalawags in a train coming close behind and the bodies robbed of rings. On very, very rare occasions, some reverted to cannibalism and dug up the bodies and ate them.

But still they came.

Two

"He ain't a-comin' back," Bum said to Red Hand. "Preacher got him. Bet on it."

The renegade Indian looked into the distance and was silent for a moment. Red Hand was no friend of Preacher; their paths had crossed on more than one occasion, with Red Hand coming out the loser each time. Red Hand knew from bitter experience that the mountain man called Preacher was a savage fighter and could be totally ruthless toward his enemies.

Red Hand turned to face the outlaw Bum Kelley. "He was a Dog Warrior. One of the best in my band. I sent him to test Preacher. To see if he had lost any of his skills. He has not." The Indian smiled. "Now you send one of your men to kill Preacher on the trail while he scouts."

Bum knew he was being tested by the renegade whose own people had banished him from the tribe. If he didn't send someone after Preacher, Red Hand and his men would just leave. And he needed the force of Red Hand's group if any attack against the train was to succeed.

Bum had picked up two more men who were running from the law in California. Waller and a man named Seedy. He suspected Luke had sold them all out back at the fort. Not that the fool had that much to tell anybody.

"You're right," Bum told Red Hand. "That's what I'll do, for a fact."

"When?" the Indian demanded.

"Today."

Red Hand smiled. "Good. Good! Then when your man does not return, we shall be even, won't we?"

Goddamn strange Injun logic, Bum thought, but managing not to lose his smile. "That's right, Red Hand. We'll be even."

Bum walked to the fire and poured coffee from a battered and blackened pot. He looked at his men, one at a time. Finally he settled on one man. "Rod, pack you a kit for several days and go kill Preacher. Take him out on the trail, away from the train. If you don't kill him, don't bother comin' back here. You understand that?"

The outlaw nodded his head and walked to his horse, saddling up. He knew perfectly well that if he didn't kill the mountain man, he wouldn't be alive to even think about returning. With men like Preacher, you only get one chance. Sometimes not even that many.

He put some panbread in the pocket of a coat he'd taken from a dead man back up the trail, and swung into the saddle. With rifle in hand, he rode away from the camp without a look back.

"He won't be back," Moses said quietly, looking into his coffee cup. "And you know it."

"Maybe he'll get lucky," Beckman said, rubbing his leg. Damn wound still bothered him. "And kill that goddamn Preacher."

"You're dreamin' ifn you believe that," Slug said. "Rod was sent 'cause that damn Injun didn't come back, that's all. You know how Injuns think."

"You reckon Red Hand will go back down yonder and bury that buck?" Leo asked.

"Hell, no," Bum said. "This bunch don't pay much attention to their tribes' customs. 'Sides, we don't know for sure that he's dead."

"He's dead," Beckman said flatly. "And we all know it. He

went on a fool's mission with Preacher prowlin' around the train. And don't sell Trapper Jim short neither. He can be as mean as a cornered Puma."

"Shut up," Bum warned him.

"Preacher's just a man," Bull said. "He's just one man, that's all."

"Why," a mover asked Preacher as the train rolled along, "would one Indian attack an entire wagon train?"

"Yes," another asked, walking alongside Preacher's horse. "Why? That's foolish."

"If he'd a been lucky, if his medicine had been good and he'd brung back a scalp or a woman for them to hop on, he'd a been a big man in his bunch," Preacher told them. "Injuns slip into each other's camps all the time and steal horses and people. They been doin' it for hundreds of years. Slippin' into an Injun camp is tough, slippin' into a wagon train full of pilgrims is easy."

"Unless someone like you is around."

"That's a fact." Preacher stood up in his stirrups. "Little bit of a river up ahead. We got to cross it. It won't be no problem les' it's over the banks, and I don't think it is. See you boys."

He rode up to the head of the train and walked his horse alongside the mounted Swift. "Hold the wagons here, Swift, so's the animals won't smell the water and act up with it so near. I'll ford this river and check it out. You can rest your folks some while I'm gone."

As rivers go, it wasn't supposed to be much of a river. But there had been a lot of rain that spring, and the winter had been terribly harsh, with a lot of snow, so the rivers were running over their banks.

"Well," Preacher said to Hammer, "we gonna be here for a couple of days, ol' hoss." He rode back to the train to break the bad news to Swift and the others.

"Is this the best place you know of to cross?" Swift asked.

"Yep. Banks is too steep for miles up or down. And I've

been up and down for miles." He looked at Swift. "Come on. Have a look-see. Then you can decide whether you want to build rafts or try to rope and float them across."

"I say," Richard said, as he and Edmond rode up. "May we accompany you men?"

Swift shrugged his shoulders. "Suits me. Let's go."

The river was high and full and running very fast. "Rocks?" Swift asked.

"No," Preacher told him. "Like I said, Injuns been usin' this spot to cross for hundreds of years, and whether you believe it or not, they's some of the best engineers in the world."

"What do you mean?" Edmond asked.

"Most of the roads in the U-nited States started out to be Injun trails. Then the white man come along and widened them for wagons. White man makes the mistake of thinkin' that Injuns is dumb. Injuns is far from bein' dumb. They just don't think like we do. Gimmie your ropes, boys." He tied them together, using knots Richard nor Edmond had ever seen (many trappers had worked on keelboats and Preacher was no exception) and then tied one end to a sturdy tree. Preacher smiled and said, "See you directly, boys," and plunged Hammer into the waters. He held his rifle high above his head to at least keep the powder dry on one of his weapons.

Hammer scrambled up the bank on the other side and Preacher jumped off, securing the other end of the rope to a large tree. "Get your people to buildin' them rafts!" Preacher shouted across the water. "Start emptyin' wagons. We got to make 'em lighter. We'll build rafts and float their possessions acrost."

Swift waved his hand and turned his horse. Preacher picketed Hammer and swiftly began drying out and reloading his pistols and his spare Hawken. This was no time for wet powder, not with Bum and Red Hand liable to pop up at any minute. And Preacher knew Red Hand and how the renegade thought. Red Hand had lost one of his people, so that meant that he would expect Bum to send one of his men in. Injun logic.

No way that any of those hooligans and ne'er-do-wells in Bum's gang would have the courage to try Preacher alone and face to face, so he would have to be doubly cautious at all times, for an ambush or a sneak shot in the back.

He quickly dried and readied his weapons, then called to Richard and Edmond. "First raft over, send my kit with it. I ain't a-crossin' again."

"Will do, Preacher," Richard shouted, and turned his horse sharply on the slick bank. The horse started to slip as it struggled to keep its footing and failed, sliding slowly down into the river, Richard frantically waved one arm, the other hand gripping the saddle horn.

"Well, if you're that anxious to join me," Preacher shouted. "Come on acrost." He shook his head. "Gawddamn pilgrims."

While Richard retired to the bushes to strip down and dry off, Preacher built a fire and a lean-to for that night's shelter. Swift stayed on the other side, getting operations ready over there. It was not a complicated move getting wagons across swollen rivers, but it was a dangerous one.

"Does this river have a name?" Richard asked, stepping out of the bushes with leafy branches held in strategic places about his body.

"Called the Raft," Preacher told him. "Just down the trail a few miles is what's called the California Trail. Some take that route. But she's a dangerous one. Swift done right in stickin' with this trail."

The sounds of axes working hard reached the two men. Men of the wagon train were busy chopping logs to build rafts.

"Do you suppose this river was named the Raft because somebody once had to build a raft to cross it?" Richard asked.

Preacher paused for a moment, a quizzical expression on his face. "I can't rightly say. But that's as good a reason as any, I reckon."

"You say the route we're taking is the correct one, Preacher. But several back at the fort urged us to change our plans and take the California Trail. Why is that?"

Preacher smiled. "Sure, they did. But it wasn't done with no charity behind the words. The Hudson's Bay people is tryin' to keep as many settlers out as they can."

"Why?"

"Fur, Richard. They don't want to see pilgrims comin' in and settlin' up the fur country. But when they told y'all this route was a bitch-kitty, they wasn't lyin' about that, ol' hoss. But it ain't near'bouts as bad as the California Trail. If we was to take the southwest trail, it leads a body through rocks, sagebrush, greasewood and smack into that gawdawful Great Basin. And that's over five hundred miles of hell. Dry, dry, Richard. Salt and baked clay. Mountains all around it that act like a damn white-hot mirror. Then you reach the Humbolt. It don't flow, it oozes. You eat dust instead of drinkin' water. Then, if you was to make it 'crost that, and that's doubtful, you got the Sierra Nevadas to 'crost, and them mountains is tough, boy, mighty tough."

Richard excused himself and slipped back into the bushes to pull on his nearly dry longjohns, then his buckskins. "And the way we're going?" he called.

"It's bad, hoss. It's bad. Injuns, rivers, storms. A lot of the time you people is gonna spend with an axe in your hand, clearing a way through for the wagons. They ain't no roads, Richard. Y'all got to cut your way through. But 'fore then, 'fore we turn to cross the Blue Mountains, you gonna see some of the wildest country you ever gazed upon. The south rim of the Snake. That's about three hundred miles of rough. Then you cross the Blues. After that, you got about two hundred and fifty miles that you got to raft down the Columbia—and ride out some wild damn rapids, or about two hundred and fifty miles that you can attempt to wagon through the Cascades. Only then will you see the Willamette Valley. And they'll be some in this train who won't see it. Believe that."

"So we have weeks still ahead of us?"

"Yeah. Weeks. If you're lucky. We have trouble and get caught in them Casades in the fall, we gonna be real unlucky. You get caught up there when the snow comes, you liable to end up eatin' each other. And it'll happen sooner or later. Some damn fools will get trapped. Bet on it."

"I would *never* resort to cannibalism!"

"You ain't never been hungry," Preacher said softly. "I've come up on folks that was tryin' to make it 'crost in the winter that was pawin' through the snow like an animal, eatin' grass and roots and bark offen the trees. If you can find grubs, eat them, they ain't bad and some even say they's good for you. I don't care for them personal."

"Those people you found . . . did they live?"

"None of the first bunch I found did. Two of the second bunch did. The others was too far gone for me to help. And the damn fools brung their kids with 'em. Turrible sight to behold, let me tell you that. And stupid, too."

"They were trying to improve their lives by moving west, Preacher."

"Well, they didn't," Preacher said shortly. "I don't like buryin' kids. Ain't right. Crazy folks to set out in the middle of the summer headin' for the blue water. You just can't tell some folks nothin'."

Richard decided to drop the subject.

"Hello the shore!" A woman's voice reached them.

Preacher looked up—Melody. She waved. Preacher grunted.

"Are you all right over there?" she called.

"Just peachy," Preacher muttered, and ignored her.

"Yes, we're fine, Melody," Richard shouted.

Then Melody started jumping up and down and pointing. She acted like she wanted to scream but no words would come out. Preacher glanced at her and without a word, grabbed his Hawken and jumped for the bushes.

"What is the matter with people?" Richard said, looking across the water at Melody, leaping all around.

"Indians!" Melody finally found her voice.

"Where?" Richard called.

161

"Behind you!" Melody shrieked.

"We ain't neither no damned Injuns," the voice came from behind Richard.

He turned around and stared at three of the most disreputable looking men he had ever seen in all his life.

"Well," the spokesman said, jerking a thumb at the man to his right. "He is. Dupre's a Frenchy and I'm called Beartooth. I'm a pure-dee frontiersman."

"I bet you can't spell that word," Preacher said, stepping out of the bushes.

"Wagh!" Dupre shouted. "Hell, no, he can't spell it. He just learned to pronounce it a week ago." He jumped off his pony and ran over to Preacher, grabbing him in a bearhug. The two men jumped around for a few seconds, each pounding on the other's back.

"Ummmm," Nighthawk grunted, watching the antics of the two.

"Beg pardon?" Richard asked him.

The Indian sat his pony and stared at the missionary.

"He don't say much," Beartooth said. "But he'll come when you call him to eat. How you been, Preacher?"

"Tolerably well, thankee. You lookin' prosperous."

"Looks don't always tell the story. Furs about played out, Preacher. We didn't make enough to write home about. If I had a home to write to, that is."

"When did you learn to write?" Dupre asked. "I been readin' what newspapers we could find to you for years."

Beartooth said, "Yeah, but you read 'em in French, you igit. I don't know what the hell's goin' on. I think you do it deliberate." He looked back at Preacher. "You a-guidin' wagon trains now, Preacher?"

"Just this one. I sorta got roped into it, you might say. After the fight at Fort Hall."

"What fight?" Dupre asked.

"Y'all heard about the epidemic?"

"Naw," Beartooth said. "We been clear to the Cascades this winter. Sold our pelts over to Fort Vancouver and then headed east."

162

"Pox wiped out the Blackfeet, near'bouts. Y'all light and set. We'll palaver later. We got to start gettin' these wagons of pilgrims acrost this stream here. If you was a mind to, you could help me."

"What fight?" Dupre asked.

"What's in it fer us ifn we do hep out?" Beartooth asked.

"Food cooked by a woman's hand."

"That's good enough for me," Dupre said. He looked at Richard's nubby ear. "What happened to you, pilgrim?"

"It's a long story," Richard replied.

"Ummm," Nighthawk said. "Eat first. Talk later."

Three

While they waited for the first wagon, aided by raft and ropes, to begin the crossing, Beartooth said, "You watch when you get up close to the Blues. Them damn Cayuses is on the prod for some reason. We had us a good fight a couple of weeks ago. Seems like of late, even the Injuns we been friendly with for years has turned meaner 'an a grizzly. Them Cayuses is all riled up about that new mission that was built last year, I think it was."

"I heard about it," Preacher said. "It's really there on the Oregon Trail?"

"Just north of it. Right where the Walla Walla forks. Man by the name of Whitman built him a church there and is preachin' the gospel to the savages. But them Cayuses ain't takin' to it real well."

"Wagon coming!" Edmond shouted across the water.

"What the hell's he expect us to do?" Dupre asked. "Swim out there and pull it in? How do you put up with these pilgrims, Preacher? They don't 'pear to know nothin'."

"I'm a patient man, boys," Preacher said with a straight face. "I come upon these poor lost children and the Lord told me to help them . . . in a roundabout way. And you all know that I have the disposition of a Saint and have never turned my back on a child of God in need of help."

Richard was listening, pure astonishment on his face.

"Ummm!" Nighthawk said, and rose to his feet, wandering off into the bushes.

"What you is is a lie," Beartooth told him. "You the most cantankerous, ornery, sulled-up, and mean-spirited man I ever met. I bet you got you a skirt on that train, that's what I think."

"Wagon coming!" Edmond shrieked, panic in his voice.

Preacher looked up. "Crap!" he said, for the raft had broken free of the ropes and was turning round and round in the swirling waters.

The mountain men jumped into the water and grabbed the ropes, straining with all their might to hold the raft. Richard, who was showing more savvy every day on the trail, grabbed the loose end that Dupre tossed him and quickly secured it to a tree.

Preacher, Dupre, and Beartooth muscled the raft around and got the other end secured. Nighthawk jumped his pony into the water and trailed another rope across the small river so the fording could continue.

"This rope's been cut," Dupre said, after climbing out of the river and shaking himself like a big dog.

The mountain men and Richard gathered around and looked at the rope.

"Cut halfway through and the strain done the rest," Preacher said. "But who? . . ." He lifted his eyes and looked across the river. The young troublemaker, Avery, stood on the other side, smirking at him.

"Everything all right over there?" Swift shouted.

"Yeah," Preacher called. Up to now, all the kid had done, and that was aplenty, was nonsense stuff. Just pranks, but mean pranks. He hadn't actual hurt anybody. But this was different. This could have resulted in a family losing everything they had and maybe even loss of life.

"Preacher, you know who cut this rope?" Nighthawk said, stringing together more words then than he had all day.

"I got me a pretty good idea. That smart-aleck boy standing right yonder. He's gonna get somebody killed 'fore this trip is over. I got me a good notion to hogtie him and dump him in the back of his daddy's wagon for the rest of the trip."

"Wagon coming across!" Swift hollered.

Preacher waved it on then turned to Richard. "Richard, you cross over and you and Edmond keep your eyes on that Avery boy. He's gonna get somebody bad hurt or dead if this keeps up."

"You don't know that he did it, Preacher. Although I certainly wouldn't put it past him."

"Let's just say he's a likely candidate. Go on. Let's get some wagons acrost this stream. And tell Swift to send a team over next. We can't muscle these damn wagons up this slope."

The men worked all the rest of that day and managed to get ten wagons, teams, and personal possessions across the river. As nightfall approached, Preacher called a halt and the mountain men sank wearily to the ground.

"This is too damn much like work to suit me," Beartooth complained. "I'm so hungry I could eat a raw skunk."

A woman placed a heaping plate of meat and potatoes and dried apple pie in front of him. Beartooth grinned up at her and fell to eating.

" 'Bout the only thing that'll shut his mouth," Dupre said. "Tell us 'bout the fight and the sickness and them that's after you, Preacher."

After they finished the first huge plates of food, Preacher told his friends all that had happened, right from the beginning, when he had found the missionaries.

"Mayhaps we could hire on this here train," Beartooth said later, after thanking the woman for bringing him his third plate of food. She had looked at the bearded, shaggy-headed, and buckskin clad man and walked away, shaking her head in disbelief. "Tell you the truth, we could use the money."

"I don't know that they could pay much," Preacher leveled with him. "These folks are all purt near broke. What money they got, they have to dole it out careful. They got to have a poke to get by in the promised land 'til they get a crop in."

The three mountain men looked at each other and reached a silent agreement. "Aw, hell, Preacher," Dupre said. "You know we ain't gonna ride off and leave you in this mess alone. We'll just tag along for the vittles if that's all they can pay."

"What you gonna do when the grub runs out?" Preacher asked with a grin.

The mountain men had all been observing carefully the silent play between Melody and Preacher. Mostly on Melody's part. She had pitched a fit to get over to be near him. Beartooth said, "Well, we'll be like you, I reckon."

"How's that?"

"Live on love!"

They worked for another full day and a half before all the wagons, teams and possessions were across the river. The rest of that day was spent reloading the wagons and getting them trail ready.

"We been lucky that no Injuns ain't fell up here on us," Dupre said, as the men sat over a small fire on the morning of the pullout from the banks of the river. "Or some of Bum or Red Hand's people. Preacher, you get the idea that someone is a-watchin' us?" Few others were awake except the sentries.

"Yeah. I get me a tingly feelin' in my back when that happens. And I've had one since yesterday."

"Not Indians," Nighthawk, the big Crow said. "White man. Wears long coat. Find thread."

"Well, damn your mean eyes," Beartooth told him. "Wasn't you gonna tell us?"

"Am not your mother," the Crow said.

Preacher grinned at the Crow. "One man, Nighthawk?"

"Yes. Very careful man. Afraid, I think."

"Now how could you possibly know that?" Edmond said, after listening for a moment.

"By the way he moves," Dupre told him. "His tracks will show if he's skittish. He's from Bum's bunch, then."

"Yeah," Preacher said, slurping at his coffee. "Dupre, you guide these pilgrims on this day. I'm gonna lay back and watch the train go. Then do some huntin' on my own."

"You take my hat and give me yourn. We'll swap horses too. That ought to throw him off."

They were both dressed in buckskins and were nearly the same size, Dupre being only slightly taller than Preacher.

When Swift tooted on his bugle, Nighthawk, Dupre, and Beartooth very nearly jumped out of their moccasins.

"Sweet Baby Jesus!" Dupre hollered, grabbing his Hawken and jumping up. "What the hell's that all about?"

Preacher rolled over on his back and busted out laughing. Springing to his feet and wiping his eyes, he said, "That's how they wake people up. He'll toot it again to signal the train's shovin' off."

"I can think of a place where he can shove it," the usually taciturn Nighthawk said, settling back down. The Crow spoke perfect English when he wanted to.

" 'Fore I joined the train they woke the people up by firin' their rifles in the air," Preacher informed his friends.

"These folks do have a sight to learn about the wilderness," Beartooth allowed.

Preacher and Dupre exchanged hats and Preacher slipped away from the campsite and into the woods long before dawn cut the sky. Nighthawk had already led Dupre's horse away and picketed it. Preacher sat on the ground, his back to a tree, and dozed until Swift honked his tooter and the train slowly pulled away.

While the train was getting under way, with people shouting at oxen and mules, mothers squalling for their kids, and the wagons creaking and grumbling and rattling away, Preacher circled and came up on the spot where Nighthawk figured the outlaw to be. The Crow wasn't off by a hundred yards.

Only problem was, he was gone.

Preacher could see that his horse's droppings were still very fresh, so the man — whoever he was — hadn't been gone more than a few minutes. He had made a cold camp, and had eaten some biscuits.

"Sloppy eater," Preacher muttered.

Preacher ran back to his horse and swung into the saddle. Mounted, he backtracked and picked up the outlaw's trail. The mountain man rode with his rifle across the saddle horn, all senses working hard.

Preacher soon found that the man he was tracking was either very sure of himself, or just downright stupid. At no time did he find where the man had reined up just to listen and look around him. He just plowed on ahead. In the wilderness, that was a damn good way to get captured by Injuns and get slowly and very painfully dead.

Preacher found where the man he tracked watered his horse and himself, propping his rifle up against a tree, some yards from the stream. No way he could reach it with a single jump. This feller was downright ignorant.

The man he tracked left the cover of timber and brush and moved his horse onto the trail the wagons were taking . . . and making as they went. Preacher swung in behind him, walking his horse. He was in no hurry to kill the man.

It wouldn't be long before the train would hit the south rim of the Snake River — actually they were already in it, but the going was still relatively easy for the route, though that wouldn't last long. If Bum and his people were going to attack, they would either do it before the train hit the rugged south rim, or wait until they were between the rim and Blues. Preacher figured it would be the latter. Probably in the Blues itself so's any patrol that come up on the ruins would blame it on the Cayuses. Preacher personal knew Chief Tamsuky of the Cayuses, and got along with the tribe for the most part. He couldn't figure why they had turned violent. That Bible-thumper who build the mission must have really riled them up.

Preacher whoaed his horse and studied the tracks. The

man he followed had been joined by at least three more riders, all of the horses shod.

"Ain't this sweet," Preacher said, dismounting and squatting down, the reins in his hand.

The riders had stood and talked for a goodly time. Preacher found where someone had knocked out the remnants from a pipe, and found the butt of a soggy stogy.

The riders resumed their trek west, and Preacher followed, soon discovering that the three new men were just as confident or stupid as the original rider. Their sign told him they never stopped to check their back trail or just to sit their saddles and listen. Stupid. Just plain stupid.

Preacher grew more cautious. He was now up against four outlaws instead of just one. Stupid and careless they might be, but one man against four was lousy odds anyway a feller wanted to cut it.

Preacher found a place to cut a ways south and into the timber, then a game trail that went due west, keeping him several hundred yards to the south of the wagon trail. He walked his horse now, staying in the grass that muffled the sound of his horses's hooves.

He picked up a sound that was not of the wilderness and reined up, sitting very still. He listened hard. There it was again, clearer this time.

Voices came to him. But so faintly he could not make out any of the words. He swung down from the saddle and checked his pistols, then took a third pistol from its saddle holster and stuck that one in his sash, to the rear. He would have to make every shot count, but Preacher was used to doing that. He had left his bow and quiver of arrows back in the wagon that Trapper Jim was driving.

He moved out, walking as silently as a ghost as he made his way through the timber and brush. The voices lost their muffled tone and he could pick out words, now.

". . . help me kill that damn Preacher and Bum'd shore welcome you into the gang, for sure."

"I been hearin' about that man for ten years," another

170

voice came to him. "I'm sick of it. It'd be worth killin' him just to get folks to shut they fly-traps atalkin' about him."

Preacher smiled and listened. He held his Hawken in his right hand, hammer back, and a .50 caliber pistol in his left hand, likewise cocked and ready to bang. The pistol was double-shotted, the twin balls capable of inflicting terrible damage upon a human body. The Hawken was a war-hoss of a weapon to fire one-handed, but Preacher was a war-hoss of a man and he'd done just that many times.

"What's so damned important about some lousy wagon train?" another man questioned. "Hell, them folks ain't got nothin' worth stealin'."

"This one do," Rod told him. " 'Sides, it's got some of the finest-lookin' white women this side of the Muddy. How long's it been since you cast your eyes upon the nekkid flesh of a beautiful white woman?"

"Lord, Lord," yet another man said. "I'm gettin' all swole up just thinkin' about that."

"We'll just keep taggin' along after the train," Rod said. "Bum and Red Hand ain't that far behind us. 'Tween the four of us, we ought to be able to take out Preacher and them other nasty lookin' men that jined him by the Raft. Then, with them gone, the wagon'll be easy. They ain't nothin' but a bunch of pilgrims and women and kids."

"What other men?"

"Three trappers come up on the train back at the river. They don't look like much to me," Rod explained.

Preacher grinned at that. Nighthawk and Beartooth and Dupre had roamed the mountains together for years. They were three of the toughest men Preacher had ever known. Besides Jedediah Smith and himself, Beartooth was the only other man Preacher personal knew who had actual killed an attacking grizzly with just his knife. There might have been others — and probably were — but Preacher didn't know them.

If these four piss-poor rogues squatting down there by the

171

trail thought they were the match for any mountain man Preacher knew they were sadly and badly mistaken.

"White women," one of the men breathed. "I can't hardly wait. After we get through with them, we can swap them to the Injuns for horses and pelts."

"What about the kids?" another asked.

"Bum and Red Hand says we kill them. You boys got any problem with that?"

"Naw. Just grab the babies by the ankles and bash they brains out agin a wagon wheel or boulder. I've done it lots of times with Injun brats. But ten, twelve year old girls make for good hoppin' on."

"You know," one of the outlaws said, "I got me an idea. See how you like it, Rod. We could take them young girls down into California and sell them to slavers. I know people who'll pay top dollar for a fine-lookin' girl. 'Specially blondes. They really bring a good piece of change."

"That ain't a bad idee," Rod said. "But that's up to Bum and Red Hand. I'll shore suggest it, though."

Nice folks down there, Preacher thought. Real gentlemen types. I ain't gonna have no trouble sleepin' after puttin' lead into these rabid coyotes.

Preacher moved closer still, his moccasins making only a faint whispering sound as he moved. He could now pick out shapes. But he wanted to get closer. This was going to be mainly pistol work, and he was still too far away by many yards for his short guns to be as effective as he would like.

"You say they's missionary people on this train, Rod?"

"Yeah. Two of the finest-lookin' females you ever seen. Make your mouth water just gazin' upon them. Hell, we been chasin' 'em for five hundred miles. That's how fine they is."

"I got to see this. I cain't hardly *wait* to see this."

Preacher warbled a bird's call. None of the four men so much as looked around.

Stupid worthless trash, Preacher thought. Outlaw

172

scum can't even tell the difference between a man's call and a real bird. Mine echoed, you idiots.

"Hell, let's ride!" an outlaw declared.

"Hell, let's die!" Preacher shouted, and opened fire.

Four

Preacher's yell startled them all. When he shot a big lard-butted, pus-gutted ruffian in the belly with his .54 Hawken, that really got their attention. The outlaw folded up like he'd been kicked by a mule and hit the ground, squallin' and bellerin', both hands holding his tore-up belly.

Preacher fired his double-shotted pistol and the muzzle exploded in fire and smoke. Both balls struck Rod in the face, and suddenly the outlaw no longer had a face. He fell back dead without uttering a sound.

Preacher dropped his Hawken and jerked out a pistol. It misfired and he found himself facing two pistols ready to discharge. Preacher leaped back into the brush just as the outlaws fired. He rolled fast, then came to his feet, holding his last charged pistol.

One of the two remaining outlaws threw good sense to the breeze and came hollering and crashing and cussing into the brush after the mountain man. Preacher opened him up from belly to gullet with his knife. He wiped the blade on the dying man's jacket and charged his weapons. He took his time, working fast but carefully. The dying man watched him and used some of his last breath.

"He's here, Jason!" he managed to gasp. "He done me in, I say. Oh, it hurts something fierce."

Preacher glanced at him and winked. "Have a pleasant journey to hell, child-raper."

"Damn your cold black heart!"

But Preacher was gone, slithering away soundlessly, working his way north of the last man on the trail, who, by now, must be getting real nervous.

"Who are you?" the last outlaw shouted. "Some brigand? Hell, join us. They's no point in anymore shootin'."

Preacher was standing about twenty yards from the man, by a tree. The man he'd belly shot with the Hawken was jerking and crying on the ground. But his cries were becoming weaker.

"It's Preacher!" the outlaw Preacher had opened up with his knife hollered weakly. "I knowed I'd seen him somewheres afore. Kill him for me, Jason. Avenge me, boy. Avenge your old partner!"

Preacher lifted his freshly-charged and cocked pistol. "Yeah, Jason," he said. "Why don't you do that?"

Jason whirled, his face pale with fright and with a very nervous trigger finger. His shot went wide. Preacher's did not. Preacher coolly fired, the ball striking the young man in the chest. He screamed, dropped his pistol, and went down, both hands holding his bloody chest, covering the mortal wound.

Preacher charged his pistol, stood for a moment listening, and only then slowly walked over to the young man, guessing him to be in his early twenties. He stood over the man, his tanned and rugged face as set and hard as his eyes. "Gonna be a big tough outlaw, huh, boy? Didn't quite work out the way you had it planned, did it?"

"The old Devil take you!" the young man gasped. "Damn you to the pits of hell for killin' me."

Preacher snorted. "Well, if it wasn't me that put a ball in you it'd been someone else, I reckon. You got a ma you want to speak any last words to?"

"Hell with her and you."

Preacher shook his head in disgust. "You're a real nogood, ain't you?"

"It's gettin' dark!"

"It's gonna get a hell of a lot darker, boy. And you can trust me on that."

"I hate you!"

"Man shouldn't go to meet his Maker with hate in his heart. That's just another mark agin you, lad."

"I still hate you."

"Whatever." Preacher turned away and began gathering up the outlaw's horses. And they were good horses too. That's one thing you could count on about outlaws—due to their way of life, they had to have horses with a lot of bottom to them, so they always stole only the best.

"You ain't gonna leave me to die alone, is you?" the young man called.

"I thought you hated me?"

"I do. But I want somebody here when I pass."

"I'll stay. But I ain't gonna get too close. I might get a hotfoot when you expire."

But Preacher was talking to a dead man. He closed the lad's staring eyes and with a sigh, dragged him and the one with no face off the trail and into the timber. Then he went to see if the one he'd carved on was still alive. He was, and moaning.

"I hate you," the man said in a surprisingly strong voice. His eyes were very bright with pain.

"This is gettin' to be like an echo," Preacher told him. "You keep sayin' bad things about me, I ain't gonna say no words over y'all's restin' spot."

"You gonna bury us?"

"Yeah. I'll pile some rocks over you so's the varmits can't worry you. You got airy person you might want to know about your fate?"

"Damn bitchy wife and a shackful of squallin' kids back in the Missouri bottoms around New Madrid."

"You should have stayed to home."

"Fine time to tell me that." He closed his eyes, jerked

176

once, then passed.

Preacher piled them all into a natural depression and tossed rocks and small logs over their bodies until he had them covered best he could . . . or wanted to. He took off Dupre's hat and said, "Oh, Lord, here these mis-begotten, worthless, trashy, no-count, and misguided souls is. Do whatever the hell you want to with them. Amen."

He sat down and built a hat-sized fire and boiled some water for coffee. While that was heatin' up, he went through the possessions he'd taken from the outlaws' pockets. Between the four of them, they had three dollars and fifteen cents cash money.

"The glamorous life of an outlaw," Preacher said, and pocketed the money.

Their sleeping blankets were all ragged and full of fleas, so he tossed them aside. But their saddlebags were filled with pocket watches and rings and brooches and all sorts of jewelry, also some gold teeth, which they'd pried out of the mouths of the dead they'd robbed. A real nice bunch of people, these four.

Preacher took the ill-gotten booty and threw it all into the timber and brush.

He sat for a time, drinking his coffee and letting his nerves settle down. He knew there was no point in kidding himself, Bum and Red Hand were not going to give up simply because he had killed another of their gang. The quick way one of the gang—now lying dead—had recruited others showed him how easy it was to find those inclined to rob and rape and murder. The wilderness was not only attracting decent men and women and their families to settle and work the land and be good citizens, it was also attracting the thieves and murderers and the like.

And it would only get worser, Preacher figured.

Preacher carefully put out his fire, poured water on what remained, and stirred the ashes with a stick to make sure it was completely out. He squatted for a time, his mind busy on the problems facing the wagon train. He did not have

177

one idea in all of billy-hell how he was going to get all those wagons through and past the south rim and then across the Snake. These pilgrims just didn't know what faced them.

Preacher knew that the missionary, Whitman, had tried it—and he guessed succeeded—the year before. But he'd been forced, so Preacher had heard, to abandon his wagons and transfer everything to pack animals. But these folks Preacher was guiding wasn't about to give up their possessions—it was all they had.

Well, he thought with a sigh, he'd just have to find a way. That was all there was to it.

"That's some fine-lookin' horseflesh there, Preacher," Dupre said, inspecting the animals Preacher brought into the encampment. "Their riders decided to walk the rest of the way and just give 'em to you, hey?"

"Something like that," Preacher replied, giving Dupre back his hat and settling his own on his head. He took the plate of food handed to him by a settler woman and sat down on the ground to eat. Nobody asked him anything until he had finished filling his stomach. Mealtime was serious business and there wasn't no point in chit-chatting until a man was done eating.

When he'd set his plate aside and hottened up his coffee, Preacher leaned back against a wagon wheel and told the others what had happened.

"The wilderness is fillin' up with scalawags," Beartooth opined. "I knowed when towns started up they'd be fillin' up with foot-padders and back-shooters and the like."

"What towns?" Preacher asked.

"Over in Oregon and Washington Territory. Why, I seen one town this last trip had more'un two dozen buildins. Dupre said one of 'em had a ladies dress shop that was spelt with two p's."

"Why?"

"Damned if I know." Beartooth scratched his woolly head.

"How many p's is it 'posed to have?"

"Boys," Preacher said, "how in the hell are we gonna get these wagons acrost the south rim and over the Snake?"

"I talked to Tom Fitzpatrick not long ago," Dupre said. "He told me how he thought it could be done. He said Tom McKay had done it last year, but they had to leave the wagons at the Snake River Gorge. I think they's a way, but it's gonna be a rough one."

"What happens when we reach the Dalles on the Columbia?" Beartooth asked. "That is one evil place."

"We portage it," Preacher said.

"With the wagons?" Nighthawk broke his silence. "It's never been done."

"It's either that or float them," Preacher said.

"I reckon we could build rafts to ferry the people."

"With the wagons on them?" Nighthawk again spoke. He shook his head. "Ummm."

"Look," Dupre said, freshening his coffee. "Let's get these folks through the South Rim and out of the Gorge first." He looked over at Preacher.

Preacher nodded his head in agreement. "We'll take 'er one day at a time. I don't know of no other way to do it. Hell with it. I'm going to sleep."

"My God!" Swift exclaimed, as he stood with Preacher and the other mountain men, looking at the brutal terrain of the Snake's south rim.

"Get the winch out," Preacher told the wagonmaster. "The heaviest ropes. We're gonna be here for several days gettin' all these wagons acrost this mess. Get your strongest men to work the winch and put others unloadin' the wagons and totin' the possessions up that trail. We ain't gonna do it by standin' here jawin'. Let's go to work."

"How many of these steep rocky trails lie ahead of us, Preacher?" Richard asked.

"Oh, 'bout a thousand or so," he replied, then walked off.

"And he ain't kiddin'," Dupre told the missionary.

"Just be glad some trappers found a way around Hell's Canyon," Preacher called over his shoulder. Laughing, he walked on.

"What's that all about?" Swift asked.

"A place you don't even wanna look at," Dupre said. "Let's get to work."

And work they did. It was either that, or turn around and take the California Trail, which no one in the party wanted to do. Using ropes and muscle and winches, and sometimes doubling the mules and oxen, one by one the wagons reached the summit of the peak . . . only to discover another seemingly insurmountable, boulder-strewn steep mountain trail was what faced them.

So they squared their shoulders, rubbed sore and aching muscles, and faced the task. The men and women worked all that day, and managed to make three miles.

Richard and Edmond had lost their city flabbiness. Their waists and hips were leaner and their chests and arms and shoulders much more muscular. Now they didn't look so stupid strutting around in their buckskins.

No one sang songs around the fires that night. Directly after supper, nearly everyone except the sentries rolled up in their blankets and were snoring in two minutes.

"You gotta hand it to them, Preacher," Dupre said. "If this bunch here is gonna be the breed comin' from the East, we gonna be all right, to my way of thinkin'. I'm right proud of these pilgrims."

Preacher nodded his head in agreement, but he was still deep in thought.

"Spit it out, Preacher," Beartooth said.

"We're goin' over the Cascades," Preacher said.

Nighthawk looked across the dying fire at the mountain man. "Still got the fast water to cross."

"Rafts. We'll take the wagons apart. I'm talkin' about right down to the box. We'll make the box waterproof with tarps and tallow. From this moment on, save the candle drippin's. We'll use that to fill the small cracks and holes in the beds of the wagons. That way, should a raft get ripped apart, the wagon beds will still float."

"You a genius, Preacher!" Dupre said. "Hell, I'd a-never thought of that. But why not just stay on the rafts and head on down the Columbia?"

"Bum Kelley and Red Hand, and them warrin' Cayuses. We'd be sittin' ducks a-bobbin' around in the river. 'Sides, if the Cayuses is up in arms, the Snakes and others will be, too. I've made up my mind. We go over the Cascades."

"It's a hard two hundred and fifty miles through them mountains," Beartooth reminded his friend.

"And nobody ever took no wagon train through them, neither," Dupre added.

"Well, boys," Preacher said, standing up and stretching. "The likes of us has been the first to do a lot of things. We've climbed up through mountain passes that no other white man ever done before us and gazed upon land that was wild and pure. We've seen the eruptin' steam holes in the high-up country and we've crossed the wild deserts to the south of us. We've drunk our fill from cold pure streams where no white man ever bellied down afore us. We're the ones who blazed the trails and forded the rivers and laid it all out and made it easier for them others we knowed would come a-snortin' and a-blowin' after we blazed the way. How many nights has we laid up in our buffler robes whilst the snow blowed all around us and was the first white men to be sung to by the wolves and the coyotes. We were, boys. Us. The very first mountain men. Nobody else 'ceptin' us. And there ain't never gonna be no one else like us. Bet on that. How can there be? We already done it.

"It was us who was the first to make friends with the Injuns—them that would let us—and the by-God first to do near 'bouts *everything* else that's been done by white men out here. We was the first. So the way I look at it, why, hell, boys, this little adventure we lookin' at now won't be nothin' compared to what already lays behind us."

181

"Damn, ain't that purty?" Dupre said. "You shore do talk nice when you're a mind to do so."

Beartooth was so moved he wiped a tear from his eye.

"Ummm!" Nighthawk grunted, getting to his feet to head for the bushes. Speaking of getting moved.

Five

"He ain't comin' back, Bum," Slug told the outlaw leader. "And them Injuns is gettin' jumpy. They ain't likin' movin' so far out of their territory."

Bum nodded his head. He was rapidly getting a gut full of the mountain man called Preacher. But the thought of calling off the chase never entered his mind. He could not, however, afford to lose the support of Red Hand. Without Red Hand's braves, they would have no chance against the wagon train.

Bum knew Slug was right: Rod was not coming back. But that didn't necessarily mean he was dead. He might have developed a yellow streak and went the other way, rather than face Preacher alone. But Bum didn't think that was what happened. Rod just got careless and Preacher finished him.

Bum went to see Red Hand. He had been working out a plan in his mind and now was the time to see if it would work.

"I wouldn't blame you if you took your people and run back to the Portneufs," Bum told the renegade. "That's a mighty mean man we're chasin'. Lots of folks is scared of Preacher. So you take your boys and run away, if you're a mind to."

183

Red Hand drew himself up tall and glowered at the outlaw. "Red Hand does not *run away* from an enemy." The Blackfoot spoke the words contemptuously. "Why would you think I would even consider such a cowardly act?"

"Well, I don't know. Just come to me, that's all. You gettin' so far away from home country, I reckon. And we ain't been doin' so good agin Preacher."

"You worry about the cowards among your own group," Red Hand told him. "And do not ever again question my courage or the bravery of my people."

"Fine," Bum said, ducking his head to hide his smile. "That suits me, Red Hand."

The Blackfoot stalked away, his back stiff from the insult against him. Bum went back to his own group. He squatted down by the fire and poured coffee.

"How'd it go?" Beckman asked.

"Red Hand wouldn't quit now no matter what happens or how far we have to travel. He's in it all the way."

"When do we hit the train?"

"Between the Blues and the Wallowa. Right along the Powder. I'll toss it to Red Hand and before it's over, he'll be thinkin' he suggested it."

"Why don't we hit them on the Columbia?" Moses suggested. "You know they got to take the river."

"Maybe not. Preacher ain't never done nothin' the easy way; so I been told. I got it in my mind that he's gonna try to take them acrost the Cascades."

"That'd be plumb stupid!" Bull said. "Ain't nobody ever took no damn wagon acrost them mountains. Ain't nobody ever goin' to, neither."

"I don't know of no one who ever tried it," Bum said. "But if anyone can do it, it'll be Preacher."

"So when do we ride for the Blues?"

"I'll give Red Hand an hour or so to get over his mad, then talk to him. I 'magine we'll pull out in the mornin'. We'll get there in plenty of time to lay out an ambush site and get all rested up."

"I liked Rod," Keyes said. "He was a good man."

"Obviously not good enough," Seedy said.

The traveling got rougher for those in the wagon train. The terrain was terrible and the mosquitos worse. Great thick hordes of them fell on the wagon train and soon everybody was slapping and cussing and scratching from the bites. The weather was just as miserable as the terrain. One day it was ninety degrees, the next day it was cloudy and cold.

Bands of Digger Indians would line up on either side of the trail, to stand in silence and watch the wagon train. Many of them begged for food.

"Don't give 'em nothin'," Preacher warned the movers. "If you do, they'll wart you forever. Them's the sorriest tribe anywheres. They'll take crickets and roaches and make a stew of it. They eat rats and the like. Most disgustin' bunch of people I ever met in all my days."

"But they're *hungry!*" Penelope said.

"They won't do for themselves," Beartooth said. "They beg and steal. They'd rather starve than work. Ignore 'em, missy. They just ain't worth your pity."

The wagon train rolled on, following the Snake over rough and rocky ground. The wagon train stopped early that day, due to several broken wheels. The ground was so rough one woman fell off the seat and busted her head wide open. The wound was not serious, but like all head wounds, it bled freely for several minutes, giving the pilgrims a good scare.

"Everybody off them wagons and walk!" Preacher passed the word up and down the line.

"My wife is with child, sir!" a mover yelled in defiance.

"Shoulda thought of that 'fore you started, fool!" Preacher muttered in disgust.

They crossed Goose Creek the next day, straight up and straight down. Most movers lost articles out of their wagons. The ground was the worst they had experienced thus far.

That night, Preacher told Swift and a few of the others, "We can expect trouble up ahead. Place called Rocky Creek. It's about twenty miles from where we're camped. Since the first big band of movers come through last year, trouble-huntin' Injuns have been hangin' around there, and they're a mean bunch. Pass the word that nobody wanders off once we're there."

When Swift was gone to pass the word, Preacher said to his friends, "We're gonna push it tomorrow. We're gonna put fifteen miles behind us. That way we'll make Rocky Crick by mid-mornin' of the next day and put it behind us."

"You figurin' we'll have trouble there?" Trapper Jim asked.

"Yeah. Somethin's got these Injuns all stirred up. I don't wanna camp nowheres near the crick."

"What kind of Injuns will these be?" Richard asked.

"Northern Paiute, probably. Maybe some Bannock. Ain't no tellin', really. A lot of them is renegades and just plain trouble-hunters. Renegades will put aside centuries-old tribal hatred and band together for protection." Preacher refilled his cup and sat back down. It was a nice evening, for a change. They were camped near a creek and everybody had bathed and washed clothes and were lounging about simply relaxing after a grueling day on the trail. Kids were playing within the relatively safe confines of the circled wagons. Mothers kept a good eye on them nonetheless.

The mountain men smiled and winked at one another. They alone knew that what they were doing had never been done before. A few wagon trains had punched through to the Columbia, for sure, but no one — *no one* — had ever taken a wagon train over the Cascades.

These mountain men would be the first to do so, something that mountain men enjoyed. Being the first.

"This is an excellent stretch of trail through here,

Preacher," Swift remarked about noon of the next day. "I feel we could make better time."

"We could."

"Then why aren't we?"

"I don't want us to have to camp on Rocky Crick, that's why. We'll do about fifteen miles and then shut it down. That way we ll hit the crick and be long past it come time to circle for the night tomorrow."

"I hardly think these savages would attack a train of this size," Swift persisted.

"I've had my say," Preacher told him, then lifted the reins and rode ahead. "Damn igits!" Preacher muttered. "Can't see no further than the end of their noses."

He whoaed Hammer up short. Not a hundred yards ahead, sitting smack in the middle of the trail, was a mother grizzly and two cubs. She had not yet caught his scent and Preacher backed Hammer up and beat it to the train.

"Hold it up," he told Swift. "And don't be tootin' on that damn bugle, neither."

"What's the matter?"

"I said, hold up the goddamn train!"

Clearly miffed, Swift rode back and stopped the long wagon train. Beartooth rode up. "What's the matter?"

"Mama griz and two cubs sittin' in the middle of the trail. She'll weigh a good eight, nine hundred pounds. We'll let them alone and they'll move directly."

Young Avery rode up on one of his father's horses. "I'll go up and shoot her," he said.

"You'll do no such of a thing," Preacher told the hulking teenager. "Who'd care for them young of hern?"

The man child shrugged his shoulders. "Who gives a hoot?"

"We do," Beartooth said. "Larn this now, boy: you don't kill something for the sake of killin'. You kill for survival or for food. You eat what you kill. You don't kill something just 'cause you—"

Avery sneered at the man and spurred his horse, heading at a gallop up the trail.

187

"Smart-mouthed little son of a bitch!" Beartooth cussed the young man.

Preacher touched his moccasins to Hammer and the big horse leaped forward, easily overtaking Avery. Preacher reached out and slapped the young man clean out of the saddle. Avery hit the ground and bounced on his butt a time or two.

"Pa!" he squalled.

"Get your butt in the saddle and get back to the train," Preacher told him.

"My pa'll whup you!" Avery said, climbing back into the saddle.

"Doubtful," Preacher told him. "Move."

"I'm fixin' to kill me a bear!" Avery said. "And you can go to hell."

Preacher jumped his horse forward and knocked Avery out of the saddle with a hard right fist to the smart-aleck's mouth. The blow was a brutal one and it smashed lips and brought blood leaking down onto the young man's shirt. Beartooth galloped up at that point and settled a loop around Avery's shoulders just as he was getting to his feet. Beartooth jerked on the rope and Avery went down again.

"Larn you some manners, squirt!" the burly mountain man said. He turned his horse and began dragging the youth back down the trail, to the train.

Preacher grabbed the horse's reins and led him along.

Avery was cussing just like a full growed man—which he very nearly was—and struggling to get to his feet. Everytime he did, Beartooth would jerk on the rope and down he would go again.

"By the Lord, you ll pay dearly for this!" Avery's pa, a man called Wade, yelled furiously upon witnessing his pride and joy being dragged down the trail at the end of a rope.

"Shut your trap or I'll dab a loop around your shoulders," Preacher told him.

"You step down from that horse and I'll give you a thrashing you're not likely to forget for the remainder of your days," the man said.

"Wagh!" Nighthawk shouted.

"There's to be a tussle!" someone in the train yelled.

"You a damn fool!" Dupre told the man. "Preacher'll clean your plow 'fore you can blink, pilgrim."

"I fought Cornish all my days," the mover told him, as Preacher slowly dismounted. "I'm not worried."

"Back away, mover," Preacher cautioned the man. "Your boy got what he deserved, and no more. It's nothin' to be fightin' about."

"You and that snot son of yours have been nothing but trouble since Missouri," a woman yelled from the train. "We should have voted to abandon you before reaching the Rockies."

A great majority of those gathered around loudly agreed with her statement.

Avery's father was rolling up his shirt sleeves and flexing his muscles. He did a little footwork in the trail to limber up.

Preacher was paying no attention to him. He had walked over to Swift to report what had taken place between Avery and the mountain men.

"Preacher," the wagonmaster said, "you'd best be wary of the man. He's a rough fellow. He ran taverns back East."

"Is that right? What do you 'spect I best do: run off somewheres and hide?"

The wagonmaster smiled. "Look at him carefully, Preacher. The man's a brute."

"He's big'un all right. I bet he'll make the ground tremble when he hits it . . . on his butt."

"My boy's been cut and bruised!" Wade hollered. "And he says you struck him in the mouth and face, Preacher. By the Lord, you'll pay for this. Turn and face me, Preacher. Receive your thrashing like a man."

"Hee, hee, hee!" Beartooth giggled. "Pilgrim says he's a-gonna thrash you, Preacher. His one or two friends on the train say he's a mighty tough man. I'm afeared for your safety, Preacher."

189

"I just can't watch it," Dupre said. "The sight of blood makes me dizzy-headed."

"Hell, that's your natural condition," Preacher told the Frenchman.

Wade was drawing a line in the trail with the toe of his boot. Preacher watched the man, amusement in his eyes.

Nighthawk was watching Wade, puzzlement in his dark eyes. White people sure did some odd things.

"Be you warned that to step across this line means you are ready for the fight," Wade said.

"Is that what it means?" Preacher said with a laugh, as he took his pistols from the sash and handed them to Swift. "Now I 'spect you gonna tell me they's rules to this here fight?"

"That is correct, sir," Wade said. "Mister Swift will keep the rules and shout out when to break."

"When to do what?" Beartooth asked.

"To give a man time to recover from a knock-down," Wade told him. "Each man will retire away from his opponent once the other man is down. The fight will continue until one man yields or is knocked unconscious."

"Is that the way they do it back East now?" Preacher asked.

"That is correct. Now toe this line," Wade said.

"Yeah, Preacher," Dupre said. "Step up here and receive your thrashin'."

Preacher suddenly screamed like a panther and leaped at the bigger man. One foot shot out and slammed against Wade's face, knocking the man down to the dirt.

Preacher looked down at Wade, looking up at him, a startled expression on his face. "Now tell me again, where it is I re-tire to?" the mountain man asked.

Six

Wade slowly got to his feet, an angry red splotch on the side of his face where Preacher had kicked him. He was trembling with rage. "You, sir, are no gentleman," he ground out. He lifted his fists and began dancing around.

"Oh, my!" Preacher said. "Now I know what you want to do." He jumped over and before the mover could throw a punch, Preacher grabbed Wade's wrists in an iron vise. Wade, red-faced in embarrassment, tried to break free. He could not break loose from Preacher's powerful grip.

Dupre, Nighthawk, Trapper Jim, and Beartooth began clapping their hands in unison as Preacher danced the man all around the trail. "You dance good, Wade. This is fun. Somebody get a fiddle and a squeeze box. Let's have us a party."

"Circle round and dipsy-doo, up on your toes and turn real slow," Beartooth chanted. "Twirl your partner around there twice, back again and ain't that nice."

"You goddamn heathen, unhand me!" Wade bellered. He struggled in vain to break free of Preacher's grip.

Dupre grabbed the first women he spied and began dancing around the trail. Others soon joined in. Someone found a fiddle and another man took out a squeeze box. Still others began clapping their hands. Up the trail, the grizzy sow lifted her huge head and grunted at the strange sounds. She moved her cubs off the trail and into the timber and stashed them safely in thick brush. Then Ursus horribilis went lumbering down the trail to investigate the strange noises in her woods. All nine hundred pounds of her.

Nighthawk was doing a little jig on the trail with several little boys and girls dancing with him.

Richard and Edmond, while taught to mightily forbid dancing as the devil's own work, were gettin into the action, patting their boots to the rhythm. Melody and Penelope were shaking various parts of their anatomy to the beat.

"Turn me loose and fight, you bastard!" Wade shrieked.

"I'd rather dance," Preacher hollered. "Ain't this fun?"

"No!" Wade screamed.

"Kick him, pa!" Avery yelled. "Trip him down on the ground!"

A mover just couldn't resist the opportunity. He leaned out from his wagon seat and conked Avery on top of the head with the handle of his bullwhip. Addled to his toes, the rash youth sank to the ground, both his eyes crossed from the blow.

"Yee-haw!" Preacher yelled, dancing around and around with his very reluctant partner.

The grizzly sow reached the top of the hill and looked down at the goings-on below her. She had never seen anything like it. She wasn't afraid of it—it is not known whether grizzlys are afraid of anything—yet something in her brain told her that this should be avoided at all costs. But not before she told the strange animals below her that this was her territory and to get the hell gone.

She reared up, standing about nine feet tall, and roared.

Horses, mules, cows, dogs, sheep, oxen, goats, and about forty cats panicked. The horses and mules reared up and fought their harnesses. The cows bellered and squalled. The goats and sheep bleated. The dogs barked. The cats howled. The oxen did their best to turn the wagons around, right there in that narrow trail, and everything got all jumbled up.

The grizzly sow took one more horrified look and ran at full speed back to her cubs. She gathered them up and headed for another, more peaceful part of the timber.

Preacher had danced Wade to just the right spot. He released the man and gave him a little shove. Wade went tumbling down the embankment and did a belly-whopper in the Snake River. Preacher looked around him, found Avery, and jerked him up and tossed him over the side. Avery rolled down the hill and slammed into his father, just beginning his climb back up the embankment. Father and son went together into the Snake.

"You son of a bitch!" Wade squalled at Preacher, standing on the trail, laughing at them.

It took the better part of an hour to get the livestock settled down and untangled. When Wade once more appeared, in dry clothing, and wanting to fight, Wagonmaster Swift told him that if he threw down one more challenge, he'd tie him to a wagon wheel and deal out twenty lashes from his whip. He had the power to do just that, and Wade knew it. Wade gave Preacher a dark look, which Preacher ignored, and returned to his wagon. Swift tooted on his bugle and the wagon train moved out, with everybody except Wade and Avery feeling better.

Wade's long-suffering wife had to struggle to hide her smile.

Preacher halted the wagon train about five miles from Rocky Creek. He ordered the sentries doubled and the wagons pulled in tight. Then he walked the circle of trains, visually inspecting each wagon. "Get dead leaves and twigs and the like and scatter them in front of your wagons. Make it several feet wide and put them three or four yards out. You wake up with something cracklin', shoot it. 'Cause it ain't gonna be nobody friendly."

"I got me a feelin'," Dupre said.

"Yeah, me, too," Preacher agreed. "I think we gonna have troubles this night."

"Injuns is all turned ever' whichaway," Beartooth said. "Snakes down in Ute country. Paiute moved up north. Blackfoot and Arapaho wandering around down here. Cayuse on the prowl. It don't make no sense to me. We seen some Hidatsa over west of here. Whole bunch of them, wasn't there, Nighthawk?"

"Too damn many," the Crow said. "And they weren't huntin' food, neither. I think they flee the fever back East."

"I keep hearin' talk of an up-risin'," Preacher said. " 'Bout tribes buryin' the hatchet and bandin' together. I reckon it's true." He leaned forward, cutting off a chunk of meat fairly oozing with fat. "Any Dog Soldiers with them?"

"Couldn't tell for certain," Beartooth said. "I hope not. I hate them damn contaries."

The Hidatsa Dog Soldiers did everything backward, hence they were called contaries. But they were fierce fighters and much feared.

A mover walked up and squatted down. "I thought the wild red savages always beat on drums before they attacked?"

Dupre and Beartooth grinned, Nighthawk looked disgusted but said nothing. "Some do back at the village," Preacher said. "Before a fight—gets 'em all worked up into a lather. But I ain't never seen no Injun totin' no drum in battle a-whuppin' on it. Although if you was to tell a contrary he couldn't, he would." Preacher laughed. "Wouldn't that be a sight to see?"

Thoroughly confused, and really wanting to ask what in the world a contrary might be, the mover sighed and stood up, returning to his family.

Very soon after supper was eaten and the dishes washed, the movers began settling down for sleep. Trapper Jim brought over a fresh pot of coffee and the mountain men relaxed, drinking the hot, strong brew.

"When you think they'll hit us?" Jim asked.

"You feel it too, huh?" Dupre asked.

"Yeah. My guess is just as soon as the people get good asleep. I don't think they're gonna wait too long."

"That's a good thought," Preacher said. "We'll just drink this here coffee and then take up positions. Our backs is in pretty good shape, backed up to the bluffs. East is clear enough. West and south'll be the way they'll hit us." He drained his cup. "I reckon it's time to go to work."

Preacher found Swift. "Get the folks out of their blankets," he told him. "We're a-fixin' to get hit by Injuns."

The wagonmaster cocked his head and listened for a moment. "But I don't hear a thing, Preacher."

"That's right, Swift. You don't hear nothin'. Now think about that."

The two men stared at one another for a moment. Swift nodded his head. "I'm learning," he told Preacher. "Takes me awhile, but I'll get there."

Preacher clasped him on the shoulder. "Good man. Now get them movers up and ready."

"I see something out there," a woman told Preacher as he walked by her wagon. "Several somethings. They're not trying to hide."

Preacher angled over to her and stood gazing out into the night. He called out in Snake.

"One third of your horses and mules," the harsh voice came back to him, speaking in English, "And one third of all your supplies. Then you may pass through."

"Forget it," Preacher returned the shout. "And don't tell me you're hungry. They's game aplenty out there this summer. We ain't botherin' you, so there ain't gonna be no tribute paid."

"You will die then. All of you."

"Sing your death songs."

The Indian shouted out some very uncomplimentary and very uncomfortable suggestions to Preacher.

Preacher heard Beartooth's laugh. "Your horse wouldn't like that either, Preacher."

"You have that stinking cowardly Crow puke Nighthawk with you?" the Indian shouted.

That prompted a long stream of invectives from Nighthawk. He told the Snake where to put his bow and arrows, his horse, his wife, his kids, his mother, his father, and all his friends.

"Wagh!" Dupre said. "Talk about a tight fit."

A bow string twanged and the arrow thudded into the bed of a wagon near Preacher.

The shapes that the woman had seen had long disappeared as the Snakes prepared to attack.

"Only cowards attack women and children!" Beartooth shouted. "None of you are fit to be called braves. I say you is all stinking coyote vomit."

"Bear-Killer will not die well, I am thinking," the Snake's words came out of the darkness.

Preacher had hunkered down. His eyes had found a shape on the ground that was unnatural to the terrain. He lifted his Hawken and sighted it in, squeezing the trigger. The powerful rifle boomed and the shape lifted itself off the ground for a few seconds, then collapsed, shot through and through.

Preacher quickly reloaded as arrows filled the night air. One mover screamed as an arrow embedded in his thigh. A child began crying and its mother tried to soothe the child into silence with calming words.

Nighthawk's rifle crashed and another Snake went down, shot through the stomach. The brave began screaming in pain as he rolled on the ground, his innards ruined.

"If we can get three or four more," Preacher told the man who crouched beside a wagon wheel, "them bucks will break it off. I don't think they's many of them out there."

Preacher was thoughtful for a moment. "Pass the word: everyone with two rifles get ready to stand and deliver. We'll all fire at once. Injuns is notional. That much firepower all at once might change their minds. Keep your second rifle at hand in case it just makes 'em mad and they charge."

The mover looked at Preacher.

Preacher shrugged his shoulders. "Life's full of chances."

Within two minutes time, all the men were ready. "Now!" Preacher shouted, and the night roared and flashed with fire and smoke and lead balls.

The movers were lucky this night. Their blind fire had hit several warriors. The Indians, never with enough ball or powder, figured that any group with so much shot and powder that they could waste it made their medicine very bad. Shouting threats and insults, they pulled back into the night.

Nighthawk laid on the ground, his ear to the earth and listened. "They're riding away," he finally said, standing up. "Heading south. That bunch is through for this night."

Preacher walked over to the man with an arrowhead sunk more than halfway through his thigh. "You got any drinkin' whiskey?" he asked.

"In the wagon," the mover said through gritted teeth.

"Get it," Preacher told the man's wife.

The woman returned quickly with a jug of rye and handed it to Preacher. "Thankee kindly, ma'am," he said. Preacher took him a long pull and then handed the jug to the wounded man. "I could say that this is gonna hurt me worser than it does you, but I'd be lyin'. You take you three or four good swallers and tell me when you're ready."

The mover's adam's apple bobbed up and down as he swallowed the raw brew. "I'm ready."

Preacher nodded at Dupre and Beartooth and the mountain men grabbed the mover's arms. Preacher got him a good grip on the shaft of the arrow and pushed hard. The man screamed as the arrow tore out the back of his leg. Preacher quickly broke off the shaft and pulled it out, then reached behind the man's leg and jerked out what remained.

The mover had passed out.

Preacher poured some whiskey on the wound, front and back, and told the woman, "Nighthawk'll take over now. Let him fix his potions and poultices and don't interfere. Injuns been usin' things like marigold and goldenseal and dandelion and nipbone and others for centuries. And they work."

"What do you suggest for a bruise?" Edmond asked, pulling up his sleeve and showing a badly bruised arm.

"I won't ask how you got it. You pick you some

bruisewort in the mornin'. That'll fix you right up."

"Some what?"

Preacher smiled. "Daisy flowers. Crush 'em up and lay 'em on the bruise. Works, ol' son."

"Pickin' handfuls of daisies on the banks of the Snake," Beartooth sang and did a little dance. "This'un I don't like, that'un I'll take."

Dupre looked at him. "I swear you too young to be gettin' senile. But you shore been actin' goofy here of late. Did you fall off your horse and bang your head?"

"Nope. I just feel good, that's all. And you best feel good too. 'Cause when we cross the Snake in a week or so, and start headin' north, feel-good time is gonna be over."

"I allow as to how you may be right." The two men linked arms and went off singing, "Pickin' daisies on the banks of the Snake . . . This'un I don't like, that'un I'll take . . ."

Then the two mountain men did a little dance step and made up some lines that caused several of the women to squeal and cover their faces with their aprons.

Nighthawk sighed and shook his head.

Seven

Preacher halted the train about a mile from Rocky Creek and he and Dupre, Nighthawk, and Beartooth rode up to the crossing. No Indians were in sight, but the four of them knew that accounted for nothing in this country.

"Quiet," Preacher observed. "But a peaceful kind of quiet."

"Right," Dupre said dryly. "Like that bird singin' yonder that ain't no bird."

"I gleamed that right off," Beartooth said. "So they're waitin' for us in them rocks over yonder crost the crick. Now, I consider that to be downright nasty, sneaky, unfriendly, and not a-tall to my likin'."

"Yeah," Preacher said with a grin. "Not nothin' like any of us would do."

"You got you an idee," Beartooth said. "Ever' time you grin like 'at, I know you got something sneaky wigglin' around inside your headbone."

"I do for a fact. Let's ride on back and get things set up. We'll give them renegades something them that live through can tell their grandkids."

"Real easy like and not in no hurry," Preacher told Swift, "I want you to pick out twelve of the best shots in the train and get them ready to load up, six in each wagon. Three to

199

a side. I want them to have at least three rifles loaded up and pistols at the ready. Beartooth and Nighthawk is on the south right now checkin' to see if we're bein' spied on. Rig the canvas so's it can be jerked up from the inside. Have Jim drive one wagon, and a damn good man on the seat of the other. We're gonna turn this ambush around."

The warbling of a bird reached them. Preacher smiled. "That's Nighthawk tellin' me it's clear. When you get your men picked out, load ever'body up on the south side of the wagons so's the Injuns won't see what's goin' on."

"Where will you be?" Swift asked.

"Me and Beartooth will be in front, Dupre and Nighthawk to the rear. What we'll do, you and me, is have a big argument on the banks with me yellin' that we can only take two wagons acrost at a time. Then we'll move 'em out."

Swift looked doubtful. "I hope this works," he finally said, with a shake of his head.

Preacher grinned at him. "Me and Beartooth's gonna be in the front. What are you complainin' about?"

Preacher walked back to where the two wagons were being prepared. With only the flaps facing southward lowered, men busied themselves off-loading the wagons' contents, making room for the marksmen to crouch. Other men were digging for spare rifles and pistols, loading them up and handing them to the marksmen. The mountain men double-shotted their pistols and checked their rifles.

"Me and Nighthawk found signs that show some lazy-butt Diggers has joined this bunch," Beartooth said. "This bunch mostly is tribal castouts. For a Digger to throw somebody out of the tribe means they really must have done something awful."

"I ain't never heared of a Digger ever throwin' nobody out," Dupre said. "Most of 'em's too damn lazy to take the time for a meetin'."

Preacher told Swift, "Make your people ready for an attack. We can't circle here, so keep everybody in the wagons, or right near them. Guns ready."

"We're ready," Trapper Jim called.

"Come on, Swift," Preacher said. "Let's us walk down to the bank and have a quarrel."

The two men stood on the banks and shouted at each other for several minutes, with a lot of finger-pointing at the other side of the creek. Finally, the wagon master threw up his hands and stalked off.

"Bring 'em on," Preacher shouted. "Beartooth, bring my horse down here, will you?"

"You think they bought it?" Beartooth asked, when Preacher had swung into the saddle.

"I hope so." He cocked his Hawken and Beartooth did the same. "We're gonna have to fire these things like pistols," he told the big mountain man with a grin. "So get a good grip on yourn. I'd hate for you to lose it and you have to go wadin' in the crick after it. Your feet's so dirty the water'd be ruint for miles downsteam."

"Wagh!" Beartooth said. "You ain't tooken a bath in so long even the fleas is a-leavin' you. I oughtta shove you offen your horse so the poor animal could take a decent breath. It's a wonder he ain't dropped stone dead from havin' to smell you."

They insulted each other while the wagons were lumbering down the trail to the creek.

"I reckon we'll play this here game out like we see it oncest we're crost," Beartooth said. "Watch your top-knot ifn you have to leave the saddle, ol' son."

"Same to you, Bear-Killer. Here they are. So here we go."

They stepped their horses into the creek and began the crossing, staying close to the first wagon, driven by Trapper Jim. They felt the attack would begin as soon as the second wagon was fully out of the creek and past the top of the embankment. The renegade Indians would, in all likelihood, be content with slaughtering those in the two wagons rather than face defeat or taking heavy losses by waiting until the entire train was over.

"In the rocks left and right," Beartooth whispered.

"Unless a rock has taken to growin' a hand."

"Yep. That's a careless Injun. Tell you what, just as soon as the last wagon s crost, we kick these hammerheads into a gallop and get past them boulders. I'll swing left and you swing right—that's the side your furthest leg is on," he added with grin, "and we'll come up 'hind 'em."

"I would tell you to keep low in the saddle," Beartooth responded with a smile, "but you so damn scrawny and poor as it is, if an Injun gets an arrow in you it'll be pure luck. Never seen a man afore that has to stand in the same spot twicest to make a shadder."

"Don't worry none 'bout takin' no arrow-points, Beartooth. They's so much lard and blubber on you it won't do no damage to amount to much."

They stepped their horses onto the bank and started up the slight incline.

"The only place Beartooth might take an arrey is in his butt," Trapper Jim called. "Way it hangs out over the sides of that saddle makes a right temptin' target."

"I don't know why I 'ssociate with the likes of you people," Beartooth said. "Way you continue to heap insults upon the poor head of this humble child of God."

"Wagh!" Preacher said, then spat. "You bring it all on yourself. Any man who'd winter with a squaw as ugly as that female you took up with back in '31 is beyond redemption. I thought you'd took up with a bear first time I come up on you two. What was her name? She Who Frightens The Sun?"

Beartooth grinned. "She cooked good and was right cosy in the robes, though."

"I 'spect she were that. 'Course you had to kill nine deer to get enough skins for her dress. First time that woman reared up in front of me I jumped ten feet in the air. I thought I done come up on a sasquatch."

"I allow as to how she were a queen compared to that Assiniboin you took for a bride back in '28."

"I *had* to marry up with her," Preacher said. "It was either that or they was gonna kill me. I'm tellin' you, her father was desperate to get shut of that girl. He didn't name her Squalls a Lot for nothin'. First time she hollered at me the whole damn tipi fell down."

The second wagon reached the crest of the bank and Preacher let out a wild whoop and Hammer took off like he'd been shot out of a cannon.

Preacher cut left and Beartooth cut to the right just as the rocks on both sides of the trail were suddenly swarming with rogue Indians.

The canvas on the wagons was jerked off and the riflemen inside leveled their weapons and cut loose with a volley. These Indians never had a chance. Taken completely by surprise, they were cut down and their blood began staining the rocks and boulders by the creek.

Preacher left his horse and slammed into a buck, knocking him to the ground. He sprang to his feet with a knife in one hand and a pistol in the other. Preacher shot him at nearly point-blank range with the Hawken and the ball passed right through him, the impact knocking the brave off his moccasins. Preacher used his rifle like a club, cracking the skull of a buck who came screaming at him.

Dropping the Hawken, Preacher jerked out two pistols— double-shotted as usual—and took two more out with them, the balls doing fearful damage to the braves.

A brave jumped at Beartooth and the huge man grabbed him by the neck and hurled him against a boulder, breaking the warrior's back with a horrible cracking sound.

Nighthawk turned as a renegade Sauk—identified by his distinctive necklace of grizzly bear claws—cursed Nighthawk for a mangy Crow dog. Many of his tribe had been pushed West by the ever-moving and encroaching whites. Nighthawk lifted a pistol and drilled the Sauk through the heart, then ran to help his friend, Dupre, who was struggling with two Indians who wore Sioux markings.

Nighthawk clubbed one with the butt of his pistol, smashing the man's skull. Dupre threw the other one to the ground and shot him in the head.

Trapper Jim had left his wagon seat, a pistol in each hand, and two dead Indians lay at his feet.

"It's over!" Preacher shouted. "Stop firin'. It's over."

Men coughed nervously and rubbed at eyes that watered and smarted from the thick gray smoke from their black powder weapons. The mountain men went about the grisly task of finishing off those warriors who were badly wounded.

"Stay in the wagons," Preacher told the movers. "This ain't nothin' you need to get involved in. It's just something that has to be done. Reload all your weapons. That'll give you something to do." He shook his head, but he was proud of the movers. They had conducted themselves well.

Nighthawk knelt down beside a badly wounded, gut-shot Cayuse and spoke in his own language. "You are dying. Do you want me to hasten death?"

"I want you to do nothing, Crow puke," the defiant warrior told him. "Except leave so I do not have to look upon your stupid, ugly face. I do not want that to be the last thing I see in this life."

Nighthawk rose. "Then I shall certainly abide by your wishes, Cayuse vulture shit."

He walked away, leaving the buck to die alone.

"You ever see so damn many tribes in one spot?" Dupre asked, as the mountain men met back on the trail. "I counted eight tribes. They's a dead Cree over yonder."

"Worries me," Preacher admitted, as Swift yelled from the other side.

"When do we cross?" the wagonmaster yelled.

"Bring 'em on over!" Trapper Jim shouted, waving at the man. He climbed back on the seat and pulled his wagon on ahead, the second wagon following.

"Worries you?" Nighthawk said, pointing to a dead Indian. "That's a Crow over there. I knew him as a good man.

204

It's hard for me to believe that a Crow would join up with such a band of puke and maggots."

The men gathered their horses and got off the trail as the wagon train began its crossing of the creek. No one asked if the mountain men were going to bury the dead Indians. By now, they knew they would not. But they did help drag them out of sight so the womenfolk wouldn't have to look at the mangled and bloody bodies.

The wagons lumbered across slowly, the creek crossing going well until a wheel came off and dumped some of the wagon's contents into the now muddy water.

"Don't try to drive them wagons around it," Preacher hollered out the warning. "They's rocks on one side and a drop-off on the other."

"Rig a skid!" Swift shouted. "Helpers down here, boys. Let's step lively now."

Melody walked her horse across the creek to sit side-saddle and watch the proceedings. She wrinkled her little nose at the smell of death that hung heavily around the ambush site, and very pointedly ignored Preacher.

"That woman wants to share her blankets with you, Preacher," Dupre said.

"She's a looker," Beartooth said.

"I'd sooner bed down with a coyote," Preacher said. "I done told that woman fifteen times to leave me be. It's like tryin' to get shut of a hongry bear when you're totin' fresh-kilt meat."

"Why don't you bed her down and then just ride off?" Dupre suggested.

"If I done that, she'd be followin' me around forever, totin' a bedroll. I can just see it now. All the rest of my days, I'd have this female followin' me acrost the plains and the mountains. No matter where I might wander, she'd be right behind me, callin' out, 'Come back, Preacher. Preacher, come back.' Lord, I'd be the laughin' stock of the West." He shook his head as his friends broke out in laughter.

Melody cut her eyes to the group of mountain men, unaware of the Indian who was only a few yards from her. He had not moved during the ambush. He lay between a rock and a small bush. He was one with the earth, conspicuous to anyone who might glance his way and actually see what lay before them. But the Indian knew that while whites look at many things, most of them actually see very little.

All around him movers strained and grunted and swore as they finally got the wagon with the broken wheel out of the creek and up the grade. No one saw the lone brave. He was going to die, and he knew it. It didn't matter. He had sung his death song hours before. He moved only his eyes as he planned out his final few minutes on this earth. Up swiftly, one short jump, and the honey-haired woman on the horse would be dead. No matter if the others killed him. That was not important.

But the horse didn't like the strange scent in his nostrils. He kept fighting the bit, wanting to leave this place, the smell of the warrior making him nervous.

Preacher looked at the skittish horse, wondering if there was a snake over there. Something was sure making that horse nervous. Melody was having a hard time controlling the animal, and Preacher knew she was a good horsewoman. Something was very wrong. He left the group and walked toward Melody, reflex making him cock the Hawken as he walked.

The Indian sensed it was now or never. He knew the legendary mountain man called Preacher, and he was proud that it would be a mighty warrior who killed him. That was good. The mountain men would tell the story and Indians would hear it. Songs would be sung about how he died. He made his move, springing off of the earth and leaped toward Melody, a war axe in one hand, ready to bash her brains out.

The horse walled its eyes and trembled, then reared up in fright, took one big jump, and Melody fell off the side-saddle rig and hit the ground, landing on her butt in a sprawl and in a cloud of dust. She cut her eyes, saw the Indian in

206

mid-air, and let out a shriek that was startlingly close to the sounds that Squalls a Lot used to make.

Preacher cooly lifted the Hawken one-handed and fired it like a pistol, the heavy ball striking the warrior just under his throat and tearing out his back. The ball seemed to stop the warrior in mid-flight. He did not utter a sound. He was dead when he hit the earth.

Melody jumped up, ran to Preacher, and flung her arms around his neck. "My hero!" she said, then passed out cold.

"Oh, Lord!" Preacher said. "I ain't never gonna get shut of this female."

Eight

Preacher handed Melody over to a gaggle of females and retreated back to his horse.

"Preacher, come back!" he heard Melody call weakly.

"Hell, it's started already," he muttered, and put Hammer into a trot. Beartooth climbed into the saddle and rode out after him, catching up with him about a half mile from the creek.

"You're a marked man, Preacher," he told him. "I hear weddin' bells in your future."

"What you're hearin' is your dried-up brains rattlin' agin each other."

"We'll come see you from time to time." The mountain man wasn't about to let up. "See how you're gettin' on, havin' to live with walls all around you."

"You best build you a wall around that mouth of yourn," Preacher told him. But he knew the ribbing was far from over. The boys hadn't even got started yet. Preacher knew he was in for it now. He cut his horse toward a stand of timber. "This looks like a good spot to light and sit and have some coffee. It'll take them movers hours to get crost that crick and this far."

"I'll start a fire and boil some coffee," Beartooth offered. "You best go over to that little puddle yonder and wash your face and hands and slick back that shaggy mane of yourn. Your ladylove'll be along shortly."

Preacher told him where to go, how to get there, and what to do when he arrived.

"Wagh!" Beartooth said with a laugh. "That shore would be uncomfortable ridin'. Speakin' of ridin', here comes them two Bible-thumpin' friends of yourn."

"I say," Edmond said, dismounting. "We've taken a vote and decided to rename the creek back there."

"Is that right?" Beartooth asked, unable to get the grin off his bearded face.

"Yes," Richard said. "We are going to erect a sign and call it Hero Creek. In honor of Preacher."

"Have mercy!" Beartooth said. "Hero Crick. You hear that, Preacher?"

Preacher muttered under his breath.

"What's that you say, Preacher?" Beartooth pressed.

"I said I ain't no gawddamn hero. That's what I said."

"Oh, but I say, Preacher, you are indeed. Why, Miss Melody would have been killed if it were not for your brave and heroic actions and quick thinking," Edmond said.

Beartooth rocked back and forth in front of the small fire. "Hee, hee, hee!" he cackled. "Gen-u-ine hero, that's what we got in our midst, yes sirrie. I be a frontiersman like Dupre read to me about, and you be a hero. Lord, what a pair." He howled with laughter and rolled around and around on the ground.

"I fail to see the humor in this," Richard said. "I must admit, I am at a loss."

Preacher looked at the two Easterners. How to tell them that what happened not an hour past was something that occurred with almost monotonous regularity in the wilderness. It became a hard fact of life that had to be faced. No one thought anything about heroics.

Preacher shook his head. "Richard, you and Edmond ride back to the wagons and guide them to this spot. Right here."

Richard stuck out his chest. "It would be an honor, sir!

Come, Edmond."

They ran for their horses.

"I bet he gets 'em lost 'tween thar and here," Beartooth opined.

"I don't hardly see how he could. The trail's fifteen feet wide and a blind man could follow it. 'Sides," he said with a smile. "He's got Jim and Dupre and Nighthawk to sorta help him along."

"We gonna be crossin' the Snake in 'bout three, four more days, Preacher. You been givin' that any thought?"

"A lot of thought. They's wagons that's crossed it, but not very many and not with the water so high. I'm thinkin' we're gonna have to raft and rope . . . and pray, if you're of a mind to."

Beartooth grinned. "Oh, everything will be all right, Preacher . . ." Beartooth noticed Preacher's hand inching toward a rock and got ready to jump. "I just know it will, since we got us a hero along!"

Preacher hurled the rock and Beartooth jumped. But he was just a tad too late. The rock caught him smack in the ass and Beartooth howled like a mad puma. Then he rolled to his feet and chased the much smaller and much more agile Preacher all over the place, until finally Beartooth collapsed on the ground.

"Ox," Preacher said, falling down beside him and relaxing on the cool ground, shaded by the stand of timber. "You and Greybull gettin' to be 'bout the same size. Fat."

"I ain't neither fat. I'm stocky built and have lots of muscle, that's all."

"Between your ears, mostly."

"Preacher?"

"I ain't moved."

"It ain't never gonna be like it was before, is it?"

Preacher was silent for a moment. With a heart that was heavy, he said, "No, it ain't, Bear. That's over. Or will be soon. It's our fault; we done it."

"How you mean?" Beartooth rolled over and up on one

210

elbow.

"Don't fall on me, you moose. You'll squash me flat as a flapjack. How do I mean? Hell, we're the ones who trapped out all the streams, ain't we? Just to satisfy some fancy lady or foppish man back East. We talked about it 'fore. Lots of times. But we kept on doin' it. We ain't got no one to blame but ourselves . . . as far as the fur, that is. The people comin' out here like swarms of locust? Well, that was bound to happen. We're a nation of movers, I reckon. And I opine we ain't seen nothin' yet. They'll be towns a-springin' up right and left and folks a-buildin' fences and roads and dammin' up cricks and rivers. Why, you know what Richard told me? He said that folks has dug a big wide ditch, a canal, he called it, that's three hundred and fifty miles long and filled the damn thing up with water so's people can float boats on it."

Beartooth reared up and blocked out the light. Preacher rolled out of the way. "He's a-lyin' to you, Preacher. They ain't nobody that damn stupid."

"He ain't lyin' neither. They call it the Erie Canal. And it cost millions and millions of dollars to build."

"Who paid for it?"

"Why, hell, I don't know. The government, I reckon."

"Where'd they get the money?"

"Do I look like a damn professor? How should I know?"

"Life's gettin' too complicated for me, Preacher." Beartooth flopped back down and the ground trembled for a moment. "I think I'll just find me a good woman who can put up with me, build me a little cabin in the mountains, and re-tar."

"You ain't a-gonna do no such of a thing and you know it. Neither am I. We gonna be ridin' the mountains 'til the day we die."

"Greybull's a-scoutin' for the Army. I heard tell that Pugh was hangin' on, tryin' to make a livin' trappin' up north of here. Him and Lobo and Deadlead. Thumbs Carroll is somewheres on the Platte. I don't know where Powder Pete and Tenneysee and Matt and Audie is."

"I thought Lobo was a-livin' with a pack of wolves that he adopted—or they adopted him?"

"He goes back to 'em from time to time. He tried to teach one to talk for five years. I think he finally give up on that. Wolf hiked his leg and pissed all over him."

"That'd be discouragin', I reckon."

The group rolled on without further mishap. The only adventure they encountered was the daily grind of surviving the oftentimes monotonous trek westward.

The second day after the failed Indian ambush at Rocky Creek, the train rattled and lumbered over twenty-two miles of trail. It was the most miles they'd ever done in one day on the Oregon Trail. The next several days were also uneventful. The following day would not prove to be so peaceful. They had to cross the Snake.

The mountain men stood on the south side of the river, gazing across its rushing waters to the north bank.

"Here's where we test the mettle," Dupre said.

"It ain't as bad as I've seen it," Preacher said. "The islands is visible and they're big enough to hold wagons to rest. I reckon a far-thinkin' man could make some money by operatin' a ferry here."

Within a few years, someone would.

"Well, let's get ropes strung and start gettin' the people acrost," Beartooth said. "I'm just hopin' we don't lose nobody here."

"If we do, maybe it'll be that damn Avery," Dupre said. "But I don't figure we'll be that lucky."

He'd been caught spying on ladies as they went to the bushes. Swift had warned the young man's father that if it happened again, he was going to lash his son. The father had said that would be done only over his dead body.

"That can be arranged," Preacher told the man.

They lost the first wagon that attempted to cross. Currents grabbed it and carried it downstream, smashing it against rocks. The team was saved, and most of the possessions had been off-loaded.

"We got two of the wheels," Preacher told the devastated man and woman. "We can build you a cart and a travois."

"A what?" the woman asked.

"I'll show you later. It ain't hopeless, people. It just looks that way," he added.

It took three days to get the entire train across the river. No more wagons were lost, but several had been damaged due to ropes coming loose or breaking under the strain. And half a dozen wheels would have to be repaired. One child fell into the river, but a very alert Richard grabbed the screaming girl before she could be swept away and lost.

"Now you can be a hero," Preacher told him. "I gladly give up the title."

"You take all the fun out of it," Beartooth told Preacher. But he stood a safe distance away as he said it.

"How much stock did we lose?" Preacher asked Swift.

"We were very lucky. We only lost a few head. And no milk cows. There'll be a tragedy here someday, I'm thinking. That's a wicked crossing."

Preacher's smile was grim. "You ain't never seen The Dalles on the Columbia."

The train rolled on, now taking a more northerly course as they put the Snake behind them. No one missed it. Indians came down out of the mountains to watch them, standing or sitting their ponies and silently watching the long train as it pushed north and west.

"Relax," Preacher passed the word the first time the Indians appeared. "Them Nez Perce. They ain't gonna bother you if leave them alone." *I hope*, he silently added. He rode over to stand in front of a mounted sub-chief and made the sign of friend.

"I speak your language," the Indian said. "So it is as we were told. The white man comes like ants to honey."

"Looks that way," Preacher told him. "And I ain't likin' it no more than you."

"Preacher has never lied to us so I will be truthful to you. The Cayuses are making war talk. And Red Hand has

213

joined with a large band of whites and now waits in the Blues. Is it you they are after?"

"Yeah. How many is they?"

The sub-chief shook his head slowly. "Plenty. Twenty-five, maybe thirty, maybe more of the white outlaws. Red Hand has gathered a large force to follow him. Bad Indians whose tribes ran them from the village. Killers all. Maybe seventy-five of them. White haters. You are going the way of the trappers—through the Blues?"

"Right through them. Blues to the west and the Wallowas to the East."

The Nez Perce nodded his head gravely, his eyes expressionless. "May the Gods ride with you, Preacher." He made the sign of friend, and he and his party were gone.

Preacher rode back to the train and reined up beside Dupre and Nighthawk. "If that Nez Perce can count, we're lookin' at maybe a hundred or more of Red Hand's and Kelley's people."

"In the Blues?" Nighthawk asked.

"Yep. You 'member where the Powder makes that big wide curve? That's a bad crossin' there. We'll be tied up the better part of two days. That's where they'll hit us. Bet on it."

"When we're all split up, half on one side and half on the other," Dupre said. "Red Hand and Bum might be worthless, but they ain't stupid."

"You got it." Preacher looked thoughtful for a moment. "Well, we can't do nothing to change it, so's let's concentrate on just gettin' there."

That was beginning to be a problem. The wagons had put hundreds of tough miles behind them, and they were all beginning to show signs of wear. Wheels were shattering nearly every day. Tongues were breaking and the pace of the trek had slowed considerably.

Preacher did not push them. He made daily inspections of the wagons and knew that the movers had to set their own pace. He could only guide them, not make them move faster.

They pushed on, crossing Canyon Creek and several days later, camping near Lucky Peak. From there, Preacher turned them westward for a time and plunged deeper into the wilderness.

"You reckon they's some boys gonna be up here at the fork?" Preacher asked Dupre.

"They wasn't when we went out that way. But that was some months back. If they is, they gonna be plumb shocked to see this bunch come a-rattlin' in."

"And be busy callin' us nine kinds of fools for bringin' 'em, too," Beartooth added.

Richard came a-foggin' up, lathering his horse. "Preacher! A child is gone. Little Patience Lander. Swift has halted the train for a search."

"Had to happen," Preacher muttered, and turned his horse, riding back to the hysterical mother, standing with a group of other women by the wagons.

This was brush and low hill country, perfect for ambushes and for Indians to sneak in and steal a horse, cut a throat, or grab a child. But neither Preacher nor any of the other mountain men believed Indians grabbed the little girl. None of them had seen any sign of Indians since Preacher talked with the Nez Perce several days back. But that possibility could not be discounted.

"We're gettin' real close to Cayuse country," Dupre reminded him.

"Yeah, that is a fact," Preacher said. "Let's start circlin' for sign. We'll find her." The mother's wailing had grown louder. He turned to Swift. "Somebody calm that female down 'fore she works herself into the vapors."

Preacher left his horse and set out walking, slowly working in an ever-widening circle. He took the terrain to the northeast. Bogus Basin lay only a few miles away, near the edge of the Salmon River Mountains.

The thing that bothered Preacher most was that some of Red Hand's people might have been spying on them and seen a chance to grab a kid and done it. The young age of the girl wouldn't make any difference to a renegade—white or red. They'd mount her and then kill her.

Behind him he heard someone shout wildly, "Lord, Lord, everybody. Mary Ellsworth's gone into hard labor. She's gonna birth anytime now."

"Wonderful," Preacher said. He paused, his eyes picking up on a track. He knelt down and studied it, his skin growing clammy. Moccasin tracks. He carefully inspected the find. Four sets of Injun tracks and one set of little girl prints. They had her. If it was a Cayuse or even Blackfoot, they wouldn't harm the little girl. They'd adopt her into the tribe. Her life would be hard, but she'd be alive. They might beat her, but they wouldn't rape her. But Preacher had him a hunch these were renegades from Red Hand's bunch.

That put a whole new light on it.

Nine

He looked back. He was a good mile from the wagon train—too far for a shout and he didn't want to fire a shot into the air. Since this was brush country, and it had been dry, the renegades would have stashed their horses several miles away—not wanting to raise a dust—and approached the wagon train on foot. So now it was a race against time.

Preacher broke into a trot, staying with the tracks. And the Injuns were running now; he could tell that by the longer strides. One of them was making a much heavier print, so he was carrying the child.

I tole and tole and tole them women to keep their eyes open for their kids, Preacher thought. *Don't never take your eyes offen them. Dammit!*

But he knew this wasn't the woman's fault. The girl had probably been riding on the sideboard—called a lazy-board—or on the tailgate and Red Hand's people just popped out of the brush and snatched her off 'fore she could set up a squall. They stuffed a gag into her mouth and set off on a run once they got clear of the trail.

Preacher was gaining on them. He caught a glimpse of brown skin not that far ahead of him. He had his Hawken and his brace of pistols. Three shots and four of them. He'd have to make every shot count, and then, when the bastard totin' the child set her down to make a fight of it, Preacher would have to be close enough to cut him.

He wanted desperately to look behind him, to see if Beartooth or Dupre or Nighthawk or Trapper Jim might be closing, but he knew he couldn't risk it. He had to keep his eyes to the front.

He was only a few hundred yards behind them now. He had heard their running footsteps a couple of times. Approaching a huge boulder, Preacher took a chance and jumped, landing on top of the boulder and kneeling down. He pulled his Hawken to his shoulder and sighted one in, compensated for the distance, and squeezed the trigger. He saw the renegade throw up his hands and fall face down into the dirt. The three Injuns left paused for a second, then took off running. Preacher was off the boulder and running hard, knowing the shot would bring the others at a gallop.

The Lander girl must have worked the gag out of her mouth and really put her teeth to work on the renegade, for he let out a fearful holler and Preacher heard the slap as he struck the child.

The one Preacher had killed, he noted as he ran past him, was a Hidatsa, and the buck carrying the girl looked to be the same. Preacher hollered out, "Beater of little girls! Does your nightime-in-the-blankets taste run to little boys, too?"

The brave stopped and turned around, his face a mask of war-painted hate.

Preacher didn't let up, he continued running toward the three Indians, now all stopped, hurling insults. "No wonder you are all lovers of men. No woman would look upon such ugliness for fear of being struck barren."

The Hidatsa threw the girl to the ground and Preacher shot him stone cold dead with one ball from a pistol that caught him in the heart and knocked him down.

"Run to yonder horsemen, girl!" Preacher shouted. "Run like the real red Satan was after you personal. Fly, child!"

One of the other renegades, a Crow, Preacher noted, lifted his rifle. Preacher hit the ground, rolling behind some rocks and working frantically to reload his pistol. The ball from the Indian's old Kentucky rifle whanged off the rocks as Preacher rammed home shot and powder and patch. Now his pistols were both double-shotted.

He chanced a look behind him and saw where Nighthawk had swept the girl up in his arms and was riding back toward the wagons at a gallop. Dupre and Beartooth were slowly circling Preacher's adversaries, cutting them off.

The two remaining renegades had disappeared, dropping to their bellies in the brush, hoping to slip away, and Injuns being what they were, the chances were good they'd do just that.

Dupre and Beartooth were staying in the saddle, scanning the area around them from that better vantage point.

"You all right, Preacher?" Dupre called.

"Dandy. Watch your butts, boys. There ain't nothin' more dangerous than an Injun who's in a trap."

"I told Hawk to tell them others at the train to stay put. We'd take care of this. He's comin' back."

Preacher had a pistol in each hand, the hammers back. He heard only the faintest of brushing sounds on the other side of the boulder. He quickly backed up and hunkered down amid some smaller rocks. He heard the rustling sound again and put it together. The buck was trying to snake up the other side of the huge rock. Preacher smiled as he heard a rifle boom. Dupre or Beartooth had spotted him, and that was that for another of Red Hand's crap and crud.

Preacher slipped from the rocks just as the last renegade rounded the boulder, a war axe in his hand and a look of raw hatred on his face. He screamed at Preacher and the mountain man put two lead balls into his chest, the impact knocking the buck back and flinging him dead against the boulder. He slid down, his blood smearing the stone.

"That's it," Preacher called.

"For the time bein'," Beartooth added.

When they returned to the wagon train, Richard met them with a grin on his face that a charge of blasting powder couldn't have removed. "It's a girl!" he said proudly.

"Mary Ellsworth just gave birth to a girl!"

"Wonderful," Preacher said. "Something else for me to have to worry about."

"Naturally, we'll have to camp here for a day or two until the mother regains her strength," Richard said.

"Oh, naturally. It wouldn't do to move on. Not a-tall. It makes sense to stay here close to them four dead bucks out yonder in the brush. Seein' as how some of their own might decide to come after them for burial and spot us here restin' and decide to attack. That makes a lot of sense to me."

He walked off, muttering to himself. But the wagon train stayed put for two days.

While they waited, Preacher thought about the re-crossing of the Snake, not that many more days ahead of them. He just didn't know how it could be done without taking days to build some rafts and ferry the wagons across.

"Got to be," Dupre agreed. "There ain't no other way to do 'er."

Preacher looked at Jim and Nighthawk. They both nodded their heads in agreement.

"And I got my doubts these wagons will hold together over the Cascades," Dupre added. "You give airy thought to that."

"I been givin' lots of head-ruminatin' to that. I been usin' parts of my brain that I ain't put to work in years. Makes my head hurt, too. Let me put it to y'all this way: if we can beat back and put a good enough whuppin' on Bum and Red Hand in the Blues, we could chance a run down the Columbia. But that's a mighty big if, boys."

"There might be some ol' boys camped on the Boise that'd lend us a hand," Beartooth said.

"*If* and *might* don't feed the bear, boys." Preacher sighed and took a slug of coffee. "I agreed to see these people through, and that's what I'll do. Or they'll bury me out here in the wilderness."

"We'll get them over the Cascades, then," Nighthawk said.

"I know trails. But . . . ?" He smiled and shook his head.

"Yeah," Preacher said glumly. "But."

When the train reached the crossing where the Boise juts off from the Snake, there was evidence that trappers had been there, but only one man remained, a trapper who'd taken an arrow in his leg and it had gotten infected. He was near death when Preacher found him, propped up against a tree, waiting stoically for death to take him.

"You don't look so good, Ballard," Preacher said. He struggled to maintain his composure, for the stench of the rotting leg was very strong.

"I feel a damn sight worser than I look, Preacher," the dying man said. "And you can bet on that." He cut his eyes to the wagon train, just then coming into view. "I heard y'all comin' for a long time. Didn't know what the hell it might be."

"How come you didn't let them take your leg, Ballard?"

"I ain't never knowed no one-legged trapper. Be kind of hard to sit a horse, wouldn't it?"

"Might be. Never gave it much thought. They's missionaries in the train. I can get some of them to pray over you, if you'd like."

"It'd beat the sound of my own voice, I reckon. That's all I been hearin' for a week. I thought I'd be long dead 'fore now. Why don't we make an e-vent of it. We can have singin' and shoutin' and preachin' and prayin'. If I set my mind to it, I reckon I could expire durin' all the festivities."

"I'll see what I can do."

"He wants *what?*" Edmond asked.

"A party and some prayin' and a jug."

"That's grotesque," Richard said. "The man needs salvation."

"What he needs is what he wants," Preacher told them. "I'll get the jug, you get to prayin' and the like."

"I'll conduct this with dignity," Edmond told the dying mountain man.

"I ain't interested in no dignification," Ballard told him.

"How dignified can I be with my leg all swole up the size of a tree and pisen all in my body? Gimmie that damn jug, Preacher."

Ballard took him a long pull and sighed. "Mighty tasty. Now git some of them women to singin'. I'll get myself all ready to pass."

"Is he serious?" a mover asked Beartooth.

"Shore. I once knowed a man who rode a hundred miles with two arrows in his stomach. By rights he should have died days 'fore he did. But he wanted to pass in the company of friends. So he hung on 'til he reached a camp. He fell off his horse, looked at us, said 'Howdy,' and died."

The mover looked at the mountain man, not at all sure he was hearing the truth. He had learned that mountain men do, on occasion, tell lies.

"Lift your voices in song, sisters," Ballard said. "And you might lift them skirts up some and show me a shapely leg, if you've a mind to. I ain't seen a white woman in nigh on two years."

"Mind your manners, sir!" Edmond admonished him.

"Go to hell, boy," the dying mountain man told him. "Preach or pray. But get to doin' something."

A group of ladies began singing.

"That's better," Ballard said. "That shore sounds sweet." He took another long pull from the jug. "Pretty women, soft singin', and good whiskey. I can see the gates of Heaven openin' up now."

"What you see is storm clouds," Preacher told him. "It's a-fixin' to rain."

"Not 'til I pass," Ballard told him. "You mind them damn cayuses, Preacher. Something's got 'em all stirred up. You got airy stogy on you?"

Preacher found the butt of a cigar and stuck it in Ballard's mouth and got a burning twig from the fire and lit it.

"Now I'm a contented man," Ballard said. "You look after my good horse, Preacher. Give my rifle and my pistols to someone who needs them. And bury me deep so's the varmits won't get me."

"I don't know of no varmit who'd want you, lessen it'd be skunk."

"Well, you might be right there." Ballard puffed on his stogy for a time, waving it in the air every now and then in time to the singing of the ladies.

Preacher had lifted Ballard's buckskin shirt and seen the deadly lances of blood poisoning from his gangrenous leg shooting all the way up to his chest. That the man had lived this long was nothing short of a miracle.

"They's some laudanum on the train, Ballard. You want me to fetch it?"

The mountain man shook his head. "No. Hard to believe, but most of the pain is gone. I think the pisen and the rot done killed it. I ain't been able to feel nothing below the waist in two days. Can't piss neither. So my kidneys ain't workin'. All in all, it's gonna be a blessin' to pass."

"Been me, I'd had one of them ol' boys shoot me 'fore they left," Preacher said.

"I axed 'em to. But they said they just couldn't do it. It was a pisen arrow, Preacher. You ever known of Injuns to use pisen arrows?"

"Yep. A few. You just got unlucky, Ballard."

"You got that right. I'm gonna let them ladies sing about one more song, and then I think I'll pass." He shook the jug. "Well, maybe two songs."

"Oh, Lord God, our Savior!" Edmond thundered, his voice drowning out the singing. "Look down with pity upon this poor wretch of a man who lies dying before You . . ."

"Make it one song," Preacher urged. "Believe me."

Ballard took a mighty slug of the hooch and wiped his mouth with the back of his hand.

"He isn't much, Lord," Edmond intoned, "and I know his life has been filled with debauchery of the vilest kind . . ."

"Yes, it has," the ladies said in a sing-song voice.

"It has?" Ballard asked. "Pray tell me, Preacher, what do them words mean?"

"It means you've enjoyed strong drink and whores."

"He got that right," Ballard said solemnly.

". . . And his soul is dark with sin, Lord . . ."

"Is that feller tryin' to get me in or out of Heaven?" Ballard asked.

"Dark with sin," the ladies sang.

"He's a savage, Lord! Just like the heathens he's lived with, and laid up with their savage women and lusted in their red flesh, Savior," Edmond's voice rippled the leaves. "Wallowing in the blankets and stroking the hot naked flesh of sweating women."

A couple of the ladies took to fanning themselves quite vigorously.

"I do recollect that Kiowa squaw that I took to one long winter. Married 'er, I did," Ballard said. "She and the boy were killed by Blackfeet whilst I was runnin' my traps. Then there was a Fox woman that was mighty fine, mighty fine." Ballard took him another long pull. "There was two or three more along the way, that I recall. But I ain't been no ladies man, that's for sure."

"Save this poor creature, Lord!" Edmond shrieked and Ballard and Preacher both jerked.

"He's just gettin' warmed up, Ballard," Preacher warned. "I'm a-tellin' you."

"I can't take much of this. I wanted some quiet prayin' for my soul. Not no revival. Listen, Preacher. They's a bunch of missionaries done built them a church just north of the Blues Ballard said. His voice was getting weaker. "They got the Cayuses all stirred up. Even some of the real small tribes is smearin' on war paint. Be careful."

"We'll do it, Ballard. You rest easy on that."

"I think I'll just give up the ghost, Preacher."

"Whenever you're ready, Ballard. I'll plant you deep. That's a promise."

"Preacher?"

"Right here."

"I can't lift the jug, ol' hoss. Ain't this a pitiful way for a man to go out?"

"I don't know of no real good way."

"You do got a point."

Edmond was shoutin' salvation and damnation to those gathered around.

"See you, Preacher," Ballard said.

"See you, ol' son."

The mountain man closed his eyes and died.

Ten

Preacher, Beartooth, Dupre, Nighthawk, and Jim wrapped the dead mountain man in his robes and carried him deep into the brush and timber.

"Do you want any of us to accompany you?" Richard asked.

"No," Preacher told him. "We'll do this private."

"I think I understand now," the missionary said.

Preacher looked at him and smiled. "Yeah, Richard, I think you do myself. You've come a far ways, and I ain't talkin' about distance in miles traveled."

"Thank you, Preacher."

Preacher studied him for a moment. "You come on and you go with us, Richard. I think you've earned that."

The men dug a deep hole and planted Ballard, covering the grave with rocks. Richard said a very short and quiet prayer, and it was over.

"When I go to the Beyond," Nighthawk said, "I want to be buried Indian way. Remember that, all of you."

"Damned heathen," Beartooth said with a grin.

"Makes me closer to the Gods," the Crow said. "Much

better than having to dig out of the earth."

Richard was thoughtful as they walked back to the wagons. "He does have a point."

Edmond was still preaching when they returned.

"Long-winded feller," Preacher remarked. "But the folks seem to be enjoyin' it. Never took to no lengthy sermons myself. I recollect my pa sayin' that he figured more souls was won in the first five minutes of a sermon and more souls was lost in the last five minutes."

Richard was in quiet agreement with that.

"Too much talk about Gods and spirits makes head hurt," Nighthawk said.

"Let's take a long look at this crossin'," Preacher said. " 'Cause it sure ain't gonna be easy."

It took five days of brutally hard work to build the rafts and get across the flood-swollen river. There were a lot of cuts and bruises and badly strained muscles, but fortunately no broken bones.

Within a few more years, the Hudson's Bay Company would have one small ferry boat operating there. The movers would pay three dollars a wagon to cross. By then, most of the area Indians would be 'tamed'—with only an occasional uprising and massacre of the set-tlers—and the Indians would swim the river with the stock, moving them along. But that was years ahead.

On the afternoon of the first day past the river, Swift galloped up to Preacher. "Two families have pulled out, Preacher. They say they're going to stay right here. They're not going any further."

The news came as no surprise to the mountain man. He'd been expecting something like this for weeks. "They's actin' like damn fools by doin' it, but I ain't gonna waste no time jawin' with 'em. Leave 'em be."

"Man, they'll die out here!"

"That's their problem. I didn't sign on to hold nobody's hand. 'Sides, they got a chance of sur-vivin' here. They's cabins all over the wilderness. Life'll be hard for 'em, but they could make it."

"That's all you've got to say on the subject?"

"There ain't nothin' else to say, far as I'm concerned."

The wagon train rolled on, leaving two families behind, standing silently by the side of the trail, waving at those who continued on. Preacher did not look back.

He had it in his mind that the movers weren't about to stay out here in the wilderness. They'd had a gutful of it and were planning on headin' back East to civilization. How they planned on getting back across the rivers and the like was anybody's guess. He could be wrong about their plans, but he didn't think so. And it was just as well, for this country was no place for cowards or the faint-hearted. The wilderness seemed to bring out the best in some and the worst in others. It oftentimes appeared to Preacher that the sometimes savage vastness seemed to know the cowardly or timid who came into it. The silent earth they were buried in was the only homestead they ever occupied.

After the brief rains that fell the day Ballard died, the sun returned and it came with a vengeance, baking the land in midsummer's heat. The trail was dust that coated wagons, animals, and people. And the stretch they were coming up on was void of water.

"Top your barrels," Preacher told them at a creek. "Fill everything that'll hold water. Your animals come first. You drink after them. Swift, we'll be headed straight north once we make this next thirty or so dry miles." He took a stick and drew in the dust. "Here's the Snake, and this here's the Burnt River. I'm takin' us right between 'em." He moved the stick north. "Once we get up here, that's close to Lookout, we'll rest. We'll be about thirty-five miles from where I figure Bum and Red Hand is gonna hit us."

"Maybe they'll have given up by then?" Swift said hopefully.

"Don't count on it," Preacher told him.

They moved on through the heat and the choking dust. That afternoon, they buried the Ellsworth baby. No one among them knew why the baby died. She had appeared to be a perfectly healthy baby.

"Damn fools!" Preacher said. "Fools to start a two thousand mile journey through the wilderness with a woman that's with child."

The mother's wailings could be heard as she stood over the small mound of earth, being comforted by other women. Richard had told Edmond that he, not Edmond, would conduct the brief service. Edmond protested, but Richard prevailed.

"Maybe they didn't have no choice in the matter," Dupre said.

"This family did," Preacher said sourly. "They sold a good business back East to become movers. Ellsworth told me he wanted a great adventure. I asked him why he didn't wait 'til his woman birthed? He just looked at me and walked off. Damn fool!"

"We stayin' the night here?" Beartooth asked.

"No," Preacher said. "We'd use too much water and we ain't got it to spare. We got to push on."

"Gonna be hell gettin' that mother away from that grave," Jim said.

"Yeah," Preacher's reply was short.

Preacher walked away, back to his horse. He cinched it up tight and swung into the saddle, riding up to Swift, who was unsaddling his horse. "Put it back on, Swift."

"What?"

"Your saddle. We're pullin' out in a few minutes."

"Man, you can't be serious! Mary is sick with grief. She's flung herself across the grave."

"Well, unfling her. Pour some laudanum down her throat and knock her dopey and put her in the wagon. Swift, I ain't tryin' to be no mean, heartless man. But we got to move. We stay here, and we use up the water. No matter what you tell these people, half the water'll be gone come the mornin'. And we won't be no closer to more water. Now get the goddamn people to their wagons. Toot on that bugle and do it!"

"I refuse to be so cruel! The mother has a right to her grief."

"Her grievin' ain't gonna change a damn thing. The baby's dead. She's with Jesus, Swift. There ain't nothin' in that hole in the ground."

"We're staying right here for the night."

"Then go to hell, Swift. You either get these people movin', right now, or I'm gone, and I won't be back. I told you from the git-go, I tell you to stop, we stop, I tell you we go, we go. And you agreed to those terms. Now I'm tellin' you, Swift. Get this train rollin'!"

Swift looked up as Beartooth, Nighthawk, and Dupre rode up. He looked at Jim, saddling his horse. "What's he doing?"

"Gettin' ready to pull out with us," Preacher told the man.

"You'd all leave us?" Swift looked at the unflinching gazes of the mountain men.

They sat their saddles silently, staring their answers at the wagonmaster.

"My God, but you're a cruel, heartless pack of brutes!"

"To your wagons!" Preacher shouted. "Let's go. Move it, people."

"No!" the grieving mother screamed.

"I said, get to your wagons and goddammit, do it now or I leave you here!" Preacher roared.

Slowly, with undisguised ill-feeling toward him in their eyes, the settlers began moving toward their rolling homes. Mary screamed and Ellsworth fought his wife. She kicked him, she slapped him, she bit him and she cursed him and fought him from the grave to the wagon. He manhandled her into the wagon and her other children held her down.

"Pour some laudanum in her," Preacher told Richard.

"Force a whole bottle down her. Knock her out, get her drunk, and tie her in." He looked at Swift. "Toot that bugle, wagonmaster. Toot it loud and toot it now."

Preacher sat his horse by the side of the trail and watched the wagons roll past, following Nighthawk, Dupre, and Beartooth. He wanted to be damn sure they all headed out. The hot looks he received bounced off him like raindrops off his fringed buckskins. When the last wagon passed, followed by the livestock, Preacher rode back to the head of the column.

"You shore didn't win no new friends back yonder," Beartooth observed.

"No. But I kept some old ones alive."

They prodded on, through the dust and the heat and the dryness, each step drawing them closer to the mountains where Preacher was certain Bum and Red Hand were waiting. When they made camp that evening, Preacher saw to it that the water was carefully rationed. They had just enough water left them to make the next crossing. They had twelve waterless miles to go before they came to Burnt River. Once they left there, it was just over thirty dry miles to the Powder.

Preacher walked the camp. Very few people had anything to say to him. That in itself did not trouble him. Preacher was a hard man in a hard land, and to survive out here, that was what it took. These pilgrims would soon discover that, or they'd die. That was the bottom line.

Preacher went back to his own kind and sat down by the fire, accepting a cup of coffee from Jim.

"We'll lose some when them renegades hit us," the trapper said. "This won't be no little skirmish. Bum and Red Hand will throw everything they've got at us."

Preacher sipped at his coffee and then nodded his head. "I've done all I know to do. I've seen to it they's

231

plenty of powder and shot. I've warned 'em what they can expect. I can't do no more."

"You know," Dupre said, waving his hand at the encircled wagons. "This is what we're all gonna end up doin' 'fore it's all said and done."

"What?" Jim asked.

"Either guidin' trains through or scoutin' for the Army. That's all that's left."

"Wagh!" Beartooth said.

"Uummm!" Nighthawk said.

"He's right," Preacher spoke softly. "What else can we do? Think about it. Another two, three years, the fur will all but be gone. Them's that's plannin' on trappin' forever is kiddin' theyselves. Can't none of us tolerate no towns or houses for any length of time. I can't see none of us clerkin' in no store. We damn shore ain't gonna get married and settle down and scratch in the ground raisin' crops — at least I ain't. So you tell me what that leaves us."

"You must make plans on returning to civilization and law and order," Edmond said, strolling up.

Trapper Jim said a very ugly word that summed up the feelings of all the mountain men.

"In the not too distant future," Edmond said, ignoring the profanity, "I can envision this trail being a wide and well-traveled road. Engineers will come in and build bridges across the rivers. There will be towns along the way. The railroads will cut through the mountains and link coast to coast . . ."

"Plumb depressin'," Preacher said.

"That's the most terriblest thing I ever heard of!" Beartooth said. "Them people best stay home. What's all them people gonna do out here?"

"Bring civilization and law and order," Edmond told him. "Raise families and build towns and schools and churches. Make a decent life for thousands of people. All sorts of factories will be built . . ."

"To make what?" Jim asked.

"All sorts of goods for the newly arrived settlers. It's the law of supply and demand. It's called progress, gentlemen. You can either be a part of it, or it will coldly push you aside. You cannot stop progress, gentlemen. It's futile to try." Edmond turned and walked away, back to his wagon.

"What's fu-tile?" Beartooth asked.

"I don't know," Preacher said. "But it sounds bad to me."

"Railroads!" Beartooth said. "There ain't nobody gonna build no damn railroad through the mountains. It can't be done."

"Melody told me they's people back East taken to travelin' in balloons," Preacher said.

The mountain men stared at him. "Now, Preacher . . ." Dupre said. "You have told some whoppers in your time, but . . . ?"

"It's true. They make a big bag and then fill it with hot air and soar up to the clouds. They ride in baskets that's got little stoves in 'em. They keep the bag filled with hot air by burnin' wool and straw and the like."

"That ain't natural," Beartooth said. "If God meant for men to soar, He'd birthed us with wings."

"How high up do they soar?" Nighthawk asked.

"I don't know. I ain't never seen one. More'n a mile, I reckon."

"What happens if the bag busts?" Dupre asked.

Preacher shrugged his shoulders. "I reckon you'd have to fall back to the earth. What the hell other direction would you go? Up?"

"Why, that'd be the same as jumpin' off a damn mountain?" Jim said. "Who'd be foolish enough to do that?"

"Them folks back East, I guess. There ain't nobody ever gonna get me up in no damn oversized picnic basket."

Jim looked around him at the rapidly quieting camp.

"Folks back East just ain't got good sense."

Preacher glanced at him. "Took you this long to figure that out?"

Eleven

When they had run the long dry miles and finally came to Burnt River, Preacher told them to rest and water up. Nighthawk had already switched his saddle to another pony and was ready to pull out for the Powder, to see what he could learn.

"You be careful, Hawk," Preacher told him. "That's a mean, nasty bunch up yonder."

"And also very sure of themselves," the Crow said. "Red Hand is an arrogant fool, and Bum Kelley is worse. I will be back in two days." Preacher nodded his head and stepped back, watching him leave.

"We got trouble," Dupre said quietly, appearing at Preacher's elbow. "One of the movers is about to go mad, I'm thinkin'."

Preacher was not surprised, and he had a pretty good idea who it was. A very soft-spoken and timid little man from New Hampshire. His wife was timid and their kids were timid. Never heard a peep out of any of them. Preacher had been watching the man as the deep wilderness closed around them. Day by day, he talked more to himself in a mumbling sort of way. He wandered the camp after dark, twisting his hands and rubbing his arms nervously.

"Winston?"

"That's him. Swift is over there talking to him now. The Big Empty got to him, I reckon."

"Let's go have a look."

The man's eyes were wild looking. His hands were shaking and his face was pale as a fresh-washed and sunshine-dried sheet. He also had a pistol shoved down his belt.

"Winston!" Swift said. "Where is your family, man? Talk to me."

"What about his family?" Preacher whispered.

"They's missin'. All of them."

Swift looked around. His eyes were not friendly. He still hadn't gotten over Preacher's insistence they move on so quickly after the Ellsworth baby's death. "No one's seen them since this morning. Winston was late getting started. The stock drovers said he didn't catch up with them until we'd been on the trail more than an hour."

"Watch that pistol of his," Preacher said to Dupre. He walked around to the rear of the wagon and looked inside. It was the awfuliest mess he'd ever seen. Looked like a pack of Injuns had gone berserk. He picked up a shirt that caught his eye. It was covered with blood. "Damn!" he whispered.

Carrying the shirt, he walked around to the front of the wagon and opened the lid to the jockey box and looked in. A small hatchet was on top of the various tools. The axe head was bloody, with several strands of hair stuck to the edge. Preacher held the axe to the light. The hair was of different colors.

"Take his pistol, Dupre," Preacher called.

The mountain man reached down quickly and jerked the pistol from Winston's belt. Winston offered no resistance. "What'd you find, Preacher?"

Preacher walked around the wagon and held up the blood-stained shirt and the bloody axe. "This."

Winston screamed and jumped up. Swift popped him a good lick that put the crazied man on the ground, stunned but not out. "The voices told me to do it. They've been talkin' to me for days and days now. I could resist them no longer. I had to do it, I say, I had to."

"Where'd you do them in, man?" Swift asked.

"Back at last night's camp. After the train pulled out this morning."

Preacher turned to Trapper Jim. "Saddle us some horses. And rig up three pack horses. We'll bring the bodies back when, or if, we find them. It'll be long dark 'fore we get there, but it's got to be done. Dupre, you ride with me."

The mood of the settlers very quickly grew dark, and some men were talking about a rope and the nearest tree limb.

"Chain Winston to a wagon wheel," Preacher told Swift. "We'll be back sometime tomorrow."

The mountain men rode easily back down the trail. There was no need to hurry, the victims weren't going anywhere. Neither man was all that anxious to find the bodies of the woman and her two daughters, for they were both pretty sure that by now the varmits had been at the bodies. It had been a horrible and shocking event, but not so appalling to the mountain men. They had seen it all before, more than once. The loneliness of the wilderness was something that not everyone could endure. The vastness of it all and the silence worked on some people. The savage land, void of accustomed amenities, had driven many people mad. They had all known trappers who had gone berserk and killed friends while they slept. This was not a land for the weak-hearted; no place for those who could not live without newspapers and comfortable chairs and lamplight and walls.

The mountain men, leading the pack horses, rode through the twilight and into the night, finally reaching the site of the previous night's campgrounds.

The vultures and the varmits had been at work all that day, but enough was left for identification. While Dupre kept the carrion eaters away with fire-brands, Preacher rolled the torn and partly eaten bodies into canvas and lashed them onto the nervous and skittish pack horses. They rode back up the trail for a few miles before making camp for the night.

They hung the canvas-wrapped bodies from limbs to keep the varmits from them and made camp away from the now odious carcasses. They were back at the wagon train by noon of the following day.

Winston was bug-eyed and slobbering. He had soiled himself and was a pitiful sight chained to a wagon wheel. During the night he had gone completely around the bend and had been reduced to a babbling idiot, or so it appeared.

Avery's father had built him a noose and was talking hanging.

"You can't hang no madman," Preacher told him. "He ain't responsible for what he done."

"We do what you tell us to do when it involves the trail," Swift told Preacher. "But I set the law of the train."

Preacher could not argue the words. That was the rule of any wagon train. He walked away and joined his friends, sitting on the ground away from the still-circled wagons. Beartooth handed him a cup of coffee.

"Dispatched each one with a blow to the head," Dupre said. "I reckon them poor little girls only had a few moments of fright. But we'll never know."

"Did he abuse them?" Jim asked.

"Hard to tell," Preacher said. "They was all some et on. I'd rather think he didn't."

"Them pilgrims has been workin' theyselves up into a frenzy," Beartooth said. "I think they're gonna hang him."

"T'ain't up to us to interfere," Preacher replied. "If it was up to me, I'll turn him loose. Injuns won't bother him. He'd survive for a time. But on the other hand, he might get his hands on another axe, or a club or rock, and do in somebody else who's comin' up behind us. Personal, I'm just glad the decision ain't up to me."

"There ain't nobody been doin' much sleepin' 'ceptin'

the kids," Jim said. "They been palaverin' all night, all broke up into little groups." He glanced over toward the wagons. "Here we go, boys. "Looks like they fixin' to take them a vote now."

"They'll be more than one," Preacher opined.

The mountain men drank their coffee and waited by the fire. Their opinions were not asked. The settlers argued and shouted and fussed and talked for the better part of an hour. A dozen times men and women alike left the group to walk over to the bodies and throw back the canvas, looking at the bodies of the woman and two girls.

Finally, Swift walked over to where the mountain men sat, drinking coffee. "We've voted. We've decided to take him with us and turn him over to the proper authorities."

Preacher shook his head in disgust. "Man, *what* authorities? There ain't no law out here. We ain't got no in-sane asylums. There ain't no jails. I don't know what the billy-hell you people got in your minds that you're gonna find when we reach Fort Vancouver. But it ain't no town like y'all think of. Either hang the poor wretch or turn him loose. Injuns won't bother a crazy person. They stay shut of them. Hell, they might even adopt him and look after him. You can't tell about Injuns. But they ain't gonna harm him, and that's a fact. You want to take him with you, fine. But he's your responsibility, now and forever. The chief factor at the post ain't gonna take him off your hands. He ain't got no way of takin' care of the poor bastard. He don't *wanna* take care of him and he ain't *gonna* take care of him. Winston is your responsibility. He ain't ourn. He's yourn."

Swift walked back to the group. Winston was howling like a chained dog.

The mountain men ground some more beans and brewed a fresh pot of coffee and smoked and chewed and waited.

The group argued and shouted and seemed to be unable to reach any decision.

"Oh, Lord," Dupre said, looking up. "Here he comes again."

"We're taking him with us," Swift informed the men. "We've voted and that's the way it's going to be."

Preacher shrugged. "Suits me. Have fun guardin' him and hand-feedin' him and bathin' him and wipin' him after he shits. 'Cause you folks sure got it to do."

Preacher walked to his camp under a tree, laid down, and went to sleep.

Since most of the movers thought it inhuman to chain a maddened person like an animal—even though that was exactly what was happening in the young nation's asylums, and would continue that way until well into the next century—Swift was persuaded to merely bind the man securely with ropes.

Of course, Winston escaped.

Preacher, laying warm in his blankets, as well as Beartooth, Dupre, and Jim, heard the man after he slipped his bonds and made his way out of camp.

"You gonna stop him?" Dupre whispered.

"Not me," Preacher said, speaking in low tones. "It's a hard thing, and these pilgrims don't wanna accept it, but the man will be better off thisaway. I seen the insides of one of them in-sane asylums one time back in St. Louie. Most pitifulest things I ever did see."

"Winter'll probably kill him," Beartooth said.

"But you never know," Jim spoke up. "Folks like that got some sort of natural survival about em. That fool over yonder in the Bitterroot's still there. And he's as silly as a gaggle of geese. Been over there for goin' on fifteen years, I reckon."

"I clean forgot about that feller," Dupre said. "But you sure right. Wonder if he still lives in a tree?"

"He was two . . . no, three year ago. 'Cause I seen him with my own eyes. He liked to have scared the crap outta me." Trapper Jim chuckled softly. "I was ridin' along, just a-followin' the St. Joe and en-joyin' the view when all of a

240

sudden this fool comes a-runnin' and a-hollerin' and a-squallin' out of the woods and a-wavin' a stone axe. My good horse damn near bucked me out of the saddle, pack horse tore loose and run off about a half a mile, and I damn near made a mess in my britches. That crazy man was nekkid as the day he was borned and his hair was a-growed down to his waist. Turrible lookin' sight. Don't speak words that make no sense to nobody. Injuns is scared to death of him. I talked to Mark Head last year and he told me seen Ol' Crazy clear down to the Red Rock one time. Ol' Crazy do get around."

"Mark ain't got much more sense than Winston," Preacher said. "That boy takes too many chances." He chuckled. "I was at the rendezvous, back in '33 or '34 when ol' Bill Williams scolded Mark for cuttin' buffalo meat across the grain."

"I heard you fit Mark once," Dupre said.

"We had us a round one time. He told me shortly after he left the Sublette party back in '32, I think it were, that he'd been in the mountains for ten years. I gleaned right off that the boy was a greenhorn and he was storyin' and I told him so. Although not that kindly. He was a good scrapper even then. But I whupped him and then we was friends and still is. If he ain't dead."

"He ain't," Beartooth said. "Least he warn't last year. He fit a grizzly over on the Grand River. The grizzly won but Mark he lay still as a log and ol' griz figured he was dead and wandered off. Them two or three others that was with him thought shore he was gonna die. But he didn't."

"The boy's too brash for my tastes," Preacher said. "I don't care to ride with him. Brave is one thing, reckless is another story. He'll come to no good end, you mind my words."*

"Reckon when some sentry is gonna look into the

*Mark Head was killed around 1847. Shot in the back outside of Taos, New Mexico.

241

wagon and see that Winston's done slipped away?" Dupre questioned softly.

No sooner had the words left his mouth when a shout shattered the quiet night. "Winston's gone! He's slipped his ropes and fled. See to your women and children. The madman is among us."

"Oh, hell!" Preacher said, throwing off his blankets. "Somebody's sure to get shot if we don't sing out."

"He's gone!" Beartooth hollered. "So y'all just calm down."

Swift ran over, looking rather foolish wearing his long-handles and nothing else. "You saw him leave?"

"Sure," Preacher said. "I'd say it was a good hour ago. He had enough sense to take a pack and a poke with him. So he ain't as crazy as you might think."

"Why didn't you stop him?"

" 'Cause we're better off without him, that's why. Now go away and let me sleep."

Swift sputtered and stuttered, so angry he could not speak. He finally stalked away into the night, yelling for a search party to be formed.

"Some of them is gonna get lost sure as we're layin' here," Jim said.

"You wanna volunteer to lead 'em out there in the night?" Preacher asked.

"Nope."

"Then shut up and go to sleep."

Twelve

Preacher lay in his warm blankets but did not return to sleep. He figured that in about twenty minutes, someone would yell that someone else was lost, and he'd have to get up anyway.

"George Wilson is lost!" came the shout, just reaching the campgrounds.

"Oh, hell!" Preacher said, throwing back his blankets. "I knowed it."

"Paul Davis is alone and lost in the wilderness!" another mover shouted.

"Naturally," Dupre said, standing up and putting on his hat. He nudged Beartooth in the rear end with the toe of his moccasin. "Get up, lard-butt. The rescuers and the searchers done got theyselves lost in the woods."

"Well, why don't they just sit down on the ground and wait 'til mornin'?" Beartooth grumbled.

Jim stuck his pistols behind his sash. "No, they got to go blunderin' around in the timber in the dead of night lookin' for a fool who's probably five mile gone from here by now."

"Oh, hush up and come on," Preacher said. "Them folks'll be shore enough lost if we don't go in there and take 'em by the hand and lead 'em out like lost children in

243

the wilderness. I wish to hell they'd all stayed to home."

"Caleb Potter is lost in the woods!" a man shouted.

"Everybody just stay where the hell you is!" Preacher shouted the words into the night. "Just sit down on the ground and wait for us to find you and fetch you back. Good God Amighty!"

"You don't have to be rude," a woman told him.

"Oh . . . hush up, woman!"

"Well!" she said indignantly, and flounced away.

It took the mountain men hours to round up all the movers and lead them back to the wagon train. Some of the men were badly shaken by the night's events. Even to men accustomed to the woods, getting lost in the deep timber at night can be a shattering experience.

"Here's Winston's tracks," Jim called, kneeling down. "He's tooken straight out north and he ain't lookin' back."

"I wouldn't neither," Preacher said. "All he's got in that numb mind of his is puttin' distance between himself and the wagon train. Is everybody accounted for?"

"Far as I know," Dupre said. "Seems like these folks would know that things looks different at night."

"Most of these folks come from towns and cities. You notice that the farmers amongst 'em didn't get lost. Come on, I want some coffee."

The train stayed put for another day, until Nighthawk returned from his scouting. The Crow swung down from the saddle and handed the reins to a boy. He walked to the fire and poured a cup of coffee.

"We're in for it, all right," he finally spoke. "Looks like every renegade west of the Little Missouri has gathered up there in the Blues."

Nighthawk was not known to exaggerate, and that placed him as a rarity among mountain men.

"That many, Hawk?" Preacher asked.

"I would say about one hundred and fifty Indians— many tribes represented—and probably fifty or more white and half-breed or quarter-breed outlaws."

Beartooth whistled softly and shook his shaggy mane. "Lord, have mercy. I've heard worser news, but I can't rightly recall where or when it was. Where in the *hell* did Bum come up with that many whites?"

"Lots of ol' boys come driftin' out here over the past couple of years, wantin' to be trappers and sich," Preacher said. "I reckon lots of them was wanted for some crime back in the organized country. They soon found out that trappin' these mountains was damn hard work. It was easier to find they own kind and go back to stealin'." Preacher smiled and the others, including several movers and Swift, noticed it.

"You find placing our women and children in danger amusing?" one mover asked.

"I find it plumb ignorant that you brung 'em out here to begin with," Preacher said, pouring a tin cup brim-full of hot, black, and very strong trail coffee. "But you did, and they're here. So that's beside the point. Red Hand and Bum, they don't like me very much. Red Hand, well, he hates whites. All whites. He hates Bum Kelley, too, but he'll work with him 'cause one's just as sorry as the other. It'd be grand for Red Hand if he could take my hair. He'd be a big man. Same for Hawk here, and Beartooth and Dupre and Jim. This showdown's been comin' for years."

"And you're looking forward to it?"

"You might say that. I ain't lookin' to get my hair tooken. But when somebody just keeps a-proddin' at me, I sorta get my hackles up and start to thinkin' about ways to prod back. Y'all better understand this now: they gonna be hittin' us all the way to the blue waters. They really gonna hit us in the Blues, probably on the Powder. They want your womenfolk, and they covet your possessions. I heared them trash I kilt back aways talkin' about seizin' the girls, ten, eleven, twelve year old, and sellin' 'em to slavers. So you folks talk and make up your minds that they just might be a lot of killin' from here on out.

Get your stomachs set for it. Break out your molds and lead and start makin' balls. You gonna need 'em," he added grimly.

They spent another day and night in camp, the movers melting lead and casting balls for their weapons. A new spirit seemed to overcome the movers, and the mountain men could sense it. The settlers had come far, and no band of wild renegade Indians and white trash was going to stop them—not this close to their final destination.

"When the train pulls out in the mornin'," Preacher said to Beartooth, "I want you and Dupre and Hawk to guide them through. I'll be doin' a little preambulatin' about on my own. This is gettin' right personal to me now."

"Sounds like you gonna be havin' fun whilst the rest of us is left behind," Beartooth said.

"I am gonna make life some miserable for them trash north of us. I'm gonna roar like a grizzly, howl like a wolf, and snarl like a mad puma."

"Wagh!" Dupre slapped his knee. "Them doin's shine mighty right with me, Preacher. You talk about ol' Mark Head bein' rash; what do you call one man goin' up agin two hundred or better?"

"I call it takin' the fight to 'em," he replied, with a twinkle in his eyes. "Preacher-style!"

Melody and Penelope, with Richard and Edmond in tow, stopped by the camp of the mountain men just as dusk was settling. It was obvious they wanted to talk to Preacher by the way they kept looking around and fidgeting like kids.

"T'ain't here," Beartooth told them. "He left out hours ago. He'll meet us on the Powder."

"Whatever in the world make him do something that brash?" Penelope asked.

"He go count coup," Nighthawk said with a grunt and a hidden twinkle in his obsidian eyes that only his friends knew was there. "Take plenty scalps. Hang on horse's mane. Impress pretty girls."

"I happen to know that you can speak perfect English, Nighthawk," Richard said. "And you can read and write and do sums. You were raised and educated in a white home. Now will you stop grunting like a heathen and speak properly?"

"No," the Crow said. "Like talk this way. Talk like white man make tongue tired."

"Oh, for pity's sake!" the missionary said. "I give up."

"Good," Nighthawk said.

"Why has Preacher gone away into hostile territory?" Edmond asked.

"He just told you," Dupre said, jerking a thumb toward Nighthawk. "Can't you hear good?"

Edmond drew himself erect and in a very condescending tone, said, "My good man, I will have you know that my auditory faculties are excellent, I assure you."

"Your *what?*" Jim asked, pausing in the lifting of coffee cup to mouth and staring at the man.

"My hearing!"

"Why didn't you say so? Preacher's gone to hay-rass Bum and Red Hand's people."

"Alone?" Melody gasped.

"No," Beartooth said. "Course he ain't alone. He's got his hoss with him. Damn, woman, you didn't think he'd *walk* up yonder, does you?"

"I meant—"

"I know what you meant," Beartooth cut her off before she got started.

"Don't you worry none about Preacher, Missy," Dupre said. "Preacher's an ol' lone wolf. He's at his best operatin' by hisself. He'll be all right, missy."

"But . . ." Melody protested.

"He *likes* it, ma'am," Jim said. "Preacher's part grizzly,

247

part wolf, part puma, and part rattlesnake. And he's mean when he's riled up. Lord have mercy, Missy, but he's mean. He ain't gonna cut them folks up yonder no slack when he goes on the warpath. He's the best they is, ma'am. I ain't never seen nobody that'd even come close to Preacher in the wilderness. You hear all sorts of talk about Carson and Bridger and Johnson and Brown and Simpson. And the talk is true for the most part. But them's explorers and guides and so-called adventurers and trappers and the like. Preacher's all of them things, too, but what counts most is he's a *warrior*. After Preacher gets done with his slippin' around up yonder and his throat cuttin', they's gonna be some, white and Injun alike, that's gonna pull out. They ain't gonna want no more of Preacher. You'll see, ma'am. All of you. Right about now, Preacher is gettin' ready to make war. And when he starts, it's gonna be right nasty."

Dupre nodded his head in agreement. "Shore is. I'd give my possibles sack full to be there, too. Hee, hee, hee," he chuckled. "Ol' Preacher gonna be sneakin' up on some right about now. They gonna be pourin' a cup of coffee, feelin' all safe and snug and the last thing they ever gonna know is how a knife blade feels cuttin' they throat. Hee, hee, hee."

Melody shuddered.

Preacher lowered the Indian to the cool earth. The dead renegade had him a right nice war axe, so Preacher took that. Standing in the darkness, he hefted the tomahawk. Had a dandy feel to it. Later on, he'd see how it was for throwin'. He wiped his blade clean on the dead buck's shirt and slipped silently on, moving closer to the dancing flame of the small campfire that was placed close to a boulder. He could see another buck sitting close to the flames, roasting him a hunk of meat.

The smell of that meat cooking got Preacher's mouth to

salivating. Bear, it was. He could tell that even from this distance. And it was just about ready for gnawin' on. He worked his way closer to the fire and stood quiet for a time, moving only his eyes. These two, the one lying dead in the timber and this one sitting by the fire, were supposed to be the forward lookouts, Preacher figured. He felt he was still a couple of miles from the main party of outlaws and renegades.

Damn, but he was hungry.

He judged the distance, hefted the war axe another time or two, and let it fly.

The head of the axe caught the buck lower than Preacher had intended — striking and embedding in the Injun's neck — but it was a righteous throw. The head drove deep, severing jugular and destroying voice box, and the Injun fell over, kicking and jerking, but dying.

Preacher hoped he wouldn't kick too hard and cause the meat to fall into the fire. The brave tried to get up, but it was all for naught. His blood poured out, weakening him, and he finally jerked his last and lay still.

Preacher moved quickly. He scalped the buck and mutilated the body, just like he'd done with the renegade in the woods, then grabbed up the meat and slipped back into the timber. He'd left Hammer picketed deep in the timber, with good graze and a bit of water so's he wouldn't get restless.

Preacher squatted down about a mile from the now-still and bloody camp and ate the bear. Preacher silently apologized to the bear for its death, then complimented it for being right tasty.

"Ay-eee!" he heard the faint shout, and knew that the bodies had been discovered. He smiled. Now the fun was really going to get good.

They'd be coming at him hard, now, with vengence on their minds. He'd mutilated those two pretty bad, and to make matters worse, had killed them at night. That meant, to their tribe, that they'd forever wander the land, unable to attain the great beyond and rest in the land of plenty.

Preacher finished the bear meat and wiped his hands on his buckskins. He wanted to belch but was careful not too. He couldn't afford the noise. There were Injuns out yonder that were just as good in the timber as he was. And they'd be moving toward him at this very moment. He stood up slowly and carefully and listened for several heartbeats.

He now had two war axes, having taken another one from the careless buck by the fire. He carefully shifted locations, moving as silently as death's own hand through the brush and timber. He came to a little fast-moving crick and followed it for a time, working his way north, staying just at the edge of the timber, just inside the Wallowas.

Preacher froze by a huge old tree as his ears picked up a very slight sound on the other side of the crick. He moved his eyes left and right. One brave, and he was a big one, much larger than the average Injun. He made his silent way toward Preacher's location. Sensing the way the Injun moved, Preacher felt he hadn't been spotted. The buck would have tensed slightly if he'd spotted Preacher.

The Injun stopped and stood tall and silent for a time. Sniffing the air, probably, Preacher thought, for an Injun and a non-Injun smell different to those who have trained their blowers to tell the difference.

The brave would have to get a lot closer than he was before Preacher dared make even the slightest motion, for at this distance, the renegade would disappear before Preacher could use knife or axe. He sure didn't want to risk a shot and have the whole damn bunch of them down on him.

The renegade slowly turned his head, and in the very faint moonlight filtering through the trees, looked right at Preacher.

Thirteen

Preacher lowered his gaze to the brave's chest. He knew that looking directly at a person can sometimes bring to life a sense that ordinarily lies dormant. Preacher remained as still as the tree he stood by. He willed himself to be a part of the tree, to be as one with the earth. It worked for him most of the time.

This time it didn't.

With almost a silent cry of jubilation, the brave spotted him and jumped for the creek and Preacher.

Preacher stepped away from the tree and flung the war axe. The heavy head took the brave in the face, embedding in his skull. The renegade threw up his hands, dropping his own axe, and fell without a sound to the ground, landing on his back.

"Pretty good axe," Preacher muttered, as he went to work mutilating the body with his knife. He scalped the Indian and stuffed the hair behind the wide leather belt that for this night, replaced his bright sash. He worked the axe out of the Indian's skull and wiped the blood away on the dead man's leggings. Satisfied with his work, Preacher moved warily but quickly away from the death scene, working his way toward where he believed the main body of hostiles to be camped.

He had left his rifle in the boot, for he did not want to be hampered by a long gun this night. He had his pistols, but this was a night for knife and axe.

He moved through the brush and timber without a sound, walking a short distance and then stopping, to listen, let his eyes sweep the terrain, and to sniff the air.

A few hundred yards later, he smelled woodsmoke. He stood silent for a moment, until he had pinpointed the location of the smoke. He turned to the west and moved toward the source of the smoke.

He stopped and sank slowly to the ground, on his belly, when he saw that there were too many men around the fires for him to take on. Preacher was a brave man, but he wasn't stupid.

He backed away from that camp and slipped around it, changing direction. He almost made a fatal mistake when he came to a clearing, then hesitated at the last second. Something just didn't seem right.

Then his eyes found what his sixth sense had warned him about. Two men, standing just inside the timber on the other side of the tiny meadow, thick with grass and heady night fragrance of summer's flowers.

White men, for an Indian would never have been so careless. Preacher waited, to see just how impatient the sentries might turn out to be. And it wasn't a long wait.

"This is stupid," he heard one say, the words carrying to Preacher plain. "I can't understand what in the hell we're on guard for?"

"Hell, don't ask me, 'cause I shore don't know," the other one replied, disgust in his voice. "Them movers shore ain't gonna try no attack, and Red Hand's done got the Cayuses offen us. I think it's plumb ignorant bein' out here when we could be warm in our blankets."

"I left me a squaw on the Payette to join this bunch. I want some pretty bangles to take back to her. We'll have our way with them mover women 'til we git tarred of 'em

252

a-whinin' and complainin' and squallin' and then kill 'em and go through they possessions."

What nice folks, Preacher thought. Just lovely. While they talked, Preacher took that time to move. He slowly circled the meadow and entered the timber, working his way up to within a few yards of the so-called sentries.

"I be right back," one of the outlaws said.

"Where you goin'?"

He mumbled something in a low voice and stepped back into the timber, unbuttoning his trousers as he walked.

He walked right into Preacher's big knife. Preacher lowered the throat-cut body to the ground, and walked right up to the remaining sentry.

"Took you long enough," the man said. "Now stand here and keep your eyes open whilst I—"

"Die," Preacher finished the statement as he buried a war axe in the man's skull. He grabbed the man's shirt to prevent the body from thudding the ground, and lowered the dead outlaw to the earth. He scalped both men and mutilated the bodies.

Preacher figured he'd pushed his luck just about as far as he cared to push it this night. He began his walk back to Hammer. He was about halfway back to where he'd picketed his horse when he heard the first shout, coming from 'way behind him. Someone had found the bodies of the two sentries.

He immediately dropped down to the earth, in some scrub bushes, and waited for a few moments, curious to see what would come of this.

"Goddamn you, Red Hand," the shout came from not too far from where Preacher lay. The voice belonged to Bum. "I thought you told me you'd fixed it with the Cayuses?"

"This is not Cayuse work," Red Hand's voice was tight with anger but still controlled. "I have the assurances of the warriors in this area that we are to be left alone."

"Well, who else would be workin' this area?" Jack Harris asked.

"Preacher," Moses said quietly. "He's amongst us, boys."

"That ain't possible!" Bum shouted. "He's good, but he ain't that good."

"Aii-yee!" the call pierced the night, as the bodies of the Indians were found.

The men began running toward the sound and Preacher slipped out of the bushes and started toward his horse, circling wide of the timber where he'd left the dead Injuns. Heading deeper into the timber, Preacher stopped when he caught movement just ahead of him. Two Indians running almost noiselessly through the timber, both of them carrying rifles. They ran past Preacher, not more than twenty feet from where he stood. No sooner had they jogged past, Preacher stepped out and continued on toward Hammer.

A shot split the night far behind him. "I got him!" someone called.

Preacher smiled as he walked. You got one of your own, you fool, he thought. What a pack of ninnies.

He reached Hammer, swung into the saddle, and headed south, following an old game trail. When he felt he had put enough distance behind him, Preacher stopped and made a cold camp for the rest of the night. He went to sleep smiling, knowing there would be damn little sleeping in the camp of Bum and Red Hand for the remainder of this night.

Preacher met the wagon train a few miles south of where the trail crossed the Powder. Two of Red Hand's warriors had made the mistake of trailing Preacher out of the Wallowas. He now had their scalps tied to Hammer's mane, in addition to the other scalps he'd taken.

"Wagh!" Nighthawk said, spying the scalps. "You had an interesting night of it, did you not, Preacher?"

"Got right borin' there toward the last," Preacher replied. "Weren't no fun left to it foolin' with greenhorns, so's I pulled out. But I reckon I did leave them in some manner of disaray, I 'spect."

"What are those things?" Swift asked, riding up and pointing to Hammer's mane. A half a dozen others rode with him, including Edmond and Richard.

"Scalps, Swift. Human hair. The top-knot, mostly. When I make war, I like to leave the enemy a little sign that it ain't nice to fool with Preacher."

"That's disgusting!" a mover said.

"Actually," a mover said, "I have read where some historians believe the white man originated scalping, not the Indians. What say you about that, Preacher?"

Preacher shrugged his shoulders. "Some tribes scalp, others don't. Most do. I 'spect scalpin's been goin' on ever since the knife was invented. That's what I think. Swift, they's a right nice place to circle about two mile ahead. Circle 'em tight, 'cause we close to the action now. Keep everyone inside and when folks got to leave the circle, have armed men with them at all times."

The wagonmaster gave the mountain man a curt nod of his head and turned his horse. The others followed, except for Richard and Edmond.

"I think them scalps of yourn done irritated the man, Preacher," Dupre opined. "They cut agin the grain of his Christian holdin's."

"It's a barbaric practice and I fail to see what you have accomplished by doing it," Edmond put his penny's worth in.

"Demoralization," Richard said.

"Do what?" Beartooth asked, looking at the missionary.

"It lowers the morale of the enemy."

"Oh. Do tell?" the big mountain man said. "Do that mean that Preacher done good?"

Richard noticed the twinkle in the man's eyes and sighed. He held a strong suspicion that these mountain men were not nearly so ignorant as they would like others to believe. On more than one occasion he had noticed lapses in their horrible grammar that led him to believe they were merely having a good time at the expense of others.

"I would have to say yes to that question."

"Wagh!" Beartooth hollered. "You a hero agin, Preacher."

Dupre put a hand to his heart and proclaimed, "My hero!"

"I think I am going to faint," Nighthawk lisped.

"I'm of good mind to just shoot all of you," Preacher said, and rode off.

When the wagons had been circled and the women were busying themselves with preparing supper, the mountain men gathered at their own camp, as always away from the main body of movers, and talked.

"I think we'll have at least one full day of safe crossin'," Dupre offered. "That'll put about half the wagons on each side of the Powder."

"That's the way I see it," Preacher concurred. "Then when the men is busy on the second day, Bum and Red Hand will hit us and they'll come a-foggin', boys. There ain't gonna be no feeler attacks. They'll try to make the first one do it."

"And they's a chance they could do 'er, too." Beartooth offered up the sobering thought. "We're gonna be spread pretty damn thin."

"Everybody that can shoot is gonna have to be well-armed," Preacher said. "We got weapons aplenty, so Jim, you check each wagon for powder and shot. Dupre, see that every boy of age and the girls, too, if they can handle a gun and they parents allow it, is armed. Beartooth, you and Hawk check out the crossin' at first light." He paused for a moment. "I shore hope God looks down and smiles on fools, 'cause we sure got a bunch gathered here. Includin' us," he added.

Red Hand and Bum were still livid over the dead that Preacher had left behind him. Some of Red Hand's renegades were very nervous about continuing with the planned fight that lay ahead of them. Preacher's medicine was too good, they warned Red Hand. There will be other wagon trains—plenty of them, so the talk goes—so why not wait? Let this one go on.

"Fools, cowards, old women, fops!" Red Hand yelled at them, shaming them. "Look around you. We are two hundred strong. Preacher is but one man. The others with him are nothing. The whites in the train are not skilled fighters. They are women and small children. No. We attack as planned."

He walked to Bum's side. "This better work, Outlaw. If the first day does not find us in control of the wagons, we will have men leaving us. Both yours and mine."

"Your warriors thinkin' that Preacher's medicine is too strong, Red Hand?"

Red Hand stared hard at the man. His dark eyes were unreadable. "Yes," he finally said. "And maybe it is." He turned and walked away.

Jack Harris had stood quietly and listened to the exchange. Now he felt he had to speak his mind. "Bum, that took a hell of a man to do what Preacher done the other night, and an even better man to slip away oncest it was done. Some of the boys is right edgy, I got to say."

Bum nodded his head. "I think Preacher's even got Red Hand thinkin' 'bout quittin'. I don't think he will quit. His honor's at stake now. But he's thinkin' on it."

"So is some of our people."

"You?"

Jack shook his head. "No. Not me. I'm in this 'til it's over. One way or the other. Way I see it, Preacher and all them others has got to die. If they was to get through and tell what they know 'bout us, the Army would be shore to send men in after us, and all that'd be waitin' for us would be a rope. And that makes my neck hurt just thinkin' 'bout it."

Bum was sure in agreement with that. "This time tomorrow, Jack, they'll be plenty of women and girls for us to be usin'. And a few of us will have gold aplenty to spend back East. Me, I'm gonna take my share and retire from this business. I'm gonna change my name and buy me a little business of some sort back acrost the Muddy and settle down. Civilization is movin' this way, and it's comin' fast. Ten years from now, they'll be people all over this area."

Jack doubted that. In fact, he doubted everything that Bum had just said. The man was an outlaw, and that was all he would ever be. He watched as Bum walked over to the small fire and poured a cup of coffee.

Get out of this! his mind warned him. *Pack your kit and saddle up and ride.*

But he knew he wouldn't do that. Knew he had to finish the wagon train and actually look down on Preacher's dead, bloated body. And the bodies of everyone on that train. He had a good thing going, this leading wagon trains to ambush. If anyone lived to talk about it, he'd be finished.

"What you ponderin' so heavy, Jack?" Bum asked him.

Jack forced a smile. "Thinkin' about all them women on the train."

"We gonna have us a high ol' time for sure," the outlaw said with a grin. "I cain't hardly wait."

Ride out! the words again popped into Jack's brain. He shook his head to clear it.

He looked at his comrades, sitting and squatting and standing in small groups. They were filthy. Clothing hanging in rags. Stinking and unshaven and ignorant. They were working ten times harder being on the

258

dodge side of the law than they would holding down regular jobs.

Too late for that, Jack mused.

He looked south. Tomorrow would tell the story. Tomorrow would either be feast or famine for them all. He touched the butt of a pistol.

Tomorrow.

Fourteen

Preacher sat Hammer just above the banks of the Powder, his eyes taking in everything around him. It was very peaceful, very serene, and very quiet. No birds sang or flew, and no other animal had been to the river for a drink in several hours, not that Preacher could tell. The silence was a dead giveaway.

"Well, Hammer," he spoke to his horse. "I reckon they just went and outsmarted themselves. I could figure maybe Bum bein' that stupid, but not an old firebrand like Red Hand. So I tell you what we're gonna do, ol' friend . . ."

He told his horse and then sat there for a time, chuckling. "Yes, siree, Hammer," he said as he lifted the reins. "They's gonna be some mighty mad outlaws and Injuns when they see what's happenin' over here."

"Are you out of your mind?" Swift yelled, jerking off his hat and throwing it on the ground. "That's the craziest thing I ever heard of."

"Not so crazy," Nighthawk said. "Not perfect, either. But it's a good plan."

"Why?" the wagonmaster demanded.

"Make them come to us," Richard said. "Yes. I see. We can have the river on two sides of us. We have access to water that way, and our main forces could be concentrated on the other two sides. Yes, we have ample supplies for an extended siege, and plenty of shot and powder. We can start gathering tall grass for the animals and keep them on short rations for a few days. I think it's a fine plan."

It was at this point that the river made a curve, much like an upsidedown V, the river wide on both sides, and narrow at the tip of the inverted V, where the trail crossed.

Swift thought about Preacher's plan for a moment, then nodded his head. "It's better than us losing a lot of people." He lifted his bugle and tooted on it.

The wagons did not circle, but rather formed up into a long rectangular box like fort, with the stock inside the box. Swift assigned young people to scoop up the mess the livestock would make. It was going to be close and odious, but all felt they could wait out the outlaws and Indians.

Men went to work immediately cutting down small trees and clearing them of branches. The logs would be used first as barricades from bullets and arrows, then, if need be, to use in the building of rafts to cross the river, although, at this point, Preacher did not think rafting would be necessary.

Across the river, Red Hand glared at Bum, his eyes hot with anger. "It is far too early in the day to stop for nightfall. Why don't they begin crossing? Why do they stop and build fortifications?"

"I don't know," Bum lied, for he knew perfectly well what the movers were doing. He had a sinking feeling in his guts that Preacher had won another round. The outlaws were slap out of supplies. They were out of coffee, beans, sugar, salt, flour—everything. They had planned on existing on the supplies taken from the wagon train. Now? He didn't know.

"We've got to attack, Bum!" Jack Harris said. "We've got to attack now, man."

"Yeah," Bull said. "We let them movers get all set over

there, and we'll never pry 'em loose from there. We're out of grub, Bum. We ain't got nothin' to eat. And as soon as the shootin' starts, there won't be even a rabbit within five miles of this place."

Bum was thoughtful for a moment. "Preacher's countin' on that. He's countin' on us sendin' people out on a hunt. 'Cause come the night, him and them other ol' boys down yonder is gonna slip out and circle around on all sides of us, waitin' for a hunter to go out for game. And that hunter ain't never gonna come back. *Goddammit!*"

"To attack now would be folly," Red Hand said. "We would have to cross several hundred yards of open land, then ford the river. They would pick us off as easily as stepping on a bug. If we wait until night, many of the new warriors who have joined us will not take part. They will not fight at night."

He walked away, to join a brave who was motioning to him. They talked for several moments, then Red Hand returned. "We are out of food." He shrugged his muscular shoulders. "Of course, Indians are accustomed to that. So what do you say now, Bum Kelley?"

"I don't know," the outlaw admitted.

"Stalemate," Richard said, standing beside Preacher, Swift and several others, as they looked toward the seemingly deserted timber across the river.

"How long could we last?" Melody asked.

"Days," Preacher told her. "The last two or three wouldn't be easy to take, 'cause the stock'll be squallin' for feed. But it'd be a discomfort to them whilst doin' 'em no real harm."

"Won't those thugs across the river go hunting for food?" A mover's wife asked. It was mid-morning of the second day camped by the river. No hostile action had been initiated by the other side, but all could see the thin tentacles of smoke from their campfires.

Preacher smiled. "Take a look around you, ma'am. You

see Beartooth or Nighthawk or Trapper Jim or Dupre?"

Everybody turned their heads and looked. "No," Edmond said. "Where are they?"

Preacher pointed to the other side of the river, as a horse came slowly walking up to the edge of the timber. A man was tied in the saddle. Using a spy glass, Swift could see the arrow still sticking out of the man's back.

"He's been scalped," the wagonmaster said. "And he's stiff in the saddle."

"Yeah," Preacher said. "And comin' from that direction, I 'spect that's Beartooth's work. It's like I been figurin'. Them folks over yonder is gettin' hongry. They slap out of supplies. I 'spect they was countin' on feedin' off the supplies carried in this train. We done spoiled their plans, turned everything topsy-turvy. Now they sendin' out hunters and them ol' friends of mine is sendin' the hunters back without their hair. Hee, hee, hee!" he chuckled. The others looked at him strangely as he chuckled in dark humor. "I do love it when a plan works out."

"Will they attack, do you think?" a woman asked him.

"They might. But if they do it'll be a hard one, in the hopes they can take us on the first run. But more than likely it'll just be a short attack to let us know they ain't forgot us and they'll be waitin' further on up the trail. If they had any sense, they'd go on and leave us be."

Preacher looked across the river. If he thought either one of the leaders would honor a flag of truce, he'd borrow a petticoat and wave it at them and palaver with them. But Bum had about as much honor as a stump and Red Hand was even worse when it come to dealing with whites. Anyway, Preacher mused, that was just a dream. Red Hand could always drift back into the wilderness, but Bum's situation was a different one. He had to keep trying until he succeeded in stopping the wagon train cold and killing everyone in it.

If the outlaw leader had had any foresight about him, he'd have had hunters out killing game and smoking and jerking the meat. But 'if' don't put a scrap of food in nobody's mouth.

So what would I do if I was in Bum's place, Preacher thought. I'd pull out right now, get a lot of distance between this place and the next point of ambush, and I'd be huntin' all the time. That's what I'd do, Preacher wound it up.

Melody broke into his thoughts as he caught the last of her question ". . . what month is it?"

"July," a mover replied. "Near the last, I think. I'll ask my wife. She's keeping a diary of our adventure."

Adventure! Preacher thought sourly. Then he had to smile and shake his head and silently ask himself this: Why are you so sour about it? You're damn sure a part of it.

Swift awakened him. "They're crossing the river, Preacher. Left and right."

Preacher was fully awake and out of his blankets just about the time the words left his mouth. He looked up at the sky. It was cloudy with no moon.

Good night for it, he thought. "Get everybody up and ready. Buckets filled for flame arrows. The women can handle that. Have the men stand ready for a fight. Assign the younger kids to load weapons. Move."

Preacher took his position by a wheel and stared into the darkness. He found him a target—albeit a long way off—and pulled the Hawken to his shoulder and let 'er bang. The man, he couldn't tell if it was an outlaw or a renegade, screamed once and fell face first into the river.

A mover fired and another scream was heard in the night, followed by a lot of fancy cussing and floundering around in the water.

One Indian got close and Swift drilled him right through the brisket. The warrior hit the wet bank and lay still. "Damned red savages!" he shouted.

"Problem is," Preacher muttered under his breath, "they was here 'fore us." Then he saw a hat that he remembered seeing miles back, long before he'd reached Fort Hall. He lifted his Hawken, sighted just under the brim of the hat, and gently squeezed the trigger.

The big ball struck the outlaw smack between the eyes and tore out the back of his head. The man never knew what hit him.

"Adam's down and dead!" a man called. "My God, the whole back of his head is blowed off."

"Forward!" Bum shouted. "Charge, men! Charge!"

A mover's wife said a very ugly word and cut loose with a shotgun. An outlaw began screaming in pain, the bird-shot taking him in the face and neck, peppering him and blinding him in one eye. He began running toward the wagons, screaming in rage and hate. The mover's wife gave him another charge, this time at much closer range. The shot tore into his throat and knocked him off his boots.

Hot bright flames began dancing in the timber on the outlaw's side of the river.

"Somebody's burnin' our possessions!" a man shouted. "Lookee yonder." He turned around and pointed.

Richard leveled his rifle and shot the man in the ass. "Wow-eee!" the outlaw squalled, and went running for the river. He jumped into the water and sat down, letting the cold river waters momentarily soothe his butt.

Preacher grinned. His friends across the river had slipped in as soon as the outlaws had slipped out and fired their camps.

"Goddamn you, Preacher!" Bum shouted. Then he began shouting out all the things he'd do once he got his hands on Preacher.

"You wanna fight me, Bum?" Preacher shouted back. "How about it, you yeller-bellied son of a bitch? Just you and me, winner take all."

Red Hand halted his men, flattening them out along the river's bank, safe from shot. "We will see what kind of a man we have joined with," he told his people.

The firing stopped. A half a dozen men, from Bum's

bunch and Red Hand's, had left to return to their burning camps, to salvage what they could and to see what had become of the guards, both white and red. All pretty well suspected they would find them dead.

Bum didn't know what to say, but he knew he had better choose his words carefully, for to an Indian, even a renegade, a challenge was something not to be taken lightly. If he screwed this up, Red Hand would take his men and leave.

"I don't trust you, Preacher!" Bum shouted from the night. " 'Sides, I ain't got nothin' to gain from whuppin' your butt."

"True," Red Hand muttered. "There is that to be considered."

"You kill me, Bum. You got one less mountain man on this train."

Red Hand smiled grimly. "And there is that to be considered, as well."

"You guarantee me when I kill you your buddies will pull off from the train?"

"I can't speak for them, Bum. Just for me. I tell you what. I'll make it a real sportin' event. I'll fight two of you at oncest. You and that sorry damn Jack Harris. Now, I can't see how you can refuse me that."

"Nor can I," Red Hand said.

"If they do not fight him, I do not wish to ride with them any longer," a Kiowa renegade said. "It is not good to be associated with cowards. Besides, I have thought for some time that there is a secret that Kelley is keeping from us."

"What could it be?"

"I don't know. But he lies."

"He has always lied. What is so different about this time?"

"The value of what is in the wagons."

Red Hand grew thoughtful. The Kiowa was right, of course. Bum had turned evasive each time Red Hand tried to question him about the wagon train. "We will see what happens this night," he finally said.

"It's some sort of trick, Bum," Jack Harris whispered hoarsely. "Don't you be believin' nothin' that damn Preacher has to say."

"Yeah, I know. But if we don't fight him, we could see Red Hand and his bunch pull away. You know that, don't you?"

"Come on, Bum!" Preacher yelled. "How 'bout it, Jack? Or are the both of you so damned yeller you got petticoats under your britches?"

The Kiowa chuckled and even Red Hand was forced to smile.

"It's a trick, Red Hand," Bum yelled. "It's nothin' but a damn trick. Don't fall for it."

"He is a coward," the Kiowa said. "I am taking my followers and leaving. Now."

"Wait! There is something in that wagon train that is of great value. The white man's money, perhaps. If that is the case, we could use it to buy more guns and powder and shot. Think about that."

"Bum Kelley is afraid of this man called Preacher."

"Perhaps that is true. But Preacher is a man that any warrior would respect. Perhaps we are confusing respect with fear." Red Hand knew he was telling a blatant lie; Bum Kelley was so afraid of Preacher he was probably pissing in his pants. But he wanted the Kiowa and his band to stay with the group. "Stay with us. When the time is right, we shall attack the wagons, seize the money, and kill Bum and his people."

The Kiowa nodded his head. "I like that. All right. I shall stay. But only if you give Bum to me. I have a thought that he will not die well."

Red Hand smiled in the night. "It is done. Preacher!" he shouted. "It is Red Hand."

"What do you want, you damn renegade?" Preacher returned the shout.

"Your ugliness is exceeded only by your ability to lie. We do not blame Bum for not taking your offer. Since

267

you are not to be trusted, we can only believe that your offer is a trick. You are trying to split our forces and it will not work. Go to hell, Preacher!"

"I never said he wasn't smart," Preacher muttered.

"Do you hear my words, Preacher?"

"Yeah, I hear you. You best break away from Kelley, Red Hand. You stay with that buzzard puke and he'll get you killed. You best think about that."

"Buzzard puke!" Bum shouted. Then he began reiterating all the things he was going to do to Preacher once he got his hands on him.

Many of the women in the wagons held their hands to their ears.

"It's over now," Preacher said to Swift. "See 'em slipping acrost the river? Ain't no use in shootin'. They're out of range."

"So we've bought some time, is that it?"

"That's about it. But we didn't lose nobody this night, and we can start crossin' the river in the mornin' knowin' we won't be attacked."

"We should count our blessings for the small things," Edmond said, walking up.

Preacher glanced at him. "Way I look at it, stayin' alive ain't no small thing."

Fifteen

"Pulled out last night and headed north," Dupre said, swinging down from the saddle and heading straight for the coffee pot. "And they didn't even look back."

"They gonna be a raggedly-assed bunch," Beartooth added. " 'Cause we shore made a mess outta they camps."

"Clothes needed burning," Nighthawk said, speaking perfect English. "Fleas and other crawling and jumping insects had infested the material."

Richard sighed as he listened to the man speak. Whenever he tried to engage the Crow in conversation, the Indian resorted to grunting and broken phrases.

"We left six more dead at the camps," Trapper Jim summed it up. "And they's several bodies floatin' in the river."

"So our adversaries, while still quite formidable, have been drastically reduced in numbers," Richard said.

Beartooth looked at Dupre. "What the hell did he say?"

"Take heap many scalps," Nighthawk grunted, hiding his smile. "Count plenty coup."

"Oh, for pity's sake!" Richard said, and stalked away.

The wagons began crossing the Powder that day and by late afternoon of the next day, all were across and the fording was accomplished with only one minor incident:

Young Avery fell off his horse and very nearly drowned because no one in the party would offer to help him. The young man and his father were universally despised among the settlers. Edmond saw what was happening and tossed the youth the end of a rope and dragged him out.

"You didn't do nobody no favors," Preacher told him.

"I couldn't just sit there and let the young man drown!"

"I could." Preacher lifted the reins and rode off.

The wagons headed north by northwest, rolling through Thief Valley, then called Grand Ronde Valley, and that night camped close to the mountains. They found good water and plenty of good graze for the livestock.

"Any of you folks ever tasted salmon?" Preacher asked a group of settlers. None had. "Not all Cayuses is on the prod. We'll run into some friendly ones and I'll barter for fish. It's right tasty. I think you'll like it."

Although it was summer, the weather was unpredictable in that area. When the movers awakened the next morning, they found the sky gray and the temperature hovering around the freezing mark.

"My God!" Swift exclaimed. "It is going to *snow?*"

"It might," Preacher told him. "Anything's possible in this country."

On the fifth day after the failed attack by the Powder, Beartooth rode up to Preacher at the head of the column. "Gettin' plumb borin', Preacher."

"I hope it stays that way."

The huge mountain man grinned. "Tell the truth, so does I. Nighthawk ought to be back today or tomorrow. Be right interestin' to find out where Bum and Red Hand is plannin' on springin' their next surprise."

"They've crossed the Columbia and is waitin' for us up to the north." He smiled. "But they's in for a long wait, 'cause we ain't crossin' the Columbia and headin' north."

Beartooth looked hard at him. "What you got ramblin' around in that noggin of yourn, Preacher? We got to cross the Columbia, man."

"No, we don't. And we ain't gonna. We gonna raft these

pilgrims acrost the Fall and stay to the south side of the river."

"You've lost your mind, man! You can't take these damn wagons thataway."

"I know a way, Beartooth. I spent two year out here, 'member? I got a way all figured out in my mind. It's gonna be rough, but we can do it."

Dupre had ridden up and was listening with amazement on his face. He shook his head. "I know the way you're talkin' about, Preach. You gonna be crossin' the Sandy four times. You best think about that."

"The Sandy ain't nothin'. Bum and Red Hand's got scouts watchin' the crossin'. Bet on that. They got people lookin' and waitin' all over the north side of the river. So we'll stay to the south. By the time they figure out what's happened, we'll be so close to the fort they dasn't attack."

"Have you told Swift?"

"No. Hell, don't none of these movers know nothin' 'bout this country. When you're lost as a goose you ain't got no choice in the matter; you got to follow the leader."

"But you said yourself they's gonna be scouts of Bum's and Red Hand's watching the Fall," Beartooth protested.

"Sure they are. But we ain't crossin' the Deschutes there. We're gonna cross further south."

"There ain't no damn place further south!"

"Yes, there is." Dupre spoke the words softly. "You're a damn fool, Preacher. You plannin' on takin' these green-horns through pure virgin country. It ain't never been done afore."

"That's what makes it so interestin'," Preacher told him with a wide smile.

"Do you realize that we're gonna have to *build* a damn road?" Beartooth asked. "The way you're talkin' about ain't nothin' but a game trail."

"Yep."

"These wagon's ain't never gonna stand the trip, Preacher."

"They'll stand it."

"You're a damn igit!"

"You wanna quit?"

"I didn't say nothin' about quittin'. Did you hear me say anything 'bout quittin', Dupre?"

"Nope."

"Fine," Preacher told him. "I'm glad all that's settled. Now you can quit your bitchin'. You know the way we're goin', so put your thinkin' cap on and close your mouth. Start thinkin' of ways to make it easier."

The mountain man shook his head in exasperation. "They *ain't* no easy way!"

"Then we'll do it the hard way." He smiled. "And we'll be the first to do it."

They crossed the Blues at its narrowest point and headed northwest. They camped at a spot that in the years to come would be called Emigrant Springs. Only a few miles north of the springs, Preacher turned the long line westward and headed for the Umatilla River.

"Normally," Preacher told Swift, "the Cayuse Injuns would be real friendly. I've stayed with 'em many times and et their food and slept in their tipis. Usually this country would be swarming with their horses. But as you can see, it's deserted. That means they've pulled 'em close to their villages and gettin' ready for war. That don't necessary mean that they'll attack us. I know the head man, and he likes me. So that's a plus. Howsomever, there are a few minuses."

Dupre smiled hugely and nodded his head. "Shore are. Like a bunch of young bucks lookin' to impress the gals with scalps, for one."

"I thought you men knew the chief?"

"Oh, we do. They probably wouldn't hurt *us*. But they might kill all of *you*."

"Comforting thought," Swift muttered. "But someday the Oregon Trail will be safe for all."

"Big Medicine Trail," Beartooth said. "That's what the

Injuns call it. Kinda hard for me to get used to callin' it the Oregon Trail."

It turned cold and the winds began blowing. If the movers thought they'd seen winds on the empty prairies east of the mountains, this changed their minds. Anything that was not secured properly — "right and tight," Preacher called it — was blown off and scattered all to hell and gone. So much canvas was ripped and torn that Preacher ordered it all taken off the ribs and stored until they were out of the wind.

They lost half a day trying to round up the livestock that had drifted, trying to find comfort from the cold winds, and two very difficult days later, during which the wagon train managed to cover only a few miles each day, another birth was recorded on the trail.

It was a very long and hard birthing, and the woman's screaming was a nerve-wracking thing for all to hear. The mother had never been very strong, and shortly after the birthing, the woman died. The husband refused to accept the baby — a little girl — blaming the child for the mother's death. She was given to the Ellsworth woman to care for. The mover flatly refused to go any further. No amount of coaxing would change his mind. He flung himself across the mound of earth that covered his young wife and wailed out his grief.

"Rainin' too damn hard to move anyways," Preacher said. "We'll just stay here and wait it out. Maybe that feller will get over his grief come a new dawnin'."

Just before a cold and rainy dawn would break, a single pistol shot brought the sleepers out of their blankets.

"I bet I know what that was," Preacher said.

"Yeah," Dupre said. "I shore wouldn't bet agin you."

The young widower had stuck the barrel of a pistol in his mouth and pulled the trigger, blowing out the back of his head. He lay sprawled across his wife's grave.

"Git some shovels," Preacher said, disgust in his voice. "Be easier digging up this fresh grave and just layin' him beside his wife. I figure that's the way he'd want it."

273

"That's sacrilege, sir!" Edmond objected.

"Oh, shut up! Don't get up in my face, Edmond. Not now. I'll hurt you, boy," Preacher told him, then turned his back and stalked off. "Any man who'd shoot hisself over a damn woman is a fool! Anybody who'd shoot they-selves over just about anything's a damn fool. Life is for the livin', 'cause when you dead, you dead a long time."

"I have never known a man that hard," Richard said, rain water dripping off the wide brim of his hat.

"Hard country, Bible-shouter," Beartooth told him. "This country feeds on weaklin's. I 'spect the day will come when this trail is lined with graves, from beginnin' to end. Three months after they're planted, won't be no trace of them. You best get used to it."

He walked off to join Preacher.

"Dig up the grave and bury Jacob beside his wife," Swift ordered. He sighed, steam fogging his breath. "It probably won't be the last one we'll bury before we reach our destination."

"I'm beginning to wonder if it's all worth it." A mover spoke the words to no one in particular.

No one responded to his words, the men just picked up shovels and began digging in the rain-soaked mound of earth.

Sixteen

The wagon train moved on, leaving behind them a lonely grave and the box of a wagon. The young couple's meager possessions were given to those most in need, the wheels taken for spares, and the canvas given to a family who had lost theirs in the high winds. They averaged about eight miles a day, the men having to literally hack a road out of the narrow trail, using axes and pure sweat and muscle.

When they reached the Umatilla River, two families announced they were leaving the train and heading northeast, toward the Walla Walla, to make their homes near the new Whitman Mission. They simply could not, or would not, endure the trail any longer. No one tried to dissuade them; most of the movers were just too damn tired to care.

The wagon train rolled on, with not one hostile Indian being seen. Nighthawk had reported that Bum and Red Hand had spread their people out north of the Columbia, in the wilderness along the Klickitat River.

"Just like I figured," Preacher said. "Time they figure out that we didn't cross the Columbia at the Dalles, we'll be so far into the Southern Cascades they'll never find us."

And as Preacher had predicted, when the train did

meet up with some Cayuses, they were friendly. Preacher bartered for enough fresh salmon to give everyone on the train a good meal and learned that only a few of the tribe had taken to the warpath. Those that had were operating—for the most part—north of the Columbia.

But the Cayuses shook their heads and made the sign of a crazy person when they learned that Preacher was going to take the wagons across the mountains south of the river.

"It cannot be done," a sub-chief told Swift. "That is impossible."

"It ain't never *been* done," Preacher corrected the wagonmaster. "But that don't mean it can't be done." Preacher talked long with the sub-chief and the man inspected the gee-gaws in the trade wagon driven by Jim. After two hours of palavering, the men solemnly shook hands.

"What was that all about?" Richard asked.

"They're goin' to help us cross the Deschutes," Preacher told him. "I gave him everything in the wagon, and the wagon. That'll be one less we got to pull acrost the mountains, and it'll give us an extra team."

"But that river is miles and days away!" Swift objected. "How do you know these savages will be there?"

" 'Cause they gave their word to me and we ain't never lied to one another, that's why. Move out, Swift." He pointed. "The promised land is thataway."

Jim was grateful to be shut of the wagon and back in the saddle. But like the other mountain men, he had his doubts about getting a wagon train through the Cascades.

"There ain't much feed in there for the livestock, Preacher," he reminded the man.

"That's true in spots."

"Mighty boggy in there, Ol' Hoss," Dupre added.

"Yep. In spots."

"Ropes is gettin' raggedy," Beartooth said. "And we gonna have to shore use them for snubbin' these wagons and lowerin' down them mighty steep passageways."

"Once we get them built," Preacher said.

Nighthawk shook his head at that. "Ummm," he said.

"Great God in Heaven!" Swift said, taking his first look at the Deschutes. "We'll never get the wagons across that."

"We'll get them across," Preacher told him. "Get your people buildin' rafts. This part's the easy part. Once we get 'crost is when the fun starts."

The crossing was made, but it was not done without loss. Several head of livestock were drowned in the river, and several wagons were lost when the ropes on a raft parted and the raft came apart. Since possessions were rafted across separately, the movers' goods were dispersed among other wagons and the pioneers could ride the mules. Preacher bartered with the Cayuses for saddles — he did not ask where they got them, although he had a pretty good idea — and one mover's wife shocked the entire train by putting on a pair of her husband's britches and riding the mule astride.

"Disgraceful," several of the women said. "How common can a person get?"

"Seems like a pretty good idea to me," was the opinion of most of the other women.

"No woman of mine would ever wear britches," a mover made the mistake of saying, and ten minutes later, his wife emerged from their wagon wearing a pair of his britches. "You got something to say about this?" she challenged him.

"No, dear," he said meekly.

Melody and Penelope looked at one another and smiled. Moments later they had changed from their now somewhat less than elegant riding habits into britches.

Dupre took a long look at the derrieres of the ladies, threw his hands up into the air, and proclaimed, "C'est bon! Magnifique!"

Preacher had spent weeks looking at their derrieres. He

had nothing to say.

"Here, now!" Swift said, eyeballing the britches-clad ladies. "I'll have none of this on my train. You women get back into proper clothing."

"Make us," Melody threw down the challenge.

Swift muttered under his breath and walked away.

"I'm tellin' you for a fact," Preacher said, "I can see the day comin' when women is gonna have the vote."

"Never!" Beartooth said. "Of course," he added, scratching his woolly mane, "I ain't never voted so I reckon it wouldn't make no difference nohow."

On the morning the train was to pull out, Preacher told Swift, "We got to get over the mountains 'fore the snow flies, and she can fly early out here. This ain't gonna be easy, I'm warnin' you of that right now. But I said I'd get you through, and I'm gonna do just that. So toot on that bugle of yourn, Swift, and let's tackle the last leg."

Swift smiled at him. "Tell you the truth, Preacher, I'm getting just about as sick of that damn bugle as you are."

The two men laughed, clasped each other on the shoulder, and walked off together, toward their horses. And while they had no way of knowing it, both of them were destined for the pages of a few history books. They would be the first to lead a wagon train over the rugged Cascades Mountains. But since that claim would always be in dispute, it would be taken out of the history books. Taken out long before the mass migration of the late '40's and early '50's.

When Preacher was told of this, he wasn't surprised, since he wasn't aware it was even in any books. His reply was typical: "Hell, I don't read about history, pilgrim. I *make* it!"

Book Three

One

O beautiful for spacious skies,
For amber waves of grain,
For purple mountain majesties
Above the fruited plain!
America! America!
God shed His grace on thee
And crown thy good with brotherhood,
From sea to shining sea!

Katharine Lee Bates

"We're gonna have about two and a half days of fairly easy travel," Preacher told Swift and a few others, after they broke for lunch. "Then you got to lighten the wagons. And I mean discard everything that ain't absolutely necessary. The folks ain't gonna like it, I know that, but it has to be. You think goin' through the South Pass of the Rockies was bad, wait 'til you see Hood and what's all around it."

Swift nodded. "I'll tell them."

"Don't just tell them. Stand right there until they do it. We're a-fixin' to go straight up and then straight down, half the time right into a bog, and we'll be doin' it over and over and over agin. Most beautifulest and gawd-awfulest country you ever will see. Start shakin' down the movers, Swift."

On the second day after crossing the river, the train came to a series of hills, long steep hills. That night, the movers began throwing possessions away in earnest. There was a lot of crying and fussing over many things that were being dumped by the trail, but in the end, the wagons were lightened considerably.

Preacher told them to stay in camp the next day and dump some more out of the wagons. "You just don't know what you're a-fixin' to get into, folks. But I do. You'll kill them oxen tryin' to get all this crap over the trail. The mules will just not move once they figure out they can't pull it. Dump more, people. Get busy. Lighten them wagons."

"Is it really this bad, Preacher?" Richard asked. "The people are very upset."

"I can't make it sound as bad as it really is," Preacher told him. "It don't make me feel like no big man makin' folks throw away things I know they toted what must seem like halfway around the world. But it's either that, or they break down or their oxen dies in the middle of the Cascades and they walk out with nothin'. Think about that."

"All right, Preacher," the missionary said, reluctance in his voice.

"Richard, have the movers wash their wagons to get all the dried mud off. You'd be surprised how much weight is just ahangin' on them wagons."

"Yes. You're right. Of course."

Preacher found the lady who was keeping a journal of her adventures and asked her if she was still keepin' her notes up. She assured him that she certainly was. "Well, ma'am, I hope you got lots of paper and ink and quills," he told her. " 'Cause you shore got a lot of scratchin' and scribblin' to do over the next month or so."

She smiled at him. "Would you like to see what I have written about you, Mister Preacher?"

"No, ma'am!" Preacher's reply was quick. "This trip's been de-pressin' enough without my doin' that."

The movers hit a dense forest of pine, fir, and redwood. Many of the redwood soared several hundred feet into the air. On the first day after entering the Cascades, the wagon train traveled only three miles. The movers fell into their blankets and went to sleep exhausted after a day of cutting and dragging trees out of the way. The trail they hacked out of the wilderness was a narrow one, just wide enough for a single wagon. Fallen trees had to be dragged out of the way, huge rocks and jutting roots had to be first hacked at and then dug out. The only graze for the livestock was swamp grass. Preacher warned them that only a few miles further they would encounter laurel, and that if the livestock ate it, they would die.

Lowering wagons down mountain sides by snubbing ropes to trees became commonplace for these pioneers, and they were all working harder than they ever had in their lives. They no longer asked themselves if it was worth it. They were afraid of what their answer might be.

Mothers put ropes around the waists of their children and led them single file, to prevent a small child from running into the thick tangle of vegetation that grew all around them. Any child lost in there would more than likely stay lost — forever.

They worked their way up hill more than a half a mile high, and then half a mile down the other side. That took a full day of brutally hard work, both for humans and animals. Slipping and sliding and cussing. Most went to their blankets without even eating the evening meal. They were too exhausted to eat.

"By now," Beartooth said, "I reckon Red Hand and

Bum will know that we didn't come crost the Columbia and they'll be hard on followin' the trail we're blazin'."

Preacher nodded his head in agreement and accepted a cup of coffee from Nighthawk. "Won't do 'em no good." He smiled and winked at his old friend. "You know where we are, don't you, Bear?"

"Tell the truth, I ain't rightly sure."

"Five more days and we'll hit the valley."

Beartooth stared hard at his friend. Then the huge mountain man's face brightened under his beard and his eyes twinkled. "By the Lord, we've done the impossible, Preacher."

"Looks that way, ol' hoss."

"You goin' to tell the movers?" Jim asked.

"No. I do that, and they'll get all anxious and in a hurry and somebody will get hurt in haste. We've made better time than I figured we would. I got to hand it to these folks. They got grit, I'll give 'em that."

"I got me a hunch that when they cross the last ridge and stand lookin' down into the valley, they'll give up any plans of goin' north crost the Columbia and just settle right there," Dupre said. "I know a little somethin' 'bout farmin', and that's good land for it. Damn shore rains enough," he added.

"We'll be hittin' that in a couple of days, I figure," Preacher said. "But the worst is behind us."

"What you gonna do when we get these pilgrims to the promised land?" Beartooth asked him.

"Loaf for a couple of days, then head back East to the mountains. I got me a little task to do."

"And what might that be, Preacher?" Dupre asked.

Beartooth, Jim, and Nighthawk all grinned at one another.

"I got me a score to settle with a feller name Bum and an Injun named Red Hand. You boys can come along if you like."

"Well, my goodness gracious!" Beartooth said. "Thankee

282

kindly for the in-vite. I allow as to how I might just do that. How 'bout you boys?"

"I wouldn't miss it for the world," Jim said.

"I'd feel left out by not goin' along. How 'bout you, Nighthawk?"

"Ummm!"

Many of the rogue Indians that had joined Red Hand had now left him. It was obvious to all that Preacher had tricked them and taken the southern route across the Cascades. Even the most stupid among them knew that to attempt to follow would amount to naught. By the time they recrossed the river and picked up the trail of the wagon train, the movers would be across the mountains and into the valley. To attack a wagon train that close to the fort would be very foolhardy.

Even many of Red Hand's own band had given up in disgust and headed back to more familiar ground. Bum's band of trash and outlaws had shrunk to about twenty-five.

On a cool early autumn morning, Bum watched as Red Hand and his people saddled up and broke camp. He walked over to the renegade.

"Givin' up?" the outlaw asked.

"There will be another time," the Indian said. "To pursue now would be pointless. We ride back east."

"Mind if me and my boys ride with you?"

"Do as you wish." He swung into the saddle. "We will cross the river just north of where the Snake flows." He turned his pony's head and rode off.

Bum walked back to where his men lay on the ground. Leo tossed a stick into the fire and said, "No women, no gold, no nothin'."

"It ain't over yet," Bum said, then smiled.

"Whut you grinnin' 'bout?" one of his men asked him.

"Well, I'll just tell you," Bum said, sitting down and

pouring a cup of coffee. "It come to me whilst I was talkin' with Red Hand. Seedy, didn't you tell me you'd been to Fort Vancouver recent?"

"Only about six months ago."

"And the brand new buildin' for the missionary's church was not in the fort?"

"Oh, no. It's a good three, four miles from there. They built it a-purpose there so's the Injuns would feel better 'bout comin' in to it."

Bum sipped his coffee and chuckled. "Bustin' our butts for nothin'. That's what we been doin'."

"Whut you mean?" Leo asked, scooting closer to Bum.

"Them folks in the wagon train don't know us. How could they? They ain't never seen us. Don't nobody at the fort know us. It stands to reason that them women missionaries and the gold is gonna be at the church. Seedy said the livin' quarters was in the rear of the buildin'. It's three, four miles from the fort. All alone, ain't it, Seedy?"

"You bet."

"Preacher and them sorry friends of hisn is sure to be hell-firin' back toward us to finish this fight," Bum said with a grin. "All we got to do is be a little careful and just head straight west from here and then cut south. You boys see what I'm gettin' at?"

"Kind of," Jack Harris said. "But ain't that sort of risky? If we're thinkin' along the same lines, that is."

"Not really. We can go in and grab the gold and the women and be gone hours 'fore anybody discovers the bodies. Far as that goes, we can kill some damn Injuns and chunk their bodies in there and burn the place down. Who'd know the difference?"

"I like that," Beckman said. "We could grab us a couple of young squaws, hump 'em 'til we're ready to go, and then kill 'em."

"Good idea," Bum said. "They's lots of fall berries now and the squaws'll be out pickin' 'em to make pemmican. Should be easy to grab a couple young ones. But we're gonna have to be real quiet about it and when the deed is done, we're gonna have to move fast and far. And we're gonna have to be careful about which tribe the squaws belong to."

"Amen to that," Slug said. "I damn shore don't want no Digger woman."

"That wasn't what I meant!" Bum admonished him.

"Oh," Slug said.

"When do we ride?" Waller asked.

"Let's give Red Hand and his boys a couple of hours to get clear away. We can be breakin' camp and packin' up now, just in case that damn renegade left someone behind to snoop and spy on us."

"What *did* you mean?" Slug asked.

"Oh, forget it, Slug!" Bum said.

"Which would you rather have on your trail, Slug?" Jack asked. "A peaceful Injun, or a Blackfoot?"

"Oh!" Slug said. "Right."

Preacher rode slowly back to the wagon train. He had not told any of them that on that day, they would be done with the mountains and looking out over the huge valley that lay south of the Columbia. They had reached the promised land.

Despite the fact that most of the movers considered him to be a sarcastic, heartless, and sour man — Preacher was none of those things — he was proud of this bunch of pilgrims. They had done what no one, to the best of his knowledge, had ever done. And he knew that all of them with the exception of Wade and his two-bit kid, Avery, would be bigger and better people for the trip. Preacher knew, too, that not all of them would survive out here.

Injuns would get a few, the fever would take a few more, accidents and other mishaps would claim still a few more. But those that would live could be proud of what they'd done.

And speaking of Avery and his pa . . .

The father had gotten all up in Preacher's face just the day before, after Preacher had raised his voice and fussed at the young man for being a laggard, which he certainly was. Lazy no-count pup. The father said when they crossed the mountains, he was gonna put a butt-whipping on Preacher that the mountain man would never forget. So Preacher knew that he was gonna have to stomp on Wade some.

Preacher was looking forward to it. He'd had a belly full of the man. No dancing this time around.

Preacher rode through the timber, figuring the movers had about five hundred more yards to go 'fore they broke free and could stand on the plateau that overlooked the valley. He carefully tucked his smile away.

Beartooth winked at him when he rode back to the train. "Gonna tell 'em?"

"Not just yet." He looked up at the sky. Not even noon yet. He looked at a man leaning on his axe and looking at him. Preacher was not well-liked and he was well aware of that fact. It bothered him not a whit. "You figure on that tree maybe fallin' down all on its own, Brewer?" he asked cheerfully.

The mover gave him a dirty look and went back to chopping.

Preacher rode up to Melody. "Come on," he told her. "I want to show you something. Richard, you and Edmond and Penelope come along."

Preacher stopped them just before timber's edge.

"This is it?" Penelope asked, looking around her. "This is the same thing we've been seeing for weeks."

"Y'all ride out there on that flat and take a good look. Go on. I'll wait here."

Preacher stepped out of the saddle, eased the cinch on Hammer, and squatted down, chewing on a blade of grass.

"*Yeeee-haw!*" he heard Richard shout.

286

"Waa-hoo!" Edmond momentarily forgot his churchly bearing.

A mover rode up, his long rifle at the ready. "My God, is it the red savages?"

"Nope," Preacher said, standing up. "You home, pilgrim."

Two

The pioneers, many of them ragged and gaunt, stood on the plateau and gazed in disbelief at the lush and green valley that lay before their eyes. Many of them wept, still others dropped to their knees and prayed, giving thanks to God for getting them safely through the wilderness. Only a few of them included the mountain men in those prayers . . . at first. Then, as they realized they never would have made it without the help of Preacher and his friends, they all formed a huge circle and linked hands, offering quiet prayers for Preacher, Dupre, Nighthawk, Trapper Jim, and Beartooth.

"We ought to be fairly blessed, I reckon," Beartooth said to his friends, standing away from the circle of pioneers.

"That's good," Jim said, "for I 'spect that we're gonna need all the help we can get when Gabriel sounds the call."

Swift decided at that moment it was a good time to rally the movers and get them down from the plateau. He gave a mighty blast on his bugle and like to have scared the mountain men out of their britches.

"That does it," Dupre said, when he had settled his badly jangled nerves. "I'm a-gonna snatch that bugle away from him and stomp it so flat not even an angel could

288

toot it."

Laughing, Preacher calmed his friend then turned to Jim. "Jim, ride yonder to the river and get one of them Injuns that's always hangin' around to canoe you 'crost and tell the Chief Factor we got a whole passel of pilgrims waitin' on this side. You might as well spend the night and ride back in the mornin'."

"See you boys then," Jim said with a grin. "I'll be thinkin' 'bout you when I belly up to the bar."

"Don't you drink up all the whiskey now, you hear me," Dupre warned him.

Jim waved and rode off toward the river.

"Are we reasonably safe from Indian attack here?" a mover asked Preacher.

"No," the reply was flat and fast given. "But you are safer here than at any other time behind you. If some of you are thinkin' 'bout stayin' on this side of the river and farmin', best thing you can do is build your cabins close together for protection."

"We are thinking that, Preacher. It's so beautiful." He stuck out his hand and Preacher shook it. "Thank you, sir." He looked at the others. "Thank you all."

"I reckon," Dupre said, after the man had left them, "that we could take a few days time to see that these pilgrims know how to notch logs and the like."

"That would be the Christian thing to do, all right," Beartooth said.

"I think you're all plumb loco," Preacher said.

Nighthawk looked at him. "Ummm!"

That night the skies opened up and it started raining.

"Never fails out here," Preacher said. "Wettest damn place I ever been in all my en-tar life. I'd sooner build me a cabin under a waterfall."

"I long for the Rockies," Dupre said. "You figure on winterin' where, Preacher?"

"I ain't give it no thought. Damn shore ain't gonna be near here, I can tell you true on that."

"You might oughta wrap your robe around that blonde-haired filly and snuggle up clost to her when the snow flies," Beartooth suggested. "She'd keep a man warm, I'm thinkin'."

"Bes' thing for you to do is close that fly-trap of yourn," Preacher told him.

"I be's hongry around my mouth," Beartooth wisely took the suggestion to heart. "I'd like to have me a bear steak right about now, just a-fairly drippin' with fat."

"Dream on," Dupre said. "That mover's woman over yonder said she was a-cookin' up mush and we's welcome to eat with them."

"I *hate* mush."*

"It ain't bad if she'll let it harden some and then fry it in fat. Get it crispy and it's right tasty," Preacher said. "My momma use to fix it thataway for breakfast. But I ain't no friend to gruel." He took a sip of coffee. "Was you boys serious 'bout stayin' around for a time and lendin' a hand so's these poor helpless children can get set up for winter?"

"Why not?" Dupre said. "You got anywheres else you got to be in a hurry?"

"Can't say as I have."

"Then it's settled," Nighthawk said.

"Oh, all right," Preacher had to grouse about it a little. "If I didn't I'd never hear the last of it. Y'all'd rag me about it forever. Personal, I think you all got your eyes on some mover's woman. That's what I think. Come the spring y'all probably still be here, scratching in the ground and plantin' taters and the like."

They were still bitching, telling the most outrageous of lies and insulting one another when the last lantern in the wagon train was turned down.

Melody and Penelope and Richard and Edmond ar-

---

*Boiled corn meal and water.

ranged for passage across the Columbia and Preacher was out hunting when they left—deliberately gone. About half the wagon train elected to cross the river to settle on the north side, the remainder choosing to remain on the south side. Despite his grumblings and sour attitude—which by now everybody knew was all an act and not the real Preacher—the mountain man really liked the pilgrims and in a way, felt responsible for them. It was a strange feeling for the normally solitary man. So the time went by quickly in the building of corrals and stables, stockades and the homes that would stand inside them. One day Preacher looked up and found that he and the others had been in the valley almost three weeks.

"Time do fly when a body's a-havin' fun, don't it, Preacher?" Dupre said with a grin.

Preacher nodded, his eyes on Beartooth who was returning from the fort, and pushing his mount hard. Dupre followed Preacher's eyes and said, "Somethin's wrong, Preach."

"I gleened that right off. Where's Jim and Hawk?"

"Out huntin' supper."

"It better not be fish. I'm gettin' mighty tired of fish."

"I didn't say they was spearin' it. I said they was huntin' it. Must be time for us to leave, you're gettin' crotchety and hard of hearin', too."

"I ain't neither."

"Is too."

Beartooth swung down. "Ol' John Billingly was at the fort, provisionin' up for the winter. He just come in from the East. Says Red Hand and his bunch was ridin' hard back to their own territory, but without Bum Kelley and his bunch. And they was two raggedy lookin' hardcases just a-hangin' around the fort. They pulled out quick when they spied me eyeballin' 'em."

"Have some coffee and tell us the rest of it," Preacher told him.

"How'd you know they's more?"

" 'Cause you wouldn't have been forcin' that poor animal of yourn to tote you so fast if there weren't. I swear if you get any fatter, we gonna have to buy an elephant from some circus for you to ride."

"You're an unkind man, Preacher," Beartooth said, pouring a cup full of brew that looked strong enough to melt a horseshoe, and probably was.

"What I am is truthful. What else is they?"

"That church that your sweetie is livin' at is located a good four mile from the fort. Plumb isolated, it is. Chief factor told me it was done deliberate so's the Injuns would come to it better."

"And Richard told me they would keep the gold at the church headquarters," Preacher said. "Do they have any fightin' men out at the church?"

"Nope. Couple of tame old Chinooks is all. They sweep and dust and the like, the factor said."

"I don't like it," Dupre said. "I don't like it at all."

"Neither do I," Preacher agreed. "I think what we'll do is this . . ."

It was an emotional farewell from those settlers who had stayed south of the river. The women and the kids squalled and the men stood brave and fought back tears. Preacher cut it short, waved farewell, and the mountain men turned their horses and rode away. The settlers watched them until they were out of sight and then with a sigh, turned and once more began preparing their cabins for the winter that was not far off.

Preacher and his friends rode east for a day, camped, and then come the morning, headed north, just in case Bum had men watching them.

"You know where they's a good crossin' on the Columbia, Hawk?" Preacher asked.

"No. But I know where we *can* cross . . . if the water's low and we're lucky."

Days later they were still looking for Bum and his gang. The Chief factor at the fort had been warned by Dupre about the large amount of gold carried by the missionaries, and the danger of an attack on the church by the Kelley gang. The factor had listened, and then informed the Frenchman that while he would do what he could to insure the safety of the missionaries, those who choose to settle far away from the fort were really not his concern.

His words sounded a lot colder than they really were. The factor just didn't have the manpower to look after everybody. No one had asked the missionaries to come out — they did that on their own. His primary concern was to protect the goods of the company who employed him.

The mountain men ran into a hunting party of friendly Cayuses and stopped to palaver with them.

"Southwest of the Lewis," the leader told them. "Just on the edge of the big timber. Many whites are camped. They are not friendly and we did not attempt to camp near them. They are not trappers. I don't know what they are . . . I think perhaps they are thieves. I do not trust them."

Preacher thanked him and they rode on.

"Five open hands of men," Nighthawk said. "That's a goodly number, but somewhat less than we faced a month ago."

"A lot of his followers have left him," Preacher said. "Maybe we'll get lucky and put an end to Bum Kelley."

Beartooth wasn't so sure about that. "That no-count's been around a long time, Preach. A lot of men has tried to put him in the ground."

"I'd settle for Jack Harris," Dupre said. "He's been givin' trappers and guides and the like a bad name for years."

"I'm greedy," Preacher replied. "I want 'em all."

Nighthawk touched the white ashes and smiled. "We're no more than half a day behind them."

"Twenty-five to thirty men," Preacher said, after walking around and carefully inspecting the campgrounds. "And a nasty bunch they is, too."

"No bloody bandages layin' around," Dupre said. "Looks like they're all in pretty good shape."

"They're headin' for the fort," Jim told them. "That sign's as clear as leaves on a tree."

"I know a shorter way," Beartooth said. "We can be there a couple of hours 'fore them."

Preacher swung into the saddle. "Let's ride."

"He didn't even say goodbye," Melody said, gazing out a window of the mission.

The afternoon was clear and bright and cool, with not a single cloud in the sky, a welcome relief from the rain that usually fell. Frost had colored the land that morning, laying a heavy mantle of white that was gone as soon as the sun touched it. Winter was not far away.

"Oh, Melody," Penelope said. "Why can't you see that he's entirely the wrong man for you? Yes, he's handsome and dashing and daring and all of that. But he's wild, Melody. He's like the wind. He doesn't belong in a house. He'd feel confined, like a chained animal. It wouldn't be fair to ask him to change his ways. He belongs to the mountains and the wild, high country."

Melody turned from the window. She smiled sadly. "I know all that, Penelope." Suddenly, she giggled. "Can you just imagine the looks on Mum's face if I should suddenly show up back East with Preacher in tow?"

The two young women burst out laughing at just the thought.

"Or better yet," Penelope said, "with all *five* of them!"

Richard and Edmond walked into the sitting room, curious to see what all the giggling was about.

"What in the world . . . ?" Edmond inquired.

"Girl talk," Melody told the young men. "You wouldn't understand."

Richard walked to the window that Melody had just left and stared out, silent for a moment. He turned to face the group. "It's odd that Preacher didn't stop to say good-bye. Swift told me they left very abruptly."

"What are you saying?" Penelope asked, walking across the room to stand by his side.

"I'm . . . not sure. But I became friends with Preacher toward the last. And I am sure that something is not right about their leaving. I just have a feeling that their sudden departure might be a ruse of some sort."

"A deception?" Edmond asked. "No. I don't believe that. What would be the reason?"

Richard spread his hands. "I don't know. It's just a feeling I have. I'm probably wrong."

"I'm sure you are," Edmond said smugly. "We shall never see those men again."

"That outlaw and the gold we have hidden here at the church, Melody said.

"What about it?" Edmond asked.

"Preacher may have received word that the gang had not given up and were coming this way. He and his friends may have gone to attack them, or head them off, or something like that."

"Pure romantic balderdash!" Edmond said with a laugh. "Melody, you became mildly infatuated with the man and had a mental fling. Put him out of your mind and settle both feet back on the ground. You'll not see that will-o'-the-wisp' again." With a knowing and not a terribly kind laugh, he left the room.

Richard stared hard at Edmond's back. "Sometimes," the missionary said, "I believe that man is not far from being a fool!"

Three

"They're about a mile ahead of us," Nighthawk said, slipping back into camp after making his silent reconnoiter on foot. "Twenty-eight of them. No guards out."

"No doubt in your mind it's Bum?" Jim asked.

"No doubt," Nighthawk said, pouring a cup of coffee from the pot set on the rocks beside a hat-sized fire.

"They's gonna be some of them no-counts out permanently 'fore the dawnin'," Preacher said, a grim tone to the words. His gaze touched the eyes of his friends. "Anybody don't want to do it this way, say so now."

The four other mountain men looked at him, their eyes hard. Dupre finally said, "I ain't got no use for murderin', child-rapin' scum. Let's do it."

The others nodded their heads in agreement, then set about gathering up their gear. They were grim-faced as they worked, for this was to be a bloody night.

There were only small pockets of law west of the Missouri River, and not a hell of a lot more law than that between the Missouri and the Mississippi. These mountain men ran wild and free, and they answered to few codes of conduct. But those they did subscribe to were the basic ones that decent men everywhere held to: Steal a man's horse in the wilderness and you set him afoot to face possible death. So stealing a man's horse called for a hanging or a shooting. On the spot. You did not lie except in jest, for here a man's word was held as tight a bond as a contract done up in some fancy law office. A man did not bother a good woman or a child (or even a bad woman in most cases). Harm a woman, and the penalty was almost certainly death. Rape a woman or child and the penalty was certain death, often in very unpleasant ways.

The mountain men led a wild and rough existence, and the justice they dealt was just as wild and rough and unforgiving as the land which they lived in and fought in and for most, eventually dying in.

On this night, the five mountain men shoved pistols behind their sashes, added war axes to that, and picked up their Hawken rifles.

They began making their silent way toward the outlaw camp of Bum Kelley. They took their time, wanting to arrive just when most of the outlaws would be getting ready to roll up in their stinking blankets. With any kind of luck this night, the outlaws would sleep forever, and the missionaries and no telling how many countless others, blissfully unaware of the danger the outlaws presented, would live normal, happy lives — or as normal and as happy as could be in the wilderness.

With any kind of luck.

The ambuscaders neared the camp, broke up, and silently moved forward, stopping their stealthy advance just at the edge of the clearing. The fires were dying down and men were grumbling about the cold as they prepared to roll up in their blankets.

Preacher spotted several thugs that he recognized, and assumed that Bum was already in his blankets. He lifted his Hawken and blew one standing man straight to Hell and into the hot embrace of Satan. The others opened fire a split second later.

The night roared with gunfire and the air became choking with gunsmoke from the muzzle-loaders.

"Now!" Preacher screamed and charged the camp, a knife in one hand and a war axe in the other.

Moses reared up from the ground, his dirty face pale and his eyes wide in fear. Preacher smashed his skull with the axe and jumped over the dead man.

Beartooth, using both axe and knife ended the life of Jennings while Nighthawk finished Halsey with an axe. Jim ended Bobby's vicious life of crime as Dupre buried his war axe into the head of Keyes.

Preacher threw his axe with deadly accuracy, the head burying deep in Beckman's skull and bringing the outlaw down dead. He fell into the fire. Preacher worked his axe free and let the man burn. They needed a little more light to work by, anyway.

Slug made the terrible mistake of trying to best Beartooth strength to strength. The huge mountain man broke the outlaw's neck and let him fall bonelessly to the cold ground.

"Damn your eyes!" George screamed at Preacher as he jumped for the man. Preacher buried his knife in the man's stomach and ripped upward. He jerked his blade free and stood over the body.

The camp fell silent. The mountain men looked around as they stood in the middle of the carnage. There appeared to be no one left alive.

Bum, Jack Harris, Leo, and Bull had jumped for their horses when the first shot was fired. They rode bareback, holding on to the mane, the horses just as wall-eyed and trembling with fear as the men on their backs.

Dipper, Waller, and Burke had run wild-eyed into the night. They left their horses and all their possessions behind in their frantic dash to get clear of the bloody ambush. No matter, they could always kill again and steal more horses. They headed for Fort Vancouver.

"Bum ain't here," Dupre said.

"Neither is that damnable turncoat Jack Harris," Preacher said.

"I count twenty-one," Nighthawk said. "Seven got away. I will see very quickly in what direction."

Preacher did some fancy cussing as he stood in the clearing of death.

"We'll track them, ol' hoss," Dupre assured his friend. "We'll get them."

"Bet on it," Preacher said in a low menacing tone.

Beartooth dragged Beckman out of the flames and tossed some water on him, putting out the burning clothing. "He smelt bad enough alive," the mountain man said.

"Three on foot heading for the Fort," Nighthawk said. "Four mounted men headed straight east."

"I'll take care of them on foot," Preacher said, reloading his weapons. "Let's get back to camp and saddle up. You boys track Bum — and you can bet it's Bum and Jack on horseback — and I'll catch up with you along the way. Hawk, leave rocks piled for me, will you?"

Nighthawk nodded and the men took off at a trot for their camp. An hour later they were hard on the trail of those who had survived the ambush.

"We got no food, no saddles, and we left most of our weapons back at the camp," Bum griped. "I ain't never been in no spot like this before."

They had stopped to get a drink of water at a little creek and to rest their horses.

"I wonder how many got away?" Leo questioned. "I seen a half a dozen shot to bloody rags in they blankets."

"I never figured Preacher would pull something like this," Bum said. "If it was Preacher and them."

"It was," Jack Harris said sourly. "And Preacher will do anything. He don't play by no rules. I tried to warn y'all 'bout Preacher. That's the most meanest man that ever walked these mountains."

"I think I seen Dipper and Burke get free," Leo said. "Maybe one more. I don't know for sure. It all happened so damn fast all I could think of was gettin' free and safe."

He looked at his hands in the faint moonlight. They were trembling. He wasn't sure his legs would support his weight if he tried to stand up.

"I'm just wonderin' if and for how long Preacher and them others will track us," Bum said.

"They'll track us," Jack replied bitterly. "And they'll track us 'til Hell freezes over."

Preacher rode directly for the Fort, taking trails those on foot would avoid. The three outlaws had to head for the fort; they had no where else to go. Once there, he told no one what had happened. The Factor might frown on folks ambushing other folks. His presense was reported to Richard, who told none of the others the news. He immediately saddled up and rode in to see the mountain man. Preacher was camped outside the walls.

"Melody was rather upset when you left without saying goodbye, Preacher," he told him.

"She'll get over it."

"Oh, my," Richard said.

"Oh, my, what?"

"Here comes that Wade fellow."

Preacher looked up and grunted. "He best keep on goin'. I ain't got the patience right now to mess with that fool."

"You there!" Wade called, his good-for-nothing son with him. "You! Mountain man. I came to call you out."

"You best go on, Wade, and leave me alone. Mess with me now and I'm gonna wind your clock."

Without another word, Wade hit him, the blow unexpected. Preacher hit the ground, flat on his back.

"Fight! Fight!" someone from the fort yelled.

Preacher slowly got to his moccasins and spat out blood from a busted lip. "All right, mover," he said, low menace in his voice. "You got this comin' to you." He faked a blow, Wade flicked a hand to deflect it, and Preacher tossed a hard right fist to Wade's mouth. The blow snapped his head back and brought blood to his mouth.

Preacher busted him with a hard left fist that landed on the side of the man's jaw and Preacher followed that with a right to Wade's gut.

Wade backed up, shaking his head and trying to catch his wind. Preacher pressed him, landing blows to the man's shoulders and face and stomach. Preacher back-heeled the man and sent him tumbling to the ground. Avery screamed curses at Preacher and jumped at him, both fists flailing the air. Preacher timed a punch perfectly and it landed smack on his nose, flattening it and sending blood squirting. Avery squalled and sat down on the ground.

"Goddamn you!" Wade yelled, getting to his boots. "That's my son you struck."

"And a piss-poor kid he is, too," Preacher told him. "He must take after his pa."

Wade swung and Preacher turned, the blow catching him on the shoulder. The blow hurt, for Wade was a big and powerful man. A bully. Like father, like son.

Preacher popped a fast left that smacked Wade on the mouth, bringing new blood to the man's lips.

" 'En 'is 'ow, Pa," Avery blubbered, both hands covering his busted and bloody beak.

"What'd you say?" Wade cut his eyes to his son.

"He wants you to clean my plow, Wade," Preacher interpreted. "But I allow as to how I got something to say about that." Preacher jumped up into the air and kicked Wade in the face, the kick knocking the man back to the earth. He landed heavily on his butt and his teeth clicked together from the sudden impact with the ground.

"Are you gonna rest or fight?" Preacher taunted the man.

Wade slowly got to his feet. His face was bloody and swelling and he was mad clear through. So far he had not been able to land an effective blow on the mountain man.

Preacher cut his eyes. The smart-aleck kid was crawling behind him, so his pa could shove him tumbling.

301

Preacher side-stepped and gave Avery the toe of his moccasin right in the gut. The young man howled in pain and fell sprawled out on the ground, gasping for breath.

Wade came at Preacher like a wild bull, his face filled with hate, and his mouth spewing out cuss words, all of them directed at Preacher and his ancestors. None of it was in the least complimentary.

Preacher stuck out a foot and tripped the man, sending him to the ground, face first. Wade kissed the grass and came up sputtering and spitting out dirt. Preacher stepped in close and hit the bigger man twice, a left and a right to the jaw. Wade staggered back, regaining his footing just at the last moment. He lifted his fists.

"Aw, give it up, man," Preacher said. "You're done."

Wade lumbered forward and took a wild swing at Preacher. Preacher sighed and popped him again, a left and a right, to belly and jaw.

Still the big man would not go down. "Come on, mountain man!" Wade sneered. "Fight! I got you whipped now."

"You 'bout a fool, Wade," Preacher told the man. "This fight is stupid. Give it up and I'll buy you a drink."

" 'Ick 'is ass, Pa!" Avery screamed, mush-mouthed, getting to his big feet.

"I 'bout had enough of you, too, boy," Preacher told the young man.

Avery told Preacher where to go and what to stick up a certain part of his anatomy when he got there.

Preacher narrowed his eyes and gave the young man the back of his hand right across the mouth. The force of the blow knocked Avery to the ground.

When Preacher turned around to face Wade, the big man was standing, grinning a bloody smirk at Preacher.

With a knife in his hand.

Four

"I really don't think you know what you're doin', Wade," Preacher told him, his voice cold and low. "But if you don't put that knife up, I'm gonna kill you, man. And I ain't gonna tell you that but one time."

The Chief Factor stepped through the crowd, a cocked pistol in one hand. "Withdraw, sir!" he ordered Wade. "Or stand and die."

With a snarl, Wade sheathed his blade and stood staring at Preacher. Wade's chest heaved and blood dripped from his busted nose and mouth. "There will be another day, Preacher," he warned. "And you may wager on that."

"Why?" Preacher asked him. "Are you that anxious to die, Wade?"

With a snort of derision, Wade shoved and elbowed his way through the crowd. He helped the light of his life to his feet and together they walked off.

"Preacher did not start this trouble," Richard informed the Chief Factor. "We were standing here chatting when Wade bulled his way up to us and demanded that Preacher fight him. The man is a troublemaker, sir."

"Yes," the man said, uncocking and securing his pistol. "Unfortunately, I know that only too well. The family has been in this area just about a month and already that

303

Wade fellow has been involved in three altercations. That son of his is no more than a common hooligan and vandal. I fear neither of them will come to a good end. The father does not seem to realize that I can bar him from this fort. And I might just do that. Good day, gentlemen."

"Richard," Preacher said, after several trappers he knew had congratulated him on a good fight and the crowd had broken up, "go on back to the church and charge your pistols and rifles. They's three bad ones headin' this way. I believe I can stop them. But if I don't, it's gonna be up to you."

"Bum Kelley and his gang?"

"Bum Kelley ain't got no gang no more. Not none to speak of, that is. The buzzards and the varmits is a-eatin' on most of his gang up south and east of Soda Peak."

Richard swallowed hard. "You and your friends did them in?"

"That we did."

Richard decided he really did not want to know the how of that statement. "The Indian renegade and his bunch?"

"Broke up and long gone."

Richard looked around him to make sure they were alone. "Bum and his people were coming after the gold?"

"That they were—and the women. I don't think you'll have to worry with Bum no more. Just as soon as I deal with them three no-counts comin' for your place, I'll hook up with my friends and we'll chase Bum down and dispose of him."

He held out his hand and Richard shook it.

"Likely as not you won't see no more of me, Richard," Preacher told the man. "You tell Melody and the others goodbye for me." He smiled. "You're a good man, Richard. I watched you grow over the weeks. You toughened up, both in mind and body." He clasped him on the shoulder with a hard hand. "You'll do to ride the river with, man."

It was only after Preacher had ridden off, that Richard realized he had just been paid the highest compliment a mountain man could offer.

"Goodbye to you, friend," the missionary whispered to the afternoon. "And may God bless and keep you and your friends as you ride the mountain passes."

Preacher didn't ride far that day. He rode north of the mission and picketed Hammer on good graze and a small pool of water and waited. Maybe he was wrong. Maybe the three survivors of the ambush were not going to attack the mission, maybe they were just heading for the closest point of civilization. Maybe the thugs were coming here to steal or beg or buy supplies and horses and then leave. But Preacher doubted that.

Although he'd never seen a tiger, he doubted one could change its stripes, and he felt the same about those who chose to ride the outlaw trail. Preacher knew that to a large degree, each man shaped his own destiny. People were not forced into a life a crime—they chose it willingly. Preacher had not one ounce of sympathy in his being for thugs and hoodlums and the like.

Preacher also knew that what he was about to do—depending on whether the trio showed up—cut across the grain of those who knuckled down and cowered under the watchful eye of any constable or sheriff's department. Man steals your horse, you hang him. Man threatened to do a body harm, you go after that person and put the harm on him 'fore he can do it to you.

He waited in the timber behind the mission.

Just after dark, he saw the three men slip to the edge of the timber and crouch down. He could hear the murmur of their voices but could not make out any of the words. He watched them point to the lamp-lighted windows of the church and living quarters.

Preacher stood and moved silently, making a wide circle and coming up by the side of the buildings, then working his way to the rear of the main building. He crouched down, his war-axe in his hand.

He smelled the man before he saw him. The man stank of filth and days-old sweat. The hoodlum came closer, so close Preacher could have reached out and touched him. He was going to do just that — sort of — in a few seconds. The man peered in through the precious glass of a back window, into a darkened room. He saw the man take a long-bladed knife from a beaded sheath.

Preacher rose like a wraith and buried the head of his axe into the man's skull. He rolled the man under the building.

"What was that?" came the hoarse whisper.

"Stubbed my toe," Preacher gruffly called.

"You're a clumsy igit, Waller. Did you find us a way in?"

"Right here."

"You see them women?"

"Yes. They's nekkid."

"Hot damn! I get first dibs."

What he got was the sharp head of a tomahawk right between his eyes.

"Dipper?" came the whisper.

"Right here."

"Waller with you?"

"Yeah."

"I seen some fine-lookin' horses in the stable."

"Good."

"Did you say them fillies was nekkid?"

"Yep."

"I'm on my way to glory, Dipper!"

"You shore is," Preacher said, as he lowered the cooling body to the earth.

One by one he dragged the bodies to a ditch far behind the church buildings and dumped them. He collapsed part of the bank over them and then threw small logs and branches over that. Sooner or later the men might possibly be discovered — or an arm or leg of them would — but

306

by that time the bodies would be so badly decomposed no one would be able to tell who or even what they had been.

Preacher looked toward the rear of the buildings, a thousand yards or more away. "You good folks rest easy now," he said. "Live a long life and be happy — compliments of Preacher."

Preacher rode away from the fort and made a cold camp. By noon of the next day, he was in the Cascades. By midafternoon, he had found the tracks of both his friends and Bum and his crud. By nightfall, he found the first small mound of stones left him by Nighthawk. To someone unfamiliar with his style of living, the stones would have been meaningless; to Preacher they spoke volumes. He made his camp and slept as soundly as he ever did.

Four days later, he caught up with his friends. They were standing over three mounds of earth.

"They kilt 'em whilst they slept," Beartooth said. "I didn't know none of these boys, but they appeared to be trappers. I reckon they had 'em a jug and drank theyselves silly 'fore they went to bed. They heads was all beat in. The rocks and clubs is over yonder, all bloody. So Bum and Jack and them others now got guns and the like. These bodies was stripped nekkid, so them nogood's now got skins on, I reckon. They taken everything so's they'll pass for trappers. How'd you do?"

"I took care of them three that went to the west and whupped Wade's butt good over at the fort."

"I'd like to have seen that," Dupre said. "What brought all that on?"

"I don't know. I reckon he was just feelin' lucky."

"You shoulda kilt him," Trapper Jim said.

"I would have but the Chief Factor butted in just at the last minute."

307

"Too bad," Beartooth said. "Let's ride."

Bum and his small party crossed over into Washington Territory, into what is now Idaho, and for the first time since the ambush, began to feel like they just might have eluded their pursuers. They could not have been more wrong.

None of them had even the faintest inkling of what manner of men rode after them. Bum and his men were thieves, murderers, cutthroats, and almost anything else that was evil and dishonest. Like so many others, they made the oftentimes fatal mistake of judging others by comparing them to self.

While no one who is even an amateur student of the West would ever write — or even think — that mountain men were paragons of virtue, most of the mountain men did operate under a loose code of conduct. They were wild and woolly and, as the Western saying goes 'Born with the bark on', yet curiously drawn to alliances and bonding with like kind. A good woman was as revered as their own mothers, so even to think of doing harm to a good woman was enough to bring their wrath down on a person.

Bum and his bunch did not realize that Preacher and his friends, if it had to be, would pursue them all the way to New York City and drive them into the Atlantic Ocean.

"I believe we can rest easy now, boys," Jack Harris said. "Preacher and them friends of hisn has played out their string."

"Yep," Leo said, stretching out on his stolen and blood-stained blankets and sucking on a cup of coffee. "I think we can relax and start pondering on another job."

Miles to the west, five hard-eyed mountain men rode their ponies, their Hawken rifles across the saddle horn.

"I think we ought to lay low for a time," Bull said. "Let

the news of this wagon train gettin' through to the blue waters git back East. Then they's people who'll come a-foggin' to the promised land. They'll have cash money and fancy wimmen and the like. Pickin's'll be fine, boys, fine."

"I agree, Bull," Bum said. "But we got to start lookin' hard for a cabin to winter in. The snow's done cappin' the low mountains. It'll be hard cold soon."

"We'll find some trapper's cabin and kill him," Leo said. "Lay in a stock of meat and jerk it. Preacher and them silly friends of hisn will think we've done left the country."

"I know a spot up on the Clark," Jack said. "Snug little cabin that'd do just fine. Trapper lives there with one of the prettiest little Injun gals you ever seen. She could keep us all happy durin' the winter and then we could kill her come springtime 'fore we pulled out. We'll catch her man out runnin' his traps and do him in quiet like."

"Sounds good to me," Bum said. "We'll head that way come the mornin'. Pretty little thing, you say, Jack?"

"Purty as a pitcher, she is. Shapely."

Preacher and the others stood over the ripped and torn body of the man. "Anybody know him?" Preacher asked.

"I think it's Parley," Jim said. "But the buzzards and the varmits been hard at work here. Kinda hard to tell."

Preacher rolled the man over on his stomach and grunted. A bullet hole in the dead man's flesh was obvious.

"Shot him in the back while he sat before his fire," Nighthawk observed.

"Four men," Dupre called from outside the small clearing. "It's Bum and them others for sure. Tracks are plain." He rejoined the group.

"We're gonna take 'em alive, boys," Preacher spoke the words grimly. "And we's gonna have us a court of law, all proper and legal like. Then when we find 'em guilty, we'll hang 'em."

"That sounds good," Jim said.

"Nighthawk, you be the judge," Preacher said. "I'll speak agin the bunch, Dupre, you defend 'em."

"Wagh!" the Frenchman recoiled. "I ain't got nothin' good to say about this pack of mad dog heathens."

"No, we got to do this right and proper now," Preacher insisted. "You just let them have they say and such as that. Then, after they's done, if you can find anything good to say about them, say it. Hell, it don't make no difference. We gonna find them guilty anyways. Jim and Beartooth's gonna be the jury."

"When the time comes, I shall don my proper robes to sit in judgement," Nighthawk said. "I have a fine buffalo robe in my pack."

"That'll be good," Preacher said. "Make you look plumb respectable." He glanced at the Crow. "Providin' you do something with them goddamn pigtails."

Five

"They's noonin' by a crick," Dupre reported back. "So careless you'd think they was havin' a picnic." The day was cold, the approaching winter already opening its hand and closing chilly fingers over the high country. The men had awakened to a hard freeze that morning. They night before they knew they were close upon the outlaws and had elected to keep a cold camp, so the smell of wood smoke would not give them away. "They got a fire big enough to roast a bear. So's I reckon we could build us a small one for coffee."

"Bum and them's got a-plenty," Preacher said. "And it's already fixed. No point in usin' up any of our supplies when come the sundown, them down yonder ain't gonna have no further need for vittles."

"You make a good point," Nighthawk said. "Perhaps it is you who should be the judge."

"You be better. You can look sterner than me."

"Of course. You are correct. I also am much more handsome and certainly I present a much more regal appearance."

"Wagh!" Beartooth said. "He's got you on that, Preacher."

"English judges wear wigs," Jim said. "I seen a drawin'

311

of 'em in a book one time. Them pigtails of Hawk's fit right in, seems to me."

"You be right," Beartooth agreed. "When do we move agin them murderers?"

"Right now," Preacher said, and stood up.

Leo decided the coffee was just about ready and dumped in cold water to settle the grounds. Suddenly he had the feeling of eyes on him. He looked around. He could see nothing.

"What's the matter with you?" Bull asked.

Leo shook his head. "Nothin'. Just had a shiverin' sort of feelin', that's all."

"That meat do smell good," Jack said. "I be hongry for a fact."

Bum was all stretched out comfortable on his stolen blankets, half asleep. He opened his eyes to the warbling of a songbird. Sure was pretty. He cut his eyes and saw something that was a lot less pretty. Beartooth, standing grinning at him from the bushes. The man had a Hawken rifle in his big hands, the muzzle pointed straight at Bum. Bum cut his eyes to Jack Harris. The man was squatting motionless, the muzzle of a pistol placed at the back of his head. Bum could see Leo staring up at Preacher, the mountain man holding him in check with a pistol. Bull was looking into the muzzle of a rifle held by Dupre.

"Well now," Preacher said. "That meat do smell good. So let's eat it up and then we'll settle down to business."

The outlaws were trussed up and dumped on the ground. They offered no resistance, and up to this point, no argument.

Preacher and his friends ate the meat and drank the coffee. Bum and what remained of his band lay on the ground and watched in silence.

Bum finally broke the silence. "Go ahead and shoot us, you sons of bitches! What the hell are you waitin' on?"

"Speak for yourself!" Leo said. "I'd a-soon delay the grave, if possible."

"The three that made it to the fort and the missionary's

church I tooken out," Preacher informed the outlaws. "They was a scabby bunch, they was."

"You recall their names?" Bum asked.

"Waller and Dipper was the only names I heard. Don't know who the other one was. Don't make no difference. He's just as dead as the others."

"You never gonna get us to no court of law," Bull boasted. "And since you ain't lawmen, what you're doin' is agin the law. You ain't got no right to hold us agin our will."

"You're wrong on all counts," Dupre told him. "We fixin' to have us a court of law. Right here." He pointed at Nighthawk. "And yonder sits the judge."

"A goddamn Injun?" Leo hollered.

"You best watch your mouth," Preacher told him. "It don't pay to make the judge mad."

Nighthawk rose and went to his pack horse, taking out a buffalo robe and slipping it on. He sat down on a large rock and said, "Court's in session. Commence the proceedin's."

"Who goes first?" Dupre asked. "Me or you, Preacher?"

"Me." Preacher wiped his mouth and rubbed his greasy hands on his buckskins. He looked at the trussed-up outlaws. "I'm the perser-q-tor."

"Prosecutor!" Nighthawk corrected.

"That, too," Preacher said. "Your honor, these here men a-fore you is scum. They's murderers and rapers and torturers. They ain't fit human bein's."

"Objection!" Dupre said.

"Hell, I ain't even got goin' good yet!" Preacher yelled.

"This is an outrage!" Jack Harris hollered. "I demand a real lawyer and a real judge. Not no goddamn Injun!"

"Objection overruled," Nighthawk said. "Proceed, Preacher."

"Where was I?"

"Not fit human beings."

"Oh. Yeah. Right. Your honor, these here four snake-heads is about as low as a human person can get. Buzzard puke is easier to look upon than these four . . ."

"I object!" Dupre hollered.

"Hell, I do too!" Bull squalled.

"All of you be quiet," Nighthawk said. "What is your objection, counselor?"

"Say what?"

"Counselor. That's what you are at this moment. A counselor. Now what is your objection?"

"I ain't really got one. Hell, I agree with everything Preacher said. But ain't I s'posed to object ever'time he says something? I seen a trial back . . . oh, twenty-five year ago, I reckon it was. Judge had him a wooden hammer and was beatin' on the table and hollerin' 'bout half the time. And one or the other of them lawyers was always objectin' 'bout somethin'."

"You are supposed to object when the prosecution brings up some point that you disagree with," Nighthawk told him.

"Oh. Well, hell. I might as well lay down and take a nap, if that's the case."

"No, you don't!" Bum yelled.

"I got to pee!" Leo bellered.

"Order in the court!" Nighthawk thundered. "Does the prosecution have anything else to say?"

"I say we hang the bastards," Preacher said.

"Yeah, me, too," Dupre said.

"You can't say that!" Nighthawk told him. "You're supposed to be defending these no-good, sorry, good-for-nothin's." He caught himself. "Strike that from the record and the jury will disregard my comments."

Jim nudged Beartooth. "That's us."

"Why disregard it?" Beartooth asked. "It's all true."

"What record?" Jim asked.

"Somebody's s'posed to be writin' all this down," Leo yelled.

"Well, don't look at me," Jim protested. "I can't write."

"Stand the accused up before me," Nighthawk said.

The four were jerked to their feet. Jack yelled, "This

ain't no legal court of law. I demand a judge. I got rights."

"I sentence the four of you to be hanged by the neck until you are dead, dead, dead, dead," Nighthawk said. "And may God have mercy on your souls."

"Halp!" Bull bellered.

"Get the ropes," Preacher said.

"I have to dismiss the court," Nighthawk told him.

"Well, dismiss it," Preacher replied.

"Let's get on with the hangin'," Jim said.

"Don't be in such a rush!" Bum squalled.

"I thought a court of law was supposed to show mercy and compassion?" Jack asked.

"We have the right to an appeal," Bull said.

"Now, that is true," Nighthawk said.

"How do we go about that?" Dupre asked. "This is gettin' right complicated."

"I think the prisoners got to go before another judge," Beartooth said.

"We ain't got no other judge," Preacher said.

Jim looked at the four. "I reckon that means that you boys is outta luck."

"Halp!" Jack bellered.

"Now what do we do?" Dupre asked.

"Hawk's got to dismiss the pro-ceedin's," Jim said. "Soon as he does that, I'll go fetch the ropes."

"I hate ever' damn one of you people!" Bull yelled.

"Vengence is mine, sayeth the Lord," Jack reminded the group.

"But He ain't here," Preacher said. "So we're actin' in His place."

"Court is adjourned," Nighthawk said, then frowned. "I think that's the correct term."

"Halp!" Leo hollered.

"They funnin' with us," Jack said, sweat dripping off his face. "They ain't really gonna hang us."

"That ain't no collar for a tie he's a-fixin' over yonder," Bull said.

Jim was tossing four ropes over a limb. The open

315

nooses dangled and swayed ominously.

The four outlaws were hoisted up into their saddles—rather, saddles they had killed the trappers for—and the nooses placed around their necks.

"You boys wanna pray?" Preacher asked, meeting their scared eyes and lingering for a moment at each man. His own eyes were hard as flint.

"Swing wide the gates to Heaven!" Leo shrieked.

"That'll be the day," Dupre muttered.

"Lord, I'm a-comin' home!" Bull shouted.

"No, you goin' in the other direction," Beartooth corrected.

"Forgive me of all my sins!" Jack Harris moaned. "All the men and women and children I've kilt and robbed and raped and done all them other bad things to."

"Disgusting," Nighthawk said.

"Goddamn you to the fiery pits of Hell, Preacher!" Bum Kelley said.

"Odd thing for a man in your position to say," Preacher told him, then whapped the horse on the butt. Bum Kelley and his bunch dangled and kicked and twisted and swung.

The men waited until the outlaws had kicked their last, then lowered them down and dumped them in a shallow ravine, collapsing rocks over the bodies.

"You wanna say something over the tomb?" Dupre asked Preacher.

Preacher thought about that. "Yeah. I do." He took off his hat and the others did the same, none of them not knowing quite what to expect from their friend. Preacher was famous for a lot of things, including his sometimes profane and always odd eulogies.

Preacher took a breath and said, "Here lies Jack and Leo and Bull and Bum. They run their race and now it's done. They was sorry crap without no class. So bend over, Satan, and let 'em kiss your ass!"

Six

Theirs was a solitary breed, and a breed that regrettably did not last long in American history. Progress pushed them aside. But on this late fall day in the year of 1837, the four mountain men lingered long over coffee that morning. No one had put it into words, but all knew that here was where the trail forked.

"Where you gonna winter, Jim?" Dupre asked.

"I got me a little cabin over on the Flathead. It was right snug last time I seen it. I reckon it's still there. I'll soon know. You?"

"I get on right good with the Nez Perce. They was a fine-lookin' squaw lost her man last time I was through there. I told her I'd be back 'fore the snow flew. I reckon it's about time to head that way. Nighthawk?"

"My grandfather is old. I will go to his lodge and we will talk of things past. He will die this winter, I am thinking. I want to see that he is buried properly. Bear?"

"I'm gonna look up Lobo and see if he's still livin' with them buffalo wolves. If he ain't, I might winter with him and let him put me to sleep each night listenin' to his damn lies. Preacher?"

"I don't know," Preacher tossed out the dredges from his cup. "I got the restless flung on me. I might head south.

Then again, I might head east. I just don't know."

"You best be makin' up your mind, ol' hoss," Beartooth told him. "The snow's fixin' to fly soon."

"Yeah. I know it." He began rolling his blankets and gathering up his kit.

Within minutes, the mountain men had packed up and were in the saddle.

"I wish I could say all this has been fun," Preacher said, "but I'd be lyin' and that's something I never do."

"Wagh!" Dupre said. "It'll be a relief not to have to smell your stinkin' feet."

"What will be a greater relief," Nighthawk said, "is not having to listen to Beartooth's stomach grumble when he does not eat eight times a day."

"Or listen to Dupre try to sing those awful French songs," Jim said.

The men smiled at each other for a moment, and then rode their separate ways without another word.

That afternoon, Preacher topped a rise. Careful not to skyline himself to unfriendly eyes, he paused and looked westward, his thoughts of Melody.

"Mayhaps I should have partook of them charms of hern, Hammer. I might have the re-grets about not doin' that some cold winter's night. But I 'spect we'll be back that way 'fore too long. I don't know why I say that, I just feel it." He settled his hat on his head and lifted the reins. "Well, good horse, you wanna go see some country we ain't seen afore?"

Hammer snorted and shook his head.

"Well, let's us go then."

And the mountain man called Preacher began another ride into the pages of history.

WILLIAM W. JOHNSTONE
THE EAGLE SERIES

EYES OF EAGLES (#1)   (0-8217-4285-X, $4.99/$5.99)
Raised by the Shawnee Indians, Jamie Ian MacCallister made
the perfect scout for Santa Ana's Mexican army, which was
fighting against rebel Texans. What lay ahead was the Alamo.

DREAMS OF EAGLES (#2)   (0-8217-4619-7, $4.99/$5.99)
MacCallister joins up with famed frontiersman Kit Carson on
the first U.S. expedition from Missouri to the wide Pacific.

TALONS OF EAGLES (#3)   (0-7860-0249-2, $5.99/$6.99)
With his sons on opposing sides in the Civil War, MacCallister
fights two battles—North against South and father against
son—as he leads the Confederate Marauders from Georgia to
Tennessee (Bull Run to Shiloh).

SCREAM OF EAGLES (#4)   (0-7860-0447-9, $5.99/$7.50)
His wife has been brutally murdered at the hands of the wild
Miles Nelson gang. Out for revenge, MacCallister's search for
justice leads him to Little Big Horn.

RAGE OF EAGLES (#5)   (0-7860-0507-6, $5.99/$7.50)
Falcon MacCallister roams the West searching for the man who
ambushed his father. The pursuit of his father's killers takes
him from Wyoming's Johnson County War to Montana.

WILLIAM W. JOHNSTONE
THE ASHES SERIES